THE ALIEN'S MISSION

ALIEN WARRIOR MATES II

GRACE KENSINGTON

1

The Denynso warriors were lined up along the center of the compound facing the meeting hall, creating a powerful wall of intensity and strength. Each wore a black band around his arm, bold white stitches creating a "J" in the center. They were silent, stoic as they stared at the front steps of the hall where Creia, the king of their people, had appeared through the massive wooden doors.

Creia wore long black robes that stood in stark contrast to the blue of his usual clothing. The white of his hair intensified the darkness of the black ribbons woven through it that reflected the woven pattern through the hair of each of the warriors that faced him. There were several moments of dark, tense silence that hung over the compound and then the doors behind the king opened slowly.

Though they remained silent, the warriors stiffened. They all knew what was coming, and none of them felt prepared to handle it. It had only been twenty-four hours since the battle and they were all still trying to cope with the effects of the horror that they had seen. To overcome it, however, they knew they had to honor what was lost so that they could internalize their pain and anger, and move forward with even greater determination. The Klimnu were gone, but that didn't mean that they were always going to be safe, or that they would forget what they had to go through in order to get rid of those creatures.

Bannack fought the urge to shift in his position in the line of warriors. On either side of him were Pyra and Gyyx, both staring unblinking at the doors as they opened. The anger that built inside him was unlike anything he had ever experienced. Even as a member of a species of warriors known for being aggressive, intense, and powerful, he was volatile and unpredictable. Younger than most of the other warriors, Bannack had not seen as many battles as the others, but this had been something that he could never have fathomed. What he had seen had scarred him in a place deeper than he understood, and as he stood there watching the first of the women appear at the door.

Tall and strong, the Denynso women seemed far more powerful than the females of the other species they had encountered, but in that moment each stood at the door with tears streaming down their faces. None made a sound despite the tears. They stayed strong, keeping their eyes focused ahead of them with the same concentration and intensity as the warriors. After standing in the doorway for a few moments, the women stepped forward and the black cloth they held between them came into view.

The cloth held a folded tunic and a small dagger in the center, and the women held it as if they could feel the strange lack of weight that usually accompanied the funeral cloth when they made their processional down the steps of the meeting hall and toward the wide lake at the back of the compound. Suddenly the king's voice broke through the intense silence that felt like it was suffocating the warriors.

"Today we honor one of our own who has fallen. Jem fought valiantly in our battles against the Klimnu and in his last moments he made the most courageous decision that he could. With his last breaths he chose to sacrifice himself for the good and the future of our kind. With his death he took with him the last of our most hated of enemies, securing for us a future that is free from their torment and primed for the joy that will come. We will never forget what he did for us and though we cannot properly honor his body, we honor his memory and the bit of him that will continue with us forever."

As Creia fell silent again, the women continued forward from their place to the meeting hall and down the imposing stone stairs. Those stairs always represented the strength and stability of the species and the security of the compound, but now they seemed to emphasize the pain that radiated through the row of warriors and the women who carried the empty shroud down them. As they descended, the women didn't make eye contact with any of the warriors. This was their way. The women carried the dead, a final symbol of nurturing and care, while the warriors stood vigil as a sign of continuous protection and respect.

Bannack could see the tears sparkling on the women's cheeks and felt discomfort in his stomach. The women of their kind were not known to be emotional and only one other time in his life had he seen one of them shed a single tear. Now they were all crying, though restraining any noise, and he knew that it was not just for Jem, the warrior who had sacrificed himself in the final battle of a lengthy war against the evil Klimnu species. They were crying for everything that their kind had gone through in their years of battle against the slimy creatures who had been so determined to capture and kill their beloved king Creia and take over the compound, and the entirety of the planet of Uoria. They were crying for everything that those creatures had put the Denynyso through, and everything that they had done to the human women who had come to the planet and become a part of the clan. It was perhaps these women, the smaller, more delicate human women, who had suffered the worst at the hands of the Klimnu in recent times, and it was them that had given the Denynso warriors what they needed to finally defeat them.

The women carried the black cloth with Jem's tunic and dagger, the personal items they had taken from his home to represent him in the absence of his actual body, down the steps and through the center of the compound, passing through the line of warriors that separated silently as they approached. Bannack felt the anger become even more intense as his eyes fell on the empty tunic. This wasn't fair. This wasn't what one of the strongest, bravest, and most selfless men to have ever been in their clan deserved for his final memorial. He deserved to have his body honored in the way of the men that came before him, and to be offered the same respect that any of the other warriors would expect if they were the ones who had given their lives to finally bring the conflict with the Klimnu to an end. It was if the slimy, vile creatures had gotten their last bit of vengeance even though they were eradicated in the battle. By giving himself, wholly and completely, Jem had saved the Denynso, but had also given the Klimnu a grasp on the history of the clan that they would never be able to shake free. Whenever someone thought or spoke of Jem, they would be forced to think and speak of the Klimnu as well.

Bannack kept his eyes forward as the women passed through the line of warriors, trying to tear his mind away from the thoughts of that final battle that had been tormenting him for the last day. They flashed in front of his eyes as if they were still happening, filling his mind with reverberations of the sounds, the smells, and the gut-wrenching pain. He remembered the exact moment that the battle had ended. It was unlike any other battle that they had ever experienced with the Klimnu. Those battles had ended with the Klimnu retreating, running away from the vastly more powerful Denynso so that they could go back to planning their next attack. This battle, however, had ended when the final three Klimnu approached Jem on a branch in the mysterious mirrored world that existed just beneath the compound.

Though Ty, a young Denynso who had just learned to utilize a hidden gift that he had inherited from his father and had never used before to step out of his usual role and become a warrior, had attempted to save him, Jem knew what was better for the rest of the warriors, the compound, and all of Uoria. He had fought the power that would have lifted him out of the battle and saved his life. Instead, he grabbed onto the final three Klimnu and threw himself off of the branch, disappearing into the reflected sky and taking the creatures with him. The Denynso didn't know where he went or what had happened to him, but they knew that he would not return.

The ending of the battle had been so sudden, so intense and final, but Bannack still felt the aggression and anger that fueled them through the fighting. Entering that mirror world had been like nothing Bannack had ever experienced. In that world he felt more powerful, more intense, and more aggressive than he ever had in any other battle. There was something brewing inside him that he couldn't fight and he felt like he was on the brink of going insane.

2

———

Bannack took his place near the edge of the lake and mimicked the position of the other warriors, reaching over his shoulder for one of the arrows tucked in the quiver on his back. His opposite hand held a bow painstakingly handcrafted from one of the trees in the forest that they had only the day before discovered was covering the mysterious and dangerous underground lair that the Klimnu had been using to infiltrate the compound with the help of a human flight attendant who sympathized with the Klimnu's hatred for the Denynso. This was a treasured weapon, but one almost never used for actual combat. Instead, it was an item that every Denynso warrior made for himself in his early life and kept as a reminder of their heritage and the ancestors. Occasionally the bows made an appearance during a battle or were used to hunt some of the species that would come to the land near the compound once a year. Most often, though, they were kept displayed within the warriors' homes and taken down only when it was time to pay homage to the dead.

The women carried the cloth to the edge of the purple

water, its color darker and more saturated than the smaller pond near the cliffs on the other edge of the compound, and lowered themselves to their knees. They moved in concert, never turning their eyes away from the intense focus directly in front of them, but moving at the same moments and in the exact same way as all of the others. The first two women lowered their corners of the cloth into the water and the women behind them handed their sections forward, passing the edges of the black shroud through all of their hands so that the first two could guide it down into the lake.

As the water took hold of the cloth and it started to drift forward, the warriors drew their arrows and lifted their bows. When the cloth made it nearly to the center of the lake, Creia walked down the row of warriors, lighting the ends of the arrows with the torch he held. The warriors lifted their flaming arrows at the same moment, pointing them sharply toward the expanse of dark blue above them, and let them fly.

The arrows hit the cloth just as it reached the center of the lake and a massive whirlpool began to churn beneath it. This majestic phenomenon was why the earliest members of the Denynso tribe had chosen this lake as the place where they would put their cherished warrior to final rest. The whirlpool began when something touched the center of the lake and would churn as it did now, pushing upward into a funnel of water that lifted the flame-engulfed cloth, tunic, and dagger toward the sky. After several seconds, the column of water lowered and the flames, along with the memorial to Jem, disappeared into the depths. They didn't know what happened to the honored men that ended up in the water, but they believed that by giving them into the water that surged under the ground and gave life to the plants that thrived on Uoria, they were giving their beloved warriors continued life.

Bannack could only hope that it was true now. Jem's death was a confounding and infuriating mystery that none of the warriors, and not even Creia or his wife, the queen of the Denynso Theia, could explain. What lurked beneath the compound was a place that seemed to directly reflect the land above it, as if a mirror had been placed just at the ground line so that what looked like branches of massive trees were actually the roots above, what looked like roots were actually branches, and what looked like water covering the floor of the massive cavern was actually a reflection of the sky. This is where Jem fell. He jumped down into this reflection of the sky, giving himself over to it without knowing what would happen, and none knew where he ended up.

Bannack hoped that even though they could not properly inter his body in the lake, that Jem's spirit would continue on through all of them and give them the strength and courage that he possessed, because even though they had eliminated the last of the Klimnu, Bannack did not believe that it would be the end of the threats to the Denynso. There would be more. There would be more battles to fight and more wars to win, and each warrior was going to need every bit of intensity and power that he could have if he was going to be able to help his kind continue to thrive and dominate their part of Uoria.

EVERYONE STAYED in their places by the lake for several minutes after the funnel of water had completely disappeared back into the lake and the surface had become calm again. The women remained kneeling in the sand, the warriors maintained their wall of defiance, and the king and queen stood stoic and calm on the opposite side of the women. Behind them, a few yards back from this ritual that they had not seen and would not understand, stood the human women who had made their home on Uoria. These women, the mates of some of the warriors, as well as the healer and the baker, were astonishing to him.

He, like many of the other Denynso, had thought of human women as weak, flimsy little creatures prone to extreme emotions and unlikely to make much of a contribution to anything. When Creia announced that he wanted to foster greater understanding, connection, and cooperation with the humans of Earth, and that humans would be coming to the planet in order to not only research them, but to help them understand humankind, many of the warriors had been skeptical, even angry. Many of the earliest visitors, primarily scientists, had only been after a sample of their blood. It was well known that the blood of the Denynso warriors was incredibly special, and that it held the key to not only their powers and abilities, but to many amazing uses. Their desire to take samples of their blood had only increased the distrust among many of the warriors.

Eden had changed that. She was the first of the human women to show up on the planet and to earn their trust. The mate of Pyra, the most powerful and revered warrior among them, Eden was not standing with the other human women. Instead, she was kneeling in the sand at the edge of the lake with the Denynso women. This was because she had faced a brutal death at the claws of a Klimnu who had made his way into the compound by guising himself as Pyra. Through his efforts to heal her, Ciyrs, the healer of the clan, had somehow changed her from a human into a Denynso woman. Though she was still small and delicate looking compared to the other women of their kind, she was truly one of them.

The other women had come in turn after her, each with her own reason for visiting the planet, and when they came they found themselves the chosen mates of Denynso men. Their courage to stay on the planet and be with the Denynso was already impressive. It was the incredible intelligence, strength, fortitude, and resourcefulness that they had shown that proved to Bannack that he and the others had been wrong. Of course, they were still far smaller than the Denynso, even Zuri and Samira, the two largest of the group, and were far more emotional as a whole than his kind, but they were also the central reason that the warriors had been able to dominate over the Klimnu in this final battle. It was these human women that found the mirror world, helped develop healing ointments that saved the wounded, and even fought alongside the warriors to enable their victory.

Bannack looked at the human women, and at Eden, her belly swollen with Pyra's child, the first of the new generation of Denynso, with respect and gratitude, but even these comforting feelings were not enough to dampen the fury and aggression that had been tormenting him since they dropped down from the moss-hidden holes in the forest into the mirror world beneath the compound. This was anger and intensity like he had never experienced, and he struggled with understanding what could be creating these feelings inside him when the other warriors didn't seem anywhere near as affected by the battle, or even by Jem's death, as he was. Though they had all expressed their own dark and painful emotions, they all seemed composed and controlled.

Soon Bannack couldn't take it anymore.

3

Bannack could hear the warriors behind him shouting as he broke out of their formation and started back toward the compound. He just couldn't stand there with the rest of the warriors anymore. He couldn't stand there and look at the kneeling women, the stoic king and queen, and the confused, hurting human women. He couldn't stand there and stare into the purple water, part of him waiting for Jem to simply swim to the edge and climb up out of it with his usual smile on his face, the funeral rite and the funnel of water somehow resurrecting him from his resting place in the reflected sky and allowing him to return to their number. He needed to get away.

He continued into the compound, picking up speed as he went so that he could put the lake and the entire ritual behind him as fast as he could. The emotions churning through him were too dark and too difficult for him to cope with, and he felt like he was losing control. Deep down, however, he knew that this was not all about Jem, or the battle. There was something else at play and it was pushing him ever forward toward the brink of his control over himself. He didn't know what was pushing him or how far he could go, but the thought of what may exist just beyond that threshold of control scared him.

"Bannack!" Pyra yelled from behind him as Bannack made it back into the center of the compound.

Bannack stopped and turned to face the other warriors as they streamed through the compound and joined him. He knew they were going to be angry with him. Leaving a funeral like that was not only extremely disrespectful to the fallen warrior, but to the rest of the tribe that relied on every member to band together during these difficult times and offer each other as much strength and support as possible.

"What?" he demanded as the massive, powerful warrior approached him.

"What the hell do you think you are doing storming out of the funeral like that?" Pyra shouted at him.

"I couldn't just stand there anymore, Pyra. With everything that just happened yesterday, how can we just stay goodbye to Jem and honor his death, and then move on like nothing happened? Like just because the Klimnu are gone, everything is perfectly fine and we should just go about our lives all happy and wonderful."

"What else would you want us to do, Bannack? The Klimnu are gone. The threat is over. It is horrible that Jem had to give his life for that to happen, but any of us would have. He sacrificed himself so that we could continue on with a future that isn't filled with all of the fear and pain and battles that they have put us through over the generations. We owe it to him to acknowledge what he did and honor him by continuing on with our lives."

"Pretending that there is nothing else that could threaten us is not honoring Jem, or anything that the rest of us went through. Jem is not the only one that suffered. We all put ourselves through brutality and pain to protect the clan and the compound. Now you just want us to think that that was it, that the Klimnu are all that could possibly ever want to get in our way or take over our land. What about the mirror world where Jem died? Can you explain that?"

Pyra fell silent and Bannack could see him stiffen. The warriors didn't want to think about that anymore. They didn't want to think about the strange, unexplainable place that none of them knew existed just beneath their feet, and what it could mean for them. Bannack saw Pyra look over his shoulder at the king and queen, who were approaching them quietly, their faces showing that they were as curious about what the warriors had gone through during the battle as Bannack was eager to talk about it and try to figure everything out.

"Is this the mirror world that the women told us about?" Creia asked.

Pyra nodded.

"We haven't heard very much about it."

"Tell them," Bannack demanded, "If you are so sure that there is nothing else to fear now that the Klimnu are gone, why don't you tell Creia, Theia, and the women about what we saw when we were down there?"

He wasn't used to standing up to Pyra like this, and usually he would expect for the head warrior to react strongly, even violently, but Bannack didn't care. He was tired of feeling like he was crawling within his own skin and that he was being ignored. It seemed ridiculous to him that they were all so willing to think that just because they had gotten rid of one source of threat in their lives that there would be nothing else. To him, the battle was only the beginning.

"I'm willing to talk about it," Pyra said slowly.

Creia nodded and turned to the others, who waited several feet away, not knowing what they should do. Eden stood slightly in front of the others, one hand rested over her growing belly protectively as she stared at her mate as if she could control his behavior just by staring intently at his back.

"Those who wish to know what the warriors and our brave human women experienced in the battle may come into the meeting hall with us and hear. Those who are not interested are welcome to go home and do what they please until dinnertime."

There were a few seconds where it seemed that the other warriors, the Denynso women, and the human women seemed to contemplate within themselves, and then with each other, whether they wanted to join in on the conversation about the battle. Some seemed to immediately know that they wanted to know what had happened. Others drifted toward the back of the center of the compound, drawn toward their homes where they could put the mourning behind them and continue forward in the Klimnu-free future that they had dreamed of for their entire lives.

Finally Bannack turned and climbed the stairs into the building, letting the others fall into step behind him. He walked into the main room of the meeting hall and took his place at one of the long tables positioned around the center of the room. Most of the other warriors, all of the human women, and a few of the Denynso women, along with the king and queen, made their way in after them and joined him at the tables.

"Tell us what happened," Theia said as the last person settled into place at the table.

They all had their eyes focused on Bannack, but he turned his gaze to Pyra. No matter what type of anger, frustration, and aggression he was experiencing, he knew that it was his position to respect Pyra. He had already stepped out of line so far that he deserved severe punishment, and it was time now that he relented and resumed the position chosen for him, which meant handing over the control of telling the story of the battle to Pyra.

"Do you remember when Zuri, Samira, and the other women went into the cave and discovered the tunnel that led down to the strange world that they described, where they saw the Klimnu?" Pyra started.

Everyone at the table nodded.

"Of course. That's why you created the battle plan as you did in the first place."

Pyra nodded in return and continued forward, describing the holes in the forest floor that were covered by moss, concealing them, explaining how they used the vines in the trees to attack the Klimnu, and recounting again the last horrific moments of Jem's life. Though Jem had gone into his death courageously, and even joyfully, it had been a crushing moment for everyone that was there. It was especially difficult for Ty, who had tried so hard to save him and who had made the decision to honor Jem's wishes and release him so that he could perform his final feat of heroism.

"Tell us what you're thinking, Bannack," Pyra said.

Bannack looked up and realized that everyone at the table was staring at him. He didn't know how long it had been since Pyra had stopped talking. He had been staring at the dark surface of the table, letting the images of the mirror world cross over his eyes again and again. He couldn't fight them, so he relinquished his mind to them, allowing himself to review them over and over so that he could clarify the details and commit them solidly to memory.

"Who made that mirror world? Was it the Klimnu, or did they steal it like they wanted to steal our compound?"

4

———

Bannack's words seemed to stun the others sitting at the table and he met their eyes carefully. He wanted what he had said to sink in and for them to really think about it. It had been something that he had been thinking about constantly since they first realized that the Klimnu were using the underground realm to infiltrate the compound. It seemed to him that if the Klimnu had had that capacity to create such an incredible, complex space, they would have had been able to put more into their attacks on the Denynso. It didn't make sense to him that a species that had spent generations so devoted to capturing Creia and taking down the entire clan, and who were known for their sparse, rough lifestyle would have put forth the effort to build something so strange, but so beautiful. It struck him as much more likely that the creatures had done what was in their nature and simply taken what they wanted rather than making it for themselves.

"How much do you know about the rest of the planet, Creia?"

The king looked older and more weathered in that

moment than Bannack had ever seen him. He didn't know if it was from the strain and stress of the battle or the realization that the peaceful future that he had dreamed of for so long was not yet guaranteed for them.

"Nothing," the king admitted, "The Denynso have been here for the entire existence of our kind. Our home has always been here. The compound has expanded since then, but it has been as it is now for as long as I can remember, and likely well before that."

"So you don't know what other types of creatures might live on Uoria?" Pyra asked.

The tremendous warrior suddenly seemed shaken. He stared at Creia with an expression on his face that seemed at once dismayed, let down, and angry. Bannack could understand exactly what he was feeling. Creia was a powerful and mighty king, one that they followed with absolute loyalty and devotion. He had been on the throne for longer than any of them had been alive, and was, in fact, the father of many of the warriors. To think that he had lived on that compound for his entire life without ever knowing what lay beyond it was disappointing and disheartening.

"It is our tradition to fight only those who threaten us. We have battled with species that have come from other planets, we have fought the Klimnu, and we have struggled against ourselves at times. There has never been the need to venture far out of our compound or to interact with any of the others that may occupy Uoria."

Pyra straightened and Bannack could see the darkness and anger roll over his eyes.

"How have you allowed us to not know what's beyond our compound? The unknown is what made the Klimnu such a brutal force, and what almost allowed them to defeat us. The entire planet is unknown to us. What if there are other creatures who know that we are here and want to come after us?"

"There has never been a threat, Pyra," Creia said sternly, speaking to his son with the tone of both a father and a king.

"Every threat comes after a time when there has been no threat."

Pyra seemed to be fighting to control himself. The anger was building inside him with such force it was visible. Eden reached out a hand and rested it on her mate's arm, looking at him with eyes that pled for him to stay calm.

"Are you questioning my choices as king?" Creia asked, the tone of his voice like a warning.

"I am questioning your decision, as someone who has been the primary focus of the violence and strategic attacks of the Klimnu, to pretend that there couldn't be other threats existing outside the compound. You say that our people have battled creatures from other planets. Why have we been so quick to wage war against species that come from other places in the galaxy, when we don't know anything about the species that live right on our own planet?"

There were several long, tense seconds and the look on Creia's face went from anger to regret.

"I wanted to do as all of the leaders before me have done, and I wanted to do what I thought was right for my people and my family. Staying in and near the compound meant staying safe. If we stayed here, we didn't cause trouble with the others that inhabit the planet. To me, that seemed to reduce the chances that we would be in danger."

"But we are warriors. We are known around the galaxy for that."

"Just because we can go to war, Pyra, doesn't mean that

we always have to. I didn't want to watch my children face any dangers that they didn't have to."

Pyra looked at Eden and then back at Creia.

"I am going to have a child of my own soon. I don't want that child born into a world that I don't understand. I have heard about the threat of the Klimnu my entire life. They have been looking for you for as long as I know. They're gone now, but how do I protect my child if I don't even know what I should be protecting him from?"

The mention of his grandchild, the first of the new generation, seemed to change something in Creia. He looked at Eden with painful softness in his eyes. She carried the hope of the future of their kind, and in that moment Bannack could see Creia shift. He couldn't let anything happen to that baby, and that meant finding out what threats could be lurking just outside the compound.

"Start with the mirror world," Creia said, his voice returning to his usual strong, steady tone, "Find out what you can about it. Find out if there are any species that live there, and then report back here. We will decide what to do about the rest of the planet from there."

Without another word, the warriors stood and started toward the door. Zuri, Samira, and Elianna followed closely behind, determined to return to where they had joined in the battle alongside their mates. Eden stayed behind, knowing that Pyra would never allow her to do something as dangerous as wander into an unknown area that had already claimed the life of one of their warriors when she was as far into her pregnancy as she was, and Leia stayed to be with her.

· · ·

THE WARRIORS KNEW that they would not be able to get down the tunnel in the cave, so they would have to go down into the mirror realm in the same way that they did before the battle. They walked through the compound toward the forest in silence. Bannack could feel the tension among them and knew that they felt the same way that he did. None of them wanted to go back to the site of the battle so soon.

When they got to the forest, Bannack watched as Ero and Pyra pulled away the layers of moss that covered the holes leading down into the mirror realm beneath the compound. Moving slowly and carefully, they climbed down one by one. Bannack followed Pyra, grabbing onto one of the dangling vines as soon as he got deep enough. He wrapped the vine tightly around his wrist and forearm to secure him, and swung over so that he could grab onto the tree.

He concentrated on each of his movements, going slowly and carefully to keep himself from tumbling down toward the bright blue reflection of the sky that looked even more like water rippling across the ground of the massive cavern. Bannack looked up and watched the rest of the warriors make their way down the trees. The human women were last, coming down even more gradually than their warriors due to their smaller size. The warriors watched them intently, ready to catch them if they stumbled. Once they made it all the way down, they gripped onto their mates, holding them closely both to keep themselves steady on the branches that stretched out across the sky and to gain strength and comfort from their presence.

As Bannack looked around, he felt the fury and aggression that had eased slightly roar back into full intensity. His stomach clenched and he felt a strange pressure building throughout his pelvis and down his thighs. He struggled against the feeling, fighting to focus on what Pyra was saying even though his voice seemed to be coming through fog at him. Bannack tightened his grip around the vines, hoping that the pain of the thick plant cutting into his palm would turn his focus from the feelings building inside him. Around him the warriors were strategizing about how to safely and effectively explore the cavern, but all Bannack could think about was the intense, almost irresistible pull he felt toward the back corner.

5

I sank as deeply down into the shadows as I could while still being able to see the Denynso and the women I assumed to be the human females that had joined their tribe. The fear coursed through me so powerfully that I felt like I couldn't catch my breath and I struggled to hold myself silent as I watched them. I had, of course, seen them before. They had been there only the day before when they had descended from the moss and struck down the pale, disgusting creatures that had been crawling through my home for many months.

I didn't think that any of them noticed that I was there. Just like during the battle, I stayed out of sight, keeping completely to myself so that they didn't know that I even existed. That was the way that I liked it, the way that it had been for several years since the rest of my kind succumbed to an illness so severe that it burned through our families in a matter of days and killed everyone that it touched. I had no idea why it spared me. There have been many times when I wished that it hadn't. It would have been much simpler to let it take me as it had everyone that I knew and loved. Instead, it left me with the memory of youngest sister disappearing into the sky as I let her slip through my fingers.

The creatures that live on the ground above me have never known that we were here. My grandmother once told me that our kind didn't always live in this cavern. We once lived where the Denynso have settled, but a brutal war with another species and a plague that threatened our very existence drove us down into the cavern, a space that the wisest and most powerful of our species living then transformed into a reflection of the land above, the land that our clan loved so deeply. They had no way of knowing that the plague followed us down. It would be many generations before it struck again, but when it did it did so with a vengeance and only I was left behind.

Now I was more alone than I could ever imagine that a person could be. I was not just the last of my kind, the last of my family and friends. I was the last of a species that had been out of sight for so long that no other species on the planet even remembered that we existed. If anything, I was a myth and a legend.

I could see the men clutching their vines tightly as they scanned the reflection of the sky that covered all of the floor of the cavern that they could see. They all emanated fear and uncertainty, emotions that none of them were accustomed to feeling, and that none of them wanted to admit to the others. They all hated to feel as though there was something that they didn't understand so close to a space that they only knew as their own. The human women were more difficult for me to decipher. Unlike the warriors, who presented themselves as cold as stone on their exteriors but in fact presented their thoughts and feelings quite readily, the women held themselves closer, protecting themselves with their own internal forces so that I had to concentrate intently on each of them to be able to see what they were experiencing inside.

Many times I had heard the legends of the Denynso warriors and their incredible might, both on the battlefield and with their mates. It was said that these massive, forceful men fought with more intensity, skill, aggression, and determination than any other creature that had ever existed among the stars, but when they found their mate, they could be tamed as quickly as a pet. The warriors went through a difficult change when they neared their mate, struggling with their anger, primal force, and arousal until their mate soothed them. The blazing heat of their skin kept all but their intended partner away from them, and once they bonded, it was permanent. I had been told that these partners shared a very special gift that enabled them to communicate with each other through their minds even when they were far apart.

I often wished that my abilities were like that. I didn't read the minds of those I saw. Instead, I looked into them and reflected back to them the essence of who they were; their thoughts, their feelings, and their struggles. Now I was struggling myself, trying to grip what the human women were experiencing as they watched the warriors slowly and carefully extricate themselves from the vines and start to make their way out onto the branches that snaked and intersected across the sky. It was those branches that were perhaps the most brilliant element of the creation of that ancestor of our kind. He designed the cavern so that it reflected the space our species knew as its home so that we could always remember what the land looked like, but with that design came protection.

Those that made their way down into our cavern would

see the branches and walk out onto them, thinking that they could make their way across the entirety of the cavern. The branches would only go so far, though, and just like the ones on the ground above, some were weak and could snap in an instant, sending whoever stood upon it tumbling into the unknown beyond the sky. There had been very few who had ventured down to the cavern in recent generations, and none in my lifetime until the Klimnu appeared. When they did, it was the first time that I had been truly thankful for the illness that had taken everyone else. Their deaths had been fast, and though it left me alone, I would have much preferred that to watching my family and loved ones go through the horrors I could only imagine those creatures would have inflicted on us if they had found our colony thriving.

As I watched them, one of the men caught my attention. He was not the largest of the group and he, like the others, were definitely under the control and guidance of the tremendous one that now stepped out onto one of the biggest branches and hunched down to stabilize himself as he made his way out a few feet over the sky. There was something about him, though, that made me not want to turn away. His hair was stark white like the hair of the rest of the warriors, but unlike them, who wore their hair in high, spiky mohawks, his was tightly braided down his back and tied with a stretch of dark fabric. I remembered seeing him in the battle the night before. He had been much the same then, exuding an energy that was wild, unchained, and volatile despite being contained within his quiet exterior.

He looked up in my direction and for a brief moment I thought that he might be able to see me. I sank back further into the shadows and watched him narrow his eyes, the energy within him send out aggressive, powerful waves that drew me in even more. Part of me wanted to reach out to them, to tell them about the cavern and unveil its secrets, but the other part was so frightened and unsure of them that I couldn't move from my spot.

The man I had been watching stepped forward onto one of the branches and my heart tightened. I knew that he had chosen one of the weaker branches and the further he stepped, the more likely he was to fall. Keeping my eyes focused on him, I crept out from behind the low hill where I had been hiding. I lifted my hand to my chest as I made my way quickly, but as quietly as I could, toward the very edge of the bank where the land on this side of the cavern would flow into the sky. They couldn't see me where I was standing. They thought that the sky filled the entire space. Knowing that made me feel more secure, but even if they had suspected that there was something beyond the gradually darkening sky, I wouldn't have stopped.

The man took another step and I heard the low creak of the wood. The growing darkness of the sky was making it more difficult for him to differentiate between the branch and the sky, and he took another step onto one of the smaller outshoots of the branch. He stumbled and I heard a gasp rise out of the human women. One of the warriors started toward him, but I acted first. I tore my necklace from my neck, opening the compact in my hand and thrusting it forward. As the reflection of the stone wall across from me came into view on the bottom portion of the mirrored compact I stepped forward into the sky.

6

———

Bannack heard the sickening sound before he felt the branch beneath his feet crack. Pyra yelled behind him and he heard the women scream. For just a moment the world slowed down and a wave of peace washed over him as if everything around him had gone quiet and calm, and his body could release. Maybe this is what Jem had felt in those seconds before he jumped.

An instant later he felt his body fall forward and he knew that he was going to drop into the sky and discover whatever existed beyond. The branch disappeared from beneath his feet and he felt his body straighten, but it didn't drift downward. Instead, there was a brief moment of falling before he hit something hard and solid. It was as though he had tripped and landed on the hard packed earth and stone of the cliffs, only harder. The impact took the breath out of him, but he didn't feel any pain. He lay still, waiting for something, anything to happen.

Chaos broke around him as the other warriors ran toward him and scooped him up, dragging him back toward the trees before he could even get his feet beneath him. The women were talking so quickly that he couldn't understand any of the words that they were saying. His mind was reeling. He was aware that he hadn't fallen into the sky like he had expected to even though the branch had broken beneath him, but he had no idea what had actually happened. Suddenly he noticed a faint, pearlescent glow across the cavern. His eyes locked on it and he felt the muscles of his stomach clench. His pants tightened painfully and a wave of confusion rolled over him.

Bannack released the vine he was gripping and took a step toward the edge of the trees again, wanting to get closer to the glow. When it didn't fade or disappear, he took another step toward it. He felt Pyra's hand grab the back of his tunic and try to pull him back, but he lifted his hand to wave him away. He didn't need to be rescued. He wanted to be near the glow and whatever was making it. Though he knew he was only inches away from the edge of the sky, he believe he would be fine when he stepped forward. There was no fear as he lifted his foot away from the trunk and stepped out into the darkness.

His foot again hit solid ground rather than the sky and the confidence built inside him. The validation of that first step propelled him forward and he took another. He could hear Pyra and the other warriors protesting behind him, but the human women argued with their mates, telling them not to follow him. Bannack didn't care whether they followed or not. He continued to walk toward the glow, knowing each time he took a step that the solid ground would be there to meet his feet. As he walked the glow grew brighter and more intense, and soon he realized that there was a figure within the light.

"Hello?" he called out softly as he approached.

There was no response, but he continued forward still. The figure became more defined as he got closer and he realized that it was not actually within the glow but behind it. It seemed to move away from him, but he wasn't worried. He took another step, allowing the slowly retreating glow to lead him forward toward the other side of the cavern. After a few more steps he felt the texture of the ground beneath him change from hard and solid to slightly softer and more resilient. As soon as his feet touched that surface, the bright glow disappeared and out of the corner of his eye he could see the floor behind him go from solid and dark back to a sky awash with stars and a vibrant full moon.

Bannack turned his attention back to where the glow had been and found a woman standing in front of him. The figure that had been standing behind the glow, she was emanating her own very soft light that didn't seem to be coming from within her, but off of her. She wore a long white dress that gently skimmed the lines of her body and stopped with a band across her chest so the soft upper swells of her breasts and her smooth, elegant shoulders were bare. Ties down the front of the dress held it just in place, making the dress and what lie beneath even more intriguing. Pale silver hair flowed to her knees and the eyes that stared back at him from a face so breathtakingly beautiful it didn't seem real, her eyes were a clear, hypnotic lavender. She closely resembled the human women, but it was obvious that she wasn't.

Without a word, she held out one slim, graceful hand and Bannack took it, resting his hand on top so that she could curl her fingers around his coarser skin and draw him closer to her. The nearer he got to her, the more intense the feelings that he had as soon as he stepped into the cavern became, only he was no longer feeling anger or aggression when he was near her. Instead, he felt a sense of power and calm, while the tension through his body seemed to only increase.

"Hello," he said, wanting to make more of a connection with the beautiful creature standing so quietly and calmly in front of him.

"Hello," she replied and her voice was like the delicate, dancing sound of raindrops hitting glass. "Are you alright?"

"Yes," Bannack replied, somewhat startled by the question.

She didn't seem to be asking about whether he had been injured, and the question cut deeply into him.

"My name is Loralia," she said.

"Bannack," he replied.

He realized that she was still holding his hand and despite the cool feeling of her skin, the touch sent warmth throughout his body. She smiled at him softly, but he couldn't decipher what was behind the smile.

"Would your friends like to come to this side of the cavern?" she asked.

"I don't even know how I got over here," Bannack replied, part of him not wanting them to come over and break the small circle of privacy that surrounded them because of their distance from the others.

"I can help them." Loralia released his hand and Bannack felt disappointment ripple through him. "It's alright," she said with a gentle laugh, glancing at him before stepping forward toward the edge of the sky, "I'm right here."

It was as if she knew what he was feeling even though he hadn't said anything, but her confirmation was soothing in a way that made him feel absolutely comfortable and secure. She turned her palm over and in the faint light coming off of her skin and the refraction from the moon he saw what looked like a silver compact in her palm. Loralia held her palm out in front of her and lifted the top of the compact. Immediately the bright glow filled the space again and Bannack realized that the inside of both sides of the compact was mirrored. She tilted the compact until the stone wall across the cavern came into view in the top mirror.

The alignment of the bottom mirror made it so that it reflected the image in the top mirror, showing the wall flat against her palm.

"It's safe now," she called out, her voice so gentle and quiet that Bannack wasn't sure if the others would hear her.

Just as he suspected, none of the warriors or the human women stepped forward.

"She says it's safe," he called out to them.

They looked back at him with uncertainty on their faces, so Bannack took a few steps forward, leaving the softer ground of the bank and stepping again onto the hard, solid ground of the sky. He knew it was going to be there without even looking down.

Bannack taking those few steps seemed enough to convince Zuri, who took let go of Ero and took one large step forward, forgoing easing out over the space and instead going right for an open expanse between two branches. Samira followed, taking a slightly more cautious step, but stopping just beside Zuri. Bannack knew that the warriors not stepping forward was not out of fear, but out of distrust. Finally the men started forward and soon everyone was walking calmly across the expanse toward Bannack.

Suddenly he heard a scream and a deep grunt. He looked toward the back of the group and saw Ciyrs holding Elianna up by her arm as she struggled, her legs kicking down through a small section of the floor that now showed the sparkle of the stars rather than the solid darkness from before.

7

My stomach sank as I watched the tiny human woman drop, but she had had enough of a grip on the Denynso beside her that he was able to catch her before she was lost. Terror rolled over me. If her falling made any of the other ones question the solidity of the ground beneath their feet, they, too, would begin falling. Instead, they all rushed forward, getting off of the expanse of reflected stone as quickly as they could and then turning angry, suspicious eyes toward me.

"What the hell do you think you're doing?" the man that had rescued the small woman who fell demanded, taking an aggressive step toward me.

He didn't feel like a warrior. He seemed gentler, calmer, more nurturing despite his attempt to intimidate me.

"Ciyrs," the woman said, grabbing him and pulling him back, "You don't know that she did anything."

I felt relief wash over me. At least this one seemed to be willing to trust me rather than immediately blaming me.

"What do you think happened, Elianna?" another of the warriors snapped toward the small woman, "She's the one that told us it was all of a sudden safe to walk on the sky, and then as soon as you do, you fall."

"Don't talk to my mate like that," Ciyrs snarled toward the warrior, turning his aggression to him instead of me.

"I'm just pointing out that it's ridiculous for her to defend this person, whoever she is, when she is obviously the one who just tried to kill her."

Suddenly everyone started talking and shouting over top of one another and I felt like I was filling with so many feelings, emotions, and energies that I was going to shatter. I held my hands up and shouted as loudly as I could possibly force my voice.

"Stop it! All of you."

The cavern fell silent and the group turned and looked at me. Bannack seemed startled, but somewhat pleased, at my outburst and he stepped a little closer to me.

"What is it?" he asked.

"I didn't try to kill her," I said, wanting to talk to the entire group but at the same time feeling the compulsion to talk only to him, "It wasn't my fault."

"Then whose fault is it?" Ciyrs demanded.

"Hers," I said matter-of-factly.

"What?" he said roughly and I noticed all of the warriors looking at him with surprised looks on their faces as if he never showed this type of personality toward anyone.

Indeed, I could see the healer within him and knew that this was not in his normal nature. When it came to his mate, however, he was far more intense and aggressive than he would ever be when he was away from her. This made me less angry at the way he had treated me, but I was still not happy.

"In order for a reflection to mean anything, you have to believe in that reflection. If you didn't know what an item was and you saw a reflection of it, you still would not know what it was. You wouldn't embrace its presence and believe in its functions because you wouldn't know about them. If you looked in a mirror and saw something that you thought was something else, you would still believe that that reflection was what you thought it was and that if it was real, it would function the way you expected it to. Reflections only have the meaning that you give them. If you don't believe in the reflection, it can't work for you. She didn't believe in the stone beneath her feet, so the stone was no longer there."

I expected for them to react strongly again, but they surprised me by seeming to accept what I had told them without further argument. Even if they had argued, there would be nothing else that I could have said to them. It was a very simple concept, though one that may be difficult to grasp for those who hadn't grown up with such rules governing their existence.

"Do you live here?" the largest of the warriors asked me.

"Yes."

"May we look around?"

It was an unusual moment, a moment of balance and control. This was a moment that I had been waiting on for years, a moment when I would no longer be alone and could possibly look forward into a life that was not isolated beneath the ground for the majority of the time, and yet a moment that I also feared. I was so accustomed to being alone and to protecting the space that had once been the home to everyone who I have ever loved that it was frightening to me in a way to think of others entering the deeper areas of the space. I was very aware that nearly every inch of the land ground was a place where someone I cared for had taken their last step or even their last breath, and I had the irrational fear that if these people stepped on those places, they would cover them and diminish the memory of those last moments.

I glanced over at Bannack and found him looking at me, evaluating me. Looking at him offered me a sense of anchoring among the others in a way that I didn't understand. It was as though the rest of the group and I were completely separate entities, but that Bannack could act as a link between us that would close the space.

"Yes," I finally said, offering my permission for them to go further into the cavern.

"This is Loralia," Bannack introduced.

"Hello, Loralia. My name is Pyra."

One by one the warriors and the women introduced themselves to me and I found myself attaching characteristics to each of their names so that I would remember them more clearly later. Zuri was incredibly strong, but adored the way that her mate made her feel feminine and beautiful. Samira held wounds that were still healing, but for the first time in her life, she felt like she belonged. Elianna was vibrant and spirited, but still had a vulnerability in her that seemed to come from an event in the recent past that shaped her now and for the future.

I nodded at each of them as they introduced themselves and tried to offer smiles that would comfort them and ease their worries about me. Once everybody was introduced, Pyra started forward, keeping his eyes trained on me as he moved further into the cavern. There was still a heavy sense of distrust around him as he moved slowly past me and then ventured deeper. The others followed him, gazing around as they moved beyond the hill where I had been hiding when they first entered and stepped down into the expansive chamber that dipped lower and contained the first collection of small buildings that were once home to my friends and family. Two tunnels led off of this chamber, each leading to another chamber containing more buildings.

Off of these chambers were two more tunnels that fed together into one narrow corridor that led deep into the cavern to the chamber that our kind used as its greatest source of protection. When there were threats, we would gather there, utilizing our mirrors to reflect a solid wall over the mouth of the cavern so that no one could enter. I spent much of my time there, forgoing the home I once shared with my parents and siblings to live in the protecting surroundings of this nearly empty chamber.

"There is a tunnel that leads off of that first room and goes up into the cliffs at the edge of our compound," Pyra said.

It seemed more a statement than a question, but I replied anyway.

"Yes. I haven't used it in many years."

"Are there any other tunnels that lead into the cavern from above ground?"

"No. The only way to enter is that tunnel and the hatches in the forest."

"How often do you go above ground?"

The change in voice made me turn to Bannack, who was still standing close beside me. There was a faintly desperate look in his eyes and I could feel the sense that he was trying to understand of the emotions rolling through him, as if knowing how often I walked on the same ground as he did.

"Never," I told him, keeping my voice as even and calm as I could in an effort to assure him.

"How do you survive down here without ever going up?"

"The cavern provides everything that I need. There are plants throughout the cavern and a stream in the middle chamber. I was born down here and have always been here."

"Will you come up with us now?"

My eyes widened and I saw Pyra look sharply at Bannack, but he didn't say anything. My warrior, for that is how I was beginning to think of him, was staring at me intently and I saw him lift his hand toward me.

I hesitated only a moment before placing my fingers against the warmth of his palm and seeing the hint of a smile touch his lips.

8

____

B annack wrapped his hand around Loralia's fingers as soon as he felt their cool touch on his palm and turned to Pyra.

"We said that we wanted to learn more about the other species that are on this planet. Why don't we let her tell us?"

Pyra agreed and they started back toward the front of the cavern, allowing Loralia to use her compact to change the glimmering night sky spread across the floor into the hardened stone of the wall so that they could walk across it. Just like he had since the first time he had walked toward her, Bannack believed completely in the safety of the ground beneath his feet and crossed without hesitation, his hand cradling Loralia's beside him. The others paused briefly at the edge and Bannack saw them take a few breaths as if preparing themselves and convincing themselves that the ground would be solid when they stepped forward.

"WHERE ARE the others of your kind?"

Loralia looked up at Creia where he sat on his massive

throne without flinching. Bannack found himself watching her in awe, admiring how she could go from an underground realm she had always known to facing the king of an above ground species without showing any sign of intimidation or fear.

"There are no others," Loralia told him calmly, "I am the last of my kind."

"What happened to them?"

"There was a plague several years ago. I am the only one to survive."

Whispers rippled through the meeting hall and Bannack turned to glare at the others, suddenly protective and defensive. He knew that no matter how Loralia was handling herself in that moment as she faced down the king, confronting a strange species that was far larger and more powerful than her, and that she had always heard were the ones who had taken over the land her kind had once inhabited after war and illness drove them underground, had to be frightening to her. He didn't want the reaction of the rest of the Denynso to upset her further.

Bannack turned his attention back to Creia, who looked at his wife in a way that told Bannack that the mates were communicating silently. Theia turned to Loralia and he saw the gentle, nurturing look in her eyes that made her the mother figure of all of the Denynso.

"You are welcome here, Loralia," she said warmly, "You may stay with us for as long as you would like."

Bannack wasn't sure how Loralia was going to react, but he saw her take the few steps up toward the platform where the thrones sat and reach her pale, lovely hands toward the queen. Theia stood from her throne and approached Loralia as if she were as drawn to her as Bannack felt, and took the beautiful woman's hands in hers.

"Thank you."

Loralia's voice was so gentle Bannack could barely hear it, but he felt a little jump in his heart when he realized that she had accepted the queen's invitation to stay. The conflict he felt when he looked at her was so intense it made his stomach twist painfully. As much as he wanted to be near her, and the intense way his body responded whenever he looked at her, he was still extremely aware that she was a completely different, unknown species. He knew nothing about her or her kind, and part of him was still extremely wary about getting close to her.

Bannack jumped when he felt a heavy hand land on his shoulder. He looked up to see Ero standing beside him.

"What are you thinking about so hard over here?" the other warrior asked.

"Her," Bannack said, nodding toward Loralia, "How is it possible that she has been living right underneath us her entire life and not only did we not know she was there, we didn't even know that there was a place for anything to live down there? From what she said, her species has been down there since long before the Denynso even existed. We have lived right over top of her kind for generations, but there was never any interaction."

"So?"

"So? Doesn't that make you suspicious? If they have been down there that whole time, they would know when the Denynso settled. Why did they just stay down there and not come up and try to make contact?"

"Maybe they didn't feel like they had any reason to. There was never any conflict, so why shake things up? Isn't existing peacefully what matters?"

Bannack looked back at Loralia.

"I don't know. It just seems weird to me. I don't know how I feel about her staying around here."

"You are the one that quite literally took her by the hand and brought her here. Why did you do that if you didn't want her here?"

Bannack sighed.

"I don't know," he answered honestly, "I just felt like it was what I should do in that moment."

Ero looked at him and Bannack saw his mouth twitch like he was fighting a smile. The other warrior nodded and his eyes traveled briefly down Bannack's body.

"Yep," Ero said, patting Bannack on the back, "I'm sure you did."

Ero walked away, heading back across the meeting hall toward Zuri. Confused, Bannack glanced down and saw exactly what had called Ero's amused attention to the lower half of his body. Muttering expletives under his breath, Bannack tried to adjust himself as quickly and subtly as he could to make his raging erection less obvious. Just as he was finishing, he saw Creia look up at him and gesture for him to come to the platform. By now both the king and queen were standing at the edge of the platform and as Bannack approached he saw them grin happily at him.

"I hear you have met our new friend," Creia said, reaching out to touch his hand to Bannack's shoulder.

"Yes," Bannack replied.

"She has accepted our invitation to stay with us and she requested that you be her guide and protector while she is here."

Bannack looked over at Loralia and found her gazing back at him, the lavender of her eyes so intoxicating he felt like he was falling into them. He felt her hand intertwine with his again and his erection twitched. The frustration and confusion built inside him and he felt painfully torn. He knew that he couldn't deny the king and queen his service as her protector, but the way his heart and body were responding to him made him feel both excited and repelled. She was at once the most beautiful and intriguing creature that he had ever seen, and something that made him uncomfortable.

"I will," he answered.

"Good. Bring her to the house where Samira was going to live," Creia turned back to Loralia, "I hope that you will be comfortable there."

"I'm sure I will," Loralia responded, "Thank you for your kindness."

Bannack gave a nod toward the king and queen and led Loralia out of the meeting hall, forcing himself to keep his eyes trained forward rather than letting them wander over to her or to acknowledge the group of warriors sitting at one long table, watching him and muttering comments as they passed. He knew what they were saying, but he didn't want to acknowledge it.

Loralia took a deep breath as they stepped out of the building and into the quiet center of the compound.

"I love the way the air smells up here," she said, "It's so different from the cavern."

"I'm glad you like it," Bannack replied gruffly, not turning his eyes toward her.

Finally they arrived at the simple house on the same row as the other homes the Denynso reserved for the scientists and students who had been invited to visit Uoria as part of the exchange program. He opened the door for her and stepped back to allow her to enter in front of him.

"Will you come in with me?" she asked gently. Bannack hesitated. "It's the first night that I've spent away from the cavern in my entire life. I don't want to be alone just yet. Please just spend a few minutes with me."

No matter what he tried to tell himself, Bannack couldn't resist her request. He stepped forward into the house and let Loralia close the door behind him.

"The solar panels collect energy throughout the day so you can use the lights and heat water for a shower."

Bannack turned back to Loralia and saw her staring at him.

"Why are you fighting it?" she asked, taking a step toward him.

9

I could see the confusion flicker across his eyes, but the intense feelings were still radiating toward me as I walked slowly toward Bannack. His gaze traveled along me, exploring the curves and planes of my face and the dips of my body, but I could still sense the internal struggle that was keeping him from admitting what was coursing through his mind and his veins.

"Fighting what?" he finally asked me, his voice strained slightly.

"What you are feeling right now."

I was only two steps away from him now, close enough that I could feel intense, powerful heat pulsing off of his body and see the swell in the front of his loose-fitting pants.

"Can you read my thoughts?" he asked defensively, obviously uncomfortable with not only the concept that I would be able to get into his mind and read what was there, but what the implications of that ability would be if I was to be able to do it.

Still staring at the front of his pants, I bit my bottom lip and shook my head slowly, finally lifting my eyes to his.

"No," I said, "but I can sense what you're feeling. I can look into you and see and feel what is inside you. I know what you're thinking about right now, and I want to know why you are fighting it."

He didn't respond and I lifted my hands to the ties at the front of my dress. I released them slowly and carefully, deliberately looking into his eyes as I did. The ties stretched from my neckline down to the center of my stomach and I loosened them all the way down. Once the ties had fallen loose, the bodice of my dress slipped down, revealing my breasts. Bannack cleared his throat and looked away, but I didn't stop. I could feel my hair sweep across my bare back as I carefully pushed the dress down over my hips and let it pool at my feet. I was barefoot as I always was, so when I stepped out of the soft white fabric and gently kicked it aside, I was standing in front of Bannack in only a pair of thin, finely woven panties that tied at either hip.

"Why do you keep fighting?" I asked again, taking another step toward him so that only one more step separated us.

Bannack shifted where he stood, looking around as if he couldn't find something to rest his eyes on so that he didn't look at me.

"I can't feel this way about you," he finally said and I felt a little flicker in my belly.

"Feel what way about me?" I asked.

He looked at me and the confusion in his eyes had turned dark and mixed with the desire coursing through his body.

"You know exactly what way," he nearly snarled.

"Of course you can feel that way," I said.

"And why is it so easy for you to just say that?" he asked.

The tension in his voice said that he was being sarcastic, but at the same time he was truly asking me.

"Because," I said, taking hold of the strings on either side of my panties, "you already do."

I pulled the strings, releasing the ties and letting my panties fall free away from my body. I could feel what was inside him more intensely in that moment than I had in any other except for the very first moment when I saw him in the cavern. I had known immediately and the feeling building inside me was something that I had never experienced. The longer I looked at him, the more I realized that what I was feeling was not a matter of a simple reflection. I had fallen completely under his spell and I was helpless to resist him, even if he was trying to resist what he was feeling himself.

Bannack's eyes shifted briefly into a dark orange and I saw his hands clench, tightening into fists as if he was fighting to control his body as much as his mind. I closed the space between us with a final step, bringing us close enough that my breasts brushed against him and I could feel his erection straining toward me. I reached up and touched his cheek, guiding his face so that he looked down into my eyes. The pad of my thumb stroked over his lips and Bannack's eyes drifted closed. I could feel the breath stream from his lungs and ripple from the inside of my wrist down my arm. The warm feeling made my nipples tighten and I felt a tingle slip down between my thighs.

I walked around Bannack further into the house, making my way toward the furniture arranged in the middle of the main room. After a few steps, Bannack followed me. We didn't speak, but our hands expressed more than words could have in that moment. He approached me and I took the end of the tie that closed his pants in one hand. As I loosened it, my warrior cupped one of his hands around my breast and ran his thumb across my nipple, making it ache. His pants slipped down his hips to his feet and he stepped out of them and his soft boots at the same time. As he pulled his shirt off over his head, I rested my palm against his long, hard shaft and wrapped my fingers around it. I stroked him carefully but insistently, watching my hand in awe as it moved across his erection.

I felt his finger tuck under my chin and lift my face up to his. There was a still, quiet moment, and then he leaned forward to touch his lips to mine. The kiss filled me as if it gave me breath, satisfying something deep within me that I hadn't even known needed fulfillment until I saw him for the first time. Our mouths moved across each other languidly, tenderly and carefully discovering the feeling and taste of each other's lips and welcoming each other's tongues to slip between, tangling and exploring.

Bannack stepped forward, pushing me back so that he could turn and sit down in the large chair I had been standing beside. Our mouths parted and I could hear our heavy breaths filling the space around us, accentuating the silence we had maintained. Bannack's strong hands turned me and eased me back so that I sat on his lap, moving my hair aside so that it cascaded down his thing and along the front of the chair. His body cradled me, surrounding me in his warmth and the strength of his presence. He wrapped his arms around me and I let my head rest back against his shoulder.

We remained still for several long seconds, our breaths synchronizing as his heartbeat created an enticing yet comforting rhythm against my back. His hand flattened in the middle of my chest and smoothed its way down my body, pausing in the dip between my hipbones. I could feel myself trembling and my breath caught in my throat as he applied gentle pressure. No one's hands had ever touched me and I found myself overwhelmed with the sensation of his body so close to mine and his hand easing down between my thighs.

Bannack's other hand carefully parted my legs to give himself better access, keeping his grip on my thigh as if providing stability. The first touch of his fingers in the warmth of my body sent shockwaves through me and I cried out, arching off of him so that he took his hand way from my thigh and rested it on my belly, easing me back down into his lap. I let the strength of his hand on stomach relax and reassure me, and my body rested down against him. Releasing the tension in my thighs, I allowed my knees to fall open further and welcomed his touch. Bannack's fingers explored my hot, wet folds, building dizzying sensations and tension throughout my hips, thighs, and lower belly.

Suddenly the feelings shattered within me and a cascade of intense tremors rippled through my body. My hips lifted up out of his lap and I felt his strong, powerful erection slip from behind my back to in front of me. I tucked my hand around it, pressing it against my body so that he could feel the warm wetness that he created. Acting purely on instinct, I rolled my hips, letting my core run along his length until I could hear him groaning behind me. I wanted him inside me in a way that I had never wanted anything. I lifted my hips, readying myself to guide him to my entrance, when I felt Bannack's hands suddenly tighten on my hips.

"Stop."

10

Bannack held his shirt under his arm as he rushed out of Loralia's house, tying the strings on the front of his pants and trying to block her voice out of his ears. He could hear her behind him, shouting for him, calling for him to come back, but he forced the sound away and kept forging ahead, dropping his shirt down over his body and setting out at a run. The thoughts and emotions rushing through his mind had reached a fevered pitch when he felt the intoxicating, entrancing warmth of her body against him and he just couldn't let himself keep going. As much as he wanted her, and it was far more than he could ever have imagined wanting anyone or anything in his entire life, he hadn't been able to silence the conflicts and questions raging in his head.

"Bannack!"

A different voice forced itself into his consciousness and he paused to turn toward it. Ero was running toward him across the compound. Ero was always running. It was something that he had done since he was young to combat his own feelings and escape whatever was bothering him at the moment. He used to run out of fear and anger, but since he had found Zuri he ran only to amuse himself and when he was needed.

"What is it Ero?" he asked, the question coming out sharper and angrier than he had intended.

"Pyra told me to get all of the warriors in the meeting hall."

"For what?"

"I don't know. He seemed really serious about it, though."

"Does he know that Creia assigned me as Loralia's protector?"

"Why would that have anything to do with him wanting you at the meeting hall? Besides, if you are her protector, why aren't you with her?"

The question fell like a rock into Bannack's gut and he shook his head, trying to shake the images of the time he had just spent with the gorgeous, confounding creature. Ero seemed to know not to push the issue and the two warriors hurried toward the meeting hall in silence. When they got inside, the main room bustled with voices and an argument seemed to be going on at one of the long tables.

Suddenly Pyra jumped up onto the table so that he was visible above the heads of the other warriors and Denynso men who had gathered around him. Bannack looked around and saw Creia sitting silently on the platform, staring at the men with a look on his face that was at once worried and pleased.

"If you aren't brave enough to come with me, then don't," Pyra shouted and some of the warriors shouted back at him, "I'm going. The king has given me permission and I am going to take it. I've already discussed it with Eden, and she agrees that we don't want to bring our baby into this world until we know what kinds of threats, and what kinds of opportunities, may exist outside of our compound. She may be close to delivery, which means that I need to go soon if I am to be back by the time the baby arrives."

"Where are you going?" Bannack shouted up toward the warrior.

Pyra looked down at him.

"I'm going to explore Uoria outside of the compound. There are other species out there that we don't know anything about, and I want to change that. Eden, Leia, Elianna, Zuri, and Samira all came here from Earth because the humans want to know more about our kind, yet we haven't even gone so far as the other side of our own planet to find out what might be there."

"When are you leaving?"

"Three days. I need the time to get together all of the supplies that I might need while I'm gone." He straightened and looked out over the group of warriors. "Who's with me?"

There was defiance in his voice, a sense of strength and defensiveness that seemed to come from the idea that there were things he couldn't protect his mate and future child from because he didn't know what they were or what they might do. It enraged him, and as the fiercest and most aggressive of the warriors already, that was intimidating to see.

A few of the other warriors yelled back up to him, but Bannack turned and ran toward Creia's platform.

"Are you alright, Bannack?" the king asked as he approached.

"May I have permission to have a leave from my responsibilities to Loralia and go with the other warriors?" Bannack asked, ignoring Creia's question.

The king hesitated.

"She is new to our compound, Bannack. She specifically

asked if you would be her guide. That must mean that she trusts you."

"I understand that, but I feel that I would be better serving the tribe if I went with the warriors and helped explore the planet. I'm sure that the human women would be happy to keep an eye on Loralia and help her get accustomed to the compound. They would probably do better than me anyway."

"Why do you say that?"

"Because they're different, too."

"Different?"

The king seemed to be testing Bannack in some way, but he didn't have the patience to explore what he might mean.

"They aren't Denynso. They are a different kind, so they know what it's like to be a strange species among the tribe. It might make her feel better to spend some time with them."

"I'll give you permission to go with the warriors, Bannack, if you are able to convince the women to take on your role as protector. But listen carefully when I tell you to think about your decision, and your reasoning, carefully."

Bannack nodded his thanks and ran back across the meeting hall. He couldn't get the taste of Loralia's lips or the feeling of her body on his fingers out of his mind no matter how hard he found them, and he knew that he had to get to the women so that he could get them on his side and start preparing for the journey. He, like the other Denynso, had never ventured away from the compound, but right now getting as far away from his home, and from Loralia, as possible seemed like the only thing that he could do.

He got to the edge of the table where Pyra stood and shouted up at him over the voices of the other warriors who still seemed to be locked in a debate over whether they should go at all. Many thought that it would better serve them to concentrate on building up the defenses of the compound before they started searching for threats.

"Where's Eden?" Bannack asked.

"She's at the bakery with Samira. Why do you need her?"

"Creia says that the only way I can go with you is to get the human women to agree to watch over Loralia while I'm gone."

"Why?"

"She chose me as her protector."

A smile crossed Pyra's lips, but Bannack refused to acknowledge it. He pushed away from the table and ran out of the meeting hall toward the bakery. The smell of fresh, hot bread greeted him as soon as he opened the door.

"I need your help," he said and saw Eden jump slightly where she was sitting on a high stool near the counter where Samira was rolling out long ropes of dough to form into braided loaves.

"Is everything alright?"

"I want to go with the warriors to explore Uoria, but I need someone to watch Loralia while I'm gone. She chose me as her protector and guide, and the king says that I can only have permission to go with Pyra if you will agree to watch over her while we're gone."

The two women exchanged glances. If he didn't know better he would think that they were communicating with their minds in the same way that mates could. Eden's hand wandered to her belly like it so frequently did and she seemed to press into a certain area as if she could feel the baby through her skin.

"Are you sure that's what you want?" Eden asked.

Bannack was growing impatient with being questioned. Everyone seemed to think that they knew something he didn't, and it frustrated him. He nodded, not wanting to give her the satisfaction of acknowledging her seeking tone.

"I want to know what's outside this compound. I'm tired of seeing the same things and going the same places. There's more out there and I want to know what it is, but the only way I can do that is to unload Loralia."

"You're the one who brought her here."

"So I've been reminded," Bannack said through gritted teeth.

"If you're sure that's what you want, Bannack, I'll be happy to help her get used to the compound."

"Thank you."

Bannack stepped back out of the bakery and took a deep breath of the night air, hoping it would cool the burning on his cheeks. He didn't know what he wanted anymore, other than to get away.

TBC

(To be continued in Part II...)

THE ALIEN PROMISE

1

———

I didn't know how to feel or what to do. I stood at the doorway to the house, what was meant to be my new home, staring into the darkness for what felt like hours after Bannack left. Finally I stepped back into the house and closed the door behind me, pressing my back against it and sliding to the floor so that I could curl my knees against my chest and rest my forehead against my folded arms. Everything around me in the Denynso compound was strange and unknown, and now suddenly I was feeling a pain that I never knew existed, with an intensity that was far beyond anything I thought that I could ever feel. The air around me felt oppressive, while the places on my body that Bannack had touched now felt cold and abandoned. I felt empty inside, both in that my heart felt torn from my chest and in that my body still ached for him even though he had left so abruptly. I couldn't understand what had just happened.

I sat against the door, letting the darkness of the coming night close in around me without moving to turn on any of the lights throughout the space. Everything had been going so perfectly. The feelings that I had experienced for Bannack since the first moment that I saw him had grown within me until they felt like they were burning in my belly and overflowing within my chest, creating a sense that made me at once overwhelmed and elated. I had been so young when the rest of my kind had died off due to the horrific plague that scourged our home that I had never had the opportunity to feel love, or even real attraction, to anyone. I had seen my parents together and how they felt about each other was obvious. I could remember even then how they would hold hands, gaze at each other, and find any excuse to be close to each other, even after they had spent more than half of their lives together. I hadn't understood that until I had seen Bannack.

Being alone in the mirrored realm that existed beneath the Denynso compound had been isolating and lonely, but I had grown accustomed to my life alone underground. Over the years I had become absolutely comfortable with not having anyone else with me, and even felt that I preferred the quiet and isolation because it meant that I could live exactly as I wanted to and have no one and nothing to tell me otherwise. When the Klimnu invaded, the terror had been more that they would change my lifestyle than that they would hurt me, and I had managed to stay completely out of the way the entire time that they were down there. Even when I saw the human woman and the Denynso traitor, and then the other human women, come into the mirrored realm, I felt no compulsion to interact with them. I had hoped that the Klimnu would simply tire of my world and leave me alone so that I could go back to my simple, independent life and not have to worry about anything else.

The moment that my eyes touched Bannack, however, all of that changed. Everything around him disappeared. I couldn't perceive the other warriors or the slimy, disgusting creatures that were battling them. It was as though nothing else in the entire world mattered in those moments but this beautiful warrior who in a single second changed everything about how I felt about life. Suddenly I didn't want to live completely alone underground anymore. I didn't want to continue on with the lifestyle that I had built and evolved into after my family and friends had died. I didn't want to be left to my own devices, or to have a life that was totally my own. In that instant I could understand why my parents spent nearly all of their time together, and why when my father died, my mother followed him only hours later even though she had barely been sick.

He, of course, didn't know it, but I had watched the entire battle between the Klimnu and the Denynso. I had followed him carefully in each of his movements, making sure that he stayed safe as he fought. I didn't even know his name then, but I could feel the intensity of his presence and the energy emanating off of him in a way that I had never experienced. In the final moments of the battle, I had saved him. He stumbled while trying to approach Jem, the incredibly courageous warrior who had given his life to ensure the future of his people, and a moment later caught himself. He thought that he had simply managed to find his footing and regain his hold on the vine that was coming from the tree where he stood. In reality, I had reflected the surface of the tree so that he could step steadily onto it before finding his way back to his original stance.

The action had been risky. I nearly betrayed my existence in that single moment, but I was willing to do anything in order to ensure that he got through the battle safely. It was a decision that I had made impulsively, without really thinking, and it hadn't struck me until I saw him again the next day and had the compulsion to again save him from tumbling into the reflection of the sky by creating a floor of the image of the stone wall that it was him that I had saved. It was as if I was reacting to a memory that I hadn't made yet, a thought or a feeling that I had deep within me that wasn't really there but was waiting to be there. It was difficult even for me to explain, but something that I wanted to feel more of.

The glow of my skin was even more evident in the room now that I was cloaked in complete darkness and I thought about the first time that Bannack saw me. He had felt something when he got down into the mirrored realm. Something within him had told him that things were changing and that he was about to experience something that would forever change him, but no matter how hard I tried to look into him, I couldn't figure out exactly what that was. When he noticed my glow across the sky, however, that feeling had intensified and I knew that he felt the same draw and need about me that I was feeling about him.

He had trusted me then. He had given himself over to me and to the unknown that waited when he took a completely unafraid step away from the branches that crossed the reflected sky and created the only source of stability that they knew down in my world, and onto the stone floor that I had made for him. There had been no sense of fear in him, or even unsureness. It was as though he knew, even if he had no concept of what or who I was, that he was safe as long as I was there.

What had happened between that moment and the moment when he ran out of the house and into the darkness of the night without a single word of explanation? He had taken my hand in my world beneath the compound, led me out of the ground and literally into a world that I had never once seen or experienced. I had offered myself to him in the way that he had offered himself to me, stepping into something that I had only heard about and never once witnessed myself, for the first time in my solitary existence truly wanting to go above ground, and for the first time in the years since I had become accustomed to being alone that I had wanted to put that life behind me and share life with someone else.

In those moments I felt a connection between us that was only growing with each second. Resistance had begun to build inside him, though, and he had started to fight the feelings that I knew he had when he looked at me. He didn't need to say them. I could feel them when he touched me, when he rested his mouth to mine, and when he tucked his hand between my thighs to create unimaginable sensations and emotions within me. Just before I welcomed his body into mine, however, he moved me off of him and started to dress. I had dropped my dress over my head and tied the laces as quickly as I could, but it wasn't fast enough to stop him from crossing to the door, his shirt clutched in his hand, and running out into the darkness of the compound.

My own voice screaming after him was reverberating in my mind and tears like I hadn't cried since I was a small child pooled beneath my eyes and poured down the skin of my arms where my head rested. He had given me no explanation, offered no reason for suddenly leaving me in the silence aching for him, but in that moment I felt more alone than I ever had.

2

———

Bannack paced outside of the bakery for a few minutes, not really knowing what he was supposed to do with himself, and trying to convince himself that the decision he had made was the right one. After all, he had been the one to bring up the fact that the Denynso, including Creia, the king who they all looked up to and thought of as being the most powerful and knowledgeable of them all, didn't really know anything about the rest of the planet of Uoria or what types of species inhabited their planet. It had been this assertion and his insistence that they find out what was going on that brought them back down into the mirrored realm that they had discovered during the final battle with the Klimnu. If that hadn't happened, they never would have found Loralia at all, and the rest of the warriors, particularly Pyra, wouldn't have agreed with him about how important it was to go out and find out more about the planet.

The fact that the warriors were now planning on leaving the compound for the first time and going on an exploration of the rest of the planet so that they could see what they might discover and potentially identify future threats to them was based entirely on his determination and his recommendations. It was only logical and fair that he be permitted to go along with them. He had not asked Loralia to request him as her guard and protector while she was in the compound. While he had been the one who had asked her to come up above ground in the compound with them, it had not been his idea for the king and queen to invite her to stay with them once they found out that she was the only one left of her kind. He should not be held responsible for the wellbeing of a creature who he didn't know and who he had not pledged his loyalty to until forced.

The more he paced and the harder he thought, the closer Bannack was to convincing himself that asking the human women to take on the responsibilities of taking care of Loralia and making sure that she got assimilated to her new surroundings so that he could join the other warriors in the quest outside the compound was not only fair, but truly his only choice. If he had agreed to stay behind with Loralia rather than going with Pyra, Gyyx, Ero, and the others, he would have compromised his position as a warrior and presented himself as being a coward. He also would have shorted himself an opportunity to learn things that no other Denynso had ever known, possibly putting himself and the rest of the compound at risk should he ever come into contact with one of the species that the warriors found during their explorations.

Even though he had made himself believe he was fully justified in walking away from his responsibilities with Loralia, he still couldn't entirely convince himself that walking away from her, or more precisely running away from her, after he brought her home was the right thing to do. He was incredibly torn, more conflicted than he had ever been in his entire life. Loralia was the single most beautiful thing that he had ever seen, and even before he had laid eyes on her, his mind and body had started responding to her presence. Just being near her made his defensive, aggressive instincts kick in stronger than they ever had even in the many battles he had faced. As soon as he saw her, he was instantly entranced by her. She was ethereal and gorgeous in a way that was truly indescribable. The gentle glow of her skin, incomparable lavender color of her eyes, and flowing silver hair made her look as though she were not quite real, as if she were a delightful figment of his imagination conjured in a moment of near-death to soothe and comfort him.

The touch of her hand and the smell of her skin, though, told him that she was absolutely not a figment of his imagination or some wonderfully lucid dream. She was incredibly real, real in a way that he could not quite fathom and was not ready to believe. Loralia created in Bannack feelings that he didn't want to admit to himself much less anyone else, and the more he felt them, the more he wanted to force them down into himself so that they couldn't be felt, seen, or experienced. This was not the way it was supposed to be. He had not waited his entire life to find his mate only to find himself falling for a creature that belonged to a species he hadn't even known existed until that day.

He hated himself for the betrayal of his mind and body, and for not being able to control himself. He hated himself even more than that lack of control had led him to nearly mating with her. If he had waited just seconds longer he would have felt her body envelope him, and he would have known for sure if she was what he feared his mind was trying to tell him that she was. Bannack had not been ready for that moment of clarity. He didn't know which answer he dreaded more, or how he would have responded to either one. In that moment all he knew was that he needed to get away from her, and that he didn't want to be in the same room with her again for a very long time.

Even as he thought that, though, he knew that he was lying to himself. No matter how hard the two sides of him struggled and fought, he couldn't deny that he still felt incredibly drawn to Loralia, and that more than anything he wanted to be near her.

"Bannack."

He heard Eden's voice from behind him and he turned to look at her. She had her hand rested protectively over her swollen belly like she usually did and the little bit of weight that she had gained in her face during her pregnancy made her look softer and gentler than she had when she first arrived on the planet.

"What's going on with you?" Eden asked, lowering her voice as though she wanted to keep the conversation private.

"What do you mean?" Bannack asked, trying to force his voice to sound casual.

"I know you, Bannack. I know when you aren't telling the whole truth, and right now a big part of you is lying. Asking me and the other girls to take care of Loralia isn't just about wanting to go wander around the planet with the other warriors. What is it actually about?"

Sometimes Bannack really hated how in tune to emotions that the human women seemed to be. The Denynso women weren't like that. They were gentler and more feeling than the men tended to be, but they were still aggressive and gruff compared to the humans. He could only imagine how much more difficult it was for their Denynso mates. Part of the mating process for their kind was creating an unbreakable link during the actual bonding.

This link made it possible for the mates to communicate with one another without having to speak, which meant that not only were the human women able to tell when their mates were dealing with an emotional situation, they could actually read their thoughts and find out exactly what was going on if the Denynso men weren't careful to control what was going through their minds. It seemed overwhelming to be that close to someone else.

"I just want to go with the other warriors," he said, "It was my idea to find out more about the other species anyway."

He realized that he sounded like he was whining, but he didn't really care. He was dealing with enough of his own confused thoughts and feelings to think about trying to seem tough and put together.

"Alright. Don't tell me if you don't want to. Just know that I know that there is something else going on, and eventually we are going to all figure it out."

She turned and headed back into the bakery. Bannack had absolutely no doubt that what the little red-haired human woman had said was the truth. They were smart, crafty, and extremely capable. Not only could they find out what he was going through if they wanted to, they would, and they would do their best to interfere until they helped him find a solution. That just meant he needed to get out of the compound and away from Loralia as quickly as possible.

3

———————

I don't know how long I sat on the floor, my back against the door to the house that was meant to be my home but was feeling more and more like a strange and unwelcoming prison with every second. Part of me wanted so much to go out into the compound and look for Bannack so that I could ask him what happened and hope that he could give me some explanation for running away from me like that. Maybe there was an element of his species that I didn't know about that had made him leave. He had asked me if I had read his mind, and he seemed frustrated and almost angry when he asked me. Perhaps there was something more to that question than I had originally thought. If the people of this species could easily communicate with each other through their minds, it was possible that one of them had reached out to Bannack and told him that he was needed somewhere else. The loyalty and sense of duty that came with being a warrior would mean that he felt compelled and inarguably obligated to go where he was needed.

Though it didn't fully explain why Bannack hadn't

responded to me when I called for him after he left, or why he didn't simply tell me why he was leaving, telling myself that there could be an explanation behind his sudden departure did soothe me in a way. I still felt hurt and upset, not so much angry as I was simply brokenhearted. I knew that the feelings that had built inside me so intensely happened very quickly, but I had never once felt like they were forced or that I was moving beyond what he was feeling as well. In that moment it struck me that even though I hadn't thought that I was moving too quickly, my understanding of the love and relationship rituals of my own kind was minimal, and I knew absolutely nothing about the relationships of the Denynso. I realized that it was possible that I had offended him in some way, and that thought made me feel sick to my stomach. The idea that in my haste to explore what I was feeling toward him I had pushed my warrior away and ended the possibility that we would ever be together made me wish that I had never come above ground.

I was just beginning to stand up, planning to go to sleep and see how I felt about everything in the light of the morning, when I heard a knock on the door behind me. My heart jumped in my chest. I hoped that it was Bannack, come back to explain what happened and perhaps resume where we had left off. I straightened my dress, smoothed away the last of the tears that were still lingering on my cheeks, and opened the door. As soon as I did, the smile faded from my face. Instead of Bannack standing outside, it was two of the human women that I had met when they came underground with the warriors along with one who had been in the meeting hall when Bannack brought me to meet the king and queen of their people.

The expression on my face must have given away my

disappointment at seeing them rather than Bannack because they all narrowed their eyes slightly and looked concerned.

"Is everything alright?" the one I remembered as Zuri asked.

I nodded, trying to muster a smile that would assure them that I was fine.

"Are you sure?" the lovely, rather heavily pregnant one asked.

If it was possible, her belly looked slightly more swollen than when I had first seen her and I could feel that she was tired and somewhat anxious. I could only imagine that carrying a child at all would be stressful, but I had also noticed that there didn't seem to be any other pregnant women, babies, or children at all throughout the compound. The youngest people I had seen were some of the warriors who looked only a few years younger than me.

"Is there something wrong with the house? Are the lights not turning on?" Zuri asked.

All of the attention coming from them was becoming overwhelming and I felt bombarded even though I knew that they had come to me out of concern and genuine desire to welcome me to the compound. I stepped back and held out a hand to invite them to come inside.

"Everything is fine," I told them, "I haven't turned on any of the lights yet."

The faint light emanating from my skin and the blue glow coming from a luminescent plant across the room filled the space with just enough illumination that I was able to see the women clearly as they came into the room. I crossed to one of the lamps sitting on a low table that was similar to the types of lights that I had down in the mirrored realm and touched its base, hoping that it would turn on, which it did. The new light in the room seemed to put the women slightly more at ease and they all came further into the room.

They didn't want to say it, and they tried very much to be as subtle as they could, but they were all scrutinizing me closely as they approached. Though they were happy to welcome me into the compound and do whatever they could to help me assimilate, they were also somewhat wary of me, an emotion that each carried in a slightly different way.

I could feel that Zuri focused heavily on the way that I looked, identifying the differences between us and feeling at once uncomfortable and guilty about that feeling. The image of Ero, a man I assumed to be her mate, flickered through her mind and the discomfort eased. Leia, the smallest of the women, was fascinated by my differences, but also carried a sense of defensiveness and distance that came from dark memories of the first time she encountered a species that was not her own, dark memories that she shielded closely within her.

The pregnant woman was the most difficult. She was at the same moment the one who seemed most willing to welcome me and the most nurturing, but also the most hesitant. Carrying the child within her had heightened both her natural sense of curiosity and desire to learn about the world around her, but also of fear and suspicion. I could sense that as much as she wanted to think of me as just another woman who had found her way into the Denynso compound, she was also nervous about encountering another species that she didn't understand and that she had had no time to learn to trust.

This was perhaps the most difficult part of being around other creatures again. When I was alone I had no one's emotions to contend with but my own. I could feel and experience only what was impacting me at that moment and work through them in the way that was right for me. When I was with others, I could feel and experience what they did, forcing me to acknowledge their true impressions of me and of the world around them. While it was possible for me to control it and block myself from reflecting the thoughts and feelings of others, I had never built that skill when I was younger and now it was an incredible challenge for me to not tune in to others when I was struggling with my own emotions. This meant that right when I was at my most vulnerable, my mind betrayed me and allowed even more emotion in, often putting me in painful, difficult moments when I was at my least capable of tolerating them.

"I'm Eden," the pregnant woman said, stepping toward me cautiously, "I don't think that I've introduced myself yet."

"Hello," I said, "I'm Loralia."

"I know. We just wanted to come see you and let you know that we're excited that you decided to stay with us. There aren't enough ladies around here."

The three women laughed and I felt myself smile. Despite their hesitance, it was nice to hear that they were happy that I was there.

"Thank you."

"We know what it's like to leave the home you've always known and suddenly become a part of the Denynso," Eden continued, "and we want you to know that we're here for you and we're looking forward to spending time with you while Bannack is gone."

She gave me a soft hint of a knowing smile, but I couldn't even force one back at her.

"What do you mean while Bannack is gone?" I asked,

barely able to push the words through the hard lump forming in my throat.

Eden, Zuri, and Leia looked struck and exchanged glances.

"He didn't tell you?" Leia asked.

"No."

"He is leaving with the warriors."

4

———

Bannack walked into the meeting hall with a sense of relief, but at the same time, a feeling of longing and emptiness that made him wish that he could simply turn off his emotions and face the world completely blank and cold. It was that way that the warriors marched into their battles, emotionless, aggressive, and without feeling or compassion. He wished that he could maintain that throughout the rest of his life as well so that he didn't have to deal with feeling like this anymore.

It made him feel better to know that Eden, Zuri, and Leia had gone to see Loralia and welcome her to the compound, but he knew that them going to see her meant that she would soon know that he was leaving and abandoning his guard and protector responsibilities. He knew that this was going to hurt her, and as much as he was conflicted about how he was feeling about her, he hated the idea that he was causing this creature that had already gone through so much even more pain. He didn't want to be her impression of life above the ground, but he didn't have a choice. He had made a single impulsive decision by walking out across the sky and toward the pearlescent glow that had seemed to call to him, and in that decision he felt like he had given over control of himself.

He no longer felt like he could think clearly or make the types of rational decisions that he once did. Though volatile and unpredictable, Bannack had always been one to understand his own motivations and compulsions, even if none of the other warriors, men, women, or even rulers of the Denynso understood them. He didn't like the feeling that these were things he couldn't think his way through and that for the first time his heart seemed to be making decisions that his mind didn't understand or condone.

Some of the other warriors were milling around in the meeting hall talking about the upcoming trip. A few of them were still questioning the decision to leave the compound and go on the quest, and others were trying to convince them that it was the right thing for the entirety of the clan. Bannack had no interest in trying to build up their ranks or muster more support for the trip, especially if that meant delaying their departure more than the three days that they already had planned. He simply wanted to get their plans in place, prepare, and leave.

Bannack felt a hard pat on his back and spun around defensively, taking an aggressive step forward even before he saw who was standing behind him. Ty, a gentle giant in every meaning of the phrase, stepped back, a startled look in his deep orange eyes. The shade of his eyes was a recent development, a color that had formed only in the couple of weeks since the massive baker had discovered his mate in the beautiful, brilliant, and very young Samira.

"I'm sorry," Bannack said, shaking slightly to try to release the tension that had built in his body.

He felt like he had been wound up, the pressure inside

him building almost unbearably and just waiting for its release. It was similar to the feeling that he got when they were marching toward battle, but deeper and more intense in a way that he couldn't quite understand and hadn't ever experienced.

"Are you doing OK, Bannack?" Ty asked, "You haven't really seemed like yourself since the funeral."

Bannack wanted to brush off the comment and just try to pass it off as being devastated over Jem's death like the rest of the tribe, but he knew that that wouldn't work. Ty, like the others, had known Bannack their entire lives and it would take much more than a flimsy excuse to get them off of his back if they really wanted to know what was going on with him. He let Ty guide him over to one of the long tables where no one else was sitting and slumped down onto the bench.

"I can't think straight," Bannack admitted, "I feel like my mind is going in a thousand different directions and all I want to do is get on our way so that I don't have to think anymore. Why do we have to wait three days?"

"Because it's going to take that long to get all of the supplies together that we need. Besides, we want a little bit of time to say goodbye to our mates properly. It might be a while before we see them again and we'd like to make sure that we have plenty to think about while we're gone."

The young man gave a laugh, but Bannack couldn't muster the same reaction. He glanced down at his hands, suddenly feeling even more uncomfortable at the mention of the other men's mates.

"What are you thinking about so hard over here, Bannack?"

Pyra and Ero came up and settled onto the benches, Ero beside Bannack and Pyra across the table from him beside

Ty. All three of the men were staring at him, and Bannack felt the same desperate need to get away that he had when he was standing at the funeral. He knew that that was not really an option now, however. He looked into the faces of each of the men and thought that perhaps talking to them might be a good thing. It could help him to sort through whatever was running through his mind and gain some clarity so that he knew how to move forward.

"I just can't seem to get a hold of my brain recently."

"Why not? Is something going on?" Ero asked.

"I just have all these thoughts and I've been feeling particularly aggressive and angry lately. Ever since the battle, I just feel like I can't keep control of myself."

Out of the corner of his eye Bannack saw the other men exchange glances.

"Are you feeling like you want to kick the living hell out of just about every guy that gets near you, including us?"

"Well, I did just almost punch Ty in the face because he came up and patted me on the back."

"And are you having any other interesting changes? Physical changes, perhaps?"

Bannack squirmed on the bench. He was rethinking how good of an idea it actually was to get the other men involved in this conversation. Ero glanced down at Bannack's lap and Bannack saw him grin and look back at Ty and Pyra.

"I can definitely confirm that he is."

Pyra gave a short, knowing laugh and shook his head at Bannack.

"So who is she?"

Bannack felt his stomach turn. It was exactly what he had been dreading hearing from any of the men. He shook his head, refusing to make eye contact with any of them.

"Come on, tell us," Ty said.

Ty had always been the kindest and most romantic-minded of the Denynso men, a nurturer rather than a warrior though he had recently embraced his incredible inherited power and joined in the final fight against the Klimnu, and looked far more excited about the situation than Bannack felt.

"It has to be one of the Denynso women," Ero speculated, "There haven't been any other girls who have come around here recently."

There was a pause and then Bannack saw Pyra staring at him.

"Except Loralia."

Bannack shook his head again, but there was no use, they had figured it out and now he had nowhere to hide.

"Oh, shit," Ero said, "It is her. You have a thing for the weird little mirror creature."

Bannack knew that he meant it teasingly, but his anger at that statement nearly overwhelmed him. He stood sharply, slamming his hands down in the middle of the table and glaring down at Ero.

"I do not have a 'thing' for her," he snarled.

"Your reactions to her seem to beg to differ," Ty pointed out.

"Have you slept with her? Your eyes aren't orange."

"No, and they wouldn't be even if I had. There's no way that my intended mate is some freakish creature from underground. I am meant to bond with a Denynso woman, like I'm supposed to. I'm not going to fall for some other species, especially one that I know absolutely nothing about."

As soon as the words came out of his mouth, Bannack saw the other men tense. A stiff moment of silence fell over the table as each of them stood slowly from their benches. He met their gazes in turn, seeing a darkness in each of them that he hadn't anticipated.

"Another species?" Pyra snarled, his hand clenching into a fist beside him, "You mean like humans?"

5

———

I could hear the women still talking around me, but it was as if their voices were lost in some kind of fog that was closing in on me. I was trying desperately to process what they had just told me, but no matter how hard I tried to work through it in my mind, I couldn't force myself to let it sink all the way in.

"Bannack is leaving?"

I repeated my question, hoping that somehow I had mistaken what they had said, but deep down knowing that I had heard them exactly right.

Leia came up beside me and rested a hand on my arm. So small and fragile looking, she had a presence that was strong because it had to be, like a delicate flower that had been forged out of pure steel. It was the fire and chisel that created her as she was.

I felt them guiding me towards the furniture in the middle of the main room of the house, and I allowed them to. I had no reason to distrust these women and in that moment they were my only source of information about Bannack and what was happening around me.

"The warriors have decided to leave the compound and explore the rest of Uoria," Leia explained.

"After the battle with the Klimnu down in the mirrored realm they all realized that none of them, not even the king, knows what the rest of the planet holds, or what types of threats there might be out there. They're unwilling to just sit around and wait to find out if there is another species out there like the Klimnu that might want to destroy the Denynso and take over the compound. It seems that discovering your existence made them even more insistent," Eden said softly.

"Why me?" I asked, looking into each of the women's faces in turn.

"You have lived under the ground that they walked on every single day and they had no idea," Zuri said, "It upsets them that they are known for being the best and most fearsome warriors in all the galaxy, yet they were unable to protect their compound from invasion, and didn't even realize that there was an entire other species living just beneath their feet for as long as they have been around."

"My mate, Pyra," Eden continued, "is especially worried about our child. He or she is the very first child born of this generation of the Denynso, and Pyra doesn't like that he doesn't know what could be out there that might pose a threat to his baby."

"He or she?" I asked.

I had never heard that particular phrase used before, and it struck me as strange that she would use it to refer to her unborn child.

"We don't know what the baby is," Eden explained, "We have no way of knowing. If I were going through my pregnancy back on Earth there would have been ways for me to know long ago if I am having a son or a daughter. The Denynso don't have those ways, though."

There was only a hint of stress in her voice. With the words she had said I would have expected to feel bitterness, or even anger, coming off of her. Instead, I just felt nervousness and the sweeping love that came over her as she mentioned her mate, just like the love that Zuri had felt when she thought of Ero.

"Do you wish that you were back on Earth rather than here with the Denynso?" I asked.

Eden looked at me and shook her head emphatically.

"Absolutely not. Uoria, this compound, is my home, much more so than Earth ever was even though that's where I was born and raised. I didn't know it until I came to this planet as a scientist sent to do a project for work and met Pyra, but this is where I was always meant to be."

I envied the confidence and absolute security that radiated off of her. She had total conviction in what she said, and her heart fully believed every word of it. This really was where she belonged and she couldn't imagine leaving.

"There are other ways than the Earth ways to tell what child you are carrying, you know."

Eden tilted her head quizzically at me and rubbed her belly tenderly.

"The midwives told me that they don't have any kind of technology that can show the baby like they do on Earth, that they take care of it through their own forms of medicine. None of them have ever been able to tell what a woman was having until it was born."

"Ah, but that's the Denynso," I said, smiling for the first time since Bannack had left, "and I'm not a Denynso. My kind has always been able to tell. I could find out for you now if you'd like to know."

Eden nodded and I could feel the hesitance she had felt toward me disappearing. She was learning to trust me, and as she did, the other women did as well. It was a nice feeling, something soothing and comforting in a time when I needed those feelings more than I had in my entire life.

I gestured for Eden to lie down on the couch and I sat beside her, perching just on the edge so that I was close enough to rest my hands on the sides of her swollen belly. It took me a moment to orient myself to the positioning of the baby. Once I did, I reached up to my neck to take my compact, but realized that it wasn't there. I looked around frantically, terrified that I had lost it somewhere between climbing up from out of the ground and removing my dress for Bannack.

Leia dipped down and scooped something up off of the floor.

"Is this what you're looking for?" she asked.

Relief washed over me and I nodded. Before she handed it to me, she opened the sides of the silver compact, revealing the two mirrors within it.

"What is that?" Zuri asked, walking over to look at the compact more closely.

"Please don't touch it," I said sharply when Zuri lifted her fingers to touch the mirrors, "I was born with that compact and I will die with it. If it's broken, there is no way to replace it and I will no longer have the abilities that it gives me."

I hadn't meant to sound angry, but it terrified me to think of my compact getting broken. It was the one remaining link that I had to my family and to my kind. Without it, I would lose everything within me that made me me. I didn't know how to function without it.

"I'm sorry," Leia said, leaning forward to hand me the compact.

"It's alright," I replied, hoping to calm the fear that had started to build in her, "Do you remember when the other woman, Elianna, stepped out onto the floor and it turned back into the sky? I explained that it was a reflection and that she had to believe in what the reflection was showing her in order for it to be real?"

"Yes."

"This," I held up the compact so that she could see it clearly, "is how I made that reflection. This compact enables me to do many things, and one of them will be to tell Eden what type of little one she should be expecting very soon."

The mention of the baby broke the tension in the room and the women all smiled. I opened the compact and placed it with both mirrors flat against Eden's belly close to where I knew the baby's head was positioned. I flattened my palm against the mirror and concentrated on what the mirror was reflecting to me. It was far more difficult to reflect a baby, especially one that was unborn, because they don't know yet how to understand what they are feeling and associate it with concrete thoughts. Instead the compact reflected the essence of the child back to me. This was the inarguable elements of that baby that were stitched into him from the moment of his conception and that would stay with him throughout his entire life. These were the very core of a person, the basic foundation on which all of that person's thoughts, feelings, and perceptions would build.

Having gleaned all I needed to from the reflections of the compact, I closed it, and carefully looped the repaired chain back around my neck. I smiled at Eden.

"You will have a son," I told her, "A boy with the power and spirit of his father, and the strength and courage of his mother. He will have within him the capacity to do amazing things."

Eden had tears sparkling in her eyes and I knew that my description had surprised her. She didn't think of herself as nearly as strong and courageous as she truly was, but I knew that through this baby that she was carrying, one that would be entering the world very soon, that she would learn to see herself in the way that she was made and to see herself in him.

6

————

Bannack could see the fury in the other men's eyes and he immediately regretted what he had said to them. Not wanting the situation to turn into a conflict within the entire clan, he stepped away from the table and left the meeting hall. Either Pyra, Ero, and Ty would follow him and they would hash through the situation on their own outside, or they wouldn't follow and he could escape into the darkness of the night and deal with his feelings alone like he had been for the last couple of days. He honestly wasn't sure which one of them he would prefer to happen.

As soon as he stepped outside, he realized that the other men had, in fact, followed him and they were seething with so much anger it was almost as though he could feel the waves of energy rolling off of them. He didn't pause on the stairs leading up to the meeting hall but continued down into the center of the compound, bringing him closer to his house and further from the rest of the tribe.

"What did you mean by that?" Ero asked.

The youngest and smallest of the warriors, Ero had

always been teased and bullied for his size. This had made him bitter and angry over the years, creating in him an unpredictable violence that often led him to major conflicts with the other warriors and even non-warrior members of the tribe. When he met Zuri and she became his mate, much of this anger and instability disappeared, replaced by a sense of confidence and control. That new control, however, seemed to be gone now as the temper returned and his eyes flashed aggressively at Bannack.

"I didn't mean anything by it," Bannack said, trying to brush off the comment that he made even though he knew it was completely out of line.

"You obviously meant something by it," Pyra said, stepping closer to Bannack, "You said that there was no way that you were supposed to mate with a species other than the Denynso. Do you think that there is something wrong with other species?"

"It's not that, Pyra," Bannack struggled to find the right words to express what he had been feeling, but they seemed to die and disappear before they could get from his mind to his mouth.

"Well, it seems to be exactly that," Ty said, showing uncharacteristic anger on his face, "It seems like you're saying that the only acceptable mates for us are Denynso women, and that you are too good to have a mate that isn't one of them."

"Let me remind you that each one of us, as well as Gyyx and Ciyrs, found mates that are most certainly not Denynso women. We fell in love with humans, a species that none of us knew anything about any more than you know anything about Loralia's kind."

"You knew something about them," Bannack snapped back, "We have encountered humans before; even had them come and stay with us for a few months at a time. You might not have known a lot about humans before the women came, but you knew something. You had spent time talking with humans and you had heard about them from Creia. They weren't a complete unknown."

"Why does that matter?"

"With Loralia, I know nothing. Absolutely nothing. We didn't even know that there was a species that existed below ground, much less what they are like. So how am I supposed to be OK with the fact that apparently I am falling for her when I don't even know who or what she is? Mating with a Denynso woman would mean that I understood her. I would know what she is, where she came from, and how we were going to live our lives together. We would have a shared history and the same perspectives. It would be easier and more realistic to bond with her and stay bonded with her because we would be able to know each other more quickly and more easily."

"So you think that because our mates are human women and not Denynso women that our bonds are not as close as the men who have Denynso mates? Or that somehow our relationships are not as good, or as 'realistic'?"

"Be honest, Pyra," Bannack said, staring directly into Pyra's raging orange eyes, "Don't you feel better knowing that Eden is technically a Denynso? Didn't it make you happy that Ciyrs somehow changed her from a human to one of us?"

"I was happy that he saved her life and that I wasn't going to have to live without her. I didn't care what she was. All I cared about was that he got the Klimnu toxins out of her and kept her alive. If that meant turning her into a Denynso woman, that was what it would take; but I wouldn't have loved her any less if she had woken up still completely human."

"After everything that's happened in the last few months with the Klimnu and Jem, and now with the idea of going out into the other areas of the planet to find out what else is out there, I just don't think I'm ready to even think about having a mate, much less having one that I will have to learn everything about."

"Do you really think that any of us was really ready when we found our mates? Or that we didn't have to learn everything about them, too?"

"If you haven't noticed, those five women might all be humans, but they are in no way exactly alike. Each one of them is so different it barely even matters that they are the same species," Ty said, "I know that being with Samira doesn't mean that I understand Eden like Pyra does, and that Ero wouldn't be able to trade Zuri for Leia and just expect that Gyyx would be able to pick right up with her without any problem. That's part of finding your mate. You have to learn her and she has to learn you. Remember, you're just as much a different species to Loralia and she is to you."

That statement struck Bannack harder than he would have anticipated it would have. He had been so wrapped up in how conflicted he felt about her that he never stopped to think about how Loralia perceived him. She hadn't shown a single moment of hesitance when it came to him, and had given herself over to her feelings for him immediately, never once worrying that he wasn't one of her kind, or even that he was a part of a species that had taken over the land where her kind used to live, something that the Denynso would have responded to with violence and anger. She had soothed him and offered herself to him in a way that was so trusting it now made him feel sick at the way that he had treated her.

"What am I going to do?" Bannack asked, looking at the men around him.

The anger in their eyes faded and he could see compassion build in their expressions. Each of them had been through their own personal struggle when they were finding their mates, and they knew how difficult it was to overcome those feelings. Ero had even had to go so far as to travel from Uoria to Earth, becoming the first of his kind to ever travel through space, in order to find Zuri and apologize to her after offending and hurting her so deeply that she had left the planet only a day after arriving. They understood what it was like to be unsure of the intense, all-consuming feelings that came with finding their mates, and now he needed them to tell him how to get through it.

"What in the hell is wrong with you?"

A shriek from across the center of the compound pulled Bannack's attention away from the other men and he saw Eden stalking toward him with a ferocious look in her eyes. Somehow her belly made her look even more intimidating, like a mother animal ready to fight something that was threatening her nest. Bannack took a step back, but Pyra stepped up behind him, forcing him to stay in place and confront the fiery redheaded woman.

"What?" Bannack asked.

"You didn't tell Loralia that you were leaving?"

"Um."

"You just left her? You brought her to her house, she brought you inside, and then you just ran away?"

"Is that all she told you?"

It was bad enough that they knew that he had run out on Loralia. Bannack didn't want to think that she had shared with them everything that had happened leading up to him gathering his clothes and running harder and faster than he could ever remember running in his life.

"Oh, no," Eden said, shaking her head with a spiteful half-smile on her face, "but I don't think that my baby is old enough to hear that story more than once in the same evening."

"I thought that you said you didn't bond with her," Pyra accused from behind him.

"I didn't," Bannack insisted.

"Not completely," Eden said, and then mercifully stopped.

"I know what I did was awful," Bannack said, taking a step toward Eden as the other two women ran up to them, "and I want to make it up to her. I'm dealing with my own issues, but I'm working through them and I don't want to hurt her any more than I already have. I want to tell her how sorry I am before we leave."

"Well that's really sweet, Bannack, but it's not going to be quite that easy."

"Why?"

"She left," Zuri said.

Bannack felt like a rock hit his stomach.

"What do you mean she left?"

"After she told us what you did, she decided that she didn't want to be here anymore. She said there's nothing for her up here and that she wanted to go back home where she didn't have anyone to hurt her."

"Damn it."

"What are you going to do?" Ty asked as Bannack walked around the human women in the direction of the forest.

"I have to go find her."

7

———

I had only been away from my home for a matter of hours, but it somehow seemed like I had been gone for months. Everything seemed cold and empty, like the cavern itself had forgotten what it was like to have the touch and presence of a living creature inside of it. Even though I had lived in that cavern since birth, I entered into it with a sense of trepidation hovering just in the back of my mind. Nervousness pricked at me as I slid down through the hole in forest floor just above the mirrored realm and made my way down the large tree toward the reflected branches that made roots across the sky that had become the floor.

Something had changed within me and suddenly I didn't know where I fit anymore. The walls and crevices that had always welcomed me and had never inspired even a moment of fear now seemed strange and I wondered if I was going to be able to continue on with my solitary life in the way that I had for so many years. It was amazing how much something as simple as stepping above the ground and experiencing the presence, companionship, compassion, and betrayal of other creatures could change everything that

I knew about myself, the world, and my perceptions of existence within it.

I slid down the vines on the tree, letting them carry me until my feet hit the solid wood of the tree branches. I looked down at the reflected sky, the black expanse streaked with the murky, pinkish grey clouds that broke up the sky and muted the stars both above and below me. For the first time I found it as strange as the Klimnu, the Denynso, and the humans had found it. I had always known that our world was a mirror of the one above it, and that what we saw was not what they did, but it wasn't until I had actually stepped onto the ground and saw, for the first time in my entire existence, the sky stretch over my head rather than at my feet that I felt the odd tug within me that said I was questioning something.

Just as I had told Elianna when she nearly fell into the sky through the stone floor I had created for them by reflecting the wall behind them into the expanse in front of them, the entire existence of my kind was based on belief and trust. We had to believe from the very first moments that we drew breath that what we saw was what it was, that it would behave the way that it was meant to, and to never question it. Questioning, wondering, even for a moment, could mean death. In not questioning, however, we never encountered the possibility that what we thought we were reflecting, how we were perceiving a situation, could possibly be wrong.

I was wondering about that now as I stood at the very edge of the reflected sky and pondered what it was that I was seeing. If that was the reflection of the sky, did that mean it was only the reflection of the sky as I perceived it? What if I didn't believe that it was the sky, that I believed it was glass, would that make a difference in how it behaved?

Could it be that what I was seeing was not actually what was on the floor of the caverns, but what was being reflected by the caverns, meaning that there was something else actually there?

I knelt down by the edge of the sky and experimented by dipping my hand down into it. Like it always had, my hand slipped beneath the edge of the tree and into the cold space. I withdrew it and reached for one of the clouds. Holding tightly to the vine, I leaned slightly forward so that I could scoop my hand through the pink and grey streak that was like a faint wash of paint across the blackness. When I pulled my palm back, I watched as the pink and grey melted into cold water against my skin. It was just as I would expect it to be.

I sat back against the tree and closed my eyes. I remembered what I had thought I felt when I was standing in front of Bannack. In him I had seen the same desire and need for me that I had felt for him. I had believed that that desire was as intense and irresistible for him as the feeling that I had when I looked at him. I could only believe that because I had no other option but to believe it. Now, though, I realized that I did have another option. I could question what I believed about Bannack, and if I could question that, I could question what I believed about everything, including that the sky was all that existed on the floor of the cavern. Holding onto that feeling about Bannack, the realization that what I had seen in him wasn't really what was inside him, but what I wanted to see, I opened my eyes again and looked at the floor of the cavern.

This time I didn't see the sky. When I looked at it in those dark, silent moments I saw a pane of glass. No longer were the stars struggling to glimmer through the clouds. Instead, I saw only darkness, as if I was looking through it into the abyss deeper in the planet. I closed my eyes again, took a breath, and when I opened them I saw an expanse of thick, white ice.

I reached out over the ice and felt the cold rising up off of it, tingling against the skin of my palm. Releasing the vine that had been tethering me to the tree, I stood and stepped out onto the ice. The cold was almost painful against the bare bottoms of my feet, but I reveled in it, enjoying the sharp, undeniable feeling that told me I had created what I wanted to from my own perceptions. What I had told Elianna was absolutely true. She hadn't believed that the floor would be solid, so it turned back into what she had been told it was, and what she believed it to be, the sky. When I believed that sky to no longer be the sky, but glass, it had become glass. And now it was ice.

I didn't need my mirrored compact anymore to create what I desired. I only had to believe in my ability to change my perceptions and the perceptions of those around me, and I could create whatever I desired.

I walked across the ice until I reached the expanse of dark ground on the other side and continued forward, not glancing back over my shoulder to find out what happened to the ice when I looked away. The corners of the cavern still looked strange, but I forced myself not to look at them. I kept my eyes focused ahead and climbed my way down into the second chamber so that I could go back into my house.

The solar panels hadn't had the chance to power the lamps since I had left, so I had to rely on the soft glow from my skin to illuminate the room around me. I walked into my bedroom and removed my dress, not bothering to dress again as I made my way out of my house and toward the hot spring toward the back of the chamber that I had adopted as my bath. I sank down into the water, allowing it to soothe my muscles and ease the tension that had built within me.

I dipped my head back into the water to wash my hair and then braided it into a long plait down my back, and then twisting it up so that I could knot it around itself. The air of the cavern was cool around me as I climbed up out of the hot water and made my way back to my house, allowing my skin to dry as I walked. I felt like I was moving through a still, untouchable image, as if nothing was moving with me or responding to my presence. It was as if the emptiness inside me had extended out and taken the energy and light from everywhere I ventured.

Once I was back inside my house I reached into the bureau against my bedroom wall and pulled out a nightgown. I was just dropping it down over my head, intending to crawl into my bed and allow the world to disappear around me, when I heard a voice echoing through the cavern.

8

"Loralia!"

Bannack wrapped his arm through the vines hanging from the trees and called out to Loralia again. His eyes were focused on the massive expanse of ice that stretched across the cavern where the reflection of the sky had been when he was last in the underground world. He screamed for her again, not sure if he should even attempt to step on the ice, and remembering what she had said about believing in the reflection in order for it to be real. Considering he had no idea what it could possibly be reflecting in order to appear as a block of ice, he couldn't bring himself to believe in its ability to withstand his weight.

Finally Loralia appeared on the other side of the expanse much as she had the first time he saw her. Her body gave off the same soft glow, but this time it wasn't being entranced by the glow that made him want desperately to cross the cavern and be near her. This time it was knowing that she was inside that glow, emanating it from her smooth, soft skin and her hypnotic eyes that made him need to get over to her. He could feel his body responding with almost painful intensity and his heart pounded just knowing that she was close again.

"Bannack?"

Her voice sounded confused and she didn't step any closer to him.

"Loralia," he said again, "I need to talk to you."

"I don't have anything to say to you," she said.

The words made him feel like his heart had constricted and he couldn't force any breath into his lungs.

"Please," he said, taking a step down the trunk of the tree and toward the edge of the ice, "I just want to tell you that I'm sorry. If after that you want me to leave and not ever come back down here, I will. It will be the hardest thing I ever do in my life, but I'll do it if that's what you want, as long as you just let me talk to you for a few minutes now."

Loralia looked down at the ice and saw it breaking. Long, fine cracks appeared across the surface, forming patterns like lace until the pieces started to melt away, disappearing into the blackness of what was once again the reflected sky. She had created the ice to keep him away, but the sound of his voice and the desperation in his words told him that she hadn't been wrong about what she had reflected from him. It was questioning it that had brought her to the truth, however, just like questioning the sky had brought her to the ice that now melted into the stars. She wondered if outside it was raining.

"Please, Loralia," Bannack said again, "Let me come over to you."

There was a moment of stillness between them and Bannack watched as her eyes explored the sky that now stretched across the cavern, and then lift to him. He was worried that she was just going to tell him to leave and that he would never see her again, or maybe that she would make a floor for him to walk across and then make it fall away right when he was in the middle of the room so that he disappeared to wherever Jem had gone when he fell during the battle. To be honest, he really wouldn't have blamed Loralia if she decided to do either. He realized now how horribly he had treated her, and if she refused to have anything to do with him after it, it would be completely justified.

Loralia's slim, graceful hand lifted slowly to her neck and rested on her compact for a few seconds before she loosened the chain and took the small silver compact in her hand. She opened it and focused it on the wall behind him just as she had the first time that he saw her. The sky disappeared, replaced by the dark grey of the stone.

"Is it safe?" he asked.

"Is it?"

Bannack knew exactly why she was asking. She had already done what she could do to get him across to her, just as she had done everything she could to reach out to him and connect them. Now it was up to him. He had to trust in the solidity of the floor beneath his feet just as he had to trust in himself and in her. If he didn't, there would be no way for them ever to be together.

Taking a deep breath and keeping his eyes focused on Loralia's, Bannack stepped forward. The ground was solid beneath his feet and he continued ahead. He walked in silence, crossing to her with deliberate slowness to prove his absolute trust and confidence in the floor and in her. When he was within a few steps of the edge of the expanse, he stopped and reached his hands out to her. This would be the moment, the moment when he would lose his trust and fall victim to the struggle within him again, the moment when he would let the conflict inside him rise again and send him tumbling down into the sky.

Instead, the ground stayed secure. He didn't waiver in his desire to have her in his arms and as she stepped forward to join him on the solid stone that had replaced the sky. He knew that as long as she was there with him, the stone would stay exactly where it was. The sky was transient, always changing and shifting, never staying the same as if it didn't know exactly what it wanted to be. The stone, though, was absolute and definite. It was strong and solid, and never changed.

This is what he felt now as Loralia walked toward him, reaching out to rest her cool, soft fingers against his palms so that he could hold them and draw her forward into his arms. What had once been transient like the sky was now like the stone, and he would never again allow himself to deny her, even for a moment.

"I'm sorry," he whispered into her hair as he cradled her against his chest.

Loralia pressed herself closer against him and he heard a gentle sigh slip from her lips.

"You don't have to wonder who you are, Bannack," she said.

The words struck him and he leaned back to look at her.

"What do you mean?"

"You worry that you don't fit what you are supposed to be; that you don't live up to what people expect of you. You wonder if you are really who everyone has always told you that you are, or that you should be."

It was something that Bannack had never expressed to anyone, a feeling that he had carried within him his entire life and never given voice to, even to his closest family and friends. He understood now that it was not her that had caused all of his struggle, but himself. It wasn't that he was upset about her being another species that he didn't know anything about, but that he didn't know himself well enough to trust that he could be the mate that she deserved.

"You are a warrior, just as you were born to be. You are strong, you are brave, and you are powerful."

As she spoke, Loralia's hands drifted from Bannack's shoulders down his chest. He felt her fingers exploring his body through the fabric of his clothing as if memorizing the curves and planes so that she could remember them even when they were apart. He wrapped his arms around her waist, pulling her against him so that she could feel more of his body and how much he needed her. Suddenly she drew in a breath and looked down.

"What is it?" he asked softly.

"Did I do something wrong? Did I try to go too fast?"

Her voice sounded thin, almost like she was afraid to ask him the questions. He took her hands in his, pulling them off of his chest and holding them between them, giving them a slight shake so that she would look at him. He hated that she thought that it was her fault that he had run away from her, and he was going to do everything that he could to show her that it wasn't true.

9

———

The look in Bannack's eyes nearly took my breath away as he stared deeply at me. His eyes were flickering from their usual greyish blue shade to orange and back, and I could feel intense, searing heat pulsating from his body. It was so hot I felt like it should have burned me. Instead, it tingled across my skin and made my breath deepen.

"You did nothing wrong," Bannack said.

His voice was low and rumbling, deeper than it had been any other time he had spoken to me.

"Are you sure?"

Bannack glanced down at my lips and then back into my eyes. Without saying anything, he leaned forward and caught my mouth with his. The kiss was even deeper, more intense than our first, like it was going beyond his lips against mine to connect us on another level. As his mouth moved against mine, he pulled me closer and I could feel the hardness of his body pressing against my belly. My breath caught in my throat and I arched my back to push more firmly against it. Bannack let out a soft groan and I started guiding him off of the stone and toward the second chamber of the cavern. I wanted to bring him home with me.

We walked along in silence and I could feel his passion growing with each step. I led him past the house that I occasionally visited, where I had changed my clothes after bathing, and through the rest of the chamber toward the large, protective chamber in the back of the cavern. This was truly my home, the place where I truly felt the most comfortable and the most at ease, and this was where I wanted to be with him.

"Is this your home?" he asked as we stepped into the chamber.

"Yes," I told him, "I have a house, but this is where I consider myself at home. This is where I feel safe."

Bannack gave my wrist a gentle tug so that I curled back into his arms. He pressed a kiss to the top of my head and then another to my cheekbone.

"I will keep you safe," he whispered, "I will always keep you safe."

His lips touched the side of my neck and I felt a shiver travel through my body and settle between my thighs. I ached for his touch again and could feel the warmth building as my body prepared for him. The tip of his tongue grazed across my skin. The feeling made my body tremble and I grabbed onto his upper arms, holding them to give myself stability as his mouth continued to explore along the side of my neck and down into the curve between my neck and shoulder.

I felt Bannack's hands smooth down the sides of my hips and onto my outer thighs, gathering the sides of my nightgown with his fingers so that he could slip his hands beneath the hem. He moaned as he realized that I wasn't wearing anything under the nightgown and I felt him fill his hands with my flesh, kneading gently as he met my mouth again with another intense kiss.

His mouth moved across mine with depth and need, but not intensity. He moved slowly, carefully tasting me as his hands massaged into my muscles and pulled me ever closer so that our hips met and the irresistible pressure of his erection against my belly made me whimper into his mouth. His hands swept up, tossing my nightgown aside. I had been wearing nothing else, and again I was completely bare in front of him. I reached up behind my neck and loosened the chain that held the compact I had reattached to its hook. Gently placing the compact down on top of my nightgown, I turned back to him.

"You are the most beautiful thing I have ever seen," he whispered.

"Let me see you," I whispered back, reaching forward to release the laces that tied up the front of his pants.

Bannack stepped back and took off his shirt, letting it fall to the floor beside my nightgown. He looked at me and I stepped closer to him, bringing my hands back to the laces on his pants. They loosened easily beneath my fingers and I eased his pants down his hips so that they fell to the floor. Bannack stepped out of them and took off his boots. Finally he was as bare as I was. There was nothing between us anymore and I indulged myself by touching the front of my body to his. The heat of his skin drew me in and I ran my hand down his chest and along the chiseled, rippling muscles along his side.

"You are beautiful," I said quietly, admiring every bit of him that my fingers touched.

"I know that I don't deserve to be with you," he said,

nuzzling his face in my hair, "but if you will let me, I will do everything I can to earn you. Starting with worshiping every inch of you."

With that, he swept me into his arms so that my hips nestled against his, my core cradling his erection and my breasts crushed against his chest. I wrapped my arms around his neck and my legs around his waist. He was so tall that holding me like that had me several feet off of the ground, but I wasn't afraid. I knew that I was never safer than when I was in his arms.

"How did your kind choose a life mate?" he asked, his labored breath making his voice low and sultry.

He held me with such ease, seeming to need to put forth no effort to keep me nestled against him. His mouth dropped to the side of my neck again and I closed my eyes briefly to savor the feeling.

"They were tied together," I finally managed to say.

"Tied?" he asked, lifting his mouth just long enough to speak before kissing along my collarbone.

I nodded, tilting my head back to encourage his mouth to my neck again.

"The women wove braids out of pieces of cloth and a treasured friend would tie their wrists together and say a blessing over them."

"Will you do that with me?" he asked, his lips tracing along the front of my neck until they reached the soft dip between my collarbones.

"Yes," I said, leaning back a little further to grant him more access.

"Until then, can I show you how the Denynso bond?"

"Yes."

Bannack tightened his grip on me and started to walk

forward. By the direction he was moving I knew he was headed toward the long, low bench that ran along the far wall. A few moments later he lowered himself to his knees and rested me back against the plush cushions, carefully drawing my legs from around his waist so that he could sit back on his feet. He gently parted my thighs, draping one leg over the side of the bench and the other over his shoulder so that I was totally open and vulnerable to him.

"This time," he said, running his hand down my thigh toward the wet heat he had been creating with every touch and every kiss, "when I touch you, I want to be looking at you."

Just those words made me feel like I was edging beyond my control and I pushed my hips closer to him, opening further to surrender myself completely to him. Bannack brought his hand the rest of the way down and drew the pads of his fingers through my core, sending shivers through my body. He pressed deeper, parting my folds so he could explore me as he gazed into my face.

I watched as Bannack dipped his fingers into his mouth, drawing them across his tongue before reaching down again and slipping them into me. I gasped at the feeling, so overwhelmed that I at once tried to pull away from it and push deeper into it. He moved patiently, easing his fingers deeper into my tight, untouched body and moving them slowly so that he massaged my upper wall. He groaned in response to my body arching up toward him and the whimpers pouring from my chest. I gripped his arm, digging my fingers deeply into him as he continued his deliciously torturous exploration.

Almost unbearable pressure was building throughout my belly, thighs, and hips and I felt the same desperate need for him that I had in the house in the Denynso compound before he left. Just before he allowed the tension to release, however, he carefully withdrew his fingers. I gasped at the emptiness and searched his face, worried for a moment that he was going to leave again. He smiled at me and drew his fingers through his mouth again, removing my slick fluids from his skin.

"Not yet," he whispered, "Be patient."

I wasn't feeling particularly patient, but I nodded, willing to give all of my trust and control over to him and allow him to guide me. I wanted to please him in whatever way he wanted, and whatever way that I could. He eased my leg down off of his shoulder at the same time that he took my hand and gently led me up into a sitting position. I moved by instinct when he stood, lowering myself to my knees in front of him. Bannack stroked my face tenderly before tucking his hand around behind my head and guiding me forward so that I opened my mouth and welcomed his erection in against my tongue.

His long, hard shaft felt incredible in my mouth, and the deep sounds rolling over me like thunder pushed me even further. I let my mouth glide along him, savoring the feeling of every ridge and vein, and the warm, salty taste of his skin. I felt like I could have continued on like that for the rest of the night, but suddenly Bannack's hand tightened on my head and he gently pulled me back away from him. I looked up at him and he eased me to my feet.

Bannack sat on the bench behind him and drew me forward until I straddled his hips much as I had in the house, but this time I was facing him rather than looking away. Wrapping one arm around my hips, he lowered me down toward his lap. I felt the tip of his erection touch my opening and drew in a breath. He paused only for a moment, then led me the rest of the way down so that I settled against him, enveloping his shaft deep within me. My head dropped back and my mouth opened to cry out, but there was no sound. The feeling of him filling me so completely was so intense I could only gasp for breath.

We sat still for several seconds as my body adjusted to holding him.

"Relax for me," he whispered.

I lifted my head so that I could look into his eyes again. Letting his beautiful face soothe me, I relaxed my muscles and let him sink even deeper into me. His hands came to my hips and he began to guide them, rolling them in slow circles. Bannack sat up straighter so that our bodies touched and rested his hand on my lower back. Bracing himself against the bench with his other hand, he rocked my hips into a faster rhythm. As our bodies moved and slipped across each other our sounds blended and swirled, filling the space around us until I could perceive nothing but what we were creating together.

His body nurtured me back into the sense of dizzying pressure, but this time the desperation wasn't there. I had him within me and I couldn't imagine there was anything more incredible. Suddenly, though, I realized Bannack began to grunt deeply and thrust intensely up into me, coaxing me closer to the edge of my control, and then pushing me over so that I screamed his name and contracted around him at the same moment that he cried out, throbbing and pulsing as hot streams filled me.

I held Bannack as tightly as I could, letting my tremors embrace him as he continued to pulse within my body. I sobbed for breath and clung to him, burying my fingers in his hair and rocking my hips subtly as I rode out the last waves of my climax. His mouth slowly trailed down onto my breast and suckled at one nipple, then the other, before lifting up to cover mine.

We kissed languidly as our bodies cooled and then he parted our lips to nuzzle his nose against mine.

"Come home with me."

10

———

Bannack kept his eyes closed as he asked the question, part of him worried that Loralia wouldn't be as willing to go back above ground, and that he might have to try to get used to living down in her world. When she didn't answer, he opened his eyes to look at her. He saw her eyes widen and he smiled.

"They change color after we've found our mate," he explained, knowing that the orange of his eyes had surprised her.

As much as it had worried him that he was going to have to learn about an entirely new species in order to be with her, he realized that it felt completely natural to explain the Denynso to her and let her explain her kind to him. He enjoyed discovering the new things about her and looked forward to each new detail that he would uncover in their lives together. She still hadn't answered his question and he looked directly into her eyes, trying to make the connection that the Denynso were able to make with their mates. He didn't hear anything.

Tilting his head quizzically at her, he tried harder to make the connection.

"What?" she asked.

"What are you thinking right now?"

"What do you mean?"

"What are you thinking right now?" he repeated.

"That that was incredible," she admitted, "and wondering how long it will be until we can do it again."

He laughed softly.

"Soon," he told her.

"Why did you want to know what I was thinking?"

"When my kind find our mates and bond, our minds connect. We're able to reach each other's thoughts and communicate just by thinking. I can't hear your thoughts."

"So I'm not your mate?"

Loralia sounded devastated and confused, and Bannack felt her start to pull away from him. He held her tighter and pulled her against him again.

"No, no. You are. If you weren't, my eyes wouldn't have changed. We just can't read each other's thoughts."

"Could it be because I'm not a Denynso?"

"The human women are able to communicate with their mates."

Bannack worried that she was going to be upset, but she smiled at him.

"I guess you are just going to have to settle for trusting and loving me."

"I do," he replied.

"Which one?"

The smile had faded from her lips and she was looking at him in a way that felt like she was looking into his soul.

"Both. I trust you," he leaned forward and touched a kiss to the middle of her chest, "and I love you."

"I love you, too."

Their mouths met again and he drew her as close to his body as he could. He was still buried deep within her and he felt himself hardening again. Loralia began to roll her hips slowly, and he carefully turned her, resting her on her back and coming down on top of her.

Two DAYS later Bannack stood in the row of warriors in the meeting hall, his eyes fixed on Creia even though his thoughts were focused on the table behind him. He knew Loralia was sitting there among the human women, gazing at his back. Even though he still couldn't listen to her thoughts or communicate with her with his mind, he could feel her. He could sense her presence and it was at once empowering and soothing. With her near him he was calm and in control, but felt stronger and more powerful than he ever had.

"Many times we have come to this room to honor the courage and bravery of our warriors," Creia said from his platform, "but tonight it is for a different reason. Our men have walked into battle without fear and have come back victorious. They have always protected our home and our kind, and have offered up their lives to ensure we can live comfortably. Tonight they prepare for a challenge that none have faced. Tomorrow these warriors will leave the compound and be the first Denynso to venture out onto Uoria. We don't know what adversities they may encounter or what threats they will find. Tonight we feast for tomorrow we watch them walk toward something even more frightening than the risk of death: the unknown. I know that each of them is prepared and that they will show the same strength, determination, and mastery that they have in everything else that they have done."

Bannack's spine straightened even further at his king's words. He dreaded leaving Loralia after having just found her, but now more than ever he understood the need for their journey. He had promised her that he would keep her safe, and he intended to do everything in his power to ensure that he kept that promise.

TBC

(To be continued in Part III...)

THE ALIEN'S SURPRISE

1

______

"I think that's going to be enough, Babe," Ty said, taking another loaf of bread from Samira's hand and shoving it down into the bag sitting on the counter, "There's going to be food on the trail."

"Can you be absolutely sure of that?" Samira asked, her eyes sparkling with the tears that she was fighting to hold back, "You have no idea what's out there. Can you be absolutely positive that when you walk out of this compound that you are actually going to be able to find enough food to keep you going while you are away?"

Ty looked at his mate rushing around his bakery, gathering the loaves of bread she had baked for him, and felt his heart constrict. The truth was that he really didn't have any idea what it was going to be like when he and the Denynso warriors left the compound to go explore Uoria and find out what types of species, plants, and land existed outside of the small area of land that they had always occupied. Their kind had never left the compound and had existed completely within their small area of the planet without really considering what might be going on outside their boundaries.

When they fought the wars that made them famous around the galaxy as the most fearsome and aggressive warriors in existence, it was against species that came to their planet and infiltrated their space.

It was one of these battles that had made them realize the desperate need to get outside of their compound and explore. In that battle, the final and brutal clash with their long-time enemies the KIimnu, they discovered that there was an entire realm right beneath their feet, a mirror of the land that existed above it, that had been home to a species that they had never even known was there. The idea that a species of creatures had lived right under their compound as long as they had been there without any of the Denynso, not even the king, even knowing that they were there was terrifying, and they realized that they would never be able to protect themselves or their families properly if they didn't know what was going on on the rest of the planet.

Now the warriors along with Ty, the nurturer and baker of the tribe, and Ciyrs, the healer, would be leaving the next morning on a quest that would take them into the furthest unknown regions of the planet so that they may make contact with other creatures and find out what else grew and existed on their planet. It was a frightening prospect, one that could be extremely beneficial to the Denynso and the humans that had come to live with them, or one that could put their entire clan, compound, and existence in danger.

Ty watched Samira draw a small paper-wrapped package out from under the counter and place it in front of her. His heart squeezed even harder as he looked at her, her shoulders trembling as she couldn't hold back the tears any longer. He knew that his mate, this beautiful human woman that had been the biggest surprise in his life and the greatest thing that ever happened to him when she appeared just weeks before, was worried about him and his safety as he embarked on this journey. If he gave himself the time to really think about it, he would probably be worried about it, too.

He needed to do this, though. It was only recently, and through the support and love that Samira poured out to him from the moment that she met him was the reason he had been able to fully embrace who he was and the power that he had within him. His entire life the large, imposing Denynso man had focused entirely on taking care of the clan. He was the one who made sure that they had the food that they needed and that they recovered after battles. He was not a warrior. He had not been born to be one. A treasured, unique power he had inherited from his father and that he had hidden deep within him from the time he was a child, had proven that he was more than just a nurturer. Through uncovering and embracing that power he was able to step into the role of a warrior and join the ranks of the others as they marched into the final showdown with the Klimnu. It was his ability to move and control objects with his thoughts that had enabled him to be a powerful and unexpected force against the slimy, disgusting creatures that had been the bane of the existence of his kind for generations.

Now he needed to offer that same support and help to the warriors as they went out into the world to try to understand it better, and find more ways that they could not only improve the life they had, but to also protect themselves into the future. Samira had completely changed everything for him, and he was unwilling to let her be in danger if there was anything he could do to change it. They already planned on going back to Earth after the quest to marry the way that humans did, further solidifying the bond that had connected them as lifelong mates within the Denynso tribe. He couldn't in good conscious let himself do that if he didn't know that he could bring his wife and the potential future mother of his children back to a place that was safe.

"What's that?" he asked softly, trying to calm her with his voice.

"I made it for you," she said, sliding the package closer to him, "I've been working on it since right after we bonded. I just finished it last night."

Ty released the twine she had tied into a bow on the top of the package and unwrapped the thick brown paper. Inside was a complex-looking box comprised of gears and metal components. A small dip in the top caught his attention. He ran his finger across it and looked up at Samira.

"What is it?" he asked.

Samira smiled now, the expression a welcome break from the tears that streamed down her face and made her large eyes look deep and sad. She reached into her pocket and withdrew something, clutching it tightly in her hand. Taking a deep breath, she turned her hand over and opened her palm, holding it out toward him. Nestled in the middle of her palm was a gold ring, the metal antiqued and the design complex and beautiful. A series of prongs in the center held a dark red gem.

"I know that you probably don't know this because there's no reason that you should, but on Earth when people get engaged the girl usually wears a ring. It is just part of the whole ritual. Then both of them wear bands when they actually get married. Well, this was my great-grandmother's engagement ring and it was passed down through the family to me. I thought that since we are doing things a little differently than other human women are, that maybe I could give you an engagement ring instead."

Feeling tears starting to prick painfully in his own eyes, Ty took the ring from her palm and looked at it closely. Even though Samira was taller and larger than all of the other human women except for Zuri, the ring was still too small even to fit on Ty's pinky. She giggled when he tried to push it down toward the first knuckle of his pinky.

"No. It's not for you to wear," she said, "Let me show you."

She took the ring from him and nestled it down into the dip on the top of the metal box she had given him. As soon as it settled into place, the gears started to turn and Ty heard her voice coming through to him, telling him that she loved him and missed him and couldn't wait to have him home.

"This is incredible," he said when her voice stopped.

He was in such awe of her. He knew that Samira was incredibly brilliant and that it was the reason she had come to Uoria in the first place, as a way to expand her knowledge and to help the Denynso healer Ciyrs create healing ointments for the warriors, but it still stunned him. She was so young, and yet her beautiful, graceful hands were able to create something like this.

"If you push the button on the bottom, there are a few more of the voice discs that you can play. Just take out the ring, twist this top panel counter clockwise until it releases, lift it up, remove the disc that is in there, put in a different one, twist the panel back into place, and then put the ring back in and it will play just like that."

"Oh, just like that, huh?" Ty asked.

Samira laughed and looked down shyly. She often forgot how smart she was and that other people weren't able to understand the things that she did with almost no effort.

"If I were you, I'd listen to those discs by yourself the first time. There are a couple of them that may not be... appropriate for the other warriors to hear."

"Oh, really?" Ty said, lowering the box back onto the surface of the counter and walking around to Samira.

He slipped his arms around her waist and started guiding her backwards toward the door to their house, taking off his bag and putting it on the counter as they went.

2

———

"The way I see it, this trip can't be any more difficult than going all the way to Earth to find you and getting into it with Samira's stepfather," Ero said, cuddling closer to Zuri.

"At least when you went to Earth, you knew what you were getting yourself into," she said, wrapping an arm around his waist and tugging him closer.

"No, I didn't," Ero protested, "I didn't know anything about Earth other than that you were there. None of us had ever been there. In fact, none of us had ever been in a spaceship. I was so worried about not ever seeing you again that it didn't really matter to me that I was going to a completely different planet that I didn't know what it looked like or how I would make my way around. I hadn't met too many humans in my life, and most of the ones that I had were not exactly pleasant."

"Were you scared?"

Ero thought about the question carefully. He didn't really know how to answer. He was being totally honest when he said that it didn't matter to him when he climbed on that ship that he was going all the way to Earth to find her, but when he thought back on it he knew that it wasn't so much that it didn't frighten him, but that it didn't matter to him that he was frightened. It had been his fault that Zuri had left Uoria only twenty-four hours after she had arrived with the intention of being the first professor to come to the planet to be a part of the exchange program the king, Creia, had planned with the university on Earth. He had hurt her so badly with a comment that he made about her to the other warriors that she had left, even after they had bonded for the first time. It was his responsibility to go after her and convince her that he loved her and needed her to come back to Uoria with him to be his mate. It still seemed like an unimaginable gift that she actually had.

"I know that you don't want me to go, but isn't this exactly what you wanted to do when you came here?" he asked.

Zuri gave a huff as if he had put voice to something that she had been trying to avoid.

"I don't think that's really applicable."

Ero laughed.

"Really?" he said, tickling her playfully, "You don't think it's the same thing that you wanted to know everything you could about the Denynso and to teach us about humans so you came to be a part of the exchange program? Actually, you know what? You're right. It's not the same. You came all the way from another planet to find out more about Uoria and the Denynso. I'm just leaving the compound."

"It's not the same thing. There have been scientists coming to Uoria to study for years. I at least had some kind of idea of what I was getting myself into when I came here. I knew I was coming to a specific compound to interact with a certain species. I definitely didn't have all of the information or know exactly what the Denynso were like, but at least I had a few reference points. You have absolutely no clue what you are walking into. You are literally just going out and wandering around on a planet that not a single member of your kind has ever walked around on, essentially just hoping that whatever you find is not going to kill you. I'm sorry if I don't find that terribly comforting."

Ero lifted up on his elbow and gazed down into Zuri's face. Her thick blond hair rippled around her lovely, round face, still flushed, and her bare shoulders. Large blue eyes gazed up at him and he had to take a moment just to look at her. His mate was truly the most beautiful woman he had ever seen and part of him still couldn't believe that she was really his.

"This is something that I have to do, my love."

"But why?"

"Well, not only is it my responsibility and my duty as a warrior of the Denynso, but I have been thinking a lot about the future and what it might hold for us. I don't want to get to that point knowing that I didn't do absolutely everything that I could to make sure that our future is safe and happy as possible."

"What point?" Zuri asked.

Her voice had become soft and when he looked into her eyes he knew that she knew what he was thinking about, but needed to hear him say it. Ero rested his hand on Zuri's stomach and rubbed it gently, looking down to watch his palm follow the curves of her belly and the swell of her hipbones.

"When we will have a little one of our own. Seeing Pyra and Eden get ready for their baby has made me think about how wonderful it would be to see you carrying our child, and to get to be a father. I didn't have a chance to have a good relationship with my father growing up to really make any memories with him, and I know that I want to be able to do that for someone."

Even though his parents had died when Ero was very young, talking about them and the relationship with them that he had missed out on throughout his life brought the same deep sadness that it always had. He had always been the orphan of the Denynso, but also the smallest among the warriors. These factors had combined to give him a bitter, angry attitude and a propensity for distrust and violence as he got older. The other warriors had never missed the opportunity to tease and bully him about his size, and it was this bullying that had pushed him to the cruel comments he had made about Zuri. It had been the horrible moment when he realized what he did to her that it finally occurred to him truly how deeply the teasing had impacted him. When he saw the painful look in her eyes he saw all of the hurt that he had experienced and knew that he had just done the exact same thing to her that the warriors had done to him all those years.

Zuri let out a long breath and rested her hand over Ero's on her stomach.

"I've been thinking about that, too," she admitted.

Ero grinned and rolled over onto her, capturing her mouth with his and exploring her with his tongue. He pressed into her, hoping that he would be able to memorize the feeling of every inch of her body beneath him when he was away and lonely for her.

"Let's get started now," he growled into her ear and Zuri laughed.

Ero felt her hands pushing on his shoulders and he complied with the pressure, letting her ease her back onto his side on the bed.

"Hold on there," she said, rolling out from under the blankets, "Let me give you this first."

Ero groaned in protest as she got out of bed, but let himself enjoy watching her naked form wiggling its way across the room to the desk against the wall. He let out a grunt of appreciation when she bent over to look in the drawer and Zuri glanced over her shoulder at him. She smiled before straightening and making her way back over to the bed so that she could hand him what looked like a large book.

"What's this?"

"It's a field journal. I brought it with me from the university and I want you to bring it with you on your trip. I planned on recording all of my observations about the Denynso in it so that I could present them to the university board when I went back. "

"We're just like big giant specimens to you, aren't we?" Ero teased.

"Yes. You're my favorite, though."

Zuri leaned over and kissed him. Ero tossed the journal over to the bedside table. He was happy that he would have it with him when he left the compound and needed to feel her with him, but in that moment she was there, close enough for him to touch and kiss, and he was going to take absolute advantage of it.

3

Eden ran her hand down the back of Pyra's head, stroking the long white hair that he usually wore in the customary Mohawk of the Denynso men but was now laying soft. His breath tickled on her bare skin as he whispered to her belly, but it was so sweet that she didn't want to giggle and stop him before he was finished. He was explaining to their baby why he had to leave and that he was going to get back as soon as he could.

"I just want you to be safe," he whispered, running his hand along the side of her belly as he spoke, "and that means I have to go out there and find out if there are any scary things that I will have to fight off for you. I don't want you to worry about me. You just stay in there and concentrate on getting all big and strong. I'll be just fine and when you're ready, you'll come out and we'll run and play and I'll teach you how to climb a tree."

Eden laughed then and her enormous mate looked up at her.

"What?"

"I don't think that climbing a tree is something that will

happen directly after birth." She stopped, realizing that there were still many things that no one knew about her pregnancy or the baby that she was carrying, "Right? I mean, this will be a baby, right? Like a small baby. Not a toddler that will be able to get up and walk around right after birth?"

Pyra returned her laugh and stroked her belly again.

"I don't think so, Babe. I, for one, have never actually seen one, but I'm fairly certain that Denynso babies are small and baby-like. I don't think walking around is a thing for a couple of years, but that doesn't mean that I can't start planning now."

He leaned down and kissed the swell of her belly, closing his eyes briefly. Eden could feel his hand pressing more firmly into her skin as if he were trying to get close enough to the baby to touch it even through her body.

"You can plan anything you want. He's going to be yours."

Pyra sat up sharply and looked directly into her face.

"He?" he asked.

Eden immediately regretted what she had said. She had been so careful not to say that, but now there was no way that she could just scoop the words out of the air and put them back into her mouth. He had already heard them.

"I don't know for sure," Eden said cautiously, drawing out each of her words as carefully as she could to make sure that Pyra heard her and understood what she was saying. She didn't want him to get his hopes up when she wasn't entirely sure that she believed it herself, "The midwives don't have any way of knowing what the baby is."

"Then why did you say 'he'?"

Eden sighed. She wasn't sure how her mate was going to respond to her little experiment with Loralia a few days before. It wasn't the custom of the Denynso to try to find out what a baby was before it was born, but when the strange and mysterious creature who had come from the mirrored realm beneath the compound told her that she could tell her what her baby was going to be, Eden's curiosity had simply been too much for her and she couldn't say no.

"When the girls and I went over to Bannack's house the other night to meet with Loralia, she was telling us about her kind. She was fascinated by my belly and she asked if I knew if the baby was a boy or a girl. I told her that the midwives didn't have any way of finding that out, but I mentioned that if I was going through my pregnancy on Earth, my doctors would be able to tell me what it was."

"They could?" he asked, seeming both fascinated and a bit upset that this was not something that was available on his planet.

"Yes. So she told me that she would be able to tell me."

Eden thought about the gorgeous and completely unexpected woman that was Loralia. The very last of her kind, she had been living in the hidden realm under the compound her entire life, but had been alone for many years. When the young, impulsive warrior Bannack brought her up into the compound it had been the first time that she had ever been above the surface of the ground. Though she hadn't had the opportunity to spend much time with her, Eden had felt a connection with this misunderstood creature, and was thrilled that she and Bannack were now mated.

Pyra had been staring at her expectantly, but Eden was still unsure whether she wanted to tell him what Loralia had said.

"And?" Pyra said, widening his eyes like he was trying to encourage her forward, "What exactly did she say?"

He looked so excited that Eden couldn't help but smile.

"She put her mirror against my belly and told me that the baby is a boy."

Pyra looked delighted and he bounded to the head of the bed to gather Eden in a tight hug.

"A boy? Really?"

"Yes. She said he will be a strong warrior just like you."

"I'm so excited," he said, rubbing her belly again, "I mean, I would have loved a daughter, too, but having a son..."

His voice trailed off as if the emotion he was feeling was just too much to try to condense into words. Eden felt a surge of pride at that moment that was difficult to explain. She loved that she was carrying her mate's baby, and that she had the privilege of being the mother to the first of the new generation of Denynso, but watching Pyra at that moment as he slithered back down the bed and rested his mouth to her belly again, it all felt even more meaningful. Giving Pyra a son felt like the most important, precious, and valuable thing that she had ever done, and she felt so blessed to be able to do it, even if she was still somewhat fearful of the unknown about her pregnancy.

"My son," Pyra whispered against her skin, "My boy. Your Papa loves you, little one."

Eden reached carefully under her pillow, trying not to disturb Pyra as he continued to whisper to the baby, and took out the braided ribbon chain she had been keeping there. On it was a pendant cast from iron that looked like a hand cradling a heart in its palm. A smaller heart in the center of the larger heart featured an inlay of copper so that it stood out against the other pieces.

"I want you to bring this with you," she said to Pyra and he sat up, looking from her face to the pendant in her hand,

"I designed it a couple of weeks after I found out I was pregnant. Jem," she paused and choked back the painful emotion that suddenly tightened in her throat at the mention of the warrior who had died in the recent battle with the Klimnu, "crafted it for me."

A brilliant blacksmith, Jem had taken her vision for the pendant that would represent Pyra holding her and their baby and crafted it into something so beautiful it had taken her breath away when she saw it. She had intended to give it to Pyra when the baby was born, but now that he was leaving with the other warriors, she wanted him to take it with him so that he could have them close to him even while he was far away.

Pyra took the pendant from her hand and ran his massive fingers along the design.

"Thank you," he said softly, "I can't tell you how much I am going to miss you. I feel like I'm not going to be able to breathe without you."

"I'm going to miss you, too," Eden said, "I can't bear the thought of sleeping in this big bed without you. I'm going to be alone more nights with you gone on this journey than I was when I first got here before we bonded."

The mention of their first bonding brought a flash of heat to her cheeks. That had been such a tumultuous, emotional time, but as Pyra lifted up to lie down beside her and pull Eden in against her so that he could cradle her in his arms, she knew that she would never trade a single second of it.

4

———

Leia's hand clutched at the sheets beside her, her knuckles clenching so hard into the fabric that they whitened as she pulled it away from the mattress. Her eyes closed as her head dropped back against the pillow and her back arched up off of the bed. Gyyx flattened one massive hand into the middle of her chest and pressed her back down, holding her against the mattress with just enough pressure that she could feel his dominance. This sent even more of a shiver of excitement and arousal through her and she couldn't hold back the cry of pleasure as her mate flicked his tongue through her hot, wet folds again.

Gyyx had spread her thighs against the bed and pushed them up so that she was fully open to him, making her totally vulnerable to his touch. He pushed them up a little higher now, using the very tip of his tongue to concentrate fast, intense strokes directly on the pearl of hypersensitive flesh just at her peak. The sensation rolled through her like thunder, sending nearly overwhelming ripples of pleasure all the way along her body. Leia writhed against the bed, but

Gyyx was far larger and far stronger than she was, and the pressure of his hands ensured that she would stay exactly where he wanted her for as long as he wanted her to stay there.

Of course, there was nowhere else that she would want to be in that moment. She reveled in being at her mate's mercy and in the way that he could so masterfully manipulate her body to create feelings within her that she had never experienced before.

Just as Leia felt like she was going to lose all control, Gyyx pulled his tongue away from her body and pressed a series of soft kisses along the inside of her thigh. He was allowing her to cool, to come down from the spiraling heights of pleasure he was sending her into so that he could just bring her right back there again. It was delicious, delirious torture.

She felt him guide her legs down and his hand slide from her chest down to one of her hands so that he could ease her up to a sitting position. As he did this, Gyyx came around to her side, changing positions with her so that he lay with his head on the pillow and guided her to kneel in between his slightly spread legs. Leia bit down on her bottom lip as the position brought her right into view of his powerful erection. Her mouth watered as she looked at it and she couldn't resist running her tongue from its base to the tip. There was already a crystalline drop of fluid collected there and she licked it up, allowing the tip of her tongue to dip inside just briefly.

Gripping the base of his cock in one hand, Leia traced the edge of the crown with her tongue, pausing for a moment to concentrate her licks on the bundle of nerves on the underside of the head just as he had concentrated on her. As Gyyx began to groan beneath her, Leia started to stroke with the hand that was holding him, gliding her palm and fingers along his hard, thick length as she continued to memorize his ridges and veins with the tip of her tongue. The taste of his body made her shiver, making her want him even more.

Suddenly Gyyx sat up and grabbed Leia by her upper arms, turning her and laying her down on her stomach so that she faced the foot of the bed. He climbed over her, balancing on his hands and the balls of his feet so that he didn't press too much of his tremendous body down on her tiny frame, and she felt his erection gliding along her thighs as he rolled his hips to stroke against her without entering her. Leia whimpered and lifted her hips, displaying herself to encourage him to fulfill the ache within her that he had created with the skilled ministrations of his tongue.

Gyyx complied suddenly, pushing deeply inside her in one hard thrust that elicited a scream of pleasure from deep in Leia's chest. The warrior growled and lay forward so that Leia could feel his body full enveloping hers. It was a primal, comforting feeling that encouraged her to lift her hips and grind them into him. His hands came up under her, cupping at the front of her throat in another show of dominance that made Leia feel so close to the edge that two more hard thrusts sent her body shuddering through an intense orgasm that left her gasping for breath.

Her climax did nothing to slow Gyyx. Instead, he tightened his grip around her throat so that her back arched slightly and pulled up onto his knees for better leverage so that he could slam in her with such speed and depth that each stroke was almost painful. That fine line between pain and pleasure, however, is what drove Leia crazy and she let the sounds pour out of her, panting, gasping, and crying out as she gave her body over to Gyyx in the hopes that he would still be able to feel her when he was gone.

Suddenly she felt his entire body tense and heard him let out a strangled moan as his cock pulsed wildly within her. He stayed buried deeply inside her as the tremors continued to flow through him, spilling hot streams that she could feel filling her. Finally he lowered his hands from her throat to her chest and carefully rolled them over to their sides, remaining inside her as he curled around her.

Even though she would have liked him to, Gyyx never let himself collapse down on top of Leia. She was so small and delicate-looking, particularly compared to him, that he was always convinced he would crush her if he let himself rest on top of her completely. Instead, he curved around her, cradling her body close to his so that she was surrounded by his warmth and the intoxicating smell of his skin.

His lips touched her neck and traveled up, following the curve of her jaw until he reached her ear.

"I love you," he breathed, pulling her a little closer to his chest and stomach.

"I love you, too," she said back, kissing the arm that was draped tightly around her.

Leia couldn't help but smile as she allowed herself to drift away on the waves of pleasure still rolling through her. It had taken so much to convince Gyyx that he was not going to break her if he made love to her the way that she wanted him to, but now that they had bonded, he had stepped into the dominant, aggressive role that drove her wild and brought out every primal instinct within her. She loved his strength and his power, and the way he knew how to use them to give her such incredible pleasure. She felt fully and completely safe with him, which made it even better when he exerted himself so strongly.

When their bodies had relaxed and cooled, she carefully extracted herself from his arms and walked over to the large black artist's bag she had propped against the wall. Reaching inside the main pocket, she withdrew what looked like a small scroll. She brought it over to the bed and climbed under the covers to meet his body where he had also cuddled down into the bed.

"This is for you to bring with you so that you can look at it and think of me whenever you're lonely."

Gyyx took the scroll from her and unrolled it carefully. She heard him let out a sigh as he saw the picture.

"This is beautiful, Leia," he said, turning to kiss her tenderly, "Thank you."

"I wanted to frame it for you, but then I figured that you probably weren't going to have the space in your bag to bring along a framed picture, and even if you did, you weren't really going to be able to find a place to hang it while you were traveling around." She looked down at the picture and reached over to run her fingers along the pencil and acrylic sketch. "This is the sunrise that I saw the first morning that I knew you. I remember it being the most beautiful sunrise I had ever seen, and I know that that's because it was the first one I had ever seen now that I knew you existed in the world."

Gyyx tucked his hand around her face and stared into her eyes. She saw intense emotion there, and she knew that he was worried about her. Them coming together was a difficult and nearly tragic experience that neither of them liked to talk about very much, but both knew was something that was lingering right around them. They had found each other only because the Klimnu had high-jacked the university shuttle she had ridden from Earth, kidnapped her, and help her captive, torturing and tormenting her, for 57 days in a dark, dank prison on the other side of the compound, in one of the areas so close to the edge of their territory that many barely considered it the compound and others would never even venture. This is what compelled him more than anything to join up with the other warriors in order to go out onto the planet and find out what other creatures Uoria might harbor.

"I will think about you every single minute while I'm gone," he said.

"No, you won't," Leia said, kissing the tip of his nose, "'and that's perfectly fine. There are a lot of other things that you will need to focus your attention on. What matters is that you know I'm thinking about you, too, and when you look at the drawing I want you to know that I love you and can't wait to have you home."

5

———

Elianna buried her head against Ciyrs's shoulder and held him tightly around his neck as he continued to rock her hips against his. She cradled him inside her body, enveloping him as though protecting him in the most powerful way she knew how. His skin was slick and warm with sweat and she felt it mix with her own as they both came down from their climaxes, maintaining the link between their bodies and allowing their breath to stream and blend between them as they preserved these last precious moments in each other's arms.

She kissed the side of his neck and let out a long sigh that seemed to pull with it all of the emotion that she had experienced since coming to Uoria. It had been like nothing she had imagined. When she left Earth to come to this strange and barely-known planet it was with the intention of helping humans learn more about Uoria and the Denynso. As a journalist she planned on writing a series of reports that would help to illuminate this species as the people of Earth got accustomed to the idea that the government and the academic sector were planning on not only making direct contact with the species, but cooperating with them. Knowing the reputation of the Denynso as the most powerful and skilled warriors in the galaxy, the goal was to bring some of them to Earth to fight and to train armies, while also allowing humans to go to Uoria to share parts of the Earth culture and visit the planet as tourists.

Elianna had had her own thoughts about these plans, but she had primarily kept them to herself. She wanted to remain as objective as possible, just as her career demanded, and that meant not contemplating a future in which the inhabitants of this far-away planet showed up on Earth and roamed freely, teaching humans to be even more violent and aggressive than they already were, and in which humans flew off to Uoria on cute little family vacations thinking that they would relax and make some fun memories, when they really had no idea what was awaiting them.

When she arrived, however, Elianna's resistance to other people and pain from abandonment in her past had nearly kept her from accepting Ciyrs as her mate. He had been patient with her, though, guiding her through the difficult and confusing first moments of their connection that would eventually seal them together. Before they could fully mate, however, a member of the Klimnu had masqueraded as Pyra and stolen her, bringing her to a dark, disgusting prison just on the edge of the compound, a place where she would learn that the Denynso never went. There she was tormented and tortured, the only comfort she got came in thinking about Ciyrs and reaching out to him through her mind.

It wasn't until the Denynso came for her that she discovered he had transferred some of his incredible healing power to her, but with the ability to heal came the ability to destroy. As much as she wouldn't want to admit it, she had delighted in the ability to wrap her hand around the bony, slimy neck of the vicious creatures who had made her life a living hell for the entire time that she had been there, and had nearly killed the frail, tiny woman that she had found battered and bloody, crawling through the halls of the prison, and watch them burn.

This had changed her forever. Suddenly life was not about writing articles and bringing back information to the people of Earth so that they could learn more about a planet that would remain a novelty. It became learning about the people that were now her family, giving herself over completely to the man that she loved and who she knew was her lifelong mate, and offering the gifts that she had just discovered to helping heal and protect the Denynso.

Now as she wrapped herself around Ciyrs, reveling in the feeling of the only man who had ever been inside her, she couldn't imagine a single moment of her life without him or without Uoria. She felt more at home and at peace here than she ever had on Earth, and it was as if his presence and the abundant, never-ending love that he gave to her had soothed all of the pain and emptiness she had suffered throughout her life. The thought that he was leaving with the warriors to explore the planet was gut-wrenching and she didn't want to think about it. She wanted to continue to hold him and let him protect her in his massive arms, ignoring the eventuality, and pushing back that moment when he would have to say goodbye.

Suddenly the first rays of sunlight started trickling through the slight gap between the curtains over their bedroom window and she knew that she couldn't put it off any longer. Her mate, the healer of the clan, was a vital component of this mission and he would still need to gather all of his supplies so that he could meet with the warriors at the main hall to be ready to leave after breakfast.

She climbed off of him slowly, savoring the feeling of his body stroking against hers as it left her, and crossed to the bureau on the far wall to pull out a dress that she dropped over her head. Out of a small drawer in the bottom of the piece of furniture she pulled a book tied with a green ribbon. When she turned back around Ciyrs was tying the strings at the front of his pants. She waited while he put on the rest of his clothing, and then stepped forward to hand the book to him.

"I brought this notebook with me from Earth. It was supposed to be where I was going to make my notes for my articles, but after I met you, I realized that I was never going to go back there so I didn't need to write them. Instead, you gave me the confidence to do something that I had never told anyone that I wanted to do, but that I had been dreaming of for my entire life."

Cirys untied the ribbon and lifted the hard front cover of the notebook. She watched him read the first few lines of her neat, precise handwriting and then look up at her.

"What is this?"

"I wrote a book. It's not quite finished yet, but I want you to bring it with you and read it. You'll be the very first person to read anything that I've written other than articles, and you can help me decide how to end it."

Ciyrs gathered Elianna into his arms and hugged her close to him. She breathed in the smell of his body and listened to the rhythm of his heart, wanting to internalize that sound so that she could replay it in her mind whenever she thought of him while he was gone.

"I will be thinking about you every day. I'll get home as soon as I can."

"I know you will."

As Ciyrs released her, she glanced down at the bed. It was going to be next to impossible to sleep without him beside her. The bed looked so big, empty, and cold already and she dreaded nightfall when she would have to climb in and try to will herself to sleep alone.

"Come to the shop and help me pack up the healing ointments and other supplies?" he asked.

Elianna nodded and let him take her hand, intertwining their fingers as he led her out of their house and through the compound toward the building that held his shop and clinic. This was where they healed the sick and injured, and where they had worked with Ty's brilliant mate Samira to create powerful healing ointments that had gotten them through the last battles with the Klimnu. She knew that the bottles and tubes that he packed in his large bag would be integral to the trip, but she didn't want to think of the suffering that they would end.

As they packed his supplies and checked the list of items that he had made the day before, Elianna could hear the compound outside coming to life as the Denynso started heading for the meeting hall to eat breakfast and say final goodbyes to the men.

6

———

"**I** can't believe that I just found you, and now I have to leave you."

Bannack tightened his hands around Loralia's and stared into her still-startling lavender eyes. He had spent only three days with her, and one of them had been spent trying to find her so that he could apologize and convince her to come back with him. Now he was going to be walking away from her, leaving her in a strange place that she didn't know so that he could explore the rest of the planet for an indeterminate amount of time. Though it had been his idea in the first place for the warriors to go outside of the compound and explore Uoria to find out what other types of species existed beyond their boundaries, now that he was only minutes away from leaving, it made his stomach feel sick.

"Everything is going to be fine," Loralia soothed him, stroking the tip of his nose with hers, "You are going to go and discover amazing new things, and I will be here getting used to my new home. The women have been very kind to me and I'm sure that they will continue to do everything that they can to make me feel welcome and to help me assimilate to life up here."

His mate was truly incredible and Bannack couldn't help but stare at her in amazement. This creature, the last of her kind, had not only lived completely on her own without any contact from other species for years after her family and friends died from a mysterious plague that had spared only her for reasons that even she didn't understand, but had also left the only home that she had ever known in order to come above ground and be his mate among a strange species and in a world that she had never experienced. He might be a warrior, but Loralia by far had more courage than he ever would.

"I just feel horrible for even suggesting that we go do this so soon after meeting you."

Loralia shook her head.

"This is something that needs to be done. If it wasn't for the bravery and curiosity of the Denynso, the Klimnu never would have been eliminated, and you never would have found me."

"Well," Bannack said, squirming a little against the bench, "technically it wasn't the bravery and curiosity of the Denynso. It was the bravery and curiosity of the human women. They're the ones that went down into the tunnel after we found it, and they're the ones that went back and figured out that the Klimnu were using the mirrored realm to get to us. We just kind of went along with it."

Loralia laughed and Bannack felt his heart soar. He had struggled to think that he was ever going to find a mate, and then when he found her, he had fought even harder against himself, trying to tell himself that he was not the type of person that could mate with a species that was not his own. Of course, that was just his own fear and questions about himself talking and quickly the other warriors and their human mates showed him how wrong he was. He would never be able to thank them enough for pushing him to listen to what was truly in his heart and not what was going through his mind.

"I love you, Bannack," Loralia said, "and when you leave here, you will carry my love with you. But I also want you to bring this."

She reached into the small pouch that she wore on one hip and withdrew what looked like a slightly larger version of the compact that she wore around her neck and that held the mirrors she used to manipulate the space around her. It hung from a chain that looked like it was made of a long braid of her hair. Bannack took the compact into his palm and stared down at it. It didn't shimmer like hers did, but looked heavy and dark like the deeply scrolled metal hadn't been touched in many years.

"This compact," she said, touching it gently with her fingertips, "was my father's. He was an incredible man, and so are you. My hair connects this compact to mine. If you need me, just open the compact and reflect the braid in the top mirror for a few seconds. Mine will let me know that you're calling for me, and when I open my compact I will be able to see anything reflected in yours, and you will be able to see anything reflected in mine."

This was the most amazing gift Bannack could have imagined. He had been struggling knowing that unlike the other warriors and their mates, he was not able to connect with Loralia through her mind and communicate with her through their thoughts. It had made him feel like they weren't as tightly linked as the others, though he knew that he loved her with the same intensity as the other men loved their women. This compact, something that she had treasured for so long, was not just a reminder of her for when they were apart, but also a tangible way for him to connect with her in a manner that was completely unique to them.

"Good morning, everyone."

The deep sound of King Creia's voice brought the attention of everyone in the hall toward the platform where the king and his queen, Theia, stood. They looked out over the clan gathered in the meeting hall with the fondness and pride of parents overlooking their children. Several of the warriors were, in fact, their children, but even those who were not theirs by blood were adored by the kind and caring king and queen.

"This morning is very special for all of us, Creia continued. Today is the first day of a time of discovery that will change the future for every one of us. Through their selflessness, courage, and determination, our warriors and healer will do what no other Denynso has ever been able to do; learn what exists beyond our compound boundaries and what it means for our clan. The journey may be long and difficult, but I have absolute faith and confidence in each one of them that they will be successful and make us all even more proud of them, and of our kind, than we already are. I want each of them to know that our thoughts are with them and that we will all be eagerly awaiting their return. For now, everyone enjoy breakfast and spend some time together. They depart in one hour."

Creia nodded and stepped back, walking down off of the platform with Theia so that they could go to their nearby table and eat. The meeting hall cooks had placed trays overflowing with food into the centers of the long tables and everyone was starting to eat, but Bannack didn't have much of an appetite. He was too busy regretting everything that he had done and said in the first day that he knew Loralia. Though she had forgiven him without question, he felt like he was never going to be able to let go of those lost moments with her.

"Don't hate yourself, Bannack," Loralia said.

Though she couldn't read his thoughts the way that the other mates could read the thoughts of their Denynso men, Loralia was able to perceive the feelings and emotions of the people around her, making it possible for her to always know what he was going through.

"I lost so much time with you."

"It was only a day, Bannack, and every moment that you suffer with that is another moment that you are taking from us. Stop thinking about what has already happened and can never be redone, and think about what has yet to happen and what could be. I love you. Nothing is going to change that."

"I love you, too," Bannack said, leaning forward to kiss her.

As she gazed back at him he realized that everything she had said she meant with her whole heart. For the first time, he let himself let go of what had happened and gave himself over completely to the powerful, consuming love that he felt for her.

7

———

The compound felt eerily quiet without the men. Loralia and the human women stood in the center of the compound long after the warriors had marched out of sight, disappearing into the darkness of the forest that bordered that edge of the compound. The Denynso women and the monarchs had walked away, returning to their daily activities, within just a few moments of the last man marching out of sight, but the humans and Loralia couldn't seem to pull themselves away from where they stood. These had been the spots where they were standing when their mates had given them their final kisses goodbye and stroked their faces, imparting their warmth and expressing their love even without words. They didn't want to move and break the beautiful, precious space they had created with their men.

Finally Samira sighed.

"I don't think that standing here is going to make any difference, guys. They aren't coming back today."

There was a brief pause and then the rest of the women started laughing, happily breaking the painful tension that they had all been feeling. They needed that moment, that first second that forced them to have a thought that wasn't their mates' voices and the touch of their skin. None of them wanted to do it. They all would much rather continue feeling their men close to them, but they had no idea how long it would be before the men would be back and if they didn't push themselves out of that frame of mind, they would all just allow themselves to waste away. They knew that they wouldn't be able to get through this on their own. It would take the strength of all of them to support each other and take care of the compound while their mates were gone.

"Loralia," Eden said and Loralia turned to her, "I haven't had a chance to tell you that I'm really happy that things worked out for you and Bannack."

"Thank you, Eden."

"I am, too," Zuri offered, "I heard what happened between you two and I wanted to tell you that you aren't alone."

"What do you mean?"

"I know it can feel like him being resistant to accepting you as his mate was him rejecting you, and that that can be really hurtful. I just don't want you to think that things were so easy for the rest of us."

Loralia looked at each of the women. She wasn't sure how to feel about the conversation. She had just that morning told Bannack that he needed to let go of what had happened between them at the beginning of their relationship and let them move forward into the future together, but at the same time she found it comforting to hear that these women had also coped with challenges when they were finding their way with their mates in the Denynso compound.

"It wasn't?"

"We should have told you that when we first came to see you that first night you were on the compound. It probably would have made things much easier for you," Zuri said, "The truth is that finding a mate is something that the Denynso men look forward to their entire lives, but it can be a really scary and uncomfortable experience for them. They can get really violent and aggressive, even more so than usual, and they feel like they can't get their minds straight. That's really hard for all of them, but sometimes they have a lot of their own issues to work through, too."

"I wasn't exactly the most pleasant person in the world, especially to Pyra, and basically told him that I didn't like him and didn't want anything to do with him," said Eden, giving a short laugh and looking down at her hand stroking across her belly.

"I was a virgin who was terrified of Ciyrs and had a really difficult time trusting him," Elianna offered, "and when I was kidnapped by the Klimnu, he had to deal with knowing that I was being tortured and not being able to find me."

"I had been held by the Klimnu for almost two months and tortured, and was in a coma when they brought me back to the compound," Leia said, her voice sounding strong even though it was still difficult for her to talk about her ordeal in the prison, "Gyyx spent days with me and he finally had to..." she hesitated, "excite me to get me to wake up. Even then he was terrified to touch me because I'm so small and he didn't want to hurt me."

"Ty resisted how he felt about me as hard as he could because he thought I was too young for him. I came here with Zuri when she came back to Uoria and Ty was my guide and protector. I had to force him to acknowledge that we were meant to be together."

Loralia nodded, appreciating how these women were opening up to her and feeling more confident in her new place in the compound. She turned to Zuri, the final woman in the group to tell her story. Zuri looked slightly startled as if she had forgotten that she hadn't told about her early days with her mate.

"Oh," she said, "Ero thought I was fat."

The women laughed and together they started walking back toward the houses. Loralia was processing the connection that she was feeling to these women, trying to remember what it was like to have friends to spend time with and people to rely on. She had spent so much time alone that she was finding it harder than she would have imagined just relaxing in their company and enjoying having the friendship. She knew it would take time for her to really feel like she was a part of them, but she had already begun to feel a strong loyalty to the Denynso and was looking forward to spending more time with these women.

8

The acrid smell of the burned building still lingered in the air even though it had been weeks since the fire had burned the Klimnu prison to the ground. An impending storm threatening the sky had made the air feel wet and heavy, seeming to magnify the strong smell of the burned prison.

The Denynso men trudged toward the prison, all of them feeling reluctant to go back to this far corner of the compound, a site that held so many horrific memories for all of them. This had been the site of a brutal battle with the Klimnu, a clash that started when one of the creatures came into the compound disguised as Pyra and kidnapped Elianna, holding her in the prison and torturing her because they knew that her pain would radiate out to her mate, luring the rest of the Denynso to the prison so that they could attack.

The Klimnu hadn't been prepared for the fury that the warriors held that night, or the power and intensity that their actions had inspired in their healer, Ciyrs. Between the two of them, Ciyrs and Elianna had laid waste to more of the slimy creatures than a few of the warriors combined. They had hoped that it would be the end of the conflict, but, of course, it wasn't. Now as they stood only a few yards away from the black, sooty remnants of the prison, each lost in their own thoughts, it was as if they were walking into that battle again.

Bannack felt his muscles tightening as if preparing him in case he needed to attack. Around him the raindrops started to fall, cooling his skin but increasing the solemn, eerie feeling around the prison.

"Come on," he said, starting to walk toward the rubble again, "we're almost to the boundary of the compound."

They all walked toward the prison, going at an angle so that they walked around the perimeter.

"Wait," Pyra said suddenly, "What's that?"

Bannack followed the direction where he was pointing. He saw that the several rainstorms that had occurred over the weeks since their battle with the Klimnu had washed away enough of the ashes to reveal what looked like the edges of a trapdoor in the foundation. Pyra climbed into the remnants of the prison and toward the trapdoor. Bannack followed, watching carefully where he stepped to avoid stepping on something that might injure him if it suddenly gave way, broke, or splintered upwards.

By the time he had gotten to the edge of the trapdoor, Pyra was already on his knees digging with his fingers around the edge.

"Help me," he grunted.

Bannack reached forward to pull on the edge of the door. The heat from the fire seemed to have melted some of the metal, but after a few minutes of pulling, the weakened door broke and the two warriors were able to toss the pieces of door away. They stared down into what looked like a black abyss. It was so dark that they couldn't see the ground and there was no way of determining how far the fall would be between the door and the floor.

"Does anyone have a light?" Pyra asked.

Ty reached into his bag and withdrew a stick loaded with a solar power cell. Bannack took it and activated it so that it sent a wash of light down into the hole. Even with the light there wasn't anything to see. Pyra took his bag off of his shoulders and handed it to Bannack, then jumped down through the trapdoor.

"What the hell do you think you're doing?" Ero yelled, dropping to his knees beside the open trapdoor and staring down into the darkness.

Bannack swept the light back and forth until it fell on Pyra, crouched on a dark stone floor at least twenty feet down.

"It's a trapdoor," Pyra said, "It had to be close enough to the floor to let people actually get down here. Come on. Jump down."

Bannack went first, followed close by Ero. They stepped out of the way so that most of the other warriors could follow. A few had pulled out their own lights and soon there was enough illumination that they were able to see they were in some kind of dungeon.

"Well, it was close enough that we could get down, but that doesn't make any sense for the Klimnu. They're not anywhere near as big as we are. How would they get down here without breaking themselves?"

Pyra gazed up at the open trapdoor like he was pondering what Ty had just asked.

"I'm not sure. Anyway, let's look around. I didn't even know this place was here when we were here."

The group split off so that they could explore the

dungeon more efficiently, breaking up so that everyone had a light with them. They had been exploring the dark, damp hallways for nearly an hour when Ty discovered a door on an otherwise blank wall. Unlike the other doors that looked like they had once belonged to cells, this door was solid. He stepped back and directed a hard kick into the middle of the door, causing it to splinter.

Pushing aside the broken pieces of door, Ty stepped inside the small room and shined his light around. It looked like an office; a large desk on one wall, rows of bookshelves on another, and the back corner filled with what looked like stacks of drawers. Ty approached the drawers cautiously and pulled one open. It was filled with folders of documents and he pulled several out so that he could spread them across the surface of the desk.

"Hey, Pyra," he yelled a few minutes later after going through a few pages of the documents he had found in the folders.

Pyra stepped into the room and shined the light he had borrowed from another warrior after giving Ty back his on the desk.

"What did you find?"

"What do you know about this prison?" Ty asked, flipping through the fragile, aged pages of a book that looked ancient in his hands.

"Not much. I didn't even know it was here until the Klimnu attacked. I'm guessing that they built it so long ago that no one remembers it."

"I don't think they built it at all."

"What do you mean?"

"Look at this."

Pyra came around the side of the desk and Ty turned the book to show him what he was reading.

"Holy shit."

"I know."

"What's going on?" Ero asked, coming into the small room.

"This prison wasn't built by the Klimnu," Pyra told him.

"What do you mean?"

"Ty just found all of these books and papers. It looks like the Klimnu were just about as gracious with this prison as they were with the realm under the compound. Apparently this prison has been here for hundreds of years, which means that it was built before the Denynso were living on the compound."

"How could we not know that?"

"I don't know. Creia said that our kind has never made contact with other species except in battle. If it was there when the Denynso settled the compound, they either didn't notice it, or the species that built it was already gone by the time they came."

"How is that even possible?" Ero asked.

"I don't know."

"Look at this."

Pyra had pulled another, smaller book out from the stack of papers that Ty had taken out of the drawer and held it open to the other warriors. It looked almost like a military log, but was more extensive, like the person keeping it was both tracking the events and journaling about them as his way to express his thoughts and emotions.

"This says that the species that built this prison built it during a war with another species that they had been in conflict with for years. They used this prison to hold people who they captured during battle, but the other species found out and infiltrated the prison, freeing all of the captives and killing many of the Covra."

"The Covra?"

"That's what it says. I've never heard of that species before."

"What happened after that battle?"

"This says that the Covra knew that they weren't strong enough to fight off the rest of what they call the Light Ones, so they locked them."

Pyra stopped and looked up at the other men, a confused look on his face.

"Locked them?" Ty asked.

Pyra turned the page and read for a few seconds before looking up at them again.

"It says that the Covra can lock an entire area in place. It's like the whole place is frozen in time. They at once exist and don't. Time passes around them, but it doesn't impact them. They locked the entire kingdom of the Light Ones in that moment and never made any plans to release them."

Pyra met eyes with Ty, and then with Ero.

"What if they're still there?"

9

"What do you mean?" Ero asked.

"There's a map right here that shows where everything was when this all happened." He pointed at a large area outlined toward the upper corner of the map. "What if the kingdom is still there and the Light Ones are still stuck there, just like they have been since the Covra locked them?"

Silence fell in the room as the three men pondered what Pyra had just said. It was almost unfathomable that what that journal said could be true. After what they had all seen Loralia achieve with her mirrors, they were far more willing to accept that there were things that existed right on their own planet that they didn't understand, and species that could accomplish truly astounding things. The idea that one of these creatures could literally stop time for an entire other species, and that that frozen kingdom could still be persisting in its fully locked state just as it had been for years was too much for any of them to wrap their minds around.

"Pyra?"

The voice of another of the warriors made them all turn to the door to the office. Lynx stood there, leaning into the room with the glow from the light in his hand directed at the floor.

"What is it, Lynx?" Pyra asked.

There really isn't much down here. A bunch of cells. A couple of old chains."

"Tell the men to find a way to get back up out of the trapdoor and gather up outside. Our little adventure here is taking a detour."

"Where are we going?"

"Back in time, it looks like."

TWENTY MINUTES later the men had managed to find a nearly rusted-out metal ladder that looked like it was once attached to the bottom of the trapdoor so it could be used to climb in and out of the dungeon and had gathered right outside in the soft rain. Though the fact that the Klimnu had not actually built the prison originally explained why the structure was built as it was, the existence of the ladder seemed to make the dungeon make more sense.

Pyra gave them a brief overview of what they had found out in the office in the dungeon and told them that they were going to follow that map and see what they could find in the place that marked where the kingdom of the Light Ones at least once stood. Lynx watched him push the stack of papers and books he had carried out of the dungeon into the bag that he had returned to his hip and headed out toward the furthest boundary of the compound, past the wastelands and toward the complete unknown.

The rain intensified as they walked, starting to beat down on them in stinging streams that hurt as they bit into

Lynx's exposed skin. It was that fearsome type of rain that made you want to stay inside, drink something hot, and wait until it was over. The men didn't have that option, now. They had committed themselves to this mission, and now it seemed to be taking on even more meaning that it had when they had first started. When he first agreed to go along with them to explore Uoria, Lynx never would have imagined that they would be gone from their homes for only a few hours and already have learned of two species that they didn't know existed up until that point, but also a whole history of the planet and their own compound that none of them had known.

Though he hated himself for thinking it, and wouldn't ever have admitted it in those first few hours, Lynx was starting to change his perception of Creia. Like the other warriors, he had been raised believing that this man was the most powerful and wise of all of the Denynso. Part of a bloodline known for their extraordinary longevity, he had ruled for many decades and had faced many of the earliest battles and conflicts in the ranks of the warriors. It had been Creia who had shown the strength and courage to banish the Klimnu because of their greedy, vicious ways rather than letting them intimidate him into helping them. With all of this history and knowledge, however, he somehow hadn't known about the mirrored realm that existed just beneath the compound he had called home his entire life, or about the prison in the wastelands.

At least, he told them that he didn't know. The longer that they walked, the more footsteps that they put between the area of the compound that they knew and themselves, the more Lynx wondered how honest Creia had really been with them. Was it possible that he had known about the prison and the apparently brutal, drawn-out conflict that had existed there so long ago? Had he been completely honest with them when he told them that their kind had not made contact with others outside of the battles waged on the soil of their own compound?

Lynx felt painfully guilty for even entertaining those thoughts for a second. As a Denynso warrior, it was his responsibility and birthright to honor, respect, and obey Creia without question. He was meant to follow him and do as he ordered no matter what. The thought of questioning him for even a second would be something that the other warriors, or the king himself, would never have tolerated.

The young warrior was so lost in his own thoughts that he didn't notice the rest of the warriors had stopped and he ran directly into Gyyx's back. The larger, older warriors turned and glared at him, but turned back to face ahead of him without saying anything. Lynx stepped around to stand beside Gyyx and looked to where Pyra was standing several feet in front of the rest of them. A tall wall of weathered, ancient rocks stood just in front of him. It was the far boundary of the Denynso compound, laid by the very hands of the first of the clan. They had built in there to protect all who lived within it, intending, as the warriors had all been taught from the time that they were little children, that none would ever come inside the boundary to take the compound from them, no species not welcomed by the Denynso would come within the space without quick and brutal retribution, and that none of their kind would ever step beyond it.

They were prepared now to break free of those restraints; to be the first to go past the boundary and take back the freedom of existence on the entirety of the planet of Uoria.

10

———

"This is your last chance, men," Pyra said, his voice rumbling through the silence that had formed around them, "Once we go over this wall, we are out of the compound and facing things that none of us know or understand. There will be no turning back. If you aren't ready to do this, tell us now and you can go back. Think very hard about your decision, because it is one of the most important that you will ever make."

Pyra's glowing orange eyes burned into each of the men, giving them time to think about the implications of moving beyond that boundary and walking out onto the rest of the planet. Though they were feared throughout the galaxy, each of them was very aware that the compound had protected them, had guarded them. When they went beyond that wall, there was nothing left to surround them and keep them safe. Of course, that wall had also failed them when it came to keeping the Klimnu from attacking and tormenting them. It hadn't been enough to prevent the betrayal of the traitor Ullie, and it hadn't guarded them from the work of the flight attendant who had cooperated with him and the slimy, disgusting Klimnu to nearly spell the end of the Denynso.

Lynx could feel that the rest of the warriors around him felt the same way. They could no longer put their total blind trust and confidence in that wall. It was time that they took responsibility for themselves.

When none of the men told him that they wanted to turn back, Pyra nodded at them, his face not smiling but carrying an expression that offered a hint of strength and pride. He tilted his head back to evaluate the wall and then reached onto the side of his bag to untie a grappling hook. The other men followed suit, taking their hooks from their bags and preparing the ropes. A few moments later the Denynso stood in a long line in front of the wall.

At Pyra's command, they swung their hooks over the top of the wall and waited until they felt them catch in the stones on the other side. Moving in the perfect, nearly choreographed rhythm they had trained into their ranks, the men used the pressure of the hooks and the strength of the ropes to steady them as they climbed up the wall.

Lynx stopped when he reached the top of the wall and gazed out over the land that lay on the other side. It looked much like the far areas of the compound where there were no buildings or roads, but somehow despite its similarities, it still seemed sparser and unwelcoming.

Not wanting to be the last to be off the wall, Lynx dropped down on the other side of the wall and went through the same procedure as all of the other men, recoiling their hooks and attaching them back to their bags for use the next time that they may need them. Pyra didn't say another word, but waited until all of the men had come over the wall, and then started further along the open field. Lynx could see his gaze focused intensely on the stands of trees that dotted the field and the tall, coarse grass to either side of them. It was as though their leader were on edge with every footstep, just waiting for something to come out at them.

Pyra consulted the map in the book in his hand every few minutes, occasionally calling back to the rest of the men about which direction they needed to go, or about how far he thought it would be. Lynx followed silently, preferring to keep himself vigilant about what may be lurking at any corner rather than responding when any of the men spoke.

They had been walking for what felt like hours when Pyra suddenly slowed and all of the men followed his gaze to a towering, ivy-covered stone archway a few yards ahead of them. A worn, crumbling stone wall very similar to the one that they had crossed to leave the compound but older and of darker-colored rocks stretched out to either side of the archway and Lynx could see that it, too, had been taken over by the plants of the area that seemed to be trying to reclaim that space.

"This is it," Pyra said almost under his breath, "I can't believe it's actually here."

The men stood in stunned silence for several long seconds, not entirely sure of what they should do from there. They had come this far looking for the kingdom to see if it actually existed, and now that they had found that it did, and that it was still there, they didn't know what to do next.

"Are we going inside?" Ero asked.

Lynx watched Pyra nod.

"The only way to find out if all of this about the Covra and the Light Ones is real is to go in there and see if we find a kingdom that has been locked in time."

"How do we know that if it is all real, that we will be able to go in there at all, or that if we can, that we won't get locked too?" Ty asked.

"We don't," Pyra responded simply, "We don't know any of that. We can't just walk away from it, though. The whole point of us leaving the compound was to find out what else existed on this planet. Well, this is what else exists here. We can't stop now. We have to keep going and find out exactly what happened in there, and what is still happening, whether that means that all of the stuff in these books was just a bunch of made-up stories and that is an abandoned archway to an empty kingdom that no one has lived in for centuries, or that it is all absolutely true and waiting right inside there is an entire species that hasn't changed in longer than any of us have been alive."

"What if something does happen to us, though?" asked one of the warriors from the back of the group, "What about Eden and the baby?"

Pyra's eyes flashed at the mention of his mate and their unborn child and Lynx saw his back straighten and his shoulders square forcefully.

"My mate trusts me. She put her faith in me to find out more about Uoria so that I will be able to protect her and our baby well into the future. As for the baby, my child will know that I didn't stop at anything to make sure that my family was safe, and that I never cowered away from a challenge or a risk. I never want to look my baby in the eye and know that I didn't do absolutely everything that I could to complete my goal out here."

"And if we do find the so-called Light Ones in there," Ciyrs interjected, "there is a possibility that we could help them. They might not have to be locked forever."

As if this conversation propelled him, Pyra suddenly took off running, closing the space between himself and the archway in a matter of seconds. Ero, Ty, Gyyx, and Ciyrs followed closely after. That is when Lynx started running. Closing his eyes briefly against the fear that had settled into his stomach, he pushed himself to run as fast and as hard as he could, crossing through the archway mere seconds after Pyra had disappeared beneath the stone.

As soon as he passed through the archway, Lynx slowed and stopped. He looked up and for a moment he was afraid that Ero had been right and that they had all been locked right along with the kingdom and the Light Ones within it. Soon, though, he realized that he could think and move and he took a few more steps into the kingdom, gazing around with a sense of absolute awe. It was as if he had stepped into a painting.

11

———————

The kingdom somewhat resembled their compound, with what looked like rows of houses along a main road and a larger building positioned in the distance. Everything seemed more tightly positioned than the compound, however, and there was a greater sense of formality. Rather than the soft dirt that covered the roads in the Denynso compound, the roads here were covered in broken rocks that had been smoothed around the edges to fit in close together. The houses looked larger and more elaborate, too, with strange design elements that Lynx didn't understand.

What was undoubtedly the most fascinating part of the kingdom that they now wandered into, however, was the people. All around them were still, silent people, their bodies shaped into the postures of normal life, but none of them moved or breathed. It truly looked like they had been stopped, crystallized into a single second of their existence, and had not moved since.

"Everyone spread out," Pyra said evenly, slipping the book that held the map to the kingdom into his bag so that his hands were free, "Explore as much of the area as you can, but make sure that you keep contact with at least one other of us. We don't need anybody getting lost."

At that command, the men slowly dissipated, wandering in their own direction further into the kingdom as if each of them were drawn toward a certain place. It was unnerving to see the people scattered through the space, their eyes open but unseeing, their bodies primed for action but unable to move. There was a large garden in the center of the houses and Lynx saw several people in it, tending to crops that were still perfect after all this time. One woman leaned over, her hand just cupped around a vegetable she intended to pick while a man nearby rested with his arms crossed on top of a tall gardening implement. Lynx sighed, musing that that man could not have imagined how long his break was actually going to be when he stopped his work on that fateful day.

To one side Lynx could see a small group of children playing, locked in their laughter and joy, and he had to turn away. It was too painful to see the innocence of little ones stolen from them because of a war between adults, a conflict that they would never understand.

Turning his back toward the children, Lynx walked toward one of the houses. It drew him in in a way that the others didn't, and he felt compelled to go inside. He called out to Ty who he saw walking along at the end of the street, letting him know that he was going inside the house so that someone knew where he was should the rest of the men decide to leave the kingdom before he got out of the house, or if there was something inside that might threaten him.

He didn't expect the door to open as easily beneath his hand as it did. When it opened fully, he stepped inside the cool, airy house and looked around. Just as the outsides of the homes were more complex in their design than the Denynso homes back on the compound, they were more complex on the inside as well. Multiple rooms stretched out from the front entryway, and a set of stairs headed up to another floor. He followed his instincts and let them pull him to the stairs, keeping him focused on the landing above him as he climbed them.

At the top of the stairs Lynx let the strange, tight feeling in his belly guide him toward a room at the center of the hallway. The door was partially open and when he pushed it the rest of the way open, he felt his heart constrict.

It was a bedroom with pale yellow walls, airy white curtains on the window, and a large canopy bed tucked in one corner. On that bed lay the most beautiful woman that Lynx had ever seen, and as soon as his eyes rested on the long strands of coppery hair spread across the pillow, her pale, delicate face, and full, pink lips, he felt everything inside him unravel as an overwhelming sense of love, desire, and the need to protect her took over.

Lynx walked cautiously to the side of the bed and gazed down at her face, so perfect and calm in the sleep in which she had been locked. It made no sense, but he felt completely and inarguably in love with her, the same intense, immediate feeling of soul-wrenching attraction and need that the other men had described when talking about meeting their mates. This was a woman who had lived generations before he was even born, and yet Lynx felt inextricably connected to her, as if all this time she had been lying here sleeping, waiting for him to come find her.

Something on the nightstand beside her bed caught Lynx's eye and he picked up a silver-framed picture that looked like a younger version of the woman in the bed standing with two older people in front of a large house that resembled the houses along the main street, but much larger. Lynx flipped the frame over in his hand and released the brackets that held the picture in place. When the backing came off of the frame, he rested it carefully on the nightstand and took the picture out so that he could look at the back.

Visit to the homeland

Earth

Rain, 22 years

Lynx gasped as he realized what the inscription meant. These were not some strange, unknown species that they had never encountered. These were creatures with whom the Denynso were becoming quite familiar.

The Light Ones were humans.

Taking the picture with the intention of showing it to Pyra, Lynx took a final look at the beautiful woman, whose name he could only guess to be Rain, and then turned to the door to leave. Before he could take another step, however, a series of deathly sharp black spikes came around the door-frame, cutting into the wall as they gripped into it to pull massive black bodies like gruesome spiders into the room and toward Lynx.

TBC

(To be continued in Part IV...)

THE ALIEN'S LOVE

1

———

Lynx's mind was spinning. He didn't know what to think or how to react. He could hear the walls cracking and tearing as the massive creatures pulled themselves into the room, following each other so closely that they filled the doorway and crawled over one another grotesquely as if they couldn't wait to get to him. Lynx could only relate them to the spiders that Zuri had shown them pictures of while she was describing Earth and some of the types of life that lived there, but these were far beyond the small, scurrying bugs that she had shown them. Even the largest of those were miniscule compared to the gleaming creatures and their sharp, spiked legs that dug into the walls and ceiling as they crawled into the room.

As they moved toward him, Lynx stepped closer to the bed where Rain, the *human,* lay frozen in her calm, sleeping state. He had to protect her. He knew that this beautiful, delicate-looking woman, this lovely human that at once baffled and intrigued him, was meant to be his mate. It didn't matter to him that she was from a species that was not meant to have even visited Uoria before they started to arrive at the Denynso compound to research and learn, and even then were supposed to have been limited just to their area of the planet. It didn't even bother him that she had been lying here, frozen in her sleep, for longer than he had been alive. It was confounding and beyond his realm of comprehension, but at that moment the only thing that mattered to the warrior was making sure that the woman that lay in front of him was safe from these fearsome creatures crawling toward him.

There were seven of them now, leaving deep gouges in their wake as they moved across the walls and ceiling. He had seen gouges like that in the lower portion of the house when he had first arrived, but he had thought nothing of them. He had been far more concerned with the fact that in their desire to explore the planet of Uoria and discover what types of beings might share it with them, the group of Denynso men had found that there had been a long-running feud between two species that ended in one of them, the Covra, locking the beings they knew as the Light Ones, and that Lynx now knew were humans, in time, and that they were then roaming through that locked kingdom discovering everything that had stopped in the span of a breath, decades before.

Now what he worried about was Rain and how he would protect her. She couldn't move. As far as he knew, she had no awareness of what was going on around her. It was his responsibility to ensure that she was safe and that these creatures didn't harm her. He could continue to process the fact that she was human later. Right now he had to think quickly and get rid of these monsters.

Lynx stepped back toward the window that overlooked the street and could hear muffled screaming coming from the rest of the settlement. The creatures seemed to have found the rest of the Denynso men. Like the others, Lynx rarely carried weapons. They preferred to fight with their bare hands. And like the others, occasionally he carried a dagger that he had crafted himself. This dagger, however, he had left tucked in the bag he had been carrying as they walked from the compound, and he had dropped that bag to the floor near the door to the room.

He heard another scream from one of the buildings across the street and the frantic sound mobilized him. Lynx took a long stride across the room and dove toward his bag. He could feel something sharp grazing his back as he grabbed onto the bag and pulled it up against his chest. A fearsome hissing sound above him told him that he had angered the creatures, and he felt the sharp, piercing feeling in his back intensify.

Lynx reached into his bag and pulled out his dagger. In one fast movement he rolled over onto his back and slashed at one of the creatures. The tip of his dagger bit through the leg that was digging into his back and vibrantly green blood splattered down on him as the leg splintered off of the rest of the creature's body and skittered across the floor. The injured creature let out a horrific screeching sound and pulled back away from him, but even as Lynx saw the gleaming black thing withdrawing away from him, he watched as the open wound in the leg healed itself over and the limb started growing back.

Out of the corner of his eye Lynx saw one of the larger creatures climbing over the smaller one above his head, moving toward Rain where she lay on the bed. Lynx tightened his grip on the dagger and scurried backwards across the floor toward the edge of the bed. The large creature came toward him and he slashed at it with his dagger. Since he had watched the other creature heal itself so quickly, he didn't know how the larger one would react to his threats, but it was all he could do.

The creature took another step toward Rain and the fury built inside Lynx with an intensity that he had never experienced. He pulled himself up higher and changed his grip on his dagger so that it was pointing directly at the bulbous black eye at the front of the rounded body. He could see the reflection of his blade in the surface of the eye and as he leaned toward the creature, it stepped back. Lynx took another step forward and lay a protective hand on Rain's leg.

As soon as his hand touched her, Lynx felt his entire body tingle and saw a flash of bright, vibrant light. The room around him disappeared in the light and then reappeared, but it looked different. Sunlight, the type of dark, rich light that came with a late afternoon, made the room appear to glow. Out of the corner of his eye Lynx saw movement and he turned. Against the wall stood a vanity table with a large, curved mirror and at the table sat Rain.

2

———

Lynx started to reach toward Rain, and saw her look up into the mirror as if she could sense his presence. In the reflection in the mirror he could see just how beautiful she was, the sparkling blue of her eyes like nothing he had ever seen. As she looked into the glass, however, he realized that she wasn't looking at him, but something over her shoulder. He hadn't noticed anything, so he continued to watch.

Rain drew a brush through her long hair and then settled it onto the surface of the vanity table. She stood, the thin fabric of her nightgown skimming the curves of her body and brushing against the floor as she walked the few steps to the bed and slipped beneath the covers. Just as she settled her head onto the pillow and her body relaxed, he saw one of the massive black creatures climb out from under the bed. Lynx screamed, but it didn't do any good. The creature lifted one sharply pointed leg, the tip glinting even more gruesomely in the sunlight, and plunged it into Rain's stomach.

As suddenly and inexplicably as the vision had

appeared, the room around him seemed to melt and Lynx found himself standing back where he had been. It must have lasted only a few seconds, but Lynx felt like it had changed him completely. Something like that had never happened to him before. He wasn't even entirely sure what had happened, but those few moments had confirmed to him that these spider-like monsters were the Covra.

"Why?" he screamed at the one closest to him, and he saw it recoil as if it wasn't accustomed to hearing a spoken voice.

Lynx slashed at it with his dagger and the creature stepped backwards. He lunged forward and drove the tip of the blade toward the Covra's eye. It scurried backwards more quickly and Lynx rushed around the edge of the bed. The few moments of seeing Rain awake and vital had infuriated him to a level that was almost blinding, and he roared as he went after the Covra.

The louder he got, and the harder he slashed toward their eyes, the faster the creatures scurried toward the door.

"Lynx!"

Lynx heard Pyra's voice shouting up to him from the lower floor of the house. The deep sound of the lead warrior was encouraging. He knew that Pyra had survived and that he was not alone. A moment later Lynx heard Pyra's footsteps pounding up the stairs toward him, accompanied by another set. The horrific screeching of the Covra filled the space as Pyra and Bannack came into the room slashing at them with their own daggers. Green blood splattered the room and pieces of the creatures littered the floor.

"Their eyes!" Lynx shouted.

Pyra and Bannack turned their hands on the handles of their daggers, creating a tighter grip that allowed them to direct the carefully honed tips toward the rounded black domes of the Covra's eyes. The three warriors held their blades out toward the spider-like creatures, and for a moment they seemed to be retreating. As the room fell silent, however, the Covra's splintered limbs and the pieces of their round bodies that had fallen away under the edges of the Denynso's blades grew back and the monsters started to advance toward them again.

"Where are the other men?" Lynx demanded.

"They are fighting others of these creatures throughout the rest of the settlement," Pyra told him.

Lynx noticed that the Covra had stilled when they started speaking, and on instinct, he started again.

"These are the Covra," he told Pyra, pushing forward slightly with his blade held toward the eye of the closest creature.

"The Covra?" Pyra asked.

"Yes. The creatures that we read about in the prison in the compound. The ones that built the prison and locked this settlement."

"How could these things build a prison?" Pyra asked.

"I don't know, but they did, and now they are back here."

The men had managed to force the Covra back toward the door and they were scurrying away from them now, running along the walls and ceiling until they disappeared into other rooms and out of windows. Them being out of sight did not provide any relief for Lynx. He knew they were there, he knew now that they existed still and that they could appear out of seemingly nowhere. He didn't know how they had managed to make them retreat, and it was not comforting to him that he didn't know when they might return or how they could make them leave again.

The screams and hisses from outside had faded away as the Covra in the house disappeared and soon they were replaced by the shouts and frantic yells of the other Denynso. Pyra and Bannack started to run down the stairs toward the door to the house, but Lynx hesitated. He didn't want to leave Rain behind. Now that he knew that the Covra could return at any time, he felt like she was vulnerable. He rushed back into the room and knelt down beside the bed.

A moment later Pyra came back into the room.

"Lynx, come on. We have to find the other men. What are you doing?"

"I can't leave her," he said, gazing down at Rain.

"What do you mean you can't leave her?"

"This woman is supposed to be my mate."

He glanced up at Pyra and saw the look of confusion and shock cross his face. Finding their mate was something that the Denynso men waited for their entire lives. Unlike other species who may be able to mate with any number of others, the Denynso had one single mate. This was the only woman that existed in the entire universe who they could create a bond with, and the only one who they ever would create a bond with. They would look for that one woman throughout their entire lives, and when they found her, they immediately knew. After that, the bond was for life. This was something that they all knew from a very young age, and it took on even more serious meaning for Lynx now that he realized his mate was someone who may never again open her eyes.

"Lynx, this woman is locked in time. She has been here since long before you were even born, and she may be here on into eternity. You are just reacting to everything that's going on."

"No," Lynx said, feeling the defensive aggression building inside him, "Rain is my mate. She has been waiting for me for her entire life, and for mine."

"Rain?" Bannack asked, stepping into the room behind Pyra.

Lynx realized that the others didn't have any idea what he had discovered about these people, the Light Ones as the Covra had called them, and he debated with himself whether he should tell them. He worried that if he let them know that he knew they were human, they would not be as inclined to help them. Even though several of the Denynso, Pyra included, had mated with humans, there was still deep-seated controversy about how much interaction and connection the two species should have. The thought that they had been living on the planet all along, and that Creia had either not known about them or had been lying to them, could cause them even more difficulty than they were already facing.

Not telling them what he had seen, however, didn't seem like an option.

"I saw her," he said carefully.

"What do you mean?" Pyra asked.

"When the Covra were in here, I touched her, and I could see what I think were the last few seconds before she was locked."

"What did you see, Lynx?" Pyra demanded.

The force behind the words made Lynx feel even more defensive and he straightened his spine, pressing his chest toward the larger, older warrior. Suddenly Pyra's eyes widened.

"Lynx, you're bleeding," he said.

Lynx looked down and saw trails of his own blood sliding down his arm and dripping onto the floor beneath his feet.

3

———

"**T**here's something wrong."

Elianna jumped up from the chair where she had been sitting and rushed across the room to Eden. She dropped down onto her knees next to her and rested her hands on the other woman's rounded belly.

"There's something wrong with the baby?" she asked frantically.

There was still so much that they didn't understand about Eden's pregnancy and every tiny twinge or moment of worry could bring panic to the other women. This was the first pregnancy for this generation of the Denynso, and even though Eden had technically become one of their kind when Ciyrs had saved her from near death, there was much of her that was still humanlike and no one knew how much of her pregnancy would resemble each of the species.

"No," Eden said, rubbing her belly as if to calm herself and the baby resting inside, "There's something wrong with Pyra."

Elianna's eyes widened and Eden could see the fear in them.

"What? What's happening?"

"I don't know," Eden said, straightening in her seat. "I can't communicate with him."

She concentrated hard on her mate, trying to make the connection that would allow them to speak to each other through their thoughts. It was a precious gift that the Denynso enjoyed with their mates, something that allowed them to connect in a way that was far deeper and more meaningful than the connection that they had with any of the others of their kind. She had learned, though, that this connection was not something that was always available. She couldn't just glance into Pyra's mind whenever she wanted to. If he was concentrating too hard on something else, or purposely did not want her to be able to see into his thoughts, she would not be able to. She knew the same went for her, but she rarely closed him out. The fact that she could sense that there was something wrong with him but was unable to decipher exactly what it was, or to communicate with him, frightened her.

"Try Ciyrs," Elianna said.

Eden looked into her friend's eyes. She could see the lingering pain there that the small woman always tried to conceal, but occasionally made itself sharp and inescapably known.

"You can't get to him?" Eden asked.

Elianna shook her head.

"Try him, please."

This was another of the extraordinary things about Eden that made her stand apart from the other mates of the Denynso despite them all being quite close. She was not only the first of the human women to come to the planet and find her mate in one of the tremendous warriors who guarded the compound and waged war against other species throughout the galaxy. She was the first to find herself pregnant with the child of one of the warriors. And she was the only human that the Denynso healer Ciyrs had brought back from the brink of death after a gruesome encounter with one of the Klimnu. It was during that interaction that she had been turned into one of them, and in turn she had formed a link with Ciyrs that was just like the one she had with Pyra.

It was the only such link that existed in the Denynso. Usually only the men and their mates formed the link that allowed them to speak through their thoughts and feel each other's emotions. Eden and the healer, however, had created that link and still maintained it. Their bond was nothing like hers with Pyra, or his with Elianna. It was not romantic, but rather she saw him as her most treasured friend, like a brother that she had never had during her time on Earth. The link had extended to her and Elianna, but they rarely used it. The fact that she and Ciyrs were connected in such as way was already difficult for their mates, even though both Pyra and Elianna had expressed time and time again that they understood that they didn't represent a threat to their bonds. Out of respect for their mates, however, Eden and Ciyrs agreed to stay away from each other's thoughts as much as possible, only entering them in times of emergency.

Ciyrs?

Eden sent out the call to Ciyrs, barely breathing as she waited for him to respond.

Please, Ciyrs, talk to me. Elianna says that she can't get to you, and I can't get to Pyra. I know that there's something wrong. Talk to me.

She got no response and the fear that had been building inside her sharpened to an almost painful edge. She hadn't wanted Pyra and the other men to go out into the rest of the planet to explore. The battles with the Klimnu were still so fresh and raw in their minds, and the death of Jem was still so painful. The thought of them leaving the compound, venturing outside of the boundaries for the first time of any of their kind, was terrifying to her, especially as she moved further along in her pregnancy. She was so scared that something was going to happen to them and that she would be without Pyra, a thought that made her feel empty and hollow inside. She had left everything that she had ever known on Earth to stay on Uoria to be with him, something that she would do again in a second if she had to make the choice, but the thought of losing him was far more difficult and painful than walking away from anything she had known in her life before him.

"They've only been gone a day," Eden said, trying both to convince herself and Elianna that everything was fine, "What possibly could have happened to them? They are probably just sleeping."

Even as the words came out of her mouth, though, she knew that she didn't believe them. She had reached out to both Pyra and Ciyrs when they were sleeping before and they had woken up immediately. She had learned to enter their thoughts carefully enough that she would be able to tell if they were dreaming, something she did with tremendous caution after some of the dreams that she had stumbled into when connecting with Ciyrs, and she knew that as forcefully as she had just tried to connect with both men, they would have woken up.

"Where are the others?" Elianna asked, "Maybe they can get to their mates."

"Zuri said that she, Leia, and Samira would be down by the water. They've decided to do more of their research while the men are gone."

"They aren't going back to Earth, are they?"

"Not for any longer than Samira and Ty's wedding," Eden paused, not wanting to say out loud what the worrisome little voice in the back of her mind was saying, questioning whether that wedding would ever actually come to pass. "But I think that it distracts them. Their whole lives on Earth were the university and their teaching or studies. Maybe it helps them not think about their mates."

The two women had started out of the house toward the water and Eden could feel Elianna staring at her as they walked.

"Do you ever miss your work?" Elianna asked.

Her voice was low, as if she was trying to keep what she had said just between her and Eden, though the compound was nearly deserted now that the men were gone. The human mates still had little to no contact with the Denynso women, except for the midwives, and for the most part the five of them existed on their own.

"No," Eden said honestly, "That job, as proud as I was of it, was awful. My boss was... horrible."

She realized as she said this that she had never really told the other women how she had made her way into the Denynso compound. As the first to become a part of the clan, she had watched the other women join them one by one, but she hadn't really opened up to them about her experiences before she made the decision to stay with Pyra.

"What happened?" Elianna asked.

Eden sighed. She had wanted to leave her past behind her, to keep it firmly on Earth so that she didn't have to deal with it any longer, but she knew that it wouldn't help her to pretend like none of it had ever happened.

"My boss, Ryan, was not a nice person. He wanted what he wanted and he was going to get it, or make everybody's life miserable. I wouldn't date him, so he decided to send me on what he thought was a death mission."

"What?" Elianna sounded horrified.

"Yeah. A bit of an overreaction if you ask me, but that's what he decided to do. He knew that the Denynso had very strict rules about human visitors, particularly scientists, and he sent me here with the specific instructions to go against those rules."

"What did he want you to do?"

"He wanted me to bring back a sample of Denynso warrior blood so that he could analyze it and find out what makes them so powerful. Of course, that is the most serious rule that the Denynso have. To Ryan, either I would be successful and he would be able to get to the source of the Denynso power and possibly create his own race of superior warriors through genetic engineering on Earth, or I would get caught and they would kill me. Either way, he would get something that he wanted; success and fame, or revenge."

"Where is he now?" Elianna asked.

Eden glanced over at her. She honestly hadn't thought about him in the months that she had spent on Uoria. It was as if he didn't exist anymore.

"You know, I have no idea. It's possible that the research lab thinks that I'm dead and they've brought him up on endangerment and espionage charges."

The thought delighted Eden on a level that she didn't necessarily want to admit to anyone, and it made her feel a little less awful about herself when Elianna laughed.

"That would serve him right," she said.

Eden laughed.

"It would. I'm sure that he would absolutely love a few decades in one of the prison tech camps."

The thought of Ryan chained to one of the expansive computers in the technology prison camps, forced to work from morning until night working systems so basic they would drive him mad, was enough to assuage all of the anger she had for him, and she found herself smiling as they walked on toward the pond at the far end of the compound.

Her smile faded, however, when she saw Loralia running toward them, her long braid bouncing on her back as she rushed down the dirt road, her compact held tightly in her hand. Suddenly Eden remembered why they were walking toward the water and all of the fear and heartache came rushing back.

4

Pyra held Lynx down on the floor, pushing his arms down against the wood with nearly all of his strength. Even though the younger warrior was smaller, the ferocity that was suddenly pouring out of him was making it more difficult than Pyra would have imagined for him to control his thrashing. As soon as he had mentioned the blood dripping from Lynx's back, the other warrior had seemed to snap, suddenly becoming aggressive and violent toward him and Bannack. He was hissing in a way that was almost like the Covra, and no matter how loudly Pyra shouted his name, he stared back at him through eyes that looked dark and unrecognizable, as if they were not registering the meaning of the word.

Behind him Bannack gripped a silver compact in his hand and stared into it. The compact looked like a larger, heavier version of the one that Loralia carried and Pyra wondered what Bannack could possibly be doing with it as he struggled to not only fight off Lynx's violent reaction, but to understand what was causing it.

"Loralia!" Bannack suddenly gasped.

"Bannack?" Loralia's voice came into the room and Pyra shot a shocked look at Bannack, "What's wrong?"

"Something's happening to Lynx," Bannack said into the compact, "We don't know what's going on."

"What happened?"

"I can't get into the whole story right now, but he's been injured and now he seems like he's completely out of his mind. He's fighting Pyra and we can't get him to calm down. He looks like he's trying to kill him."

"Show him to me."

Pyra forced his knee into Lynx's chest to give him more control over him and watched as Bannack came closer and held the compact at an angle as if reflecting Lynx in the mirror.

"What are you doing?" Pyra asked.

"If anyone would be able to figure out what's going on with him, it's going to be Loralia."

"How was he injured?" Loralia asked through the compact.

Her voice sounded slightly strained, as if she knew something but didn't want to actually say it until she knew for sure that she was right.

"We encountered another species..."

"The Covra," Loralia said before Bannack could even continue his sentence.

"Yes," Bannack said, "You've heard of them?"

"Yes. A long time ago. I didn't know that they still existed. You need to get Lynx to Ciyrs as fast as you possibly can."

"What's wrong with him?"

"He's been infected by the Covra. They are fairly weak creatures. They have their talons, but their greatest form of defense is infecting those they are fighting. If they can get their venom into another creature, that creature forgets what it is and tries to kill anything near it. The effect lasts until the venom is removed, or the infected creature is destroyed."

"I don't understand. If they can turn whatever they get near into killing machines, how are they weak? Why aren't they able to just destroy whatever comes their way?"

"They used to, and then other species realized that it takes many, many years for them to reproduce, and that they have a very specific vulnerability. They were once feared more than anything on this planet, but several generations ago they came in contact with an enemy that took that power from them. They found that vulnerability and were able to stave them off."

"The Light Ones," Bannack said.

"I don't know," Loralia admitted, "I only know what my grandfather told me. He said that their numbers were greatly diminished and that they had to wait for the next generation to be born before they would be able to fight again. They haven't been heard from since."

"You don't know what their vulnerability is?"

"No, but you need to get Lynx help now. The longer you wait, the harder it will be for Ciyrs to remove the venom. If you wait too long, Lynx will kill until he is killed."

"Thank you," Bannack said, "I love you."

Pyra watched him snap the compact closed and look down at him. His arm muscles were starting to burn from forcing Lynx to stay in place on the floor and he was pushing down into his chest with his knee so hard that he worried he was going to break his ribs.

"How are we going to get him to Ciyrs?" Pyra asked, "If I let up even a little, he's going to get off this floor and that dagger is far too close to him for my comfort if Loralia is right about him being infected."

"You're going to have to hold him while I go find Ciyrs. Where did you last see him?"

"He went into a building down the street. I don't know where he is now."

Bannack looped the braid of Loralia's hair that held the compact back over his neck and ran out of the room. Pyra listened to his footsteps pounding down the stairs and fade as they left the house. He could only hope that he was able to find the healer in time to save Lynx. He didn't want them to lose one of their men on the first day of a trip that he was supposed to be leading.

THE BLOOD WAS RUSHING through his veins so hard that Bannack could hear it in his ears as he ran out of the house and back out onto the dusty street. He could hear the voices of the other men coming from the buildings and down the street, and he struggled to decipher Ciyrs's among them. He had heard the guilt and worry in Pyra's voice, but he felt like he was the one that should feel guilty. It was him that had first pointed out that the Denynso knew almost nothing about the planet that their kind had always called home, and that by never leaving their compound they had made it so that none of them knew what types of creatures might exist beyond it. It had been him that had first suggested that they should go out and explore. Pyra might feel like as the leader of the Denynso warriors, it was his fault if anything went wrong, but Bannack knew that if he didn't find Ciyrs in time, he was responsible for whatever horrors followed with Lynx.

Bannack saw Ty coming down the street toward him and Bannack ran for him, reaching out and grabbing the other man's shoulders as soon as he was close enough.

"Have you seen Ciyrs?" he demanded.

"What?" Ty asked, "What's wrong?"

"Have you seen Ciyrs?" Bannack asked again, staring intensely into the baker's eyes. "Lynx is injured and needs him now."

Worry rolled over Ty's eyes and he shook his head.

"I haven't seen him."

Bannack let go of him and continued down the street. Around him he saw the other warriors streaming out of the buildings and coming onto the street from other areas of the settlement. Many of them had the vibrant green blood of the Covra streaked across their skin or soaked into their clothing. They all had confused, horrified expressions on their faces that told him that they were just as stunned by what had just happened as he was.

"What the hell were those things?" someone asked from one side.

"Did you see their legs grow back?" another voice asked.

"Where did they go?"

Bannack continued to run down the street, his heart pounding so hard that he could feel it in his throat and he felt like he was going to get sick. This isn't what he had in mind when he suggested that they go out onto Uoria and discover what was waiting outside their compound walls. When he first mentioned it, it was motivated by his painful emotional response to Jem's death and the fear that came from the fact that he died in a place that none of them even knew existed. When he went to Pyra and told him that he wanted to go with them, it wasn't truly out of a deep need to understand what was on the rest of the planet, but out of fear of his feelings for Loralia and his desire to escape from her. Through his haste and selfishness he had put the warriors in more danger than they had ever been in.

With their other enemies, they had known what they were facing. They knew what the creatures were and how they could defeat them. Right up until they were in the mirror realm coming up against the Klimnu for the final time, they were always on their home ground, comfortable and secure in knowing where they were and the resources that they could use to fight. Now they were somewhere they had never been, surrounded by unfamiliar landscape and facing enemies that they didn't know and didn't understand. The Covra were gone for then, but they could show back up at any moment, and without even knowing what their vulnerabilities were, the Denynso had little chance of defeating them.

5

—————

Loralia looked at each of the women, gauging their reactions to the conversation she had just had with Bannack. As soon as he had begun to contact her, she had sought out the other women, feeling that if something had gone wrong on the quest with one of their mates, they deserved to know as soon as she found out. She was beginning to know and trust these women, and she didn't want to do anything that might hurt them in any way, or cause them to distrust her as the others had when they first encountered her, and that included keeping anything that she knew about the men or their quest from them for even a moment.

Eden looked back at her with one hand over her mouth, the other cupped around the front of her belly in the protective stance that she assumed most of the time. Zuri looked dumbstruck, looking up at them from where she knelt by the side of the water just as she had been when Loralia, Eden, and Elianna rushed up to her after Loralia found the other two women nearly at the pond. Elianna was trembling, one hand gripping Leia's hand beside her as if seeking out the support of the tiny woman.

None of them said anything for several long seconds. Loralia didn't push them and she avoided reflecting their feelings, not wanting to delve into the private moments that each of them were having. She didn't know what they were thinking or what they were feeling, but she was quickly learning that the human women were not as open to having their emotions explored as her kind was. She was trying to learn to rely not on her ability to decipher the feelings and emotions of those she encountered, but rather their words and actions when she wanted to interact with them.

"Be honest with us, Loralia," Leia said carefully, "How much danger are they actually in?"

Loralia wasn't sure how she was supposed to respond to that question. The truth was that she had told Bannack everything that she knew about the Covra. The fearsome creatures were something that the older ones of her kind had told stories about when she was younger. Her grandfather was known for weaving elaborate tales in the tradition of Loralia's kind, meant to both frighten the young ones in the delightful way that they enjoyed, and to teach them about the history of the planet. Many of these stories had long since left Loralia's memory, but the ones about the Covra had always lingered with her. Something about creatures that were so different from them and fought in such a vicious manner had deeply bothered Loralia, and she had never forgotten what her grandfather had said about them.

"I wish that there was more that I could tell you," she said, "but what you heard me tell Bannack is everything that I know about the Covra. I don't know what species they encountered that finally found their vulnerability, or what that vulnerability may be. All I know is that Ciyrs doesn't have a lot of time to get the venom out of Lynx before it will be too late."

"Will he kill Pyra if he gets away from him?" Eden asked.

Her voice was low and soft, but controlled. It was the voice of a woman fighting to maintain her composure, refusing to allow herself to give into the emotions that were threatening her so that she was as calm and even as possible to ensure she didn't miss any critical information about the mate for whom she lived and breathed. Loralia wanted to comfort her, but she couldn't lie to her.

"Yes," she replied.

Eden looked like she had been struck. She stepped back slightly, shaking her head as if she could make the situation go away by denying what Loralia had just told her.

"Ciyrs will get to him," Elianna said confidently, "He will. And he will get the venom out and heal him. He is the best healer that has ever been, and he brought all of his oint-ments and supplies with him. There is nothing that they could encounter that Ciyrs would not be able to heal."

Loralia nodded, allowing Elianna's words to comfort her. She longed for the ability to communicate with Bannack through her mind the way that the other women could communicate with their mates. Though they had not been able to connect with them that day, they knew that at some point soon they would be able to reach out with their minds and feel what their mates were feeling, know what they were thinking, and send their own thoughts to them. She only had her compact and the shared link that it created with Bannack. Though she was incredibly grateful for that, it was one of the things that made her feel separated from the other women. They had been truly welcoming to her since she had made the decision to join the compound with Bannack, but Loralia still felt like they existed in two entities; the five of them and her. Though they were getting closer and the human women were doing what they could to make her feel like a true part of the clan, there was still enough space between them that Loralia felt like she was looking into their experiences rather than truly being a part of them.

"Is there anything we can do?" Zuri asked, standing up and brushing the dirt off of her knees.

"All that we can do is wait to hear from them again and hope that the next time that we do it will be with good news about Lynx," Loralia said.

Eden shook her head.

"No. That's not enough. I can't just sit around and hope that Ciyrs gets to Lynx and gets the venom out of him before he tires Pyra out and kills him."

"What do you want to do?" Leia asked.

"We have to go talk to Creia. He might not know much about the rest of Uoria, but he knows more than the rest of the Denynso, and far more than us. Maybe if we tell him what the men told us and what Loralia knows, he will be able to tell us more and we can piece it all together."

There was a moment of unspoken agreement amongst the women and they all started toward the meeting hall together, hoping that when they arrived the king would be able to tell them something that could ease their fears and help them to feel more comfortable with the men being gone for longer.

They expected that Creia and his queen Theia would be in either their sitting room where they held formal meetings or in their living quarters when they arrived, but when the women got to the meeting hall fifteen minutes later, they found the king and queen standing on the front steps as if waiting for them.

"Oh! Hello, ladies," Creia said happily, holding out his hands in greeting, "I just sent Zsilvia to find you."

"Is everything alright, sir?" Zuri asked.

"Of course!" Creia said, "I just wanted to make sure that you are ready for the arrival of the new teacher."

Loralia glanced over at the other women and saw them all exchanging quizzical looks.

"New teacher?" Zuri asked.

Loralia had learned a little about the university exchange program that had brought Zuri, Elianna, Samira, and Leia to Uoria, and she had assumed that even though the women had decided to make the planet their home rather than returning to Earth at the end of what had been intended to be a few months' stay, that the program would continue. From the way that the human women were reacting, however, it didn't seem that they knew anything about this new teacher.

"I didn't know that the university was sending any other teachers," Samira said, looking at Zuri, who shook her head as she continued to stare at Creia.

"Neither did I. The plan was that I would be the first professor to come and then when I returned and shared my research with the rest of the university, we would plan for more teachers to come here and students from the compound to go to Earth."

"We received communication from the university a couple of weeks ago saying that they were sending another professor to join you," Creia said. "I told you about it that day."

His voice had lost some of the jovial happiness that it had had as they approached and Loralia felt herself fall back into her protective default of reflecting the emotions of the king so that she could prepare herself for what may be happening. The man felt frustrated, but also slightly confused, as if he wasn't entirely sure about what he was saying. He seemed to be thinking through the situation, going back through the memory that he thought he had of telling Zuri about the impending arrival of the new professor, and finally settling on disappointment.

"I'm sorry," Zuri said, "I really don't remember."

"Zuri, of all people I would think you understand the importance of this program to Uoria and to the Denynso. I know that your path changed when you came here and you have decided to stay with us, and of course we are all delighted that you have found your home and your mate among our people, but that means that in order for the program to continue and our hopes of cooperation with the humans of Earth to come to reality, we have to have another professor come."

Beside Loralia, Zuri felt stung and embarrassed. Loralia looked at her and saw the blonde woman nodding, her pale cheeks suddenly aflame with color.

"Of course," she said in a voice that sounded somewhat defeated.

"Good. Please do what you need to do to ensure there is a cabin prepared for the shuttle arrival. With the men gone, I am having Zsilvia act as escort and guide, so if possible find a home that is close to hers."

The king turned away and went back into the meeting hall, leaving the women looking up at Theia.

"You will have to forgive my mate," she said soothingly, "He feels anxious with the warriors gone. He wants you to make sure everything is ready because he trusts you. He trusts you more than he does any of the Denynso women, and that is saying a lot."

She said this with a type of conspiratorial note in her voice that made the five human women more at ease, but Loralia could still feel a sense of guarded worry coming off of Zuri.

"I really don't remember him mentioning another professor to me," Zuri said.

"To be honest, Zuri," Theia said, "He might not have. With all of the chaos that has been going on around here, he might have only thought that he mentioned it to you because he intended to. If it helps at all, I was there when he communicated with the university and they said that this professor is very excited to join you and be a part of the program."

The Denynso queen smiled kindly at the women and then turned to join her mate in the meeting hall. Zuri turned to the other women, shaking her head.

"I really don't remember anything about this new professor," she said.

"Neither do I," Samira agreed.

"Is that a problem?" Loralia asked, venturing to join the conversation that she had been trying to follow but didn't quite understand.

"We found out that a human flight attendant who had been on every shuttle from Earth had been helping the Klimnu and was instrumental in them being able to take over your mirror realm. If it hadn't been for her, none of us would have gone through the things that we did at the hands of the Klimnu. The only one of us who they didn't attack is Samira, and that's only because she came here just before the final battle. If they had had the opportunity, they would have tried to get her, too. It makes it very difficult for us to trust."

She hadn't meant to, but Loralia felt herself take a step

back from the rest of the women. Eden held up a hand as if to stop her.

"She didn't mean..." she started.

Loralia shook her head.

"No, it's alright. After everything that all of you have gone through, I don't expect you to trust me immediately."

She turned to walk away from them, wanting to be back in the little house that she shared with Bannack, when she heard Zuri's voice again.

"We really are happy to have you here, Loralia. I hope you know that."

Loralia nodded, but continued on her way back home.

6

———

Bannack was nearly at the end of the main street of the locked settlement when the door to a building beside him opened and Ciyrs stepped out. He was so relieved that for a moment he wasn't even able to move, but when the healer started in the opposite direction, Bannack reached out and grabbed ahold of his shirt.

"Come on," he said, starting to pull him down the street back toward the house where Pyra and Lynx were.

"What's wrong?" Ciyrs asked.

"Lynx has been injured. We need to get there as fast as we can. I'll explain on the way."

Apparently understanding the urgency of the situation, Ciyrs started running beside Bannack, weaving in and out of the other warriors and the people locked in time as they made their way back down the street. Many of them shouted after them, but they didn't pause. As they ran, Bannack explained as concisely as he could what had happened to Lynx and what Loralia had told them about the venom. He was relieved that the healer had his bag still strapped across him and was already digging through its contents by the time they reached the front door to the house.

Bannack could hear Pyra and Lynx still struggling on the floor above them and despite the ferocity of the sounds, he was relieved because it meant that the huge lead warrior had managed to maintain control over Lynx and the infected man had not broken free and killed him. As long as they could hear the grunting and thrashing, he knew that they still had time.

They climbed the stairs two at a time, and when they entered the bedroom, Ciyrs dropped his bag to the floor. He held a strange-looking contraption in one hand.

"Where was he injured?" he asked.

Pyra's eyes snapped up to him as if he hadn't even noticed that the other men had come into the room.

"His back. I don't know how bad it is."

"Bannack says that it took several minutes for the reaction to start."

Pyra let out a loud grunt and forced Lynx back down onto the ground. By now both men had bloody gashes in their arms and Pyra had blood streaming down his face from where Lynx had apparently reared up and broken his nose.

"Yes. He didn't start acting like this until the Covra were already gone and I pointed out that he was bleeding."

"Hopefully that means that they didn't get too much venom in him and that I'll be able to get it out easily."

"Have you ever heard of this before?" Bannack asked from the doorway.

"No, but I've dealt with other venomous creatures. I'll do the best I can. Pyra, when you feel like you have enough control, flip him over onto his belly. Bannack, come around the side and as soon as he's over, grab onto one of his arms and help Pyra hold him. This is going to be painful, so make sure you are holding him down hard enough and expect some screaming."

He said it all with such calmness that Bannack almost thought that Ciyrs was joking, but when he looked at him, he could see the intensity in the healer's eyes and he knew that he was absolutely serious. Bannack hurried around to Lynx's other side, poised to help Pyra hold him down. A moment later Pyra released the hold that he had on Lynx with his knee in his chest and let go of one of his arms so that he could flip the man over onto his belly. Lynx thrashed, nearly forcing Pyra back, but Bannack grabbed hold of him and together they were able to fight him back to the ground.

They held him in place long enough for Ciyrs to press the contraption to the long gash down Lynx's back and start turning the handle at the top. Lynx let out a primal scream and his entire body tensed. Ciyrs turned the handle faster, seeming to intensify the drawing of the venom the more the warrior responded. Finally Lynx's body relaxed and he seemed to collapse onto the floor. Bannack could see his eyelids fluttering over his closed eyes and hear his labored breath, but his body didn't move even as he and Pyra started to ease their grip on him.

"You can let go," Ciyrs told them, seeming to notice how cautiously and reluctantly the two men were releasing their hold on Lynx, "He's going to be asleep for a good while. I'm going to have to heal him up now, and all of that takes a lot out of you." Ciyrs gestured for his bag and Pyra handed it to him, "Where do you want me to take him? He's going to have to have somewhere to lie down."

Bannack watched as Ciyrs started pulling bandages and

healing ointments out of his bag and setting them on the floor beside Lynx's prone figure.

"Here," Pyra finally said.

Bannack and Ciyrs both look up at him sharply.

"Here?" Ciyrs asked, "Why?"

Pyra gestured at the bed against the wall, the one with the woman that Bannack had completely forgotten even existed. It looked even stranger now to see her lying there, not reacting in any way to everything that had just happened around her.

"He says that she is his mate."

"But she's..."Ciyrs started to protest and Pyra held up a hand to stop him.

"I'm well aware," Pyra said, his voice sounding tired as if the fight with Lynx had taken everything out of him physically and emotionally, "but it is none of my business who he thinks is his mate. We all know what it's like when we first found our mate. It might not have been the easiest thing in the world, and it might not have made terribly much sense at the time, but we knew. Even those of us who tried to deny it," he shot a glare at Bannack, who tried to pretend he didn't see it, "and if being with Eden and watching all of you find your mates has taught me anything, it is that we never know what's going to happen. If he thinks that this woman is supposed to be his mate, I think that he should be here with her. If nothing else, make him more comfortable so he heals better."

Bannack and Ciyrs nodded, and Bannack could only imagine that the healer was thinking back, just as he was, about when he found his own mate. It wasn't an easy process, and one that changed his life from the very first moment that it started. As hard as he had tried to deny his immediate and intense love for Loralia from the first time that he saw her, he had felt the changes that came over him even before he had laid eyes on her. The intensity, aggression, and anger that had coursed through him had been like nothing he had ever experienced, and though he was able to explain those feelings away as being a part of his reaction to the impending battle, he had not been able to give the same explanation to the overwhelming arousal that had come over him as he approached the underground mirror realm and did not ease until he had finally accepted his love for Loralia and completed his bond with her.

If Lynx had experienced anything like Bannack had when he first met Loralia when he saw Rain, he could only imagine how difficult it was to compound that with not knowing if he would ever see her alive, and then to be infected by the Covra. Being near Rain was the best thing for him as he went through his challenging recovery.

"If the two of you could step back a little," Ciyrs said, holding his hands out to guide Bannack and Pyra back away from Lynx, "I'm going to heal him now."

Bannack and Pyra followed the instruction, taking a few steps back away from Lynx so that Ciyrs could kneel closer to Lynx's prone form. He was not breathing as hard now and his eyes had started to settle, but Bannack knew that wouldn't last. Ciyrs could heal virtually any injury or illness if he got to it fast enough, but the process was neither simple nor pleasant most of the time. The healer pulled Lynx's tattered and bloodied shirt off and tossed it aside before positioning him so that his back was fully accessible.

Ciyrs rubbed his hands together and took a breath before placing them over the gash on Lynx's back. A faint glow appeared under his palms and a moment later Lynx let out a low groan. His body writhed and Bannack could see his hips rise up slightly. It was one of the uncomfortable reactions to the healing process, an unexplained level of arousal that was nearly as sudden and intense as the reaction that came from being close to meeting their mate. This reaction was the primary reason that the warriors preferred to be alone when they were getting healed, and why, even though Ciyrs had been able to transfer some of his impressive healing abilities to his mate when he first healed her, he didn't like it when Elianna healed the men.

After a few minutes of Ciyrs keeping his hands over the gash in Lynx's back, he pulled them away and checked the injury again. Reaching back into his bag, the healer withdrew several bottles and a handful of long bandages. Bannack watched him coat the gash with several thick layers of ointments and ground plants and then look up at Pyra.

"Help me sit him up so that I can bandage him."

Pyra crouched down beside Lynx and propped him up, helping Ciyrs stabilize him as he wrapped the bandages tightly around his body. When he was fully bandaged, the three men lifted Lynx off of the floor and carefully placed him on the bed beside the woman locking in her sleeping state. Though there was enough room on the large bed to place him so that he wasn't touching her, Pyra tucked him under the covers and moved Lynx's hand so that it rested against Rain's arm. Bannack was glad to see this simple gesture. Even though neither of them were conscious, maybe the physical contact would provide some level of comfort and peace.

7

Lynx bit down into his bottom lip, withholding a groan as he tried to control himself. He could feel the softness of Rain's mouth making a slow, torturous path down his chest from the soft dip between his collarbones. She followed the touch of her lips with the gentle, almost imperceptible glide of her tongue. When her mouth reached his belly, she let her tongue dip into his navel, and the feeling sent a shiver through his body.

He had never had a craving like he did at that moment, but he didn't want to rush the delicious feelings so he gripped the sheets beside him and squeezed his eyes closed to keep himself from taking her head in his hands and pushing it down.

As if she could sense his need, Rain traced her mouth down the rest of his belly at a slightly faster speed, occasionally following the slick of her tongue with the nip of her teeth against his skin. Finally he could feel her hot, moist breath ripple along the length of his erection and just that one simple sensation caused him to arch his back off of the bed. She waited until he relaxed again to let her tongue trace along him, pausing to concentrate for a few delirious seconds on the sensitive bundle of nerves tucked just under the head before parting her lips further and taking him fully into her mouth.

The feeling nearly overwhelmed him and Lynx continued to struggle to control himself. He wanted to sit up, grab Rain, throw her down, and mate with her until he could no longer move, but at the same time he was reluctant to give up the incredible sensations she was creating inside him and also didn't want to frighten or upset her. It was a delicate balance, at once wanting to take complete control and having enough trust in her to give himself over to her. The combination of the relinquishing control and the hot, intense feeling of her mouth along his cock was something that Lynx had never experienced, but his body moved and reacted on instinct, his hips slowly and subtly rolling to push himself deeper along her tongue to encourage her to suck him harder.

Finally he couldn't control himself anymore and he lifted his hands from the bed, gripping her shoulder with one and burying the other into her hair so that he could guide her into a faster, deeper rhythm. Part of him worried that he had gone too far, that he had exerted too much aggression and dominance over her, but Rain seemed to enjoy it, letting out a soft moan and relaxing her mouth to welcome the thrusts of his hips. As she lowered her body to accept him deeper, Lynx felt her nipples graze against the skin of his thighs and his arousal threatened to topple over.

He pulled her back so that he withdrew from her mouth and took her by her upper arms. Coming up off of the bed, Lynx turned Rain so that he could lower her down onto the bed with her head resting on the pillows where he had just been lying. Her body stretched out beneath him and the impossible, crystal blue of her eyes stared up at him with such openness and trust that he felt his emotions swell almost painfully in his chest. The urgency dissipated as a need to savor and cherish her took over. Lynx lowered his head and touched a kiss to her throat and then another to the soft dip between her collarbones where he could feel her fast heartbeat pounding up at him from beneath her skin.

There was a need for her inside him, something that he could never have explained or even understood before that moment, and he sought to fulfill it completely. His hands stroked down her body, dipping into her curves and memorizing the soft swells of her hips, breasts, and belly. His tongue slid out from between his lips to run a long, slow lick from the valley between her breasts up to the tip of her chin. Her skin tasted warm and salty, her breath rang in his ears, and he could feel her body trembling beneath him. He wanted to experience her with every sense and meld with her into one existence.

Lifting up again to stare into her eyes, Lynx eased himself over her and settled his hips between her thighs. Her long, smooth arms wrapped around his neck and he felt her draw her knees up as if welcoming him into her body. He took a long breath and began to push his hips forward, but just before he sank into her, his eyes snapped open and the entire beautiful image dissolved around him.

Deep, radiating pain in his back overtook the pleasure her mouth had given him, and cold sheets replaced her trembling body. Lynx sat up sharply and gasped at the pain that intensified in his back. His hand came to his chest and he felt the rough bandages. Suddenly things started coming back to him. He remembered the fight with the Covra and the pain of his injuries. He remembered watching Bannack and Pyra fight alongside him. Then he remembered the sudden, all-consuming feeling of hatred and aggression toward the two men. He could feel only the need to destroy them, and then there was blackness.

Lynx dug the heels of his hands into his eyes, rubbing at them to try to clear his mind. He was aware of the feeling of a mattress beneath him and a thick blanket covering from his hips over his legs. His upper body was bare except for the bandages and the cool air of the room sent a chill across his skin. When he pulled his hands away from his eyes he could briefly only see bright colored sparks dancing in the darkness, and then they faded into hazy vision. The room around him was dark, but light from outside came in through the window, allowing him to see what was around him. He glanced down and saw Rain lying beside him, her position unchanged since when he first saw her. Having her so close to him was comforting and he ventured to run his fingers down the curve of her cheek.

As soon as his fingers touched her, Lynx experienced the same sudden flash of vision that he had had the first time he touched her, giving him the same glimpse into the last few seconds of her being awake before the Covra had come out and locked her right there in her bed. Something about the vision struck him strangely this time that hadn't occurred to him the first time. He touched her again, letting himself experience those moments again, and came out of them wondering why she had crawled into bed when the sun was still up and the room was filled with the rich light of late afternoon.

Suddenly he realized that he didn't know where Pyra, Bannack, or any of the other men were. He needed to know what had happened between the moment when he was overcome by the desire to kill them and when he awoke beside Rain. The vivid, intense dream about Rain repeating torturously in his mind, Lynx carefully climbed out of the bed and left the room.

Feeling on edge and worrying that the Covra would suddenly appear again, Lynx took a few steps down the hallway before he heard Pyra's voice from downstairs. He was speaking in a hushed tone, but even speaking as quietly as he could, Pyra wasn't able to keep his voice much lower than what many people would consider a normal conversational tone, and Lynx moved toward it feeling comforted that he didn't feel the compulsion to attack his friend.

"Lynx!" Ciyrs said when Lynx turned the corner from the stairwell into a large open room toward the back of the house.

He didn't remember when the clan's healer had arrived at the house, but he was relieved to see him. He wasn't sure what had happened to him or what exactly Ciyrs had done to ensure that he woke up out of it feeling relatively normal, but he was incredibly relieved that he had been there. From what he could remember feeling in the moments before everything went black, it was very possible that he might not have survived the incident had his friends not acted quickly to ensure that he did.

"It's good to see you up and about, buddy," Pyra said from a couch near a fireplace on the back wall.

"How long have I been out?" Lynx asked, settling gingerly onto another couch beside Bannack.

"A while. Are you feeling alright?" Bannack answered.

"Other than the horrible stabbing pain through my back and being confused as all hell, I think I'm doing fine. Tell me what happened."

As Lynx listened to Pyra and Bannack recount their battle in the bedroom against the Covra and then his sudden descent into a murderous rampage and then Ciyrs's healing, Lynx found his mind continuing to wander back to Rain. He couldn't keep this thoughts off of her, from the look of her lying there locked in her sleep in the bed, to the dream he had had about her as he lay beside her after being healed. As his mind flashed back and forth between the images, something that Pyra said snapped him back into the conversation.

"What?" he asked.

Pyra looked at him quizzically.

"What?"

"What did you just say?"

"I was just saying that you said something about their eyes and then the creatures started leaving, but we didn't know why."

"She didn't see them, so she couldn't fight them," Lynx muttered.

"What are you talking about?" Pyra asked, but Lynx was already on his feet.

"Where are all of the others?"

"They are in the other houses. We decided to stay here for the night before we keep going in the morning so that you could rest."

Lynx was shaking his head and starting for the door before the others could even get up to follow him.

"No. We aren't leaving here until we figure out what's going on, and I think I can help us do that. I need to find Ero."

8
___

Lynx ignored the mutters and the shouted questions when he ran into the main room of the third house down from where he had awoken and rushed directly to Ero where he crouched in front of the fire, prodding at the glowing embers with a sharpened iron rod. The night outside was dramatically colder than the day had been and Lynx could still feel the sting of the air on his skin as he grabbed hold of Ero's back.

"Ero, I need you to come with me."

"Seriously, Lynx? You scared the shit out of me. I could have fallen into the damn fire." He glared at Lynx for a moment before his expression suddenly changed to one of shock, "Lynx! Are you OK? We've all been sitting around scared you weren't going to wake up."

"I'm fine. I need you to do me a favor."

"What do you need?"

"Remember how you were telling me that Zuri sent her journal with you?"

"Yeah, I have it in my bag upstairs."

"Could you get it and come with me?"

Without asking for an explanation, Ero rushed out of the room and Lynx heard his footsteps go up the stairs and down the hall. He could only assume that the house was laid out in essentially the same way as the one where he had been and that Ero was headed to one of the row of bedrooms on the upper floor. A few seconds later he heard the footsteps approaching again and Ero appeared back in the living room gripping the journal and a pencil.

"What do you need me to do?"

A few of the other men in the room had stepped slightly toward him as if waiting for him to include them in what he was saying to Ero, and Lynx turned to them.

"I need everyone to bring their torches and their light sticks. Anything they have that glows."

Lynx waited while the men gathered their light sources from the supplies that they had brought and then led them out onto the street. The warriors who had taken up residence in two other houses along the street came out to meet them, but Lynx told them that they could go back inside and rest. He needed the light, but he didn't need that big of an audience. The men he had already gathered would be enough for what he needed to do.

"What are you doing, Lynx?" Pyra asked as he caught up with Lynx walking toward the front of the compound.

"We need to know what happened to the people here."

"We already know what happened. They got locked by the Covra."

"Right, but there has to be at least one person who fought. One of the Light Ones had to have tried to fight back when they were locking everyone throughout the settlement. We need to find him and see what he did."

"You've lost me."

Lynx stopped in the middle of the road and turned to

look directly into Pyra's face so he could make sure that the larger warrior was listening to him and would follow him.

"I told you that I could see the last few seconds of Rain's life." He felt strangled by the words that he had just said. He didn't want to think that it was true. "The last few seconds before the Covra locked her," he amended, "What if she's not the only one who I can do that with? If there's something about me that lets me see that for all of the locked people, we can piece together exactly what happened."

"It might not work that way," Bannack said.

"Ty can move things with his mind. Ero is impossibly fast. Ciyrs can heal. If they can do those things, why is it so hard to believe that I might have something like that, too? If there is even a chance, we have to try."

"He's right," Pyra said, looking out over the men who had gathered, torches glowing with the flames that they had picked up from the fireplaces and solar-powered light sticks adding their illumination to the pool of light that surrounded them, "This is why we came out here. We want to know what else is out here, and this is part of it. We have to find out what happened."

Lynx led the men to the front of the settlement, wanting to keep what would likely prove to be a long and exhausting search through every street and building as organized as possible. They gathered at the front gate and he turned to the rest of the men.

"We'll start here and head down the main street first. I'm guessing that's where most of the people will be. We'll work our way down, going into all of the buildings, and then we'll figure out where to go from there."

As one of the youngest and least experienced warriors, it

felt strange to be taking charge in this way, but Lynx knew that he was the only one among them that had the ability to learn what he could about their last moments, and possibly discover how they would be able to reverse the lock and free the entire settlement from the imprisonment they had been suffering unknowingly for so many years.

In the darkness, the unmoving forms of the locked people looked disturbing and Lynx felt himself recoiling from them even as he approached the first person, a man who was frozen mid-step toward the main street. A few of the warriors held up their lights to illuminate the man's face and Lynx could see that his expression didn't seem frightened or anxious, more like he was just walking toward the settlement and was locked without him ever knowing what was happening, just like it was with Rain.

Lynx stepped up to the man cautiously and stared at him for a few seconds, questioning for a moment if he really wanted to do this. It was one thing to look into the last few moments of consciousness for the woman who he knew to be his mate, but this man was a complete stranger, someone who carried no connection for Lynx, and he didn't know if he wanted to go so far as to delve into the privacy of what happened to him right up until he was locked. He knew that he had to do it, though, if the Denynso were ever going to accomplish what they set out to do, and if he was ever going to have a chance to release Rain and be with her in reality.

Apologizing to the unknown man in his mind, Lynx reached out with both hands and rested his palms on the man's arm. Immediately he got the same sensation that he had when he first touched Rain. The world around him seemed to brighten and fade at the same time, and suddenly he was standing not under the cloak of night and the glow of the torches, but in the thick sunlight pouring like amber out of the sky. It was the same late afternoon sunlight he had seen coming through the window of Rain's bedroom in his vision of her last few seconds, and something pulled at his heart as he realized in the seconds that he was experiencing with this man, Rain was down in the main street in her home, brushing through her hair, and readying to climb into bed where she would lie for decades. He wanted so desperately to break away from where he was standing and run down to her house, to fight the Covra that were going to climb out from under her bed, and to protect her from her fate. Something told him, however, that he couldn't do that. He was stuck right there, unable to control himself in the space or anything that was going on around him.

To his side he watched as the man who he had just touched walk from the gate leading into the settlement. He walked calmly with the casual gait of someone who didn't have anything troublesome on his mind. He certainly didn't look like someone who was on guard or worried about an impending battle. The man took several long strides and then Lynx saw one of the Covra scurry through the gate and lash out at the man, digging the end of his sharpened leg into the man's back just as he had done to Rain's stomach. Without even so much as a groan, the man stopped, his foot not quite touching the ground and his eyes still cast down as they opened after blinking. It happened so quickly and then the Covra was gone, rushing down toward the settlement as Lynx saw others starting to climb through windows and across roofs. He couldn't figure out where they were coming from, but they were swarming the settlement at an incredible rate, and none of the Light Ones, the humans whose existence on the planet had either been forgotten or covered up in the generations since this moment, seemed to notice that they were there.

. . .

SEVERAL HOURS later Lynx took a long breath and approached the final person standing on the second street they had explored. Ero stood beside him, the journal in his hands already halfway full of the notes that he wrote down each time that Lynx came out of his vision. They had started the exploration with enthusiasm, talking and sharing ideas as they moved their way along the main street. After more than a dozen people and little information, though, their talk had started to fade. Now Lynx only talked when something extraordinary happened in one of his visions, which meant that for the most part they were walking along in silence.

As he looked at this next person, a woman who seemed locked in the stance of suddenly turning and looking over her shoulder at something, Lynx thought he heard a rustling in one of the buildings to his side. They had just been in that building, however, so he turned back to the woman.

"This has to be it for the night," Pyra said, "We need to sleep. We can keep going as soon as we wake up in the morning."

Lynx gave a defeated sigh and started to lift his hand toward the woman. He heard the rustling sound again and he noticed that the other warriors seemed to be looking around like they heard it, too. It fell silent again and Lynx reached toward the woman. Just as he started to touch her, he could see the first spiked leg of a Covra coming around the edge of the front doorway to the building beside them. Before he could say anything, his palm touched the woman's arm and he disappeared into the vision of her last moments.

The woman was walking away from him and he could see the shadow of a Covra behind her. It was another moment, one like he had had dozens of times since he started looking into these moments, when he wanted so badly to be able to call out to the person, to warn her of what was coming.

Suddenly, almost as if she could hear the screaming in his head, the woman whirled around and confronted the creature. Her eyes flashed as she swung her arm around, bringing a blade up around her and driving it deeply into the eye of the creature. The Covra let out a horrific sound that was between a hiss and a scream, and reared back, pulling its pointed legs up as if ready to strike, and then suddenly collapsing and dissolving into a slick pool of vibrant green blood that seemed to soak down into the ground almost instantly. From one side another of the creatures approached the woman and she shouted. It stumbled back at the sound of her voice and instead of running, she advanced toward it, continuing to yell as she slashed at the creature with her blade. She caught that one in the eye as well, and Lynx watched it recoil and dissolve just as the first.

He was beginning to feel hope when he heard a scratching sound from behind the woman. She turned, glancing over her shoulder, and in an instant before she could even react, a Covra buried its leg into her, locking her in place.

As the vision disappeared around him, Lynx felt himself knocked to the ground. For a moment he had a sense of panic that the Covra had gotten to him again, but he could feel the weight of something massive on top of him and knew that another of the warriors had tackled him to the ground. He heard shouts and felt the weight lifted away from him so that he could roll over and look up to get his bearings about what was happening around him.

The small group of warriors that had come along with him seemed locked in a battle. Three Covra hissed and scurried around them while Ty and an older warrior named Vax growled and rushed toward the other warriors. Lynx knew that they had been infected and that they needed to get rid of the Covra that were there so that they could get these two back to the house for treatment.

"It is their eyes!" Lynx yelled and noticed that the Covra recoiled as if they could understand what he was saying, "Get them in the eyes!"

"Lynx, Bannack, go after the Covra," Pyra commanded, "Ero, Gyyx, Ciyrs, help me."

The warriors split off to follow their orders without question. Out of the corner of his eye Lynx could see Pyra pull off his shirt and the other men follow suit. They tore the garments into long strips and wound them around their hands, tightening the fabric so that it was taut between their grip. Pyra surged forward toward Ty, slamming his shoulder into his belly to flatten him onto the ground. The sudden movement took the infected warrior off guard, causing him to pause for a moment as he tried to catch his breath and get his bearings.

Pyra took advantage of this momentary pause to flip Ty over onto his stomach and use the strips of fabric from his shirt to bind Ty's wrists together. Ero and Gyyx copied his movements on Vax, looping the fabric around his wrists to bind them together and then pulling them back as Pyra did with Ty to attach them to his ankles.

As they did this, Lynx and Bannack advanced toward the Covra. For the first few steps, the creatures seemed to be retreating, then they paused in the still, angry silence of the night air and started rushing toward the two warriors, their hissing sound seeming to rattle through their bodies as they came toward them with their gruesome legs creating deep rivets in the ground and gouges in the side of the building.

Lynx pulled back his blade and brought it over his head with all of the force that he could gather. The Covra in front of him tried to move out of his way, but was blocked by the one standing beside him. The tip of Lynx's blade dug deeply into the creature's eye and he watched it split before the Covra pulled away from him, stumbled back, and dissolved into the ground just as the ones in his vision had. Beside him, Bannack mimicked his action, destroying the Covra in front of him. The final one started scrambling up the wall of the building, and Lynx jumped onto a barrel positioned beside one of the windows and leapt up so that he crossed the path of the Covra, planting a kick in the middle of its body before it could disappear onto the roof. Its body tumbled to the ground beside Bannack, who immediately turned and drove his blade down into the bulbous, gleaming eye.

9

———

"Bannack, you need to slow down."

Loralia held the compact as steady as she could as she rushed across the compound, struggling to decipher the words that Bannack was yelling at her through the glass.

"We figured out that they can only be killed through their eyes," he repeated.

"Their eyes?"

"Yes. Lynx thought that all along, but we spent all night... never mind. I'll explain it all later."

"Are the rest of the men alright?"

"Ciyrs is healing Ty and Vax right now. I think that he got to them in time and that they will be fine. Right now we need to figure out how to get rid of the rest of the Covra. We destroyed those three, but there have to be more. We can't risk them coming out and infecting more of us. If one of them got Ciyrs, there would be nothing that anyone could do."

"Do you know how to lure them to you?" Loralia asked.

"No. They just show up. Do you remember anything else

that your grandfather used to say about the Covra? Anything about when they would come or how you could get them to come out?"

Loralia scoured her mind, trying to recall everything that her grandfather had said, every story that he had told about the creatures and how enemies defeated them. The ground pounded beneath her feet as she ran toward the forest.

"Silence," she said, suddenly remembering one of the stories as she dropped down onto the ground and moved aside a section of moss to reveal the hole leading down into her mirror realm.

"Silence?" Bannack asked.

"Yes. One of the stories that my grandfather used to tell was about how the greatest enemies of the Covra had a power that would weaken the creatures and was the only thing that could reverse their greatest defense, and that silence was their comfort and their joy."

"What was the greatest defense?"

"He never said."

Bannack didn't respond and Loralia dropped down through the hole into the home that she had had her entire life before she met Bannack and agreed to go above ground to be his mate.

"Locking them," Bannack said a moment later, sounding as if he was speaking more to himself than to her.

"Locking?" she asked.

Loralia listened while Bannack told him about the warriors visiting the prison that they had thought belonged to the Klimnu but they discovered actually belonged to the Covra, and how they found out about the kingdom that the Covra had locked. He detailed the Light Ones and how they appeared to be frozen in place in the same breath that they had been drawing when the Covra attacked them. As she listened, Loralia tried to understand what he was telling her, and what she might be able to do to help him. She had gone to the mirror realm to surround herself in what was familiar, hoping that it would help her to think clearly. She could feel that her mate was frightened and upset, and she wanted to do anything that she could to help him.

She moved deeper into the caverns, exploring the chambers and venturing into areas that she hadn't visited in quite some time. Suddenly she saw something that made her heart pound faster and a smile come to her lips for the first time since the day that Bannack left.

"Do you remember what I told you about the compact?" she asked, looking into the mirror at him.

Bannack nodded.

"Whatever reflects in your mirror, reflects in mine."

"Yes. And do you remember what happens when something reflects in my bottom mirror from the top?"

"It becomes real."

Loralia nodded and looked back across the cavern.

BANNACK CROUCHED DOWN behind the barrel he had pulled into the middle of the street and glanced over at Lynx who sat beside him. The others had remained in the buildings on either side of the street, poised beside the windows and doors to watch what was happening, but staying out of sight.

"Are you sure that this is going to work?" Lynx whispered.

"It has to," Bannack answered. "In order for it to, though, you have to believe that it will. Loralia can only make this happen if you completely believe that it is going to work the way that she intends it to. If you don't, it won't exist, do you understand?" Lynx nodded and Bannack nodded back at him, "Good. Now we have to be completely silent."

The two warriors fell silent and Bannack glanced down at the compact in his hand. Loralia's face gazed up at him from the glass, her beautiful lavender eyes calm and focused. Nervousness flooded through Bannack, but he knew that he had to steady himself so that he could do his part of Loralia's plan properly. After several minutes of waiting, he heard the rustling sound that told him the Covra were approaching. The sound seemed louder and deeper than it had before and Bannack knew that meant there were more of the creatures this time as if they had sent more to seek revenge on those who had destroyed three of their number just hours before.

"They're coming," Bannack mouthed to Loralia, not making a sound.

Loralia nodded. Bannack lifted up slightly so that he could look over the barrel and watch the Covra approaching.

"Patient," Loralia mouthed to him.

Bannack watched until they were close enough that they would be able to see him clearly and then stood, pulling Lynx up with him so that they were standing in the middle of the street, open to the swarm of creatures approaching. He could feel Lynx tense beside him, but Bannack stood steady. Lynx adjusted his grip on the blade beside him. It was meant as both a ruse and a backup plan just in case Loralia's idea fell through. They waited for a few more tense seconds, the time seeming to drag past as they allowed the creatures to get dangerously closer. Bannack's heart pounded in his chest and his head felt like it was swimming. If this didn't work, the entirety of the group could be killed, many by each other's hands.

In an instant, the plan mobilized around him. The Covra climbing along the outside walls of the buildings got close to the windows and doors, and the warriors inside started to shout. As they yelled, the creatures paused and started to retreat from the sound. They started moving backwards back down the street, but several of the warriors streamed out of the building and made a line across the street, blocking them with a wall of sound. The creatures turned and started scurrying more quickly toward Bannack and Lynx, unable to go anywhere else.

"Are you ready?" Bannack asked, looking down at Loralia.

"Just hold your compact so that the bottom mirror is straight upright and the top mirror is tilted toward it. Go!"

Bannack turned the compact in his hand and held it as Loralia instructed. There was a moment when nothing happened and he felt his stomach turn, but he closed his eyes and forced himself to believe with every bit of his existence that she would create exactly what she intended to. His eyes still closed, Bannack suddenly heard the hissing, screeching sound of the Covra dying. He opened his eyes and found himself staring at a massive slab of brown and grey rock.

After several long seconds the screaming stopped and a chilling quiet settled over the street. Finally it broke with the sound of Loralia laughing.

"We might not be able to communicate with our thoughts, my love, but how many of the other warriors can do that?"

Bannack could hear the other warriors cheering and shouting, but it took a few moments before he was able to get his thoughts together enough to walk around the stone slab toward the cheering. When he did he saw the green blood of the Covra soaking into the dirt of the road, dripping from the rock spikes protruding from the front of the slab.

"What is that?" he asked.

"The floor of one of the caverns," Loralia told him, "I used to play on them when I was younger. I remembered how sharp they were."

"You are incredible."

"No, darling, you are."

"What, now? Is this thing just going to stay here?"

"If you think that it is part of settlement now, then it is. If not, when you close the compact, it will disappear."

"Then it will stay, forever a reminder of what destroyed the Covra."

Suddenly Loralia's eyes grew dark.

"This isn't the end, Bannack," she said solemnly.

The words hit him and the sound of the celebrating warriors seemed to fade.

"What do you mean?"

"I can still feel them. They're angry, Bannack. There's more to come. You need to save the Light Ones or very soon they will be lost forever."

TBC

(To be continued in Part V...)

THE ALIEN'S GUEST

UNTITLED

Book 5 – The Alien's Guest

1

———

Lynx dropped his bag back to the floor of the bedroom and looked around. It looked different now bathed in the first faint streaks of early morning light. He could see the stains of the Covra blood on the walls and the floor, and a piece of one of their legs sat next to the bed as a grisly reminder of the battle that had happened there the day before. The air was still heavy with the smell of the healing ointments that Ciyrs had used to seal up his wounds after the healer had drawn all of the venom out of his body, and just that scent brought a shiver down Lynx's spine. He didn't want to think about what he had gone through with the Covra or in the aftermath. All he wanted to do was climb back into bed beside Rain's locked, sleeping figure and rest.

His body still weak from the healing process and even more tired now that the adrenaline from the battle in the middle of the street had seeped out of him, the warrior removed his shirt, kicked off his boots, and very carefully climbed into the bed so that he could resume his place close to the wall. Rain was still locked, unmoving and unchanged from the first moment he saw her, but he found such great comfort in being near her. His body surged with aggressive, all-consuming desire that confirmed to him yet again that this beautiful woman was intended to be his mate. Then his mind filled with anger that he had to look at her in this locked state without any idea of how he could remove her from this frozen state that the Covra had put her in so many years ago.

Wanting at least a moment of seeing her breathing, Lynx drew himself closer to her and rested his hand on Rain's stomach. He felt the intense, pulling feeling through his body that he had become accustomed to after spending the night going through the town and touching each of the locked people so that he could see their last moments before they were locked. It had been exhausting, but it had enabled him to determine the Covra's weakness and, with the help of Bannack's truly astonishing mate, create a plan that would eliminate them. At least, that is what he thought he was doing. Once they were gone, however, Loralia had confided that she knew the battle with those terrifying creatures was far from over. There was more to come.

Lynx couldn't think about that now. He was lost in the moments of Rain's life just before the Covra crawled out from under her bed and locked her in her sleeping state. They knew now that the Covra had done this because they were weakened and knew that they would be unable to defeat the Light Ones, the inhabitants of this settlement. Instead of continuing to fight or surrendering, they chose to lock the Light Ones in place just as they were in the moment they were attacked. What Lynx didn't understand was why the Covra had chosen just to lock them in place and not to kill them. Once frozen, they were completely vulnerable to anything that the Covra wanted to do to them. No matter how weak the creatures were, they could have found a way to destroy humans that were unable to move in any way. There had to be a reason that they had kept the Light Ones alive other than just the fact that they held a tremendous grudge and enjoyed coming back to explore the settlement and cast their gleaming, vulnerable eyes on the people that they were holding in indefinite suspension.

When the vision of Rain's final moment was over, he settled down beside her and stared into her pale, peaceful face until his eyes couldn't stay open any longer and he fell into a deep sleep where he hoped he would meet her and be able to hold and touch her as he had wanted to since the moment he first saw her.

WHAT FELT like only moments later, Lynx heard the door to the bedroom open and he sat up sharply, ready to throw himself back into battle, but it was only Pyra standing at the entrance to the door staring at him.

"The men are awake," he said, then glanced toward Lynx's lap, "It looks like you are, too."

Lynx looked down and saw the blanket tented up, balanced on the raging erection he had been sporting nearly continuously since the first time he laid eyes on Rain. He took a pillow from behind him and slammed it onto his lap.

"It's her," he said, tilting his head toward Rain, "I can't help it."

"I know," Pyra said, the hint of a smile coming through his stern exterior, "Trust me. I remember what it was like when I first got around Eden. That was miserable. I was hard all the time, no matter what I did, and I was so pissed off at everything that I felt like I could have killed whatever got in my way. She was not the biggest fan of me when she first met me, either, which didn't make the whole situation any easier. At least she can't yell at you."

He said it playfully, but as soon as the words came out of Pyra's mouth, Lynx felt anger roll over him. Pyra's expression dropped as he obviously saw the change come over Lynx, and he held up a hand as if to show that he meant no harm by the comment.

"You're right," Lynx said, "She can't."

"I'm sorry," Pyra said, "I didn't mean..."

"Let me get dressed and I'll meet you downstairs."

Pyra closed his mouth and nodded before turning and leaving the room, closing the door behind him. Lynx was smaller and less experienced than Pyra, but the younger warrior could tell that his leader was not willing to put him to the test. A Denynso warrior who had found his mate but had not yet completed the bond was an unpredictable and volatile creature, and adding the tension of being away from their compound, the battle, and the seemingly hopeless locked state of the Light Ones was only working to push Lynx toward an edge that could have disastrous results.

Once Pyra left, Lynx looked down at Rain. She was the most beautiful thing that he had ever seen, with coppery hair that shimmered in the sunlight and lashes so long they curled on her pale cheeks. Her full lips held the tiniest hint of a smile, that touch of expression that made someone looking at it wonder if he was actually seeing a smile or if he was just imagining it because the rest of her face was so peaceful and lovely. It was a smile that Lynx had seen on sleeping faces before, but hers was so entrancing he couldn't seem to take his eyes away from it. He wished that he could see what she had been dreaming in that second that the Covra locked her; that he could know what had given her such a sense of peace and contentment in those last moments.

Lynx suddenly heard voices drifting up the stairs from the floor below and realized that all of the warriors must have come to meet at the house after Ty and Vax woke from their healing. He knew he couldn't stay in bed and continue to stare at Rain, as much as that was exactly what he wanted to do. He had to go downstairs and be a part of the confusion, the questions, and the chaos that had ensued since the first Covra had arrived. Usually the Denynso were incredibly organized, strategic warriors, but this had thrown them completely out of control. Not only were they far away from the compound that was the only home that any of them had ever known, but they were up against an enemy that they didn't understand and fighting to save a people who they didn't even know if they could save. They had managed to come together to lure the Covra and force them into the spiked wall that Bannack created with Loralia's help, but now they were at a loss. They didn't know where they were supposed to go from there, and they would need every single one of them to figure it out.

Moving carefully to prevent jostling Rain, Lynx climbed out of bed and dressed. He longed for a hot bath, but he knew that was going to have to wait. For now he would have to settle for running Rain's brush through his tangled white hair and hoping that Ty had gotten enough of his strength back to make sure that there was breakfast for them to eat while they were talking.

Before he left, Lynx took another glance at the photograph that was sitting on the table beside Rain's bed. He still hadn't told any of the other warriors what he had discovered on the back of that picture, and he was still unsure if he should. Releasing the picture from the frame again, he slipped it into his bag and started downstairs to the waiting men.

2

The warriors were gathered around the living room, making the space look small with their massive size only magnified by the fact that that there were so many of them there together. Lynx stepped into the room and all of their eyes turned to him, burrowing into him with the intensity that said they all expected him to do something, but he wasn't sure what that was. He paused at the door and looked back at them, for the first time distinctly aware of the pairs of orange orbs that stood out against the contrasting blue, green, and grey ones that stared back at him. He had caught sight of his own eyes in the mirror above the vanity in Rain's room while he was brushing his hair and noticed that they were still their usual shade. He wondered if they flickered orange when he was near her like he had seen happen to some of the other men in the early days of them finding their future mates but before their bonding was complete.

This thought brought painful tightness to his throat and a rock to his belly. Would he ever be able to complete his bond with Rain? Would they ever be able to look into each other's eyes and truly be together, or would he be left to long for her for the rest of his life knowing that she was there, but frozen in place for eternity?

An even worse thought hit him then. He suddenly wondered if when they destroyed the Covra they also destroyed the link that kept the Light Ones alive.

"We have to figure out how to unlock them," he said without waiting for any of them to say anything to him first.

"That's exactly what we were just talking about," Bannack told him from his spot near the fireplace where the other men had seemed to be watching him before Lynx came into the room.

"How long have you all been here?" Lynx asked.

"Only about an hour," Pyra told him, "Ty and Vax were still sleeping after their healing and we thought that after everything that you went through last night you could probably use a little bit of extra rest."

Lynx nodded.

"Thank you," he said, knowing that they were probably right. The night before had been rough on him and his body still felt like he could use more sleep, "What were you saying about unlocking the Light Ones?"

He was still cautious about the way that he spoke about the people of the settlement, keeping with the name for them that they all already knew from the information they found in the abandoned, burned prison rather than revealing that he knew anything else about them that the others did not.

"You were there when Loralia told us that the Covra aren't gone. There are more to come and she is pretty positive that they are going to be strong enough that the Light Ones aren't going to be able to survive when they come."

"So what do we do?" Lynx asked.

Bannack let out a deep sigh and looked at Pyra.

"We don't know," Pyra said, "We were hoping that there was something more you could tell us about them, something else that you noticed when you were watching their last few moments. Anything."

Lynx shook his head.

"I told you everything. I can't think of anything else that I saw that would have any meaning. I only saw them locking them, not waking them up."

"And they locked them by stabbing them with their legs just like they did when they were fighting us?"

Lynx shuddered as he remembered watching the Covra's sharp, gleaming leg puncturing Rain's belly and her body going completely still. He nodded.

"Can you show us?" Ciyrs asked.

Intense protectiveness flooded through Lynx and he felt the anger and aggression surge within him. He didn't like the thought of any of the other men, not even Ciyrs, looking at Rain, especially if they wanted to expose her belly so that they could see the injury that was inflicted by the Covra. He knew, though, that they had to have as much information as they possibly could if they were going to have any chance of figuring out how to wake the locked residents of the settlement, and that meant having to trust the other men of the tribe, particularly their healer, with his mate.

"Not all of you are going to fit in the room with her," he said.

He wanted to find a way to limit the number of the men who were going to be close to her and looking at her in such a prone and vulnerable state, but he also was trying to control his anger and not hurt any of their feelings by obviously trying to exclude them from the situation.

"Just Ciyrs, Bannack, and me," Pyra said carefully as if he

were coaxing permission to get near Rain out of Lynx and being cautious not to upset him for fear that he would rescind the permission and the hopes that they would be able to help these people would be completely futile.

"Why Bannack?" Lynx asked with a touch more aggression and suspicion than he intended to put in his voice.

"What the hell is that supposed to mean?" Bannack asked.

Bannack himself was still only a few days into his mating relationship with Loralia and it seemed that much of the aggression and temper were still lingering in him as the defensiveness in the question caused his body to tense visibly.

"Calm down," Pyra said, holding one arm out in front of Bannack as if to block the other warrior from advancing on Lynx, "This is his future mate you are talking about. Think about how you would have felt if it was Loralia lying up there in that bed completely helpless and you had never even been able to speak to her much less be with her, but all of us wanted to go in and look at her and touch her."

"Touch her?"

Lynx appreciated that Pyra was trying to explain the situation to Bannack in a way that the young and volatile warrior would understand, but mentioning that they were going to touch Rain had Lynx feeling like he was pushing the very edge of his control.

"Ciyrs might have to," Pyra said to him evenly, "We have to figure out what exactly happened to them that locked them if we are going to be able to figure out how to reverse it, if that is even possible, and that means that we are going to have to examine her as thoroughly as Ciyrs thinks is necessary."

Lynx could feel his fists clenching and releasing beside

him and the urge to lash out at the men was building again. He worried for a moment that the effect of the Covra attack was still lingering inside him and that he was going back into his completely involuntary rage that nearly had him killing his fellow warriors with his bare hands. Pyra didn't seem concerned about his behavior, however, and Lynx realized that he was just feeling what all Denynso men did when they were getting close to their mates. He wanted to hope that the fact that the feeling was intensifying meant that he was, in fact, getting closer to Rain being awake and in his arms.

"Listen to me, Lynx," Ty said, stepping forward, "If any of us understand what you are going through right now and what you want to do to us, it is the three of us who have found our mates in the last few months. We know exactly what it's like to be angry and frustrated and distrustful of everyone who we thought might be trying to get near our mates. Pyra and Gyyx have even watched Ciyrs heal their mates. Because we understand it, though, is exactly why you need to trust us."

Lynx looked at the bandages wrapped around Ty's chest just as they had been around his own when he first awoke after the attack. This man was not a warrior by birth but rather a nurturer who devoted himself to making sure that the warriors and the rest of the tribe had what they needed and were kept comfortable and happy, particularly after battles. The arrival of his mate, Samira, however, had brought things out in him that none of the Denynso had ever imagined would exist in his huge but gentle presence. He had not only become as angry and forceful as Lynx was feeling now, but he had stepped forward and agreed to use the power that he had inherited from his father but had never used to battle against the Klimnu. If Ty's mate had transformed him that much; had given him that much power, strength, and courage, Lynx knew that he couldn't just let Rain lie there for a single second longer than she absolutely had to. He couldn't risk not having something so incredible in his life in the full and complete way that she should.

3

———

Lynx nodded his agreement and started toward the door of the living room before he could give himself the opportunity to change his mind. He trusted these men and he had to keep reminding himself of that. He was not going to be able to save Rain or any of the other people in the settlement on his own. It was going to take the skills, the insight, and the abilities of all of them together to release the Light Ones from their binds.

As he climbed the stairs toward the bedroom he could hear Ciyrs close behind him with Pyra coming second and Bannack bringing up the end of their line. He didn't hear any of the other men following behind and he was relieved, happy that they were showing enough respect for him to stay in the living room while the four of them went up to Rain.

Pyra had never gotten around to explaining to him why he insisted that Bannack go along with them, but as he stepped into the bedroom with Rain and turned to allow the other men to come inside, he could see Bannack's hand mindlessly touching the large silver compact around his neck. He realized then that it was not so much that Pyra wanted Bannack up there with them as he wanted to be able to contact Loralia, and therefore the other women, if he needed to. That compact was their only true connection with the compound with the exception of the men being able to communicate with their mates through their minds, but Lynx knew that they had been so tense throughout the journey that none of them had been able to be open enough to connect with their partners.

The door closed behind Bannack and the three men looked at Lynx for a few tense seconds. It was as though none of them wanted to be the first one to say anything, or the first one to take a step toward Rain. Lynx finally stepped up to the edge of the bed and smoothed the blanket beside her. For the first time he noticed the clean cut through the blanket over her stomach and the slightest tinge of red around the edge of the torn fabric. He wanted to touch her, but this was not the moment for him to get swept away into one of his visions. In that moment he hoped that there would come a time when he would be able to touch her without that happening. He hadn't even known that he had that ability, and he certainly didn't know how to control it. Of course, if they figure out how to release the people from their locked state he would no longer have any need for the ability. Perhaps it would simply go away when it was no longer necessary.

"Can you show us, Lynx?" Ciyrs said quietly, breaking through Lynx's musings and bring him back into the reality of the moment.

"Please be gentle with her," Lynx said, "I know that she is locked, but we don't really know what that means. She may still have some awareness or be able to feel."

"I won't hurt her," Ciyrs assured him, stepping up closer

to the bed.

Being careful not to let his hands brush her body, Lynx took hold of the top fold of her blanket and gently peeled it down away from her. It stuck in place briefly before releasing and coming away to reveal the airy nightgown he saw her wearing in his vision and a puncture wound in her stomach. He had noticed the wounds on the other people throughout the settlement, but they hadn't bothered him. This, however, made his body twitch and his face feel hot and tingle with fury.

"I don't understand," Pyra said, stepping up beside Ciyrs and looking down at Rain, "What was the difference? Why did Lynx, Ty, and Vax become violent and angry when they were cut by the Covra, but the rest of these people were just locked?"

"Loralia said that her grandfather spoke of them using their enemies to fight themselves by infecting them. That is their primary method of battle."

"That must mean that they can control when they are infecting a person to turn them into a weapon and when they are locking them. It is a conscious decision, not just a biological effect."

"You saw that prison, Pyra. You can't think that creatures that were capable of building something like that would just be mindless animals. They are obviously more intelligent and more skilled than we are giving them credit for."

"Or they know how to manipulate another species into doing the work for them. I can't imagine how those sharp, pointy little legs would be able to build a prison like that. I can, however, see hands like that doing it."

Pyra gestured toward Rain's hands and a hushed moment fell over the room.

"If the Covra are able to weaponize anything that they

want to," Bannack said, "Why didn't they just do that right along? What happened that they weren't able to make the Light Ones fight each other? What could have weakened them so much that they couldn't fight, but that they could still lock the entire settlement?"

The other men shook their heads and Lynx glanced down at Rain again.

"I guess if they weren't locked by the same type of poison that the Covra use to turn people into their own personal killing machines, then you can't just use the same tool to draw out the poison and it will make them better."

"I think that would be a bit too simple," Ciyrs said, reaching forward to gingerly move Rain's gown so that he could better see her damaged skin through the cut in the fabric, "I could try it if you want me to, though. I guess it wouldn't hurt to try every option that we have. I just can't imagine that the Covra would have their last ditch effort of a war be something that could be resolved so easily."

"I don't think so, either," Lynx agreed, then took a shuddering breath to prepare himself for the next statement he was going to say, "but I think that we should try everything. I don't want to leave her locked for any longer than we have to just because we didn't try something that we thought was too simple."

Ciyrs nodded and stepped up closer to the edge of the bed. Lynx reluctantly got out of the way, moving closer to the head of the bed to allow Ciyrs to get nearer to Rain. Without taking his eyes off of the injury in Rain's stomach, Ciyrs lowered the bag from his shoulder onto the mattress. He reached into it and withdrew the same tools that he had used to heal Lynx, Ty, and Vax. Lynx couldn't remember what it felt like for the healer to use the strange instrument to draw the poison that the Covra had injected into him out of his body, but it still made him shudder to look at it. It looked painful and invasive, two things that he never wanted Rain to experience.

"This isn't going to hurt her," Ciyrs said as if he could sense the discomfort and worry that Lynx was feeling.

"What's going to happen when they do wake up, though?" Lynx asked.

"What do you mean?" Pyra asked.

"What's going to happen? If we can figure it out and we do unlock them, what will happen to them? They've been this way for decades. Are they going to wake up and be violent and aggressive and think that we are trying to fight them like the Covra were? Will they be able to understand us when we talk to them so that we can tell them that everything is going to be alright and that we want to help them? Will they even be able to survive? They are locked now and that is keeping them in this suspended state, but if we release the lock are they just going to shrivel up and die because all of these people should probably have died long ago?"

Everything poured out of him with greater emotion than Lynx had intended, but he felt like he couldn't hold back all of the questions and concerns any longer. As desperately as he wanted to look into Rain's eyes, hear her voice, and complete his bond with her, it terrified him to think about what could go wrong when they finally figure out how to unlock them. As horrific as it was to see her that way, and as heartbreaking as it was to think about never actually getting to be with her, at least when she was this way he knew that she was safe. For as long as she was locked the way she was, she was alive and he could be with her. It was a terrifying balance between wanting to preserve and destroy the same moment.

4

———

Loralia was again running through the compound, feeling the ground pushing way beneath her feet as she rushed back from the moss-concealed entrance to her mirror realm in the forest toward the bakery where she hoped that she would find Samira. She was beginning to feel like running was the only thing that she was doing since the men had left. Rather than spending the time that they were gone settling into her new surroundings and helping the other women take care of the compound and prepare for the men's return, she had been running around desperately trying to help her mate even though he was far away. In her heart, though, she knew that there was nothing else that she would really rather be doing. Being close to Bannack, even if that meant helping him fight a battle through the power of her mirrored compact and the one that she had given him, was what mattered to her most.

"Loralia!"

She heard her name and skidded to a stop in the middle of the wide dirt road that led to Ty's bakery. Her thick braid swirled and hit her hip as she whipped around, trying to find the source of the voice. She was still learning the women who shared this new home with her, and when she was so lost in her thoughts about Bannack it was incredibly difficult for her to try to decipher which of them it was just through that one word.

When she turned around for the second time she saw all five of the other women coming toward her, Zuri out in front charging ahead with all of the intensity and commanding of attention that she always exuded, and Eden falling slightly behind as she tried to contend with the large, round belly that cradled Pyra's child.

"What do you need?" Loralia asked.

She surprised herself with the ire that came through in her voice when she spoke to them, especially considering she had been seeking them out just as much as they were seeking her out now. Seeing them again, however, only reminded her of the comments that they had made when they last spoke, and the feelings of frustration and anger toward them returned. She had done nothing but be helpful and welcoming to these women since they had first entered her home, but they had admitted that they have a difficult time trusting anyone new, particularly women. Though they had tried to reassure her that they hadn't meant her, that they were only talking about the flight attendant who had betrayed all of them by assisting the Klimnu, Loralia had felt like it was one of those comments that people make that they do not even realize what they have said, when they are revealing what is truly inside them even though they had been trying not to say that particular thing.

The five women stopped a few feet from her, all of them carrying expressions that showed that they were embarrassed and regretful about the conversation that they had. Loralia tried to remember what it had been like between them on her first night in the compound. She had such a horrible experience with Bannack and they came to her, offering their friendship and their comfort. They told her that they were happy that there was another woman in the compound with them and made her feel, at least for a moment, that they were going to be her friends. Loralia fought within herself to reconnect with how that felt and to keep her mind focused on the benefits that would come from forming relationships with the mates of the other warriors. This was her life now, and she would either assimilate, or be miserable.

"We have been trying again to contact the men, but haven't been able to. We want to ask if any of them remember being told about this new professor who is supposed to be coming."

Loralia tensed.

"You are still so concerned about that?" she asked, "Could it not be possible that you simply forgot about this professor? That you put it out of your mind because you were thinking about other things?" She looked at each of the women, "Why is it so much easier for all of you, so much more natural, to question and be suspicious about everything than it is for you to trust? You pretend that you are so loyal to the Denynso, but you have heard from the king himself that the professor is coming and that he received formal word of it directly from the program and you are still so convinced of your own knowledge of what is going on in the world around you that you will not even believe him."

She hadn't meant to say all of that, but it had just come out of her. Loralia expected the other women to be angry and yell back at her, or at the very least to storm away from her. Instead, they all looked even more embarrassed as if what she had said finally gotten through to them completely.

"I'm sorry," Zuri said, offering the words with true, pure emotion that Loralia knew meant she was saying it truly from herself and was not trying to speak for the other women.

"It's unlikely that any of you are going to be able to get through to your mates. They have been in a battle."

The five women gasped and Elianna stepped up to Zuri's side.

"Did Ciyrs not make it to Lynx in time?" she asked, the words sounding as though she had to fight with herself even to get them out of her mouth.

"No, he did," Loralia answered and watched the tiny woman relax, "but the Covra are vicious and persistent. Even though they are far weakened from when they first encountered the Light Ones, they still hold a grudge. They want to come back and see them, and they are not happy that the men are there."

"Wait," Samira said, "these are the same creatures? The ones that locked the Light Ones in the first place?"

"Yes. This species is ancient. They have extremely long lives and it can take many decades for a new generation to be born. The time when they are reproducing is often the most dangerous time for them because the offspring have yet to be born, but the existing generation is getting weaker. That's what I fear is happening now."

"What do you mean?" Leia asked.

"The Covra are so old at this point that they have to be close to a new generation or the species would die off. They are also getting weaker, though they are still strong enough to fight the men. I helped them lure and defeat as many of the Covra as they could, but if they are close to their reproductive cycle finishing, there could be thousands of young, strong creatures about to be born."

"You helped them defeat the ones that were already there?"

Eden asked this as if it hurt her slightly that Loralia had the opportunity to be involved with the men in this way and the rest of them didn't, but that at the same time she was happy that there was still some connection to them when the other women were unable to use their thoughts to connect with their mates.

"Yes," Loralia answered, "Bannack and I reflected the structures on the floor of one of the caverns in my home so that the Covra would puncture their eyes on it. That is the only way to kill them."

"Are they all alright?"

Loralia looked at Samira regretfully.

"Ty was injured," she said, "but he's fine now. Ciyrs was right there and he and Pyra and Gyyx were able to get Ty and Vax under control so that Ciyrs could heal them. I'm sure that they are awake by now. That's actually why I was looking for you."

"Why?" Samira asked, obviously shaken by the news that her mate was hurt in the battle against the Covra.

"The Covra will be back. I have absolutely no doubt about that. But it isn't just the men who are at risk. They could leave and continue on their journey and likely never encounter them again. The Light Ones, however, are at very serious risk. If they don't figure out how to unlock them very soon, they might run out of time. My grandfather was always cryptic with his stories, but he did mention that when the young ones come, enemies fall. If I'm right about the new generation being born soon, the Light Ones' time might be up."

"But what does that have to do with you looking for us?" Elianna asked.

"The men don't know how to unlock them. Ciyrs tried the healing that he did to remove the toxin that caused the infected warriors to try to fight the others, and it didn't work. They read back through all of the information that they found when they went into the prison and found out about the settlement and the Light Ones, and there's nothing in there about the specific way that they unlock them. They need help."

The women exchanged glances and then Elianna nodded.

"Let's go to Ciyrs' shop. I've never heard of the Covra so I don't think that there is anything in any of his books about them, but it wouldn't hurt to look through them again. Being close to the supplies and healing ingredients might also help to trigger some ideas," Elianna said.

The women hurried to the shop and as soon as they stepped inside, Loralia took the compact from around her neck and placed it on the counter.

"Everyone come around here. You'll be able to see your men and they'll be able to see you."

The women gathered tightly around her so that they could all look into the mirror and Loralia opened the compact. She reflected the chain in the top mirror and the silver around the glass started to glow. It gave off the same pearly luminescence as her skin, growing in intensity as the compact reached out to link with the one that Bannack had. She knew that just as hers did when he reflected the braid of her hair that she had attached to it before giving it to him, her father's compact would now be pulsating with light on Bannack's chest.

An instant later the glow faded and Bannack's face

appeared in her mirror again. It hadn't been long since they had last spoken and he told her that she should go talk to the women without the compact activated and then reconnect with them when the women were ready, but she still felt the upward surge in her heart that she always did when she saw his eyes looking back at her. They were still so close to the beginning of their relationship that she could remember what his eyes looked like before they shifted completely to orange after their first bonding experience. She could remember the flickering when they would shift from their original shade to the bright orange and back again, a feature that she found so strange. Now, however, she knew that she much preferred the orange because it was an outward, inarguable sign of their unbreakable connection to each other.

5

———

"Hello, my love," Bannack said.

"Hi, darling. I have the other women with me."

"I can see that," Bannack replied with a smile, "Hello, everyone."

Loralia could hear all of the women chiming in around her to say hello to Bannack and she smiled.

"How is everyone doing?" she asked.

The compact shifted suddenly and Pyra's face appeared in the glass.

"Pyra!" Eden gasped, pushing closer to the compact.

She reached out and ran her fingers down the side of the reflection of Pyra's face.

"Hi," he said softly, "I miss you."

"I miss you, too."

"How's the baby?"

"Everything's fine."

"Good."

"I wish I could connect with you."

"I know. It's just too hard right now."

"It's like I can feel you with me."

He seemed to be starting to say something else, but Gyyx's face appeared beside his as the other warrior tried to push Pyra out of the way.

It continued like this for the next several minutes, each of the men forcing their way into the reflection so that they could spend a few moments with their mates. Finally Lynx appeared in the reflection.

"I'm sorry to be the one to break all of this up, but we really need to start figuring this out."

"Lynx is right," Ciyrs' voice came from behind Lynx and a moment later he appeared in the reflection.

Elianna reached forward and touched the image of his face. Loralia could see the tears in her eyes and had a pang of feeling for the tiny woman. Elianna and Ciyrs had been together for far longer than she and Bannack, and Loralia could only imagine that the bond grew stronger with time. As with the other women, she couldn't begin to understand how painful it was for them to be away from the men who they had spent months with rather than the mere days she had been with Bannack. Being without him felt like her heart was coming out of her chest, and in that moment she found herself in awe that the other women, or their mates, were still functioning.

"Do you have any ideas?" Elianna asked, her voice lowering as if she had forgotten the others were around her and was just talking to him.

"I've tried everything that I can think of. Do you want to look at her?"

Elianna nodded. The reflection in the compact mirror moved as Ciyrs carried it over to the bed and held it up so that the image of a beautiful woman appeared in the glass. Loralia looked at her delicate but distinct features, the flow of hair in a color that she had never seen, the soft peacefulness that made her face look relaxed and calm without a hint of knowing what was coming in the moments just after she laid down to rest.

"She's like Sleeping Beauty," Zuri said.

Loralia didn't know what she meant by that, but the other four human women nodded in agreement, so she figured that it must have some sort of meaning behind it.

"Who is Sleeping Beauty?" one of the men asked and Loralia was relieved that she wasn't the only one that wasn't familiar with the phrase.

"It's a fairy tale," Zuri said with a small laugh, "A story that we tell our children on Earth. It's about a woman that gets put into a deep sleep by an evil fairy. She sleeps for so long that her fairy godmothers put everyone in the entire kingdom to sleep. She can only wake when her true love comes and kisses her."

"How long does it take?"

"One hundred years."

Loralia heard Lynx's sharp intake of breath.

"Maybe you should try kissing her," Pyra said to Lynx, only partly sounding like he was kidding.

"It worked for me," Gyyx said.

Loralia saw Leia blush.

"You might have done a little more than kiss me," she said and Gyyx grinned.

Loralia remembered the story they had told her about Gyyx waking Leia up out of her sleep after they rescued her from the Klimnu by stimulating her. She had come out of her sleep in the middle of an orgasm, but it wasn't until she had convinced him to bond with her completely that she had really started to heal and regain her strength.

"I don't think that would work," Loralia said, "She might look like Sleeping Beauty, but she wasn't singled out. The Covra locked the entire settlement, not just her."

"That's true," Ciyrs said, "This is an ability of the Covra, not magic. There has to something, something specific, that will unlock all of them."

"We're going to go back to the other men and tell them what we found out about Rain," Pyra said.

"Rain?" asked Eden.

"That's her name," Lynx said.

Loralia could hear the tenderness in his voice and she wished there was something that she could do to reassure him. Even just hearing those few words from him, she feel his emptiness and loneliness, and if there two emotions that she understood clearly, it was those.

"We will keep working on it from here," Loralia said, hoping that that would comfort Lynx in some way, "If we think of anything, we will get in touch with you."

"I have you and the baby with me, Eden," Pyra said, pulling a pendant out from under his shirt.

Loralia watched as he held the pendant in his hand and rubbed it with his thumb. Behind her she heard Eden sigh.

"Keep it with you," she said, "I love you."

The rest of the women repeated her words to their mates, and the men returned them. Finally she was looking at Bannack again.

"We'll do everything we can," she told him.

"I know you will."

"I miss you."

"I miss you, too."

Loralia closed the compact and looped it back around her neck. As she was turning toward the rest of the women, she felt a sudden wave of worry and when she looked at Eden, she watched the color drain from her already pale face.

6

———

"Eden?"

Loralia's voice sounded like it was coming through water toward her. She could hear her, but the words were muffled and indistinct. Far more distinct was the strange pain coursing through her belly and tightening in her lower back. She felt dizzy and her vision blurred slightly.

"Eden?" Zuri said

Eden felt the other woman's hand come to her back and she pressed back into it, hoping to find some strength and balance in the support.

"I don't feel right," she managed to say, though the words sounded just as warped coming into her ears as the ones that the others had spoken.

"What do you mean you don't feel right? What's wrong?" Leia asked and Eden felt her come up to her other side.

"I'm dizzy and I have a pain in my belly."

"Oh, no," Zuri said.

"We need to get her to the midwives," Elianna said urgently.

Eden looked at Loralia and saw her serene face gazing back at her. She knew that the five of them had not done very well making her feel like she was part of the clan. Even though they truly wanted to, the five of them were still hesitant and unsure of anyone outside of their tightknit little group. The reality was that the five of them were intrinsically connected. Eden had been the first to come and was there to be an anchor within the compound for the other women to come. She had watched Elianna come and go through her brutal attack from the Klimnu, which bonded them. Elianna had discovered Leia in the prison, which connected the three of them. When Zuri came, she already knew Leia from the university, and then Zuri herself brought Samira back to Uoria after her brief visit back to Earth.

Loralia was an outlier, something that none of them understood. It was not that she was another species. They had all learned that that didn't matter. It was more that she was inexplicable and came without connection to any of them. Eden hoped very much that they would soon all mesh together.

At that moment, Loralia was a source of focus for Eden. Her lavender eyes were startling enough to keep her concentrating on them as Zuri, Leia, and Elianna supported her, and Samira held the door to make it easier for them to guide Eden out of the shop. She lost sight of Loralia as the others turned her to move her out of the shop and Eden glanced back over her shoulder. Loralia was hesitating inside the building, not following the other women.

"Loralia," Eden called, "Please come with us."

It was difficult to explain, but right then, as new waves of dizziness and pain washed over her, she knew that she wanted to have all of the women there with her.

.   .   .

A FEW MINUTES later the women helped her into the home of the elder midwife of the tribe. The tremendous Denynso woman, more feminine but nearly as large as her male counterparts, rushed into the room still drying her hands from washing them in the sink in the back room. Her eyes were wide and worried.

"Eden?" she asked, coming up to the women, "What's wrong?"

"She says she's feeling strange," Zuri told her.

"I'm dizzy," Eden said, "I feel like I can't see straight."

"Are you having pain?" the midwife, Adela, asked.

Eden nodded, not wanting to actually admit what she was going through because she felt like if she gave voice to it, it would be too real and she would have to really confront what might be happening.

"Bring her into the back," Adela said, gesturing toward the curtains that covered the large doorway leading from the main room in the front of the house to the small examination room in the back.

The women helped her toward the back of the house and Eden glanced back to make sure that Loralia was following. She laid down on the bed and closed her eyes, willing the strange feeling to pass and the pain to ease. As she lay there she felt the comfort of Pyra's presence near her and she began to relax.

"Tell me what happened," Adela said, rubbing her hands together to warm them before lifting Eden's dress out of the way and resting her palms on her belly.

"I don't know," Eden said, "Everything was fine, and then I felt a little tinge of pain in my lower belly, and then it moved around to my back. It started getting worse, and then I started feeling really dizzy and lightheaded."

As the midwife examined her, Eden rested her head back and closed her eyes again. She concentrated on the feeling of Pyra's presence, the thought of him being close to her. It was as if he were there, cradling her head and touching her belly as Adela checked her carefully for all of the signs of labor.

"It doesn't look like you are in labor right now, Adela said and relief washed over Eden, but the stern look on the midwife's face brought her back into the sense of nervousness, "But I need you to remember that we aren't entirely sure how this pregnancy is going to go. Pyra is the first of this generation to reproduce, but the problem is that you were once human."

"Ciyrs says that I am Denynso now, though. He says that my DNA has completely changed and that I am now as much Denynso as you are."

Eden was feeling slightly defensive, but she knew that it was mostly fear that was making her sound angry and sharp with the midwife who had been nothing but kind and encouraging to her since she discovered that she was pregnant.

"I know that, Eden, but we've talked about this before. You are the first person to ever be changed like that. No one else, ever, has been changed from another species to a Denynso. We didn't even know that was possible, so we have no idea what it actually means. It is entirely possible that while you are technically one of us, your body still maintains some of the traits of humans. That means that we don't know if this pregnancy will go as long as a normal human pregnancy or if it will be closer to a Denynso pregnancy.

That makes it really difficult for us to tell where you may be in the process."

"What is the difference between the pregnancies of the two species?" Loralia asked from her place several feet away from the bed where Eden lay.

"Two months or more. If she is carrying like a human, she still has some time to go. If she is carrying like a Denynso, though, this little one will be ready to come into the world very soon. There is simply no way of knowing."

Eden slid her eyes over to Loralia, catching her gaze and holding it meaningfully, hoping that she could tell her what she was thinking just through that one glance. It seemed to take a moment, and then Loralia gave a single subtle nod. Eden looked back up at Adela.

"I am starting to feel much better," she told her, "I think I just overreacted. I've never done this before, you know."

"I know," Adela said with a warm, understanding smile, "I completely understand. I am the only one that still remembers the last generation being born, and I can tell you that there was not one first time mother who did not get nervous close to the end. The dizziness and pains are not uncommon. I can't tell you for sure, but they make me think that you may be carrying more like a Denynso. Those are common symptoms for a mother that is drawing close to labor."

"If it's alright with you, I'm just going to go home now. Some rest will probably do me good."

"Of course, but prepare yourself. This child could make an appearance when you least expect it, and it is important that you are ready."

Eden nodded and looked toward the other women.

"The girls will help me get the house ready and make sure that I'm alright until Pyra comes home."

"Good."

Eden let Adela help her sit before swinging her legs over the side of the bed and standing carefully. The pain had subsided and she was feeling stronger, but she longed for the feeling of Pyra being close to her. The sense of his presence had dissipated and she reached out with her mind for the link with him. As it had been for the last few days, though, she could not make the connection. She remembered him holding the pendant in his hand when they spoke through the mirror and realized that somehow it was connecting them. When he touched the hearts that represented her and their baby, she could feel his energy pulsing toward her. The thought calmed and comforted her, giving her the strength to move forward.

"Come on," Zuri said, "We'll help you get home."

With Zuri on one side and Samira on the other, the women made their way carefully out of the midwife's home and toward Eden's. Adela watched them from the door, calling out reminders to Eden about the things she needed to be doing to take care of herself until the baby arrived.

Eden waited until they got to her house to turn to Loralia again.

"Can you help me?" she asked nervously.

Loralia hesitated and then walked over to Eden, leading her with a gentle hand on her back over to the sofa.

"I can try," she said, "Lay down." Loralia knelt down beside the sofa and took her compact from around her neck, "I don't know if I'll be able to tell you anything that I didn't tell you the last time."

"Just try."

Loralia opened the compact in her palm and brought it up to rest against the side of Eden's belly, placing her other hand on top of the swell. Eden could feel her hand pressing down as if trying to reach the baby and ease it closer to the mirror. She was quiet for several long seconds and Eden started to feel worried, then Loralia's mouth twitched into the hint of a smile.

"This baby is very perceptive," she said.

"Is it still a boy?" Eden asked.

Loralia laughed and looked into Eden's eyes.

"If he was before, he still is now. I don't think that changes," she said and Eden laughed, the moment relieving some of the tension she was feeling.

"What do you mean he's perceptive?"

"He knows that you are upset, and he doesn't want you to be."

Eden rubbed the side of her belly.

"It's alright, little one," she whispered, "I'm fine. I just want you to be healthy and strong, and I want your Papa to be here when you're born."

"He's calmer now, but he is nearly ready to come into the world and meet you."

"How nearly ready?"

"I can't tell you that. Remember, I am not positive about anything that I tell you about him. I can only tell you what I feel. I would say, though, that becoming a Denynso definitely changed how you will carry this baby and any future children you may have. I do not think that he is going to stay cuddle up inside you for another two months."

The sound of a sharp knock on the door startled Zuri and she turned away from watching Loralia and Eden. She looked around the room to make sure that all of the women were there, and then looked back toward the door. There was another hard, sharp rap on the door and she heard a deep but feminine voice come through the door toward them.

"It's Zsilvia."

Zuri crossed the room and opened the door to allow the Denynso woman in. With the exception of Samira, who was nearly as tall as she was, the Denynso women were the only females anywhere around that could rival Zuri in size. They were actually taller than she was and slightly larger, which was not something that Zuri was accustomed to. On Earth she was always made to feel extremely large and ungainly, particularly when compared to the other women who worked in the university. It had been the lingering feelings of discomfort about her size and how she compared to the other women that made her nearly walk away from the love of her mate, Ero. On Uoria, though, she felt like she fit in. In fact, it was the tiny, delicate-looking other human women who looked far more out of place that she and Samira did. Fortunately, they were never made to feel the shame and self-doubt that she had.

"Hi," Zuri said, "Is everything alright?"

Though the Denynso women were nice enough and all of the women spent time together occasionally, the women born into the tribe tended to be quieter and preferred to keep to themselves. It was unusual for one of them to show up at one of the human women's homes without there being a specific reason.

"Creia and Theia sent me to retrieve you."

"Is something wrong?" Zuri felt a sudden surge of panic. "Is there something wrong with the men? Did they hear from them?"

She didn't realize it until she was within a few inches of her that she had been advancing toward Zsilvia. She stopped and took a step back, trying to calm the suddenly frantic pounding of her heart.

"No," Zsilvia said, "They said nothing about the warriors. They didn't seem upset, but they did say that they would like for you to get to them as quickly as possible."

"Eden, do you feel up to going?" Zuri asked.

Eden shook her head.

"I think that I should stay here and get some more rest if that's ok."

"I'll let the king and queen know. I'm sure they won't mind."

"I'll stay here with Eden," Loralia offered, "I can't imagine they need to see me."

Zuri nodded and the other three women came toward her so that they could follow Zsilvia toward the meeting hall where the king and queen lived and held court. This kept them close to their people at all times, whether they were eating in the banquet hall or needed to speak with them in their meeting hall.

The four women followed closely behind Zsilvia as they made their way toward the meeting hall. Not for the first time since she had been on Uoria, Zuri longed for the convenience of the vehicles on Earth. While there certainly weren't as many individual vehicles as there had been in past generations, the availability of many different kinds of public transportation virtually everywhere made it easy to get anywhere you needed to go without having to resort to walking. This seemed especially important when even her long legs were having difficulty keeping up with the impressive stride of the Denynso woman leading their way. Zuri could only imagine how much more difficult it was for the smaller human women to keep themselves up to pace.

When they finally made it to the meeting hall Zuri noticed that again Creia and Theia were standing out on the front steps rather than waiting inside for the women to come to them when beckoned. They had eaten their meals at home rather than in the banquet hall since the men left, and this was the second time that the king and queen had greeted them from the front steps instead of inside. It was almost as if without the warriors Creia didn't have the heart to have anyone in the hall. Zuri sometimes had to remind herself that these two sweet and gentle people were not just the beloved monarchs of the Denynso compound. They were also the parents of many of the warriors. This ensured that they were suffering an extra level of pain and worry now that the men were gone.

"Hello," Zuri said as she approached the steps.

Creia looked down at her with his customary smile, but

she could see how the worry was impacting him. He seemed worn and tired in a way that Zuri hadn't seen him before.

"Ah, Zuri," he said, coming down the first few steps to greet her, "Thank you for bringing her to me, Zsilvia." Zsilvia nodded and stepped to the side so that Creia and the women didn't have to look over her. "I know that there is a still a bit of time left, but I wanted you to get here early so that there was no rushing when the shuttle arrives."

"The shuttle?" Zuri asked. Creia's face darkened and it suddenly hit her. "The shuttle! That is coming today!"

"What's going on, Zuri?" Samira asked.

Zuri turned to her.

"The professor from the university is arriving today."

"I thought that the shuttle was still a couple of days off," Samira said.

Zuri shook her head.

"Creia told me last night that he got another communication confirming the arrival and that it would be a day earlier than anticipated. Apparently they are not using the same shuttle after the incident with the flight attendant, and the new one is going through testing for the university Design and Engineering program. It is faster and more efficient than the older ones."

"Apparently."

"I'm so sorry that I forgot," Zuri said, looking back at the king, "I didn't mean to." She stopped just short of telling him what was happening with the men. It didn't feel like the right time to include him in the situation. "Eden hasn't been feeling well."

The slight angry expression dissipated from his face only to be replaced by worry.

"Eden? Is she alright? Is the baby alright?"

"Everything is fine," Zuri reassured him, "We were

visiting with Loralia and Eden started feeling strange and having a few pains so we brought her to the midwife. Adela examined her thoroughly and says that everything looks good."

"Does she think the baby will be coming soon?"

"She doesn't know. She says there is still no way to know whether she will carry to a Denynso term or a human term."

Creia nodded.

"At least she is well now. Is Loralia with her?"

"Yes. She stayed home just to be safe."

"That's good."

The king looked off into the distance for a moment and then back at Zuri.

"Sir."

Creia looked like he was about to say something, but Zsilvia's voice stopped him before the words could come out. Zuri watched him turn to the Denynso woman.

"Yes?"

Zsilvia pointed into the distance and Zuri followed her hand to see plumes of white smoke appearing over the crest at the edge of the compound.

"The shuttle's here," Zuri said.

Suddenly she was nervous. No one had told her which professor was coming, and she was worried that it might be one of the women with whom she hadn't gotten along very well while she was on Earth. Fortunately there weren't many of them, but she didn't feel prepared to not only deal with one of them for however long she decided to stay on Uoria participating in the exchange program that as of yet had scarcely gotten underway, but to also have to go through the explanations as to why she had submitted papers to take an indefinite leave of absence from the university and stayed on Uoria. She hadn't told a single person on Earth other than

Samira what had happened between her and Ero, or why she was choosing to join the Denynso. It wasn't that she meant to hide it from anyone, or that she didn't want her former coworkers or anyone else to know, it was simply that she hadn't cared enough about their perceptions of her or her choices to share it with them.

"Since the warriors aren't here, I've told the shuttle commander that you will be greeting the professor," Creia said to Zuri.

"Me?"

"Yes. You are a fellow professor and a colleague from the university. It will be comforting to see a familiar face and to have some guidance."

Zuri didn't have a chance to respond before Creia climbed back up the stairs to Theia and they both walked back into the meeting hall, likely to take their places in their main throne room so that they could greet the new teacher they way they did all visitors from Earth. It was both a comforting and intimidating moment that Zuri remembered clearly from her arrival. Thrust in front of the king and queen just moments after meeting Ero, she had felt welcomed onto the blanket, but also somewhat scrutinized. After spending time with the Denynso she knew of the threats that they had faced and felt herself being just as wary of the newcomer as she assumed they had felt about her.

8

By the time they made it to the landing platform, the shuttle had settled completely into place and the plumes of white smoke had begun to disappear into the air. The shuttle would stay there for at least 24 hours to give the crew a chance to rest and recuperate after the long journey and prepare for the equally long journey back. Zuri found herself wondering if the flight attendants had the option of undergoing the sedation process that many of the passengers did when they were on their way back to Earth. If the shuttle was empty, there really wasn't much for them to do. Perhaps, though, they were required to stay awake simply because they were working and it wouldn't seem practical to pay them for working five days when they were merely sleeping.

The door to the shuttle hissed slightly as it loosened from its position in the shuttle wall and opened out into the space above the elevated landing platform. Zuri watched as the shuttle commander, the same pilot who had been in charge of her trips from Earth to Uoria, back to Earth, and then back to Uoria again, stepped out onto the platform and took a deep breath of the cool air as if relieved to be out of the shuttle for the first time in days. Behind him came a young man and a young woman wearing the flight attendant uniform. She thought that the young man could have been the one who had been with her on one of her flights, but she wasn't positive. She didn't recognize the woman, an obvious hasty replacement for the attendant who had used her position on the shuttle as a means of betraying the Denynso because of an old family grudge.

The women shifted behind her as they waited a few more seconds for the professor to come out. It had been Zuri's experience that passengers who chose to stay awake during the voyage were usually standing right in front of the door with their luggage at their feet, ready to bolt out of the shuttle as quickly as they possibly could when the craft landed because they were so desperate to not be in the same small space, staring out of the window at the deep blackness that was the universe. To her this meant that the new professor must have taken the option given to all of the passengers and been put into a deep sleep to pass the trip. She had done it on one of her trips, and though she had to admit that it made the days pass far more quickly and numbed the pain that she had been feeling, it was not something that she would have wanted to do on her first voyage. That is something that she wanted to feel in control of and remember.

After another few seconds of waiting she saw a large suitcase fly out of the door to the shuttle and skitter across the platform followed by another, and then a smaller bag. Finally a figure stepped into the doorway and Zuri couldn't withhold her gasp of surprise. It was a man.

The whispers that came from the women behind her told Zuri that they had all been assuming the same thing;

that the new professor that would come to Uoria to be a part of the exchange program would be a woman. She wasn't sure why she had assumed that, other than that she was the only professor to have come to the planet and that the majority of the professors who had been in favor of the exchange program and voiced even the slightest interest in being a part of it were women. Even the only two students who had made their way to the program, Leia and Samira, were women. This middle-aged man's sudden appearance seemed somewhat out of place, like it was throwing the balance off track.

The man stepped forward and stretched his back, looking down to offer a grin to the women gathered at the foot of the platform, and Zuri suddenly recognized him.

"George?" she called up to him.

"Zuri!" he boomed, the lilting accent in his voice sounding both familiar and strange.

She had worked with George for a few years prior to coming to Uoria, though they were never what she would have considered close friends. She wasn't sure how she felt about him being the professor who was joining the program on Uoria, but she also didn't know how she would have reacted had it been one of the women. As she stood there watching George gathering his bags so that he could carry them down off of the platform, Zuri realized that she was feeling so protective of the compound and the Denynso that she didn't think she would have reacted well to anyone new coming. She would have just as soon cancelled the program and stopped anyone else from coming to the planet.

"Where to?" George asked as he came up beside Zuri.

"When new visitors arrive on Uoria, the first place they go is to meet the king and queen. We'll take you there."

"Sounds good."

"You might remember Samira," Zuri said, gesturing toward the youngest of the human women.

"Of course. It's good to see you, Samira."

Samira nodded and stepped out of the way so that Zuri could introduce the other two women, who exchanged pleasantries and handshakes with George. Zuri could see that all of them were looking at him with expressions that said they were feeling much of the same confusion and uncertainty as she was.

"And this is Zsilvia."

Zuri stepped back so that she could gesture toward the Denynso woman. Zsilvia had fallen back a few steps from the rest of them and looked somewhat startled when Zuri urged her forward. George reached forward and Zuri saw Zsilvia's hand tremble slightly as she placed hers against his palm. He closed his fingers around her hand and held it for a few seconds rather than shaking it as he had with the other women.

"Hello," Zsilvia said, her voice uncharacteristically soft.

"It is very nice to meet you," George said.

After a moment Zuri placed a hand on Zsilvia's arm.

"We should get to the meeting hall. Creia and Theia will be expecting George."

Her intrusion in the suspension between the two of them seemed to bring Zsilvia back into reality and she stepped away from George, her hand falling away from his and her eyes dropping to the ground. Zuri withheld the smile that was teasing at her lips and started back down the path away from the shuttle and toward the meeting hall.

9

As hard as she tried to keep her eyes focused on the king and queen, Zsilvia couldn't seem to stop them from wandering to George's back. He stood several feet ahead of her, facing the king and queen as they stood near the edge of their throne platform looking down at him just as they did with everyone who came to the compound. She was positioned on the side of the hall, taking up the position that would usually be held by the warriors who accompanied the visitors from the shuttle to the meeting hall. Though she was obviously not a warrior, she was a close as was available at the time, and it was important to maintain tradition.

"We are very excited to have you here with us," Creia said.

George nodded and Zsilvia felt her eyes travel down his body again. They didn't seem to care how much her mind was telling them to stay focused and to keep away from him, but traced the broadness of his shoulders and the definition of his back through his shirt. He was not as large as the warriors, but still the biggest human man that she had ever seen. What startled her even more than his size, however, was his age. She had anticipated him being young like the human women. Even Zuri, who was the oldest of the women to have come from Earth, was at least 10 years younger than him.

Instead of making him look weathered or worn, however, the age made him seem strong, steady, and more dignified than the young warriors. Despite his broad, willing smile and the energy that exuded from him as he carried his huge suitcases with absolute ease, he had a sense of stability and control within him that stood in stark contrast to the wound up, often unpredictable nature of the warriors. She found desperately not to think about it, but she found it irresistible.

"We have found ourselves very fond of the women who have come here before you," Theia said with a laugh and the human women standing behind George chuckled.

"I look forward to the opportunity to get to know all of you and to work toward our mutual goal of cooperation between the planets."

George's voice was different than anything Zsilvia had ever heard. The accent was rumbling, like water rushing over rocks, but occasionally added a sharp edge to a word as if it were more difficult for him to say than the others. The sound rolled through her, seeming to reach deep inside her and settle into her chest.

"Usually we have one of our warriors act as protector and guide for our human visitors, but our men have recently left the compound on a quest that will keep them away for an unknown amount of time. Since you are already acquainted with Zuri, she may act in a warrior's stead."

Zsilvia watched Zuri step forward to address the king and queen.

"With all due respect, as much as I would like to ensure that George settles into the compound comfortably and has everything that he needs to get accustomed to his new surroundings, I don't think that I'm right for the position," she said.

Creia looked at her sternly.

"Why?"

"Ero, sir," she said matter-of-factly, "I know that he would understand, but I don't think that he would like me taking on that role for another man, particularly while he is gone from the compound. I must respect my mate and his feelings."

With Zuri's mention of her mate, Zsilvia saw George look sharply at his former colleague and then back at the monarchs. Creia had a softer expression on his face now and was nodding slowly.

"I didn't think of that, Zuri, and I thank you for your honesty and your respect for Ero. I agree that it wouldn't be right for you to act as protector and guide for another man while your mate is away from the compound. He has to have someone, though. It is our law, and as you know, we will not compromise on it."

"Allow Zsilvia to do it," Zuri said.

Zsilvia felt her stomach tighten and drew in a sharp breath that she immediately hoped the others hadn't heard. The king turned his attention to her and she pulled herself up to her full height, trying to look as attentive as she could.

"Zsilvia?"

"Yes, sir?"

"Could you please come here?"

For a brief moment she wasn't sure that her legs would be able to carry her the full distance between where she was standing and the spot the rest of the group had made for her in front of the king and queen by parting and moving slightly away from the center of the room. Even worse, she feared that if she did make it up there, George would see her body trembling and feel the pulsing, intense heat she could feel forming in her skin.

Finally she forced herself to take a step forward and then another, fighting to keep her eyes locked tightly on the king where he waited for her near the edge of the platform.

"Yes, sir," she repeated when at last she made it to the spot.

Out of the corner of her eye she could see George looking at her, his eyes a swirl of brown and green that she had never seen and his full lips forming only the slightest hint of a smile. She wouldn't let herself look at him, but kept eye contact with the king, who had lowered his gaze slightly.

"Will you take on the responsibility of being the protector and guard for George while he is here? Help him settle in to his new house and get accustomed to the compound?"

"Yes, sir."

It seemed those were the only words that she was able to get past the tightness in her throat. She should have said something else, expressed herself in a more thorough and meaningful way, but she could only agree to the request, as she knew she really had no choice but to do as the king asked, and hope that she would be able to get control of her emotions before they walked out of the meeting hall.

"Good. George, this is Zsilvia."

"We've met," George said, his voice sounding slightly smoother and richer, "but I am happy to meet you again."

He said the last part directly to her and Zsilvia felt a shiver ripple down her spine. She couldn't resist looking at him then, and when their eyes met she felt a surge through her like nothing she had ever experienced. She was suddenly intensely protective, wanting to take care of him and make him as comfortable and happy as she could. An ache had begun to build low in her belly and the longer she looked at him, the more intense the feeling became.

"I'm sure you are eager to settle in after that long journey," Creia said, his voice sounding like he felt completely confident and that everything was properly in place, "I'll let Zsilvia show you to your house. I look forward to talking with you more over dinner tonight. Zuri, I'd like for all of you to eat in the banquet hall tonight so that we can welcome our new guest."

"Absolutely. We look forward to it. I will go straight back to Eden's house and make sure that she's up for it."

"Thank you."

The room fell silent and Zsilvia knew that the inevitable had come. She couldn't draw it out any longer. The meeting with the monarchs was over and she now had to live up to her responsibilities and duties as his guard and protector, which meant walking away from everyone in the hall who seemed to be acting as a buffer, giving her space and distance from George, and being alone with him.

10

———————

The ache was becoming almost unbearable as Zsilvia walked along beside George. The house that they had set aside for him was toward the far end of the compound and they had been walking in silence since they left the meeting hall. She had offered to help him carry his luggage, but he had adamantly refused and swept the suitcases and bags up off the floor as if they weighed nothing. She couldn't help but admire the defined swells of his muscles through his shirt and the way they shifted with the weight of his luggage as he walked.

"Where have the warriors gone?"

George's voice suddenly filling the silence startled Zsilvia and she couldn't seem to process what he had asked.

"Excuse me?"

"The warriors. The king mentioned that all of the warriors have left the compound on a quest and that you don't know when they're going to be back. Where did they go?"

"To explore the planet," Zsilvia answered simply, unsure of what else to tell him.

"Are they looking for something in particular?"

"They are just looking. None of the Denynso have ever left the compound and some recent unpleasant events have made it so the men want to know what else is out there."

"What kind of unpleasant events?"

"There was a war," she said reluctantly. She didn't want to talk about the Klimnu or the battles that broke down the warriors and took Jem's life, "The men decided that we need to know what other kinds of species exist on the rest of Uoria and if any of them are threats to us. Especially Pyra. He's the leader of the warriors. His mate, Eden, is getting ready to give birth to their first child."

George nodded his understanding.

"I can imagine that would make him feel very protective."

"Do you have any children?"

Zsilvia surprised herself with the question, but the need to continue hearing him speak was growing, and with it, the ache that had settled into her pelvis and was tormenting her with every step.

"No," George answered, his eyes sliding over to her, "Do you?"

Zsilvia shook her head.

"Pyra and Eden's baby will be the first of the new generation."

"None of the rest of you have children?"

"No."

"That's interesting."

She wasn't sure that she liked the way he had said that, but she reminded herself that he was a professor who had come to the planet for the purpose of teaching the Denynso about Earth and the ways of the humans that lived there, and to learn about Uoria and the Denynso. His fascination was academic, which suddenly made her feel uncomfortable, as if she was a specimen that he was examining.

They fell into silence again as they turned onto the road where his house was located and she led him to the front door. It was a small cabin just like the other ones that the Denynso had created specifically for the human visitors who came to the compound. Since the first several humans that came had been kept strictly to the six-month maximum visit duration that Creia had imposed, the cabins were simple and straightforward.

George didn't seem bothered by this as he stepped inside and looked around. There was enough daylight coming through the windows that the inside appeared bright and welcoming, but she knew that as soon as the late afternoon hit, the interior would grow dark.

"There is no electricity," she told him, "The lamps, water heater, and stove all work by solar power. There are also a few plants around that will glow so you can keep the lamps off as much as possible to conserve the power."

"Alright."

George lowered his bags to the floor and turned to face her. Zsilvia felt her body drawn to him, pulled toward him as with some unseen force. It was overwhelming and disorienting, and she felt the strange, conflicting need to both run into his arms and escape the room as quickly as she could.

"I'll let you unpack and get used to the cabin. Dinner will be in a few hours, so I will come back for you then."

She turned to the door but before she could open it, she heard George's voice coming to her.

"Can I ask you another question?"

"Yes," Zsilvia said, pausing just a step away from the door.

"What does it mean that Zuri and the warrior Pyra that you mentioned have mates?"

Zsilvia's eyes closed briefly and she let out a slow breath to calm herself. Her body was trembling and her heart had started to pound uncontrollably in her chest.

"It means exactly as it sounds," she replied, "It means that they have found their lifelong mates and completed their bond with them."

"Their bond?"

She could hear George's footsteps as he slowly approached her. She turned around and found him just a few feet away from her, his eyes smoldering into hers.

"Yes. It's how our kind make the connection and commitment with our mates. As soon as a pair of intended mates bond, they are linked together for life."

Her eyes wandered across his chest now just as they had his back when they were standing in the meeting hall. She longed to touch him. She wanted to run her fingers back through his dark brown hair and trace them along the roundness of his shoulders and the carved muscles of his arms. She wanted to feel him press against her so that she could savor every inch of his body.

"Tell me what you're thinking right now," George said.

His voice had dropped to a whisper and it sounded even sexier, his unusual accent making the words almost glide across his tongue so that they swirled around her and tempted her forward closer to him. She fought the urge, but he took another step toward her, further closing the gap between them.

"I can't," she answered, mimicking his low tone with her own voice.

"Why?" he asked.

She couldn't respond, but he seemed to already know

what she was going through her mind. He reached down and took the hem of his shirt in both hands, pulling it off over his head in one smooth movement. It dropped from his fingers onto the floor and Zsilvia's breath caught in her throat. George stepped forward, bringing them close enough now that she could feel his breath touching her face.

He said nothing but took her hands in his and brought them slowly up until they rested on his chest. His fingers pressed down lightly on hers, smoothing her hands down until they were flattened on his warm skin. Thick curls of coarse dark hair tickled at her palms and she felt the ache between her thighs turn into a tingling sensation that nearly made her whimper. George brought his fingertips to her wrists and guided her hands gently down the curve of his chest and onto his belly. She could feel the rippling muscles, but it was the hair that forced her to bite her lip in order to control herself.

Denynso men didn't have this type of hair. Their bodies were smooth and streamlined, almost like machines crafted for war. George's body was different. Though muscular like the warriors, he looked somehow more masculine and primal with the hair, and it made all of her resolves weaken. The powerful wave of need that rushed over her was unmistakable.

George released her wrists from his touch but Zsilvia didn't take her hands away from him. Instead she curled her fingers so that she could draw her nails through the hair from his chest down his belly. He moaned softly and she stepped closer to him. George's hands came to her hips as she leaned forward and touched her lips to the soft dip between his collarbones. She made her way down, kissing a trail along the center of his chest, pausing to feel the timbre of his heartbeat against her lips.

His hands kneaded into her and she could feel him pulling her forward so that she would press against him. He seemed to be feeling the same need that she was, and when her body touched his, the pressure of an intense erection against her belly sent her desire soaring out of control. She felt for his belt and unhooked it, making quick work of the button and zipper at the front of his pants so that she could push the sides apart and released his cock into her hand. George groaned as Zsilvia wrapped her fingers around his length, savoring the feeling of his hardness against her skin.

She was stroking her hand along him, allowing the fluid that dripped from the tip to make her palm glide against her skin, and his fingers were releasing the strings at the front of her skirt when a hard knock on the door make both of them jump.

"George?"

Zuri's voice called in through the door and Zsilvia felt embarrassment burn across her cheeks.

"I'm just changing," George called back to her without missing a beat.

"That's alright," Zuri replied, "I just wanted to stop by and ask if you wanted to read some of the notes that I've made since I've been here. You might find them interesting."

George was putting his clothes back on and looking at her regretfully as Zsilvia tied her skirt and smoothed her hair, trying to make herself look presentable.

"Thank you, Zuri," he said, "I'll have Zsilvia bring me to your house in just a bit."

"I'll actually be at Ciyrs' shop. She'll show you where that is."

"Alright."

Zsilvia listened to Zuri's footsteps moving away from the house and then turned to George.

"His shop is the third building on the main street," she told him softly.

"Aren't you going to come with me?"

Zsilvia shook her head.

"They don't need me there," she replied.

George reached down and took her hand.

"Maybe I do."

Zsilvia looked into his eyes and felt the rush of protective need flow over her again. His grip tightened on her hand and the warmth that had spread through her disappeared as fear replaced it. Memories crashed behind her eyes and she felt her heart constrict painfully. Suddenly she couldn't breathe.

Pulling her hand out of his, Zsilvia yanked open the door and ran out of the house, needing to be alone, yet knowing that she could never be alone with him again.

UNTITLED

(To be continued in Part VI...)

THE ALIEN'S REVELATION

1

____

Zsilvia took another small step backward into the corner of Ciyrs' shop, pressing herself to the wall in an effort to get as far back from the human women and George as she possibly could while still not making it obvious what she was doing. She didn't want to be close enough to the human man who she could not resist to start up the intense, overwhelming feelings again, but she also didn't want to make it obvious that she was trying to stay away from him. She didn't want to offend him, but perhaps even more, she didn't want to start up the questions that were bound to begin if the women noticed that she was doing everything she could to avoid spending any time alone with George. It would have struck them as strange that she was putting so much effort into making sure that they were never alone in the room together and that she kept enough physical distance between them.

George was Zsilvia's responsibility. The king himself had tasked her with being his guard and protector as soon as he arrived, and that meant that it was her duty as a Denynso to make sure that the man was safe, comfortable, and grew accustomed to the compound that would be his home for as long as he stayed on the planet. It was not her choice. Creia had originally selected Zuri to take on the position, but she had withdrawn. Though she told the king it was because she did not want to offend her mate by spending that much time alone with another man as it would require to be his protector and escort, especially considering Ero was away from the compound with the other men on their quest around the planet. Zsilvia knew that this was not the true motivation that kept Zuri from wanting the responsibility.

Zuri, like the other human women, was distrustful of George from the time that he arrived on the planet. When Creia told them that another professor was coming from Earth to Uoria to be a part of the university exchange program that had also brought Zuri, Leia, and Samira to the compound, the women had been baffled. They knew that the purpose of the exchange program was to allow people from the university on Earth to come to Uoria and educate the Denynso on the ways of the Earth and the humans that lived there, with the expectation that eventually representatives from the Denynso would also make their way to Earth in order to teach students about Uoria and their kind. They had not expected, however, for another professor to show up so quickly. Though the king himself had assured them that he had received the communication from the university announcing the arrival of the new professor, the women remained wary. The betrayal by the human woman who had been their flight attendant on the shuttle that had aided the Klimnu and put their entire compound at risk had made them nervous and distrustful. They were even having a difficult time trusting Loralia, the woman who came from the mirrored realm beneath the compound and who had been doing everything that she could to help them since she had arrived.

The distrust had only seemed to increase when the shuttle arrived a day early and the professor who stepped out was not one of the female professors who had worked with Zuri at the university, but a middle-aged man. He was stunningly beautiful, unlike any man that Zsilvia had ever seen, and with a voice that held an accent so unusual and hypnotic she felt like she could never stop listening to him speak and she would be perfectly happy. Though Zuri was familiar with him from the university, she was still completely reluctant to take on the position as his guard and Creia had handed it off to Zsilvia.

Even before she had taken on this role, however, she had been so overwhelmed with her reaction to him that she could barely contain herself. In truth, she had not contained herself, which is where the issues truly began and why she was doing everything she could to avoid being in close contact with him now, just as she had been for the three days since he had arrived. She had kept up with her responsibilities, making sure that she accompanied him to the meeting hall for meals, showing him where all of the women lived with their mates, and answering his questions about the compound. Whenever she was with him, however, she made sure that at least one of the other women was there as well so that she didn't have the opportunity to give into lust and step so close to him again.

She had nearly given into him the first night that he had arrived. Just moments after Creia had given her responsibility over George, she had escorted him to his house, struggling even then with the feelings that were building inside her. From the first moment that she saw him, those first few seconds when he stepped out of the shuttle and looked down at her from the platform, she knew that he was destined to be her mate. She could feel the need for him coursing through her body, and by the time they had stepped into his house, she was nearly breathless with her desire.

He had seemed to feel the same way, his luscious, intoxicating voice deeper and more sultry when he asked her what she had meant when she spoke of the human women and their Denynso mates. She had explained it to him as carefully as she could, telling him that the Denynso wait their entire lives to find that person who is destined for them and then once they complete their bond, they are inextricably linked to one another for the rest of their lives. She had been cautious, however, to only hint at what the bonding entailed. She knew that he understood completely, however, and in that moment he seemed fully and totally ready to take her into his arms and fulfill all of the yearnings that she was feeling for him.

Zsilvia had been nearly overcome by him, allowing him to take off his shirt and place her hands against the warm, chiseled muscles of his chest and run them through the thick, coarse hair that was so incredibly different than anything that she had ever seen. He was unlike any man she had ever seen or ever known. Where the Denynso men were towering and sleek, George was only slightly taller than Zsilvia and made thicker than the warriors, the almost primal nature of his body only accented by the hair that covered him from his chest down into the waistband of his pants.

She had not stopped with the exploration of his chest and the hypnotic, knee-weakening hair. Instead, she had given in to her curiosity, her need to discover him fully, and took his length into her hand, nurturing him with her touch. The feeling of his surging erection against her palm hand only fueled her forward and she had stepped into his arms, not moving away when he began to release the ties on her clothing. This was something that she had never felt, and something that she thought that she was never going to feel. Well beyond the age that most Denynso were when they found their mates, Zsilvia had resigned herself to being one of those who was destined to live out her life belonging to no one, and having no one belong to her.

She had accepted that, almost welcomed it, and when Zuri's voice broke through the delirium that was pressing Zsilvia forward and compelled George to reach out his hand and grab onto Zsilvia, she remembered instantly and painfully why. It had been many years since she had felt the touch of a man, and after that moment she had thought that she would never want to feel it again. What she had told George was absolutely the truth. The Denynso were a people who had one intended mate who they sought out for their entire lives. They knew immediately when they met that mate because of the intense, nearly overwhelming reaction of their minds and their bodies. The only way to soothe that burning within them was to complete the bond with their mate, linking them and ensuring that they would remain together for the rest of their lives. It was a beautiful and meaningful experience that was highly romanticized among the warriors and women alike.

What she had not told them, however, was that the bond with their intended mates was not always the only sexual experience that the Denynso had. The men very often gave in to their cravings well before meeting their mate with any Denynso woman who would submit to them, and while the men were known to be tender and loving to their mates, such was not the case with their lovers. They rarely forced themselves on women who expressly refused them, but those who were willing to accept them could expect nothing less than the intensity and ferocity that the warriors showed on the battlefield. Thinking of nothing but their own satisfaction, the men would appease themselves, and then move on, almost never even thinking twice about the women that they left in their wake.

It was one of these men, a man that now did not even remember her name, who had frightened Zsilvia into rejecting even the most innocent of interactions from the men. She had given into him, desperate for the validation and attention that it would provide her, and he left her nearly dead and feeling like her soul had been torn from her body.

A change had seemed to come over the warriors in the years since then. Zsilvia was more than ten years older than most of the young warriors, and even that one decade seemed to separate them more than she would have imagined. Though they were still far from gentle and courteous, the younger warriors did not show the same level of intensity and aggression with the women before their mates as the warriors of her youth had. Instead, most of them just ignored the women, channeling all of their energies and desires into the violence that they executed in their battles.

George's hand wrapped around her arm, however, had immediately brought Zsilvia back to that horrifying night, and to the moment when she agreed that she would never allow another man near her. She remember in that moment that George was human, not Denynso, which meant that he did not feel the compulsion and immediate, undeniable attraction and sexual need her kind did for their intended mate. That meant that he was not feeling the need to bond their souls, but simply the need to soothe his body. It was far too frightening a reality for her to embrace. As much as she wanted to touch him, breathe him in, and let him carry her away into another existence with him, her mind would always get in the way of what her heart was telling her. Her fear would always supersede anything else that she was feeling, and she would never be able to move past it. Everything within her was gone and though the moment she breathed in the scent of George and touched his skin she could feel her soul feeling her again, she couldn't let herself trust, even for a moment, that it would be any different with him and that she wouldn't be crushed yet again.

2

———

Zsilvia slipped out of the door to Ciyrs' shop and out into the cool night, taking a deep breath of the air that seemed thinner, sweeter, and fresher than the air inside the small building, but that didn't hold the intoxicating scent of George. She filled her lungs again, trying to cleanse them of his smell so that she could breathe without the overwhelming need coming over her. Her body was aching for George's touch and her skin burned as she knew it would, but she couldn't let herself stay close to him.

He had been engaged in a deep conversation with Zuri over something that he had found in one of the healer's many books, and she had taken the opportunity to walk away without him noticing. The other women were beginning to drift out of the shop as well, agreeing that they should get some sleep before getting started again early in the morning. They had been working almost non-stop for four days since the men had reached out to them from their quest, trying to find something, anything that would help them to solve the confounding issue of the locked settlement. It was pure desperation, the frantic efforts that came from knowing that if they didn't figure out a way to release them from their binds very soon, the Covra, the fearsome but mysterious enemies that had put them into their frozen state, would return and they would be lost. George had earned his way into the trust of the women by offering his knowledge and his ideas to helping them, and he stood right beside them as Eden, Elianna, Zuri, and Samira, with the help of Leia and Loralia, scoured through every bit of information that they could find in hopes that something would make sense and they would be able to help the warriors, their mates among them, find a solution.

Zsilvia continued away from the building, leaving behind the glow that poured out of the windows of the shop from the rows of candles along the walls for the darkness that existed further down the street. They likely wouldn't even notice that she was gone. It wasn't like they needed her help anyway. She had contributed nothing in the days since George's arrival had necessitated her be a part, passive and silent though she may be, of the frantic search. She wasn't a scientist like Eden, a professor like Zuri, or a brilliant student like Elianna or Samira. She felt no reason to pay attention to what was happening in their tense, fast-paced conversations or to even contemplate ideas. It would only get in their way and slow down any progress that they might be making.

"Zsilvia?"

Eden's voice stopped Zsilvia's progress and her head fell back momentarily as she bemoaned getting caught in her attempt to get away from the situation and the conversation that she knew awaited her. She turned around and faced Eden, who came toward her gradually, her speed slowed by her round belly. Zsilvia stared at that belly now, for the first time feeling jealous about the baby Eden cradled within it.

That child represented so much more than just the beginning of a new generation for the tribe, the first Denynso born in more than a decade. It was a living, growing blend of Eden and Pyra, a precious symbol that Zsilvia finally felt like she was beginning to understand and at that same time was mourning that she could never understand it completely.

Before now, children existed in her mind merely as biological products of their parents. She had only ever experienced the demanding sexual drive of the Denynso men and each child that she saw seemed to be just a reminder of that faceless pressure. Now she looked at the precious swell of Eden's body and felt a pang deep within her. Eden was literally holding a piece of her mate within her, cradling that treasure against her heartbeat and nourishing it with the flow of her own blood. She was more connected to Pyra through that child than Zsilvia could ever have imagined being connected to someone, and yet now all she could think about was how desperately she wished that she could have that kind of link with George.

"You know that George is still back there," Eden said.

It was not a question, but a demand. Eden pushed this information at her, forcing Zsilvia to acknowledge it and giving an unspoken command for a response. It seemed that even through her efforts to remain as subtle as possible, Zsilvia had not been able to get past Eden.

"I know. He seemed to be in a pretty deep conversation with Zuri, though, and I'm really tired so I figured that I would just go ahead and go. He's been back and forth from Ciyrs' shop enough times that he can find his way back to his cabin on his own, I'm sure, and even if he can't, Zuri will probably walk with him anyway."

"Zuri is not his guard and protector. That is your job."

Zsilvia felt herself stiffen slightly.

"I am well aware of that, Eden."

"So it is your responsibility to make sure that he is safe and that he gets familiar with the compound. You are supposed to stay with him at all times unless he is in his home. Creia gave you that responsibility personally."

"Creia gave it to Zuri first."

"Yes, he did, Zsilvia, but as you know Zuri asked that he remove her from that role out of respect for Ero. She didn't think that it would be appropriate for her to be in that sort of a relationship with another man, particularly one who she is already familiar with because of their time working together at the university, when Ero is away from the compound."

"Why would it matter if she was spending time with another man? If Zuri and Ero are truly mates, he should know that no other man would ever interest her and she wouldn't stray from him. Is he concerned that he perhaps picked the wrong woman?"

Eden looked shocked and dismayed by Zsilvia's bold statement.

"Ero is Denynso, but Zuri isn't. That means that she doesn't have the same bonding connection that the Denynso do. She loves Ero, but human women do not react to their mates the same way and do not automatically mate for life. It is very lucky that she was able to make the telepathic link with him."

"So he is concerned."

"It is not about Zuri, it is about Ero. She is showing her respect to her mate by not spending extensive amounts of time alone with another man. She understands that human relationships are different from those in the Denynso and she wants to show Ero as much devotion and commitment as she can by not doing anything that would even begin to look like she could be venturing too close to a personal relationship with someone other than Ero, especially when he is not around."

"I don't understand why it would make a difference. Pyra has been guard and protector for plenty of people, and he continued to play that role for women even after you came along."

"Pyra is the leader of the warriors and it is his traditional station to be escort for new visitors to the planet. He did fulfill that role, but he has not been guard and protector for anyone after me. He has always had other, unmated warriors take over that responsibility for him. Even if he didn't, I was always on the compound. It's different."

"How is it different? Just because you were somewhere on the compound and Ero is off on some foolish quest with the other warriors there is a difference in the amount of time that one mate spends with someone who is not the other mate?"

"Zuri would not want Ero to hear that she was spending a lot of time with another man, particularly a human man with whom she has a lot in common and a professional history, when he was not around and possibly feel like she was doing something disrespectful or dishonest. That is why she asked to be removed from the position and why Creia gave it to you."

"That's another thing. Why is it that Zuri gets to just ask to be removed from a role that the king gave her and he does it immediately, but I get forced into it without anyone asking me if I had any interest in giving up my time and energy to fulfill a task that is not even in my station within the tribe?"

"Every Denynso is bound by duty to do as the king asks. The king also knows the importance of maintaining the sanctity of the mating pairs and is willing to make changes in order to honor those pairs and ensure harmony and security. You wouldn't understand, Zsilvia, you don't have a mate."

The anger inside Zsilvia built to an almost frightening peak and she felt herself trembling with her efforts to control herself. She nodded slowly.

"You're right," she said evenly, "I don't have a mate. I guess that's something that I'm just never going to understand."

She turned and started to walk away but she could still feel Eden's eyes watching her.

"This is about something else."

Zsilvia felt a chill rush through her at the still, unintimidated confidence in the words. Eden was truly a force to be reckoned with. Though small and delicate-looking, she had been feisty, outspoken, and brash from the moment of her first arrival on the planet. It was this that had both startled and enraptured Pyra as soon as he met her, but also what nearly threatened them being together at all. Eden had originally come to the planet as a scientist under the assumption that she would gather information about the Denynso and bring it back to the research center where she worked so that they could investigate further. At least, this is what the king and queen had understood when they gave her permission to visit and stay in the compound on the customary visitors' limits. Almost as soon as she arrived, however, she made a confession that put her in mortal danger but at the same time, saved her.

The truth was though Eden was a brilliant and accomplished scientist, her mission was actually a cover for the unethical research tactics of her boss, Ryan. This man had managed to prevent her from gaining the renown and esteem that she deserved with a combination of taking credit for everything that she accomplished and sexual harassment. He held the future of her career in his hand, and she knew it, which was why when she threatened to tell everyone about his treatment of her and that he had stolen so much of her work, he assigned her the mission to Uoria instead. She was not to just study the planet and the Denynso, however. Eden was to find a way to steal a sample of the blood of one of the Denynso warriors and bring it back to Ryan who would evaluate it to find out what was in it that made these men the most fearsome and powerful warriors in the entire galaxy. He knew that he would be able to use the compounds within the blood for a wide variety of shady purposes, including weaponization, but no one had ever gotten off of the planet with Denynso blood.

This was because the taking of Denynso blood was the strongest of the clan's laws. Even suspecting a person of attempting to take Denynso blood for the purpose of studying it and using it for anything could result in imprisonment and execution. Eden had reluctantly realized that Ryan's motivations for sending her on the mission were doubly grotesque. He knew that either she would succeed in her task and he would be the first scientist on Earth or any other planet to get his hands on the blood of the feared Denynso warriors and be able to evaluate it, bringing him greater fame, fortune, and power than anything he could have ever imagined, or the Denynso would catch her and kill her, eliminating her as a potential risk to his reputation and source of frustration in his career and his life.

Once she realized this, Eden had made the decision to confess to the king and queen and ask for their forgiveness. In exchange for her honesty, she earned not only the devoted protection of the Denynso, but unprecedented permission to stay in the compound for as long as she wanted to. Of course, within days she had bonded with Pyra and what had begun as a visit that would last a few months turned into the dedication of the rest of her life.

Pregnancy had softened Eden somewhat, but she still had the fire within her, and this combined with the perceptiveness that all of the human women seemed to have made Zsilvia know that she truly had nowhere to hide.

"Zsilvia?" Eden said leadingly, "This is not about Creia assigning you George when you didn't want to be his guard, is it?"

Zsilvia felt the anger stream out of her, replaced by a feeling of sadness that she didn't even know how to express.

"No."

"What is it? You can talk to me."

Zsilvia looked around at the street where they were still standing. The others had gone in the other direction, moving toward their own homes which were on a row separate from the Denynso women.

"I don't know what to say."

"Is this about George?"

Zsilvia nodded. Eden's hand came to her belly, rubbing it gently as she gave a knowing nod. The Denynso woman had expected laughter or teasing, but Eden's eyes stayed calm and quiet.

"I know what happens to Denynso men when they meet their mates," Eden stopped and smiled, glancing down at her belly and gesturing toward it with one hand, "obviously. But what happens to women?"

Zsilvia laughed, thankful for the moment that broke the tension and helped her feel more at ease.

"Essentially the same thing, just in female form. The same intense, unmistakable attraction. The same type of intense physical reaction. Just instead of feeling aggressive and violent, it is something... different. I don't even know how to describe it. It is a feeling that I didn't even know existed until I experienced it myself."

"You feel like your entire world has just focused on that one person and that you are so completely, overwhelmingly devoted to him that you would do anything to ensure he was safe, happy, and cared for, at the total sacrifice of anyone and anything else."

Zsilvia was shocked that Eden had been able to put to words so closely what she was feeling.

"Yes."

"So you do believe that George is your mate."

Eden said it almost as if she had somehow tricked Zsilvia into admitting something that she had not been prepared to admit.

"It doesn't matter what I think about him, things can never go farther with us than what we have right now."

"Why not?"

Zsilvia thought for a long moment about how to form her words so that she could express herself properly. She stepped closer to Eden.

"What's it like when you have sex with Pyra?" she asked, looking into Eden's eyes even though the question obviously made both of them feel uncomfortable.

"Why do you ask?" Eden asked, trying to avoid answering her.

"I think it will help me explain the situation to you."

"Our first time was sudden and aggressive and a little painful," Eden admitted.

"But did he make you feel unsafe?" Zsilvia prodded.

"No," Eden said, "I wasn't really emotionally ready to be with him and physically it was difficult on me because it had been so many years since I had had sex with any man much less one the size of a Denynso warrior. He made me feel absolutely safe and comfortable, though. Even when I freaked out at the end of it and had to leave and take a walk, he offered to go with me. I refused, but looking back I should have accepted the offer. That is when I was attacked by the Klimnu. Of course, if I hadn't ever been attacked by them, Ciyrs wouldn't have had to heal me, and he wouldn't have turned me into a Denynso." Eden sighed as if looking back on everything that had happened to her since arriving on the planet, "Pyra took our bonding extremely seriously and even though it was very fast and sudden, I felt totally safe in his arms."

"And now?" Zsilvia continued, pushing Eden a little further, "What is it like now? Do you still feel safe?"

"Even safer. The longer I am with him, the more incredible it is for us to be together. It is like our minds, bodies, and souls were made to be together, and now that I have spent enough time with him to really understand the ways of the Denynso, and now that the Denynso part of me is really assimilating to the rest of me and helping me to think in the ways of the tribe, I realize wholly and completely that that is the way that it is. We were made to be together, and every time that he makes love to me it is a celebration of that and how much we love each other. It is unlike anything I have ever experienced."

"Denynso men are only like that with their mates," Zsilvia said plainly.

She watched confusion across Eden's face.

"What do you mean?" she asked, her hand coming up to cover her belly protectively as if she was concerned that the comment would somehow get to her child and upset it some way.

"The warriors are known for being vicious and aggressive for a reason, and it goes beyond just the intensity that they show when they are in battle. Before a Denynso man finds his mate, he is still prone to the same sexual urges as any man. Fulfilling them, though, isn't like it is when he's with his mate. Instead, he thinks only of himself and his own satisfaction, sometime to the sacrifice of the comfort and even safety of the woman he has."

Eden got an expression on her face that hovered somewhere between confusion and sadness.

"The way that Pyra talked about his and the other Denynso men's reaction to finding their mates, I somehow didn't think that they..."

Her voice trailed off, but Zsilvia knew exactly what she was thinking. She knew that Eden had assumed that because Denynso warriors react with such physical voracity when they meet their mates, it is their first experience with sexual reactions. Of course, Zsilvia knew very well that this was not the case.

"You thought that because they are so intensely sexually interested when they get near their mates for the first time that they have never had sex before?"

Eden nodded, her eyes slightly wide.

"It...it didn't seem like Pyra was a virgin, but..."

"The reason that Denynso are so interested when they

find their mates is not only to help them identify their mate, but also so that they will bond as quickly as possible. There is always a chance that intended mates will encounter each other but then not bond and lose their opportunity to be together. This is not only devastating to them, but it also means that neither of those two Denynso will ever be able to reproduce. As you may have realized, the birth rate of this species is not anywhere near as high as it should be. The warriors represent the last of the children that were born in this tribe. They cover an age gap of about 20 years, but they are all the same generation. You are so surprised that Pyra may not have been a virgin, but you yourself admitted that you are not a virgin either. I know that humans don't have the same bonding instinct as the Denynso, but it should at least have told you that there was a possibility that they could have sex outside of their bonding experiences with their mates."

"I just didn't realize that the Denynso could have relationships with anyone other than their mates. I thought that was the whole point. That the mates are so precious because they are the only other person in the world that would be able to have a relationship with them."

"That's the point that I've been trying to make. I said that they could have sex with other people before they found their mates, not that they could have relationships with them. They can't. It is not in the nature of the Denynso to be able to have an emotional connection other than friendship with anyone other than their mates. It simply cannot be done. We know that that is not the same way with humans. In fact, many humans on Earth go through several life bonds isn't that correct?"

"We don't call them life bonds, we call them marriages, but I suppose you're correct."

Eden was starting to sound upset, even angry, and that

mean that Zsilvia was getting to her, which is exactly what she was trying to do.

"The point is that humans can have emotional connections with multiple people, even fall in love several times in their lives. That means that they can have sex with people other than their life partners and it can be loving and nurturing. Denynso are not like that. The bond that they have with their mates is something unique and precious that they can only experience that one time in their entire lives. The sexual urges that they have before that bond are purely personal and selfish. It is not about connecting in any way with the other person, and has nothing to do with giving any sort of pleasure to the other person, which means they like to engage in it in the way that they engage in all of the activities that they love."

"And there is nothing that a Denynso warrior likes better than going into battle," Eden said softly as if things were starting to make sense to her.

Zsilvia nodded, catching Eden's orange gaze and holding it so that the woman would process would she had told her.

"I was one of the women that would go along with the desires of the men because I wanted their attention. My first experience was horrible, but for some reason I kept doing it with the other warriors whenever they decided that I was what interested them, what would appease them in that particular moment. I know that it doesn't make any sense and I can't explain it to you. All I can say is that there was something about their attention, no matter how violent and aggressive they were, that validated me. One night the warrior who was the leader before Pyra approached me. I felt like it was quite an honor to have him want me, considering how important he was."

"Even though you knew that he wasn't after anything from you but sex?"

"Yes. I told you, I can't explain it. Looking back, I can't understand how I could be so blind as to put myself not only in that situation, but willingly and openly in that situation. I offered myself into it. Now the warriors are not as reckless and demanding of women as they once were. To be completely honest, it is possible that Pyra was a virgin when he met you. I don't know that for sure, but the way that the men are now, most of them don't interact with the women at all until they find a mate. They put everything into their battle. If they do decide that they are going to have sex with a woman who isn't their mate, they aren't kind to her, but they are at least respectful of her ability to dictate when and how it happens. That wasn't what it was like then."

"But I thought you said that you went with the warrior willingly."

"I did, but after the first two times on the same night, I was finished. I didn't want to be a part of the experience any longer and I wanted to get as far away from him as I possibly could. He didn't think that it was a good plan for the evening, however, and made it very clear to me that he was going to do whatever he wanted for as long as he wanted to do it. By the time that he was finished, I didn't think that I was going to survive. To be completely honest, I hoped I wouldn't. It was seriously that horrible."

"I'm so sorry that happened to you, Zsilvia, but I don't understand what that has to do with why you can't be with George if you believe that he's you're mate.

"I don't just believe that he's my mate. I know for absolute certain that he is. That doesn't change that I'm terrified to get anywhere near him."

"It wouldn't be like that with George, though. He's not a Denynso. He's a human."

"That's exactly my point, though. You questioned that I would have sex with someone who I knew was only after me for that purpose and absolutely no other. It horrified you to think that I would allow myself to be used that much. George is a human, which means that he doesn't have the concept of bonding, yet he was willing to go right ahead and have sex with me within just a couple of hours of meeting me. He hadn't even had the chance to have an entire conversation with me, which means that he was only after me for the sexual fulfillment of it, just like the warriors were."

"That's not true. The reason he wanted to have sex with you immediately could have been that he was as overwhelmed by his feelings for you, the same as your feelings for him and he just couldn't contain himself."

"How can you be so sure about that?"

"Because I was in his position when I came here," Eden said sternly and Zsilvia felt herself close her mouth sharply, cutting off the words that had been trying to make their way out, "I was a human who knew nothing about the Denynso or their mating habits. I didn't know anything about the idea of bonding, much less that I would discover my mate here within just a few minutes of landing on the planet, and that the same day I would bond with him. If someone had told me that before the shuttle took off when I was still on Earth, I would have told them that they were crazy."

"But you admit that you didn't like Pyra when you first met him."

"No, I didn't. Not at all. In fact, I couldn't stand him. That didn't matter, however, when we had our first kiss. No matter what type of emotions I was going through right then, I felt a draw toward him that I had never felt toward anyone, and it was like I absolutely had to have him right then. I didn't care that I didn't think that we would ever get along, or that I thought it was ridiculous and even a little bit offensive that Creia and Theia thought it was necessary to give me a Denynso babysitter to watch over me while I got used to being here, or even that I didn't think that I was going to be on Uoria for more than just a few months. None of that mattered to me at all. All I cared about was how much I felt like I needed to be with him."

"He could treat me the same way that the warriors did when I was younger."

"I can tell you from experience that the majority of human men aren't like that. There are plenty that aren't very nice and that are extremely disrespectful toward women, don't get me wrong. If you ever feel like you need to get everything that happened to you off your chest to someone who knows what you are going through, I suggest you have a talk with Leia. She knows what you went through. They aren't out for sport, though. If George had been interested in nothing from you but sex, he wouldn't still be paying attention to you like he is."

"He pays attention to me?"

The words were both startling and thrilling to Zsilvia. She had been trying so hard to not let anyone else notice what she was feeling when it came to George, but it hadn't occurred to her that any of them might notice that there was something going on with him.

"I've seen the way he looks at you. Even when you are standing as far away from us as you can get and not saying anything to us, he does everything he can to move closer to you or to sneak glances your way. It's obvious that he's thinking about you."

4

———

"Look at this."

Lynx touched the loose bit of the desk that he had discovered again. He pushed harder into it and wiggled it slightly to test just how loose it actually was. Pyra approached him from across the dark office.

"What did you find?"

"I'm not sure," Lynx said, managing to move the piece of wood lose enough that he could stick the top of his blade into it and start to pry it away from the desk.

It suddenly gave a creak and the rest of the seam seemed to open on its own as if his movements had released something. He moved his hands along the piece and pulled with both of them, revealing that the loose piece had actually be a long, narrow drawer that had been sitting in place in the desk for so long while the people of the settlement were locked by the Covra that it had sealed itself.

The bottom of the drawer looked slightly wrinkled as if the lining had shrunk over time, and Lynx tucked the tips of his fingers under the edge of the thick, fragile-feeling paper to lift it away. As he tried to move it, though, the discolored paper crumbled in his hands. He suddenly felt the urge to pull his hands back to prevent the dust of the aged paper from touching his skin. It was a completely outlandish reaction and one that didn't make any sense, but he was unnerved by the drawer and the sudden catastrophic destruction of the paper.

"What is that?" Pyra asked.

"The lining of the drawer just fell apart," Lynx replied, shaking his hand to dislodge some of the paper dust that had gotten onto his skin.

"No, not that," Pyra said, stepping closer so that he nearly pushed the smaller, younger warrior out of the way, "There's something under the lining. It's like the people were hiding it with the lining."

The leader of the warriors took either side of the drawer and pulled it the entire way out of the desk. The people of the settlement would not have had the ability to hold the drawer like that, but Pyra's tremendous arm length and massive strength made it possible for him to pull the drawer out of its place and tip it over so that the rest of the crumbled paper fell out of the way and onto the top of the desk. Lynx had the same shuddering reaction to it lying there that he did when it fell apart in his touch, but he still couldn't understand why.

Pyra leaned over the desk and Lynx leaned with him, staring at the basic black ink drawing on another thick piece of paper on the very bottom of the drawer. This paper seemed far newer and in sturdier condition than the paper that had topped it, as if the lining of the drawer had protected this paper from the influences of the environment and kept them from negatively impacting the drawing.

Lynx had been staring at the drawing for a few seconds before he even realized what he was looking at on the bottom of the drawer. The black lines, strange symbols, and boldly shaded areas were a map. Once he figured it out, the boundaries and symbols were completely clear to him, but when he first looked at it, it was as if his mind couldn't process what he was seeing. The Denynso had never even thought of a map of Uoria. It was not something that they felt that they needed, and not something that they could create anyway because they had never been into the other areas of the planet.

Getting one from another species was nothing that they could ever have fathomed happening before now. The Denynso ancestors built the compound on what their ancestors believed to be the most beautiful and useful part of the land on Uoria, and everyone after just stayed put. They didn't interact with the other species that Lynx was now convinced inhabited the rest of the planet. The only species they had encountered were those that wanted to take over their beautiful compound, or try to show their dominance and attempt to subdue the mighty Denynso, and came to wage war with them.

They assumed that the other species that were on the planet must operate in the same way that the Denynso did in terms of cooperating with others that were not like them. Though there were plenty of the Denynso who were extremely excited about the prospect of cooperating with humans from Earth and even starting to build a relationship that would allow both species to learn from and protect the other, there were others who believed that they should remain as they always did, kind to others, welcoming to few, and completely separate. They didn't want the warriors to find any other species or to start creating plans to cooperate with them as they were with the humans from the university. They felt that their kind had always been separate from others and that was the way it should remain.

"There is another kingdom marked on here. It isn't too far away," Pyra said.

"What do these marks mean?" Lynx said, pointing to a series of lines beside the name of the kingdom.

Pyra looked at them for a few seconds and then his eyes drifted down to the bottom of the page. He pointed to a square that had been drawn several inches away from the rest of the map and that contained not only that symbol but a few others as well. Beside them were words.

"I think that this is a key to the symbols used on the map," he said, "According to this, that symbol means that the two kingdoms maintained good relations."

"Do you think that it is possible that the other kingdom is still around?" Lynx asked.

The two men looked at each other, their gazes exchanging the idea that both of them were forming at the same moment. Pyra dug his fingers beneath the corner of the hidden map and loosened it from the position where it had sat for the decades since the Covra had locked the settlement and everyone inside it. Lynx watched while his leader worked on the map carefully, loosening it gradually by moving his fingers around the edge until he was finally able to release it from its position. Fortunately it did not crumble the way that the lining had and he was able to take it out of the drawer completely intact before gingerly rolling it up so that he could carry it more easily.

Without exchanging any more words, the two warriors rushed out of the office in the ornate building that they assumed by its design and the items that they found inside had some government purpose for the people in the settlement and toward the home that they had made their headquarters. Though they had only gotten the opportunity to explore that one office in that particular building, they had been going through all of the other buildings in the settlement for days trying to find anything that they could to help them. Now that they had the map, Lynx felt like they might have made progress that would help them achieve this incredible feat that they had set out for themselves but that had begun to feel as though it were slipping further and further away.

Pyra and Lynx burst through the door to the house where Rain lived and stalked into the living room. Only a few of the warriors were there, poring over papers and other items that they had found in some of the other buildings. Lynx watched them, suddenly feeling nervous about what they may discover in those papers. If he had been able to find out that Rain and the others in the settlement were human just by taking a glance at the back of a photograph that she had sitting on the table beside her bed, how long would it take for one of them to find something in those papers that would tell them? And when they did find out, how would they react?

"Where are the others?" Pyra demanded.

All of the men sitting around the room looked up at him, their expressions telling them that they hadn't even noticed the two of them come into the house.

"They are still out exploring."

"Go find them. All of them. Bring them back here immediately."

Ciyrs, Vax, and another warrior complied, rushing out of the house and leaving their papers spread across the table. Lynx approached the papers, letting his eyes scan over the words on them as quickly as he could so that he could determine what they were. The ones those three men had been looking through seemed to be forms that the people of the settlement filled out on a daily basis. They were like journal entries, but lacking the depth and emotion of freeform versions. Instead, they contained a series of questions and blocks for the answers, giving the people just enough space to offer a few words about each of the inquiries.

What is the day? What is the weather? How are you feeling? What are your tasks for the day? How has the mission changed since yesterday? What must you accomplish by tomorrow? Do you have any new information?

Reading through the answers gave Lynx a slightly uneasy feeling, as if he was at once looking into the past and listening to the voices of the people that were locked in the settlement telling him in that moment about what they experienced in the days and months leading up to the catastrophic event that kept them frozen in between heartbeats, unchanged and unmoving, for longer than Lynx had even been alive. Before he could look any further at any of the other papers, the rest of the warriors streamed back into their house.

As soon as they settled around the room, Pyra unrolled the map and displayed it to the men.

"Lynx and I discovered this while we were exploring an office in the large building at the center of the main street. It is a map of Uoria at the time when the settlement was active and has markings for other kingdoms that they maintained good relationships with during that time. For some reason it was hidden at the bottom of a drawer under a lining."

"Probably to protect it from the Covra," Vax said, "The Light Ones probably wouldn't want for their greatest enemy to find a map that would tell them the people that they were cooperating with and that they would rely on in serious times. It would only put both of them at greater risk."

Pyra nodded.

"It shows that there is another kingdom relatively close by that they were friendly with. If that kingdom is still there, there is a chance that they might have information about the Light Ones that could help us understand them better and might give us some insight into how to unlock them."

"Do you think that we should go there?" Ty asked.

"Not all of us. If there are still Covra around and they are just hesitating coming here because of the wall, us leaving could take that away. Loralia said that the only way that that wall of spikes would stay there is if we fully and completely believed that it was there. If we leave the settlement, that belief might disappear," Lynx said, "and even if it doesn't, if we aren't here anymore, the wall isn't dangerous. As long as the Covra can see it, they know not to run into it."

"Lynx is right," Pyra said, "if we all leave, the Covra will know that the kingdom is vulnerable. If there are any adults left, they'll come back and they might not be so willing to let the Light Ones live any longer. Some of us have to stay behind and keep protecting the settlement and the people here. The rest will go on to the other kingdom and see if there is anything to find out."

"Who should go and who should stay?" Ciyrs asked.

"Does anybody have any opinions one way or the other?" Pyra asked.

"I'm going to stay here," Lynx said, "I don't want to be away from Rain. It's not that I don't trust all of you, it's just that she is my responsibility and I want to be here for her."

"That's fine," Pyra said, "Anyone else?"

"I should go," Ciyrs said, "As we found out with this settlement, we never know what we're going to find wandering around Uoria, and I should be with the ones who are going into the even more unknown areas so that I can help if there is another problem."

Pyra nodded and one by one the other men made their decisions about which of the tasks they would take on, whether they would stay in the settlement with the Light Ones and protect them while continuing to try to solve the issue of their locking, or step back out of the settlement and venture into the further reaches of what was turning out to be a much stranger and more hostile planet than they had imagined. When they had divided up, Pyra looked at Lynx.

"While we're gone, Lynx is going to act as leader for this group," he said sternly, looking at each of the men who had decided to stay in the settlement, "He has the most stake in all of this and he's going to be the one that will know best what to do to protect the Light Ones. I don't know how long we're going to be gone, but no matter how long it is, Lynx acts in my stead. You treat him with the same respect as you would treat me, and you do what he tells you to do."

The other men agreed and Lynx felt his chest tighten with emotion. It was an incredible honor, something that he never would have imagined he would have been given. Pyra had been born to be the leader of the Denynso warriors and had taken on the role when he was still quite young. Offering even the smallest amount of that responsibility and honor to another of the warriors was something that never happened, and the fact that he had chosen Lynx out of all of the men was extraordinary. Lynx was younger and less experienced than many of the other warriors, which meant that Pyra was showing even more trust in him and was relying on him even more than he would be had he chosen any other man to take on that role.

"When are we leaving?"

"As soon as possible. The longer we wait, the more

chance there is that we won't be able to find any useful information in time to help the Light Ones. Everyone who is going with me, gather everything that you might need and after lunch we will head on our way."

The men dispersed, heading to the other houses where they had taken up residence so that they could gather their supplies and prepare for what could be another arduous journey ahead of them. Though they had a map that showed them the way as they had with the settlement, it didn't point out any potential dangers that may exist between the settlement of the Light Ones and the kingdom where they were headed.

"While we're gone, I want you to do everything that you can think of to figure out how to unlock them. You are the one who is in charge now, so you tell the other men what you want them to do and they'll do it for you," Pyra said, clapping one of his massive hands down on Lynx's shoulder.

"Thank you, Pyra," Lynx said, "It really means a lot to me that you are trusting me so much."

Pyra gave a nod and started upstairs to the room he had chosen. He, along with Ty, Vax, and Ciyrs, had been staying in this house with Lynx and Rain. Lynx suddenly realized that the four of them would all be gone, leaving him completely alone with Rain. It was an odd feeling that bordered somewhere between being excited that he was going to get the opportunity to spend some time with her without the other men being in the house, and worry that every moment that he was out of that house she was going to be totally vulnerable. He considered asking one of the other men who were staying behind to come move into the house with him, but he changed his mind. Keeping Rain safe was his lifelong responsibility and he was not going to be able to rely on others to help him all the time, no matter how worried he was about her. He wondered if Pyra felt the same way about Eden, or the others felt the same way about their mates. Maybe that was what made them seem so strong when they finally found their mates. It wasn't really that they weren't that strong on their own, but that the constant worry about their mates forced them to be stronger so that the fear would not overcome them.

Zsilvia heard George call her name and for a moment she wondered if she had imagined it. The sudden change of the expression on Eden's face, however, told her that she hadn't. The smaller woman gave her a meaningful look as if imploring her to remember what she had said about George and the potential for his feelings for her, and then turned around with an enormous forced smile.

"There you are!" Eden exclaimed, "Zsilvia has been waiting for you. She thought that you had slipped out and she came out here to look for you, but she couldn't find you so I've been standing here with her chatting. You know how women are."

George looked at her quizzically and then at Zsilvia, who was startled and somewhat put off by Eden's sudden false bubbliness.

"I was inside Ciyrs' shop talking to Zuri. I thought you saw me."

Zsilvia shrugged.

"I guess I was seeing things. Did you two talk about anything interesting?"

She was trying to sound casual, not allowing the emotion that had already begun coursing through her to come through in her voice. Eden was looking between the two of them, her hands cupped around her belly and the smile on her face static as if she couldn't release the muscles enough to make the expression fade now that she had managed to force it into place. Suddenly she seemed to notice the other two looking at her out of the corners of their eyes and the smile finally broke.

"Oh!" she said, glancing back toward the glow of the shop where Zuri had just stepped out of the door, "Now that you've found him, I'm just going to go. I have to talk to Zuri about something."

She rushed away with as much speed as she could muster and Zsilvia returned her gaze to George. His eyes smoldered into hers and she felt her body getting hot. Her heartbeat increased and she felt like she was having trouble keeping her breath even.

"Are you ready to go home?" she asked.

"Sure."

They walked along together and Eden's words repeated themselves through Zsilvia's mind with each step. She wanted to believe them and to open herself enough to give George a chance, but she was struggling even to stand near him without feeling the almost painful internal tug of both wanting desperately to be with him and being frightened enough to want to run. It was as though there were two of her existing within her body and they were trapped in an ongoing fight. One of them was ready to move forward and step into an existence controlled by the moment that she was living and not what lurked behind her eyelids every time she closed her eyes. The other was still very much living in that dark, unsafe world and could not break free of her own imminent existence.

"Blood flow," George said.

"What?" Zsilvia asked, turning toward him to give him a strange look.

"Blood flow. That's what Zuri and I were talking about. You asked if we were talking about anything interesting and that's what we were talking about."

Zsilvia gave a short laugh and nodded, turning back to the road in front of them.

"Oh," she said, "What about blood flow?"

"We were thinking about these locked people and how they haven't moved or breathed or done anything since the Covra froze them in place. That got us thinking about their hearts. If their hearts aren't beating, then the blood isn't flowing through their bodies."

"So? Maybe their hearts stopped at the same time as the rest of their bodies and the blood just kind of settled where it was."

Zsilvia watched George shake his head insistently.

"No. If the blood had just stopped while it was still going through their veins, it would have pooled at the bottoms of their limbs like it does with a corpse. There would be dark discoloration along the bottoms of their arms and in their legs, and even some swelling." He shook his head again, his eyes fixed on the road in front of him as though he could see what he was talking about hovering in the air above the road. "No. The men would have mentioned something like that and they didn't. That means that it isn't just their hearts that stopped, it's everything. Their blood locked, too."

"What does that mean, though?"

"We think that perhaps if we can get their blood flowing again, it would unlock their entire bodies."

"That's amazing," Zsilvia told him, stunned that they would come up with something that complex, "Do you have any idea how you would be able to do that?"

"Not yet. Since the Denynso don't use the same technology as the people of Earth we can't use the same things that we would use there, so Zuri, Samira, and I are trying to come up with alternative ways to use the same basic principles but with the resources available to us here."

"What about Eden?"

"Her scientific background is mostly plants and animal life. She is going through some of her notes and researching as much as she can to see if there may be anything that she can think of that is applicable. She did mention that there are several animals and bugs on Earth that she has researched that use a very similar attack method to immobilize their prey before eating them. The difference, though, is that the victims of those creatures maintain their brainwaves and heartbeat while in their locked state."

They had arrived at George's cabin and Zsilvia stopped. There was a tense moment as they looked at each other, their eyes melding with such intensity it was as if the rest of the world around them had completely faded away. Zsilvia felt herself falling into George again, her heart, mind, and body magnetizing to him so that she felt like she couldn't step away. He stepped slightly closer to her and their breath lingered, blending between them and tracing down her body. His fingers lifted and she felt them gently stroke down the side of her face. It was a tender, cautious touch, yet it made her body shiver.

George stepped forward again until the heat radiating off of both of their bodies grew. He leaned toward her slightly, brushing his lips against hers. She had seen him beautifully bare and held his tempting erection in her hand, yet that kiss, the first that he had given her, took her breath away. He lifted his mouth away from hers just slightly and their eyes opened so that they looked at each other. His seemed to search hers, gauging her reaction to his touch. When she didn't move away from him, he placed his hands on her hips and held her steady while he dipped his head to kiss her again.

This time he kissed her with greater intensity, his mouth pressing down into hers and his tongue touching the inside of her lips to coax them open. The taste of him touched her tongue and made her even hungrier for him, but the pressure of his fingers on her hips made her hesitate. As she pulled back, the pressure released, but his mouth didn't move from hers. Zsilvia relaxed into the kiss, allowing the need for him to take over the thoughts that were flooding her mind.

When the kiss ended, George moved his lips from hers to her ear.

"Can I see you tomorrow?" he whispered.

His breath felt hot against her neck and her body clenched in response as if searching for him.

"Yes," she said.

Though she had expected him to ask her to come inside with him then, there was something in the question that was even more thrilling and she felt breathless answering him.

"Good," he replied.

He kissed her a final time and then walked into the house, wishing her goodnight just before closing the door. Zsilvia walked home with a smile on her lips that was unlike anything she had experienced in as long as she could remember. She couldn't wait until the next day when she could see George again. Perhaps if she fought herself hard enough, she would finally get through the horrible thoughts and be able to enjoy the mate she thought she would never have the opportunity to have.

6

———————

Zsilvia sat in the bath letting the warm water soothe her. She had coiled her hair on top of her head but the tendrils that hung around her neck curled with the steam rising off of the surface of the bath. She filled her palms with lavender soap and stroked them over her body. The feeling made her think of George and she let her eyes drift closed as she imagined that the touch was coming from his hands. The herbal smell coming from the soap only seemed to intensify the desire that built low in her belly as she thought of him and she took a deeper breath to draw it in.

Her hand drifted lower on her body and she let it sweep over her hipbones. Cupping one hand over her breast, she let the other slip lower so that it dipped between her thighs and into her folds. The sensation made her back arch and her lips part as it drew a gasp from deep in her lungs. Images of George formed behind her eyes and she focused on him, remembering him peeling away his shirt and releasing the button on his pants to allow her to touch him.

The thoughts of him moved to the way that he kissed her, his lips brushing hers tenderly. She imagined that same sensation moving along her body, tracing a trail down her neck and onto her chest.

Letting the thoughts of George's mouth guide her, Zsilvia let her fingers play along her nipples, imagining him take them between his lips and teasing them with his tongue. As her hand continued to stroke between her thighs, venturing upward to focus on the hypersensitive pearl of flesh at the top, she thought of him touching her, exploring her body the way that she had his. She thought of the coarse hair on his chest, imagining what it would feel like pressed against the bare skin of her naked body, rubbing against her as his body moved over hers.

Suddenly Zsilvia's body contracted and she cried out against the force of the climax that tore through her. The washes rushed over her, the spasms making her wish even more that he was buried inside her so that he could feel her body responding so intensely to him. Finally it eased and she relaxed down into the water, allowing it to calm her.

THE NEXT DAY Zsilvia walked to George's house, the smile on her face was soft and secretive, hiding the satisfaction still coursing through her. She longed for the first moment of seeing him, and when he stepped out of the house she saw he held a similar smile. Even if she imagined that smile, the thought made her tremble and she had to struggle to control herself.

"Are we still on for tonight after we leave Ciyrs'?" he asked, stepping forward to wrap his arms around her waist.

"Absolutely," she said.

George kissed the tip of her nose and they started

together toward the shop. As soon as they got to the corner of the road in front of the shop, however, they saw the other women coming out. Zuri was in front, the look on her face drawn and tense.

"Is something wrong?" George asked, starting to jog toward them.

"Creia said that he just got communication from another shuttle saying they will be arriving in a few minutes."

"Another shuttle?" Zsilvia asked, "Did you know that there was someone else coming?"

"No," Zuri answered, "and neither did Creia. He doesn't seem too happy about it, but he says that it is an official university shuttle so he is going to allow it to land and he will figure out what to do from there. He wants us to be there when the shuttle arrives, though."

George and Zsilvia joined the women and they rushed toward the front of the compound. The shuttle had already landed by the time that they got to the landing platform, and there was a sense of tension and nervousness among the group as they stared at the door waiting for it to open so that they could see who may be arriving unexpectedly. Finally the door hissed and slid out of the way. The captain stepped out followed by the flight attendant. A moment later a woman appeared at the door and out of the corner of her eye Zsilvia saw a broad smile break across George's face. He stepped away from her and rushed up the steps onto the platform to the woman.

"Ivy!" he cried happily, "I didn't think you were going to be able to come!"

The slim blond woman grinned at George and leapt into his arms, giving him a tight hug.

"I know!" she exclaimed, "I didn't think that I would be

able to, either, but I moved some stuff around and hopped on the next shuttle that was available."

George stepped back and took both of Ivy's hands in his. Zsilvia's heart felt like it was shattering. She watched him stare into the young woman's face, the smile on his face only seeming to get bigger with each passing moment. Who was this woman and why did he seem so excited to see her? Was it possible that it was wife? She hadn't seen a wedding band on his hand and he hadn't mentioned a woman in his life on Earth, but she knew from stories she had heard that that didn't always mean that there wasn't a woman around, just that the man was choosing not to mention it.

She sank back into the back of the group. She didn't want to see any more. Not caring any longer who might notice, she turned and ran away from the loading platform toward the meeting hall. She needed to get away from every-thing that was happening. More than that, she needed to get to Creia before the group of women and George did. They would arrive for the traditional greeting for the woman who he called Ivy and Zsilvia wanted the opportunity to talk with him first so that she could request to be removed from her position as his guard and protector.

"Absolutely not, Zsilvia."

Her heart sank even lower than she could have imagined and she took an imploring step toward the king.

"Please, sir. I don't think I can handle any more of this responsibility, especially with this new arrival. It seems that George and this woman know each other quite well and I do not want to be put into the position of guarding both of them."

"This woman's sudden and unexpected appearance is

even more reason why I need you to remain in your position," Creia said, "All of us need to be vigilant now and aware of any potential threats. Though the shuttle is from the university and they tell me that she was originally scheduled to come with George, I do not want to take any chances. You will remain in your position, and I will assign one of the others to this new woman."

"Yes, sir."

Zsilvia felt completely defeated. She didn't know how she was going to overcome this. The thought of not only having to continue to be around George was difficult enough, but having to be around him while also having to watch him with that woman was more than she could bear. She was just stepping back away from the platform when the group walked through the door. They were talking animatedly, but the sound of Creia's booming voice silenced them instantly.

"Please approach the platform."

Ivy walked toward them and Zsilvia felt even more of a pang within her. The woman was young and incredibly beautiful. Her hair was not bright and yellowish like Zuri's. It was paler and shimmery as it stretched nearly to her narrow waist. Though she was taller than the other human women except for Zuri and Samira, she was very delicate looking. Small, precise features, pale eyes, and long, slim limbs made her look fragile but in a precious, treasured way rather than with a sickly or damaged hint like Leia and Elianna had when they first encountered them.

"Hello. I'm Ivy," she said brightly.

Creia's face did not change. Instead, he leaned slightly forward toward her, his eyes evaluating her for several long seconds.

"Why are you here?" he asked.

"I'm here to be part of the exchange program with the university," she said, sounding slightly confused, "I am George's research assistant."

A bit of relief moved through her, but Zsilvia wouldn't let herself feel completely at ease about George again. Her being his research assistant did not excuse the friendly greeting or the way that she had smiled at him. Eden spoke of being a research assistant as well and that had always come with suggestions and indecent proposals that were never fulfilled because of the disdain she felt for the researcher who eventually became her boss as she moved up through the ranks within the company. Perhaps the same kinds of feelings existed for George and instead of rejecting them, Ivy had returned them. This wasn't something she was likely to share with the king within the first few seconds of meeting him.

"I was not aware that you were coming until the captain contacted me to let me know that you were about to land. I do not appreciate being in the dark about these things. It is my job to protect and control this compound and when I am left unaware of what is happening, I am not able to do that properly."

"I'm sorry," Ivy said, her voice sounding confused and slightly hurt.

"If I may, sir," George said, stepping forward toward the king.

"Yes?" the king said, looking up at him.

"When I was selected to be a part of this program, I asked that Ivy come along with me. She has been my assistant for several years now and she knows how I work. I knew that having her here would make the process of getting my research done as well as teaching whatever classes I would have the opportunity to teach much easier and more efficient. Prior arrangements, however, made it so that she was unable to come along with me on my voyage here. I had expressed my regret about that and it seems that when her schedule opened, Ivy made the decision to join me here."

"I assumed that because there was an available shuttle and I was supposed to come with him in the first place that it wouldn't cause a problem."

Creia seemed unmoved.

"I should have been informed of this decision before you left the university. The compound is at a tense and vulnerable state right now and it is not acceptable for us to have situations like this occur because someone chooses not to communicate professionally."

Ivy hung her head and Zsilvia fought off the urge to feel slightly satisfied.

"I apologize, sir," George said, "I take full responsibility for this situation. I should have been clearer with her about my instructions."

Creia looked at George and his expression softened just slightly.

"I appreciate your nobility," the king said, "and I understand how important professional relationships such as this one can be to the success of a project. If you are willing to vouch for her, I will allow her to stay, but only with the understanding that she is to do nothing and go nowhere without express permission." He turned his attention back to Ivy, "Zuri will be responsible for you. You are to go nowhere without her, and do nothing that she does not explain to you."

"Thank you," Ivy said softly.

As the group turned to walk out of the meeting hall, George tried to catch Zsilvia's eye, but she looked away. She might not have been permitted to leave her role as his guard and protector, but that did not mean that she had to be alone with him or make any personal connection with him until the time came that she was able to get out of those responsibilities.

7

———

"**I**s there anything else that you can tell me about her?"

Ero was sitting across the bedroom from Rain, Zuri's field notebook balanced on his lap as he jotted down everything that Lynx told him about the woman. Lynx glanced over at Rain and patted her leg through the blanket. He had come to know that if he touched her through the blanket he was able to have contact with her without it immediately flashing him to the last moments of her wakefulness. He thought through everything he knew about her, including the fact that she was human. He hadn't shared that with Ero and he was still struggling with whether he should. For some reason he was still having a difficult time divulging that bit of information to him. He couldn't explain it, but he was still compelled to hold that detail about her inside himself and not share it.

"Lynx?" Ero asked, breaking him out of his thoughts, "Is there anything else that you can tell me about her? Anything that might help us understand her better?"

Lynx thought for another long second. Finally he stood

and closed the bedroom door. He took a breath and met Ero's eyes.

"You can't tell anybody else what I'm about to tell you. No one. Not until Pyra comes back."

"Alright."

Lynx looked over at Rain. He rested his hand on her leg protectively and then looked back at Ero.

"She's human," he said.

He felt like he had to force the words out of his body and as they came out he knew that he was not going to be able to take them back. Ero looked shocked and he turned his gaze from Lynx to Rain.

"Human?" he asked.

"Yeah. I found out the first time I saw her." He reached into his bag and took out the picture of her that he carried around with him, "Look at the back."

Ero read the inscription that had told Lynx that Rain, and presumably everyone else in the settlement, had been from Earth. His eyes were wide when they lifted back to Lynx.

"I thought that humans had never made contact with Uoria before the first came to the compound."

"I did, too."

"Why didn't you tell anybody about this?"

Ero's tone was accusatory and Lynx snatched the picture back from his hand, holding it protectively and looking into the image of Rain's face when she was awake and smiling.

"Do you see how you're reacting to finding out? And your mate is human. Imagine how some of the warriors who don't think that the Denynso should have any contact with humans at all would react to finding out that there has been a settlement of humans on the planet for more than a century without anyone knowing. I was afraid that if I told anyone, no one would want to help me save them anymore."

"Knowing that they are human could make a difference, Lynx," Ero said, "There could be something about them that enabled the Covra to lock them for so long and keep them this way that is unique because they are human. We have to tell Ciyrs."

Lynx finally relented and nodded.

"I'll tell him when he gets back," he agreed, "Now would you mind leaving for a while? I want to have some time with her."

Ero hesitated and then nodded, standing up out of the chair and starting out of the room.

"You have to trust that the warriors will do what is right, Lynx."

"They'll do what they think is right for the Denynso and the compound. What if when they find out that the Light Ones are actually humans they decide that saving them is not what is right?"

Ero opened his mouth as if he had something to say, and then closed it again, stepping out of the room and closing the door behind him. Lynx sagged, putting his face in his hands. He felt like everything was closing in around him. He turned and lay down on the bed beside Rain, resting his head on the pillow beside her.

Gently moving the blanket aside, he rested his hand on her stomach. He felt the pull as the touch drew him into the last moments before the Covra locked her in place. It was something he had done many times before, the only way that he was able to see her moving and breathing. Though they were the same few seconds replayed time and time again, each time that he saw them he seemed to notice something a little different. He took time each venture into her thoughts to look around the room more or to listen more closely and see if there were any other details that he might catch. He was learning to control himself within the visions so that he could maneuver within the envisioned space and experience the things that he wanted to rather than just standing and watching helplessly as the gleaming black creature approached Rain's prone figure and buried the sharp tip of its leg into her belly.

The vision ended and Lynx took a breath before diving into it again. This time he controlled the stream of thought and forced himself to turn and look at the door to the bedroom. The Covra that attacked her had come from beneath her bed, but he had long thought that they were not the only ones in her house that evening. As he suspected, there was another of the creatures, this one larger and more gruesome-looking that the others, standing in the hallway, one of his pointed legs sticking just inside the door. He saw something that made his heart feel like it was going to stop.

Again the vision ended and Lynx shook his head, trying to clear it before he went back into the moments. He turned more quickly this time so that he was able to take a longer look at the Covra standing in the hallway. As he had seen the first time, there was something strange about the creature's front two legs. Rather than being smooth and black like the rest of his legs and like the legs on all of the other creatures, it seemed to be covered in translucent yellow orbs. They shivered slightly as if there was something inside them.

The next time that Lynx immersed himself in the vision he turned almost the instant that his mind materialized in Rain's room and he saw the Covra step in front of the door. Lynx turned sharply to look at the mirror and realized that

Rain couldn't see its reflection. He watched as a smaller Covra slipped in beneath the front legs of the first, pausing just long enough to touch the end of one of his legs to one of the yellow orbs attached to the front of the larger creature's leg before climbing under the bed so that it was poised to attack Rain when she laid down.

When the vision broke, Lynx was breathless. He stared down at Rain, his eyes fixed on the area of her belly that the Covra had impaled. Jumping off of the end of the bed, he ran out of the bedroom and down the stairs to the living room. Ero wasn't there. He rushed out of the house and down the street toward the house that Ero had chosen.

"Ero!" he called from the street, hoping that his voice would carry up into the house, "Ero?"

"What is it?" Ero asked, coming around the house from the backyard.

"I know why the Covra have been keeping the Light Ones alive."

He was frantic and his skin felt like it was burning. He couldn't control the breaths that were tearing jaggedly out of his lungs and his head was light.

"Calm down," Ero said, "What are you talking about?"

"Do you remember how Ciyrs said that he didn't understand why the Covra locked them for so long? Bannack told us that Loralia said her grandfather had told stories of the Covra locking their enemies, but they always killed them very soon after."

The words came out of him in a stream that he could barely understand himself and Ero stared at him as if he was having even more difficulty.

"I'm not following you."

"The Light Ones. They've been here for decades. Just sitting here doing nothing. And the Covra keep coming back, but they leave them here alive. Why? Why would they do that when they could just as easily kill them when they weren't awake?"

"Bannack said that they are weak when they get older and they lock enemies because they can't defeat them."

"Exactly. They are old and weak and waiting for the next generation to be born. Loralia even said that she could feel that there were more around and that they would soon be here to defeat the Light Ones. We've been operating this whole time on the concept that the Covra have just left them alive because they were holding a grudge and wanted to come back here and look at the people that they were holding prisoner. That's not it. They aren't here to check in on the people."

Lynx started around the house toward one of the people who was locked in the alley between it and the house beside it. It was a man who had been injected by the Covra in his back. Lynx pulled the man's shirt up and looked more closely at the area where the Covra's leg had pressed into his skin. Just as he expected it would, the area around the injury was slightly swollen and seemed to move beneath his fingers when he touched it.

"They don't care about the people. They defeated them a long time ago," he said to Ero, pointing out the area on his skin, "They knew the minute that they locked them in place that they would never wake up again, but not because of the lock. When they come back here, they aren't checking to make sure that the people are still locked or even to gloat about them being here. They are here to check on their children." He pressed into the man's skin again, causing the slightly swollen area to shift. "They are using the Light Ones as incubators."

UNTITLED

(To be continued in Part VII...)

THE ALIEN'S SUITOR

1

———

Lynx's heart felt like it was going to break through his ribs and burst through his chest. His mind spun, the thoughts rolling through it making him feel sick to his stomach as they grew and intensified in their horror.

"What do you mean the Light Ones are incubators?" Ero asked.

His voice was low and he was fighting to keep himself as calm as possible as he asked the question that was both terrifying and enlightening.

"The Covra are using them as incubators," Lynx said, "Remember how Loralia told Bannack that she could sense that they were waiting for the next generation to be born but that it would take a very long time for that to happen? She wasn't exaggerating. It takes decades. Whey they locked the people from the settlement they weren't just locking them to be cruel or to make sure that they were able to defeat them. They did it so that they would have a safe place to keep their eggs while the young inside developed."

Lynx thought back on the vision he had of how the

Covra had locked Rain. He has had that vision so many times before, but only in the last few days had he learned to control his ability to move within the space he was seeing. Instead of just being stuck in place and having to watch as the gruesome creatures emerged from under Rain's bed in order to impale her with the pointed end of one of their legs, freezing her in that calm moment as she slept, he had been able to look around the vision of her bedroom and see what else was happening in the space.

Looking around had allowed him to see the huge Covra step into place in the doorway. He couldn't understand why Rain didn't seem to see the reflection of the creature in the mirror of the vanity where she had been brushing her hair. The horror had not come when Lynx noticed that creature, however. Instead, it came when he saw that the front legs of the enormous Covra were not sleek and black like those of all of the other creatures. They were covered with perfectly spherical, translucent yellow orbs that seemed to have small forms moving around inside.

One of the smaller Covra had climbed through the legs of the larger one and gently pulled one of the orbs from the leg, absorbing it into his leg so that he could pass it into Rain's body along with the toxin that locked her into place. It had been sickening to watch, but at the same time it filled Lynx with a strange sense of relief when he thought back on it. Now that they understood why the Covra had decided to keep the people alive rather than just killing them immediately after locking them as they usually did with their enemies, they might have more of a chance of saving them.

"I don't understand," Ero said, "Why use the Light Ones as incubators? That can't possibly be the way that they always reproduce. They can't just lock entire settlements of people every time they are going to have a new generation, no matter how long it takes for their babies to be born."

Lynx shook his head.

"I don't know. I don't understand it either, but that's what's happening. All of the eggs of the new generation of the Covra are inside the Light Ones preparing to hatch. According to Loralia, that is going to be soon."

"Do you think that she might know why they would put their young inside another species to incubate them?"

Lynx thought for a moment. Loralia knew things that none of the Denynso ever had, and even though she had always been helpful and done so much to help their kind get through the adversities that they had faced recently, when it came to Rain and the rest of her people, Lynx had difficulty trusting anyone with her. The tremendous responsibility of releasing her from the binds that were keeping her in her peaceful yet brutal sleeping state rested on him, and he was going to do everything that he could possibly do to make sure that he was the one that would take care of her now and when she woke up.

"She said that she doesn't really remember all of the stories that her grandfather told her," Lynx said.

"But she remembered enough that she was able to help get rid of the Covra when they came into the settlement the other night, and that she was able to tell us that there were more coming, which is what helped you figure out that they were using these people to house their young until they are born. Don't you think that it's worth asking her?"

Lynx let out a long breath, trying to convince himself that what Ero was telling him was true. He had never felt so distrustful and unnerved in his life. It made him feel on edge and jumpy, ready to lash out against everyone that got near him. He knew that much of that feeling came from knowing that he was so close to his mate but not being able to bond with her.

"What's going on?"

Lynx looked up and saw Bannack approaching down the alley, his face stony with concern at finding the two warriors engaged in such heated conversation away from the rest of the group that had stayed behind in the settlement while Pyra and some of the others headed toward the nearby kingdom that had once been allies to the Light Ones.

Ero and Lynx exchanged glances. Lynx could see the message embedded in Ero's eyes and knew that he didn't have a choice in the matter any longer. He could exert the control and leadership that Pyra had given him when he left and refuse to tell Bannack what they were talking about, silencing Ero at the same time, but that could put his ability to help Rain in jeopardy. Ero pushed him again through the look in his eyes and Lynx turned to Bannack.

"Could you get in touch with Loralia for me?"

"Is everything alright?" Bannack asked, looking more worried.

"I need to ask her something about the Covra. I think I might have figured something out that could have an impact on the Light Ones, but I don't understand it completely and she might. Could you get in touch with her for me so that I can talk to her about it?"

Bannack nodded.

"Sure. Do you want to go inside?"

"We need to go up to Rain's room. There's something I'll need to show her."

He could see Bannack looking at him with confusion in his expression, but Lynx didn't bother to go any further into his explanation. He didn't think he had it in him to talk about the situation with Rain any more than he was already going to have to, so Bannack was just going to have to wait and hear it for himself when Lynx told Loralia what was going on and asked if she knew anything that might explain it.

The three warriors walked out of the alley and back to Rain's house. Once in her bedroom, Lynx positioned himself on the edge of the bed beside her and nodded at Bannack. Bannack took the heavy silver compact from around his neck and opened it, bending the long silver braid that acted as its chain so that it reflected in the top mirror. Within a few seconds the surface of the mirror seemed to swirl and cover over with light grey smoke before Loralia's face appeared.

"Bannack?" she said, "Are you OK?"

Lynx saw the softness in Bannack's eyes and again felt a pang for Rain. He was feeling more and more afraid that he would never hear his intended mate say his name or have the opportunity to have that look in his own eyes when he spoke to her.

"I'm fine. Lynx says that he needs to talk to you."

Loralia nodded and Bannack handed the compact over to Lynx. He took it carefully in his hand, knowing that it had once belonged to Loralia's father and was a precious gift she had given Bannack as the warriors prepared to leave on their quest around Uoria.

"Hi, Lynx," Loralia said, "Is there something I can help you with?"

"Hi. What do know about the Covra's reproductive cycle?" Lynx asked, the words bursting out of him so quickly they almost sounded like one.

"What do you mean?"

"You said that they took a long time to reproduce. What else do you know?"

"That's really all I know, Lynx. The mothers lay eggs that take decades to develop. I know the older Covra get weaker the older they get, but that the young are extremely powerful even from birth. I can't tell you much more." She paused and Lynx could see her eyes narrow as if she was looking more closely at him. "What's going on?"

Lynx took a breath and told Loralia about the eggs and watching the Covra inject them into the Light Ones when they were locking them into place. He carefully pulled aside the blanket covering Rain's stomach and gingerly lifted the nightgown she wore. He was careful not to touch her directly as that would bring him into his vision of Rain's last few moments before getting frozen in place. His stomach turned slightly when he saw the remnants of the injury in her smooth, pale skin. Just like with the man in the alley, the area surrounding the injury was slightly swollen.

Lynx turned the mirror so that it reflected the injury to Loralia.

"Do you see how it is swollen?"

"Barely."

"That's the way it looks on all of them. When you touch the swollen place, it moves. I think it is because of the eggs. I don't understand why they would be using them as incubators, though. They have to have a way of keeping their eggs protected until they hatch that doesn't involve injecting them into another species."

"I have no idea, Lynx. I'm sure there is a reason, but I don't know."

Bannack took the compact from Lynx and looked into the mirror as Lynx tenderly covered Rain's stomach and pulled the blanket back into place.

"We need to figure out why they put the eggs inside the

Light Ones," Bannack said to Loralia, "Lynx thinks that it is really important to unlocking them."

"I know." There was a pause. "I think I have an idea. I will get back to you as soon as I can. Watch the Light Ones closely. Make sure that the injuries aren't changing and if they do, reach out to me immediately."

"What are you going to do?"

"I'm going to find out everything I can about the Covra."

2

Pyra's throat burned with thirst but he continued to force his feet forward. The sun beat down on him with greater intensity than he had ever felt, making him feel vulnerable and exposed as they walked across a vast open space that seemed home to nothing but shriveled, browned blades of grass. It was unlike anything that he had ever seen. Accustomed to the deep, lush forest, towering cliffs, and wide ponds that surrounded the Denynso compound, Pyra was unnerved by the seemingly endless space of nothingness. There was nothing that changed out the space in front of him or gave him and the men he led a reprieve from the intensely hot sun. When they had left the settlement, the air around them had been cool and soft, but now they had walked into air that nearly stung on his skin.

He felt like he was walking in place, not really going anywhere, but when he looked down, Pyra could see that his feet were indeed moving, pushing the parched ground back behind him like a golden ribbon disappearing behind him, proving that he was actually going forward.

"What if this kingdom isn't around anymore?" Gyyx

asked from behind him and Pyra glanced over his shoulder toward him.

"We have to keep looking," Pyra said.

He straightened his shoulders and headed forward at a slightly faster pace, hoping that his leadership would encourage the men who followed him to keep moving ahead. It felt like they had been walking for months, though he knew it had only been two days since they left the compound. The map indicated that the kingdom should be relatively close, but they had seen no indications of any life as they had walked, making Pyra wonder if the kingdom still existed. He hadn't said it to any of the men yet for fear of discouraging them and keeping them from continuing forward, but he was truly starting to worry that the reason that they had not seen any signs of another group anywhere near the settlement, was that over the decades during which the Light Ones had been locked, the other kingdom had either fallen to some other enemy, or simply dissipated and moved on as groups tend to do.

Pyra didn't want to even think about possibly not finding anything much less talk to the other men about it. The idea that they had gone through this long and exhausting walk to find nothing was disheartening enough. Even worse, however, was the thought of having to take the walk again to make it back to the settlement only to tell Lynx that the people who he had put so much trust and hope in to help him free his intended mate no longer existed. Pyra couldn't imagine the torment that Lynx was facing at that moment. Young and volatile, Lynx had been one of the most unpredictable warriors Pyra had ever encountered. He had less experience than many of the other warriors, but what he had done had been impressive and he always put everything that he had into the battles that he fought. It was this intensity and dedication that made Pyra feel confident when he left him in charge of the others that remained in the settlement, but that also made him feel sorry for him.

His mate Eden was Pyra's heart and soul. Everything that he did, he did with her and the child that she cradled within her on his mind. He had been incredibly lucky to bond with her very quickly after meeting her. Even though she didn't like him very much when she first arrived at the compound to do her research, and to say that they didn't get along would have been an understatement, the intensity of his desire for her had been overwhelming to the point of almost being painful. Just the thought of her had pushed him to the brink of losing all of his control and his body had ached with his need to bond with her. Their first time hadn't been exactly as he would have imagined it, but at least it had happened. He had had the opportunity to take her into his arms and form the connection that would last for the rest of their lives. Lynx didn't have that chance. All he could do was look at Rain and feel that soul-crushing draw to her that would make him feel like he couldn't breathe, like he couldn't function at all without her.

The thought of the pain that Lynx was going through and the strength that he had been showing as they tried to understand the Light Ones, what had happened to them, and what they could do to possibly wake them up so that he could live his life with her, pushed Pyra to move faster into the empty space in front of them. He couldn't give up. He couldn't go back to the settlement and face Lynx without knowing that he had done absolutely everything that he could do to find the kingdom and get the information he could to help him. Leading the Denynso warriors was more than just training them to fight and guiding them into battle. It was also about being the one person they could rely on to always stand by their sides and take care of them whenever they needed it.

They kept moving, their footsteps loud against the dry dirt, and their hard, labored breath seeming to echo around them even though there was nothing for the sound to bounce off of as it pushed out of their lungs and through their painful throats. Pyra didn't notice that the ground was rising until they crested the top of a hill and he felt his heart skip. In the valley spread beneath them was a tall gate leading into a cluster of buildings and curving, intricate roads. They had discovered the kingdom.

3

———

Loralia rushed back into Ciyrs' shop where the others were crowded around the counter where they had spent the majority of their time since they had first heard about the Covra and their vicious attack on the Light Ones. Books and papers covered nearly every inch of the surface of the counter and piled on top of one another. She could sense the ebb and flow of their thoughts and emotions as they corresponded with their breaths; it was tense in the room from the intensity of their concentration. The moments ticked past, each unique and singular as they lived them, and she felt a painful tightening in her chest as she thought of how the men had described the Light Ones and the way that the Covra had stopped them in the span of less than a breath, less than a heartbeat.

What would it be like to be locked that way and then be lost for decades? What would the people who discovered them think of their lives and who they were should any one of those moments be their last? If any of these moments were crystallized as the final indication of their existence, would the people who found them years later understand them, or even have any idea of who they were? The thought made her heart hurt for the people of the settlement. Though the men were doing all that they could to understand them, to find out everything that they could about them, and to save them, what they could really know about them was so limited. They could only take what they could find and then assume the rest based on the exact moment where they had found each individual. It was as if those people were still lost. The men had found their forms and were gradually piecing together their existences, but their lives and their identities were still deeply hidden. She could only hope that if they could find out how to unlock them, they would be able to continue as they had been and live the lives that were intended for them.

The look on her face must have expressed the turmoil of emotions she was feeling because as soon as the door closed behind Loralia, Leia turned away from the counter to look at her and then came walking toward her.

"Loralia? Is everything alright?"

"I don't know," Loralia said, still gripping the silver compact, "Things have gotten more complicated at the settlement and I think that there is a way that we can help the men solve it, but I will need all of you."

Leia nodded, placing a comforting hand on Loralia's back.

"Of course. What do you need?"

"We need to go back to the prison."

As soon as she said that, Leia took a step back from Loralia, recoiling from her as if struck. Her eyes were wide with terror and tears already sparkled in them. Loralia knew exactly why she was reacting like that and took a step toward her, reaching out to offer her comfort now.

"I know," Loralia said, "I know that this is hard for you,

Leia, and if you can't go back there, I understand, but I need as much help as I can possibly get. Lynx just discovered that the Covra are using the people of the settlement as incubators for their young, but he doesn't know why. They found out about the settlement and the people locked there from papers that they found in the prison. There might be more there that they didn't find but that could explain why they put their eggs inside the Light Ones, and maybe even what we could do to save them. You can stay here and continue to look through Ciyrs' books if it would be too hard for you."

Leia looked into the distance for a few long seconds as if she were thinking carefully about the situation. Suddenly she shook her head.

"No. I am going with you. The Klimnu are gone, but if I don't go back there, they are still controlling me. I have to prove that they didn't take my entire life from me."

Loralia admired Leia's strength and courage. This tiny, fragile-looking woman had spent 57 horrific, harrowing days in the hands of the Klimnu in that very prison. The Denynso didn't even know that she had arrived on the planet because the slimy, disgusting creatures had hijacked the space shuttle in the middle of the trip and taken her hostage. For nearly two months they had tortured her, bringing her to the brink of death. She herself had even said that there were times when she had wished that she simply would die so that she could be delivered out of the brutality. If it wasn't for Elianna also being kidnapped by the Klimnu and Ciyrs going after her because he knew that she was his mate, she never would have found Leia, crawling along the stone hallway deep in the recesses of the prison, inches from succumbing but in that moment more determined to survive and defeat the Klimnu.

Her time in the prison had been incredibly difficult for

Leia, and in many ways she still hadn't recovered from it. Though she rarely spoke about it, she had offered Loralia just enough details that Loralia hadn't ever wanted to hear another. The torture had gone well past the physical pain to constant emotional and psychological torment that was in many ways far worse than what they inflicted on her body. Loralia could more than understand if Leia never wanted to be near that building again, and the fact that she would be so courageous as to not only want to go with them, but to do it specifically as a sign that the Klimnu didn't defeat her, was extraordinary.

"Do you really think that there will be anything there that the men didn't already find and that will be of some help?" Zuri asked.

"What prison are you talking about?" George asked from his position at the head of the counter.

"There is a prison at the far end of the compound that we thought had been built by the Klimnu many generations ago. It's where they held both Leia and Elianna, and where there was a battle that nearly defeated the Denynso, but it was burned down and the Klimnu ran. The men visited it again when they first started on their quest and they found an underground section that hadn't been damaged by the fire. They found an office full of documents and information about the Light Ones and the Covra, including a map to the settlement. That's how the men found the Light Ones in the first place."

"And you think that there may be more information there?" George asked.

"All we can do is try," Loralia answered, "We aren't getting far with these books and things, and if they found out how to get to the Light Ones from the prison, maybe there is more that they just didn't find because they didn't know what they should be looking for. The best we can do is go and look for them."

Loralia was worried that they weren't going to go with her, that they would think that it was a useless idea or that they needed to be spending their time focused on the information that they already had from Ciyrs' shop, but as soon as she finished talking, George straightened from his position beside the counter and looked at the other women.

"I think that's brilliant."

"Me, too," Zuri responded, "I can't believe we didn't think of it before now."

Loralia smiled and turned to Zsilvia who was huddling in her customary corner of the room.

"You're coming, too, right, Zsilvia?" she asked.

Zsilvia opened her mouth as if to respond and then her eyes moved over to George before snapping back to Loralia. She nodded sharply. Loralia could feel the pain radiating off of the Denynso woman, the heartache that filled her so intensely that Loralia was stunned the larger woman was even able to stand there. Loralia wished that she could understand what Zsilvia was going through so that she could help her. This was a time when she hated the skill that she was born with, the same skill every other one of her kind had possessed. Those who knew about it thought it was such a gift that she was able to detect the feelings and emotions of others just by being near them. They didn't ever consider that as she was feeling the pain, suffering, and confusion of others, she often had no idea why they were coping with those emotions or what she could do to help them. It was a deep level of torment that often made her concentrate on closing herself off from the people around her so that she couldn't feel what they were feeling, even if that made it difficult for her to connect with them in a personal way.

The women started to stream out of the building and, just as Loralia expected, Zsilvia hung back so that she would be the last one to leave. George lingered for a few moments, shifting papers around on the counter as if trying to stall leaving until the last second. Finally he gave up and walked toward the door, lifting his eyes to Zsilvia as he passed, but she wouldn't look his way. Loralia could feel a similar heartache coming off of George, but it was tinged with confusion, as if he either couldn't understand what he was feeling, or didn't know how to cope with the fact that he was feeling it.

Once George stepped out of the shop, Loralia sidled up to Zsilvia.

"Do you want to talk about anything?" Loralia asked.

Zsilvia looked at her sharply, the tears sparkling in her eyes a bold contrast to the steadiness of her jaw.

"What do you mean?" she asked, obviously unwilling to talk about whatever she was going through.

Loralia nodded and glanced through the glass in the door, catching a glimpse of George standing several feet away from the shop, his eyes trained on Zsilvia through the window even as the new woman, Ivy, stood by his side talking animatedly.

"Listen to him, Zsilvia," Loralia said, lowering her voice to a softer tone that would show the Denynso woman that she was speaking directly to her, "He is hurting. Let him tell you why."

Zsilvia held Loralia's eyes for a few more long seconds but didn't say anything before she turned away and walked out of the building toward the others who were waiting outside.

4
———

Pyra closed his eyes tightly, told himself that he might have imagined the sprawling kingdom beneath them, and then opened them again. The dry ground beneath his feet dipped deeply on the opposite side of the hill, opening out into a wide valley that held a settlement that looked far from abandoned. Unlike the settlement where the Light Ones lived, this kingdom didn't look overgrown, tired, or forgotten. Even from the distance where they were standing, Pyra could see that this kingdom looked like it was truly thriving. The buildings themselves looked alive and vibrant, and he could see the slight shifts in the atmosphere that indicated movement from whatever species might live there.

The men gathered around him, all of them staring down the hill toward the kingdom as if they, too, couldn't quite give themselves permission to believe that they were seeing the kingdom that they had been searching for for two days and had nearly given up on ever finding. After a few moments, they all started to run, pushing themselves with all of the energy that they had left to get down the hill and toward the massive gate that led down into the kingdom.

A road paved with rounded grey and purple stones led from the gate into the middle of a large open area that reminded Pyra of the area of their compound in front of the main meeting hall. In the center of the common area a large fountain rose up out of the ground, showering water down from several tiers carved from smooth, pale stone. Pyra rushed toward it, shucking his bag from around his torso so that he could drop to his knees by the edge of the bottom of the fountain and dip his hands down into the cool water. The men followed his lead, nearly collapsing by the edge of the fountain so that they could fill their scooped palms with water and sip it down. The water briefly burned as it hit Pyra's incredibly dry throat, but soon it soaked into the stiff, thirsty tissue and became soothing. He drank until he felt satisfied and then rose to his feet.

The rest of the men rose up with him and they looked around at the people who were slowly surrounding them. They came out of the buildings that surrounded the common area and down narrow streets that led away from it. Pyra felt himself tense instinctively, his body becoming stiff and defensive as the unknown species approached. Out of the corners of his eyes he could see the other warriors become equally tense, preparing themselves for conflict just as they always did. It was a testament both to their birthright and to his training, but also seemed like a show of the distrust and discomfort that had built within them since their conflict with the Klimnu.

As Pyra watched the species approach, however, he realized that none of them showed any signs of aggression. In fact, they all looked calm, peaceful, and even intrigued by the sudden appearance of the Denynso. The closer they got, the more he realized how beautiful they were. Each of them was almost unnervingly beautiful; flawless and perfect in a way that made Pyra both less defensive and somewhat uncomfortable. Eden was stunning, but even he could recognize the little things about her that others might see as flaws. These creatures, however, were like paintings they were so startling in their perfection and it made him wonder what about them would balance that beauty. Nothing could be that perfect. It was an inevitability of life. There was something in every creature that was flawed in some way. It was these flaws that made them real.

"Hello," one of the people said as he approached Pyra.

The man came to within a few feet of Pyra and lifted his hand, presenting his palm toward Pyra. He looked at the warrior expectantly as if there was something Pyra should do, but he wasn't sure what. The man seemed to realize that Pyra was unsure of what to do and gave a soft smile. He reached forward and took the much larger man by his wrist, drawing his hand up so that he could press his palm and fingers to his own. Once their hands met, he spread his fingers, taking Pyra's along with them.

"This is how we greet each other," he explained, "We want to welcome you to our home. My name is Rey."

"I'm Pyra, leader of the Denynso warriors."

Rey's eyes widened as his hand fell away from Pyra's.

"The Denynso?" he said with a hint of suspicion in his voice, "I have heard legends about you, but I always thought they were only myths."

Pyra felt Gyyx step up beside him and watched as he reached into the bag he wore over his shoulder. The tremendous warrior withdrew a small piece of paper that had been rolled into a tight scroll and released the ribbon that held it closed.

"Did the myths tell you of the sunrises on the Denynso compound?" he asked.

Rey glanced at him quizzically.

"Yes, of course. They are said to be the most beautiful on all of Uoria. The sun favors the Denynso and cloaks their home with its most majestic light in honor of them. The legends say it is from that light that the warriors gain their power and their intensity."

Gyyx unrolled the paper and held it out to Rey.

"My mate drew this. It was the sunrise on the first day that she was in the compound and the day that she met me."

Rey took the paper in his hands and Pyra saw his eyes glide over the picture, taking in the colors that Leia had used and the gentle strokes she had used to craft the image of the sunrise that had washed across the first day that she met her beloved mate. He nodded and handed the drawing back to Gyyx, who gazed down at it tenderly before rolling it back up and tucking it away in his bag.

"Why have the storied Denynso come to us?"

Relief washed over Pyra. He gave Gyyx a pat on his shoulder as he stepped back into the rest of the group and then looked back at Rey.

"We have never known anything about any other species living on Uoria. That's why we've come from the compound to explore the land outside of the walls. But our quest has been delayed."

"What has happened?"

Pyra looked into Rey's eyes and felt something twinge inside him. There was something oddly familiar about this man, but he couldn't quite place it. It was as though a part of him buried deep inside himself recognized him, though he was positive he had never encountered this man or any of the others in the kingdom before. He shook his head to get the thoughts away so he could focus on the conversation with Rey.

"We recently ended a conflict that we have maintained with a species called the Klimnu for quite some time. During one battle with them, we burned down a prison where they had been torturing two women. Before we left the compound, we went back to that prison and found information that led us to a settlement two days' travel from here." Pyra paused, feeling like he was teetering on a strange moment. Until he spoke he could still maintain all of the hope that he had about the other settlement. Once the words came out, however, it would be as though he had fallen through a window, unable to repair whatever damage may occur. "What do you know of the Light Ones?"

5

Zsilvia stayed at the back of the group, walking several paces behind the other women, George, and Ivy, partly so that she could remain physically distanced from them and partly so that she could watch them. As painful as it was to see them walking along together so closely, their heads bowed toward one another as they talked, she felt like she couldn't pull her attention away from them. Loralia's words continued to prick at the back of her mind. She had said that George was feeling the same way that she was, that she should listen to him. It was obvious that Loralia was special and could understand things about people that others couldn't, but what did she know about her or what she was going through with George?

As if he could hear her thoughts coming toward him, George suddenly glanced back over his shoulder at Zsilvia. She felt her desire for him surge inside her and looked away, concentrating on the ground beneath her feet rather than his sculpted body and sultry face. Finally the burn of his gaze on her faded and she looked up to see that he had turned back to the path in front of him. Ivy was continuing to talk to him, but he seemed to be ignoring her now. Zsilvia tried to ignore the feeling of satisfaction that came from seeing the delicate blond vying for his attention as he continued forward, but it gave her a sense of validation that he at least didn't want her to watch their interactions.

They had been walking for what felt like several hours and Zsilvia started feeling more nervous with every step. Like the other Denynso women, she had never been this far from the main center of the compound. They lived their lives close to their homes and rarely ventured further than they could venture in less than an hour. The further they walked, the more disconnected she felt from everything she knew and that made her feel comfortable. She felt out of control and didn't know what to expect with her next step. The trees grew denser around them and the ground became soft with moss and fallen leaves beneath her feet.

Suddenly the hint of ash and acrid air touched her nose. She shuddered at the smell and started scouring the ground in front of her for the source of the unpleasant odor. Several yards ahead she could see the charred, hunkering remains of a massive building spread across the ground like the decimated corpse of some massive creature sacrificed where it had fallen. She was horrified by the sight, immediately knowing that she was looking at the destroyed remnants of the prison that the warriors had set ablaze to frighten and punish the Klimnu after their capture of Elianna.

"I didn't expect for it to still have this smell."

Zsilvia heard Elianna's voice from the front of the rest of the group and felt her heart sink slightly at the sadness in the words. They had all been so concerned about Leia's reaction to going back to the prison where she had spent nearly two months in unspeakable torture, but no one had even considered for a moment that Elianna might have reservations about going back there. She had been kidnapped by the Klimnu after one of them had used their mystifying ability to appear as someone else to trick her into thinking that he was Pyra and then held at the prison where she fought for her own life, and then for Leia's when she discovered her broken, battered body lying in the middle of the hallway, pleading for her to help. The warriors along with her mate, Ciyrs, had come to rescue her and it was during that battle that she had discovered that Ciyrs had transferred some of his ability to destroy the Klimnu simply through his touch. Together they had reduced many of the creatures to ash at their feet. Though she had been under the control of the Klimnu for only a short time and had participated in the battle with enthusiasm, the experience had scarred her and now the difficulty was showing through.

Leia stepped up beside her and took her hand tightly in a show of solidarity and strength for their shared experience. Though the others were there to support and encourage them, only the two of them could understand what they were feeling and they needed to be there for each other to guide them through the challenge that they now faced.

"Are you ready?" Eden asked.

Despite the lingering concerns about her health and the baby, Eden had insisted she was going along with the others. Claiming she felt well again and pointing out that staying active was good for both of them, Eden had followed right along with them when they started walking toward the prison. Everyone had kept careful eye on her as they traveled, but other than her slightly slower walk, she had shown no indication of further problems. Now she was standing beside the two nervous-looking women offering the strength of her presence and encouraging them forward. The rest of the group stepped up so that they stood in a single file line staring at the remnants of the prison ahead of them, each lost in their own thoughts.

Zsilvia stood beside Loralia, separated from the group by a few steps. She could see Loralia sliding her gaze toward her every few seconds and resisted letting her emotions course through her so that the other woman couldn't sense them. She had felt exposed enough during their earlier conversation and was not ready for Loralia to delve any further into what she was going through.

The group walked forward, stepping gingerly among the scorched pieces of the prison until they found what looked like a trap door in the stone foundation.

"This must be how the men got into the prison," Zuri said, indicating the door.

George crouched at the edge of the door and ran his fingers along the edge. Zsilvia watched as his fingers found the lip of the door and the muscles through his shoulders and back tensed seductively beneath the fabric of his shirt while he lifted the door away with a deep grunt. Zuri and Samira helped to pull the door the rest of the way out of place and they entered the dark, cavernous bowels of the former prison.

The only light in the space beneath the ground was the pearlescent glow coming off of Loralia's skin. She stepped to the front of the group and looked at each of them.

"Did anyone bring a light stick?"

George and Zuri reached into their bags and pulled out the small metal tools. The smile on his face said that he had been waiting since his arrival to use a piece of Denynso technology and was excited that the time had finally come.

Eden tucked a hand into the small bag at her hip and withdrew a narrow torch and a flint.

"Pyra taught me to never go anywhere unprepared," she said, leaning over to strike the flint across the stone wall of the prison dungeon.

Eden used the spark from the flint to light her torch, throwing orange glow around the hallway and adding to the pools of light from the others who had brought along their tools.

"We'll have to split up into groups. Those with lights take someone without a light with you," Zuri said, looking at each of them as if mentally pairing them off in the way that she thought that they should be though she wasn't giving voice to her opinions. "Ivy will have to come with me. Creia has entrusted her to me so she's my responsibility. The rest of you, group up and we'll start exploring."

"I guess that means that you have to take me with you."

Zsilvia heard George's voice close beside her and her belly trembled. She turned to his smile and instinctively reached for the bag that she always wore at her hip like any Denynso would so that she could show him that she had her own light, but realized that she didn't have the bag with her. Her mind had been so distracted recently that it seemed she couldn't even think straight enough to do the things that she had done every day since she was old enough to leave home without her parents.

"You don't seem to have a light," George continued, "and as far as I know you are still my guard and protector."

"I suppose you're right," Zsilvia said, still refusing to make eye contact with him, "Where do you think that we should go first?"

George gestured down the hall and she followed along beside him, paying attention as she went to where the other groups were headed so that she could stay close enough to them that their presence would distract her from the fact that she was alone in the dark with him.

"Oh, George!" Zsilvia heard Ivy's voice from behind them and felt her teeth grind against each other, "We'll come along with you."

Zsilvia stepped back to let Zuri and Ivy come closer and continued to sink back as they walked down the hallway until she could barely see them ahead of her and could only decipher their position in the narrow, serpentine hallway by the glow of the light sticks that George and Zuri held.

6

———

"There was a war," Rey said, settling into place at a long table and gesturing for Pyra and the other men to take the seats on either side of him, "Before the battles broke out, our kingdoms were in close cooperation. We had maintained good relations since their arrival and were building our relationship and had even begun to talk about joining our communities. When the war started, all communication ended. We tried to reach out to them, but the men we sent out to them never returned."

Pyra hesitated, trying to form the right words.

"Were any of those that were alive then alive now?" he asked carefully.

It sounded like a bizarre question even as it came through his own lips, but he was quickly learning that when he thought he knew something, he was likely wrong about it. They had only been away from the compound for a short time and yet he felt like he had broadened his concepts of the world around him more in those few days than he had in his entire life. The Covra had wandered the planet for well more than a century and were still living as they awaited the birth of the new generation. Now he was facing another new species and Pyra had no idea how long they may live and if any of them had been around to witness the time of the war.

"No. The last of those who were alive then died many years ago."

"What happened to your kind after you lost touch with the Light Ones?"

"After the war there was tremendous turmoil among our kind. Discord caused the kingdom to divide. One group split off and left while the rest stayed here."

"What happened to the other group?" Pyra asked.

Rey shook his head, the expression on his face a difficult blend of sadness and bewilderment.

"No one knows," he said softly, "After they left, there was very little contact with the rest of the group. Eventually the ones who were alive at the time started to die off and the amount of contact diminished even further until all ties were completely broken. It has been decades since there was any communication between the two groups."

"Are they still living?"

Rey shrugged and shook his head again.

"We don't even know that. No one knows where they ended up and many of the children now barely even know that that group ever existed. It is fading from our history," his voice dropped even further, "and that is just fine with most of us."

Just then a woman approached the table carrying a large tray of food followed by another carrying one that held a pitcher and stacks of plates and cups. Rey distributed the dishes and began to serve the meal that the women had brought. Though Pyra was ravenous and he knew the others had to be as well considering they had left behind much of their food for the others in the settlement, he knew he needed to stay focused and keep Rey talking.

"After the war ended, why did no one ever go looking for the Light Ones, or at least for the people that you sent and who never returned?"

"The stories of our elders say that some did go looking, hoping to either find our lost ones and free them, or at least bring their bodies home for proper burial. They roamed the badlands between the two kingdoms for days, following the paths that were once clear and well-laid by those who traveled back and forth often. No matter where they looked, however, they couldn't find the settlement. It was as if it had simply disappeared."

"They went to the place where the settlement was and it wasn't there?" Pyra asked, confused by the statement.

"That's the story that the elders told. Of course, we don't know if it is entirely true. All we know is that there has never again been communication with the Light Ones and no one has ever seen those scouts again. You haven't told me why you are so interested in them and the relationship that they had with our kind."

The statement wasn't accusatory and Pyra finally felt himself starting to feel at ease with Rey and the other beautiful creatures. Though there was still something about them that struck him as odd and as though he should know more about them, he was starting to feel more comfortable with them and more convinced that they would do what they could to help their cause.

"The information that we found in the prison indicated that the Light Ones were engaged in battle with the Covra. Have you heard of them?"

Rey nodded.

"I have heard the name. Before communication with

them stopped near the beginning of the war, they sent word that creatures called the Covra were the ones who had attacked them and were trying to overtake them. We have never encountered such a species, though, and didn't learn anything about them before the communication ended."

Pyra fought to hold in the disappointment that came from that statement. Though Rey had confirmed that his kind knew nothing of the threat of the Covra, that didn't necessarily mean that they would be completely unable to help them unlock the Light Ones. He had said that the two kingdoms had been very friendly. It was still possible that enough information survived that they might still find something that could be helpful to them in their quest to unlock the people and restore the kingdom.

"When the Covra become too weakened and know that they are not going to be able to defeat the enemy that they have chosen, they lock them."

"Lock?" Rey asked.

"Yes. They possess a toxin that allows them to stop the victim in the exact moment when they were injected. It doesn't kill them, only freezes them in place so that they continue to exist. That's what happened to the Light Ones. That's why your kind was never able to restore communication after the beginning of the war. It is not because they didn't want to communicate with you. It is because the Covra isolated them and then locked them so that they were unable to reach out to you."

"Could that also be what happened to the scouts that were sent to check on them?"

"It's possible," Pyra confirmed. "They may have shown up in the settlement on the day that the Covra attacked and be frozen there with the others."

"But then why were none of the people who went after them later able to find the settlement?"

"I can't answer that. I don't know what affect the locking has on others. What I do know is that there are more of the creatures coming. My warriors were able to defeat as many as would come into the settlement toward us, but we know that there are more on their way, and we worry that when they do come, the Light Ones won't survive. The mate of one of my men is there and if we don't find a way to save them soon, he will have to watch her die and then live the rest of his life without her. We need your help."

"What could we do?" Rey asked, "I told you that we know nothing about the Covra."

"You might not know about them, but somewhere in your history, in your archives, you know about the Light Ones. Of everyone on this planet, you have the best chances of knowing something about them that could change everything. You might be able to help us find a way to release them from their binds, which would mean giving hundreds of people back their lives and giving Lynx his mate. Once they wake up, you may also be able to restore the relationship between the two kingdoms and work again toward what those who came before you wanted for all of you."

"Tell me what you need us to do."

Pyra smiled, feeling truly hopeful for the first time since setting off, and touched the pendant around his neck. He could feel Eden and her presence gave him the strength to continue.

"Bring us to whatever information you may have about the Light Ones and the war so that we can learn what we can and then go back to the settlement to tell the others."

"I will do better than that," Rey said, standing from his seat, "We'll go back with you."

7

———

Samira leaned over the papers spread across the counter. They had gathered all of the documents that they could find that referenced the Light Ones and brought them back to Ciyrs' shop so that they would be more comfortable examining them there than they would have in the cold and dark prison.

"Am I reading this correctly?" Samira asked.

Loralia leaned over the paper from the other side and even though the words were upside down she knew that she was reading the same thing that Samira was. Incredibly brilliant despite her young age, Samira was an expert in biology, but it didn't take her exceptional intelligence and vast scientific knowledge to decipher what they had found in a worn journal tucked in the back of a cabinet. It was written out very clearly in every grisly detail.

"We need to get in touch with the men right now," Eden said.

"Are you alright?" Loralia asked, taking a step toward Eden to place a hand on her back.

Eden looked up at her with wide orange eyes and nodded.

"I'm fine. It's just that I can feel Pyra so strongly. I know that he is thinking about me. They are relying on us for help, and this is the most important information that we have found. We need to tell them now and let them do with it what they can."

Without waiting for approval or confirmation from anyone else, Loralia nodded and took the compact from around her neck. The metal already felt warm in her hand as if it could sense that she needed it. She opened the compact and reflected the chain that held it in the top mirror just as she had instructed Bannack to do with his compact in the event that he ever needed to get in touch with her. The glass of the mirror seemed to liquefy and ripple, becoming opaque for a brief moment before she saw Bannack's eyes appear in the reflection.

"Hello, love," he said, "Have you found out something?"

"Yes," Loralia said, "Give your compact to Lynx. I'm going to hand mine over to Samira and Eden. They'll explain to you what we found out when we went back to the prison today."

"You went to the prison?" Bannack asked, sounding horrified that his precious mate had gone somewhere so incredibly dangerous without him.

"It was the only way that we were going to find out anything else about the Light Ones. It's where you found out about them in the first place, and I thought that maybe you might have missed something or that there might be something there that didn't have any meaning when you first started on your quest but that would mean something now that you have been to the settlement and know what is happening."

There was a pause as if Bannack was trying to decide how he felt about the situation.

"Thank you."

Loralia nodded and handed the compact over to Eden who held it so that she and Samira could look into it together.

"Lynx, are you there?" Eden asked.

"I'm here."

"You were right about the Covra using the Light Ones as incubators. That is exactly what they're doing. Because they reproduce so infrequently, they have to give birth to a huge number of children at the same time. In times when the Covra were more plentiful and more powerful, they would just lay their eggs in hatcheries and there would be nurse-maids there to care for them when they were born. Over time that changed to women who they had captured during wars and turned into slaves. It served their purposes better and acted as a form of torture for their enemies. They could not enslave the Light Ones, so they had to go for a more direct course of action to fulfill the needs of their children."

"What do you mean?" Lynx asked.

"When the Covra are born, they are extremely powerful, but they are also voracious. There is only a very small overlap between the birth of the new generation and the death of the old generation. In order to ensure that they are large enough to come into their full abilities before the death of the old generation, the babies double to triple in size every day. This requires a tremendous amount of food. The role of the original nursemaids was to ensure that they brought the new young enough food to support them in their first days and to keep them alive as they grew. When the food grew sparser and the Covra were a less powerful and feared species, the slaves stepped into the role. They were meant to bring food to the babies, but when that food ran out, they were eaten alive. The Covra were not strong enough when they were preparing for this new generation of young to enslave anyone to care for their babies, so instead, they locked the Light Ones and decided to use their bodies to protect and insulate their eggs, but also to nourish their young."

"They are going to eat the Light Ones."

Lynx's voice expressed the horror that all of them were already feeling.

"Yes. As the babies hatch, they are going to consume their hosts from the inside out. By the time the waves of hatchings finish, the Light Ones will be completely destroyed and the Covra young will be at full power. The entire planet of Uoria will be at risk."

"What are we supposed to do?"

Lynx sounded desperate at this point, frantic as if he was grasping onto the very last remnants of his hope but was feeling them slip from between his fingers.

"I don't know, Lynx. The only chance that the Light Ones have left is if you can remove the eggs from them safely before the hatchings start and then destroy them. But even then, they will still be locked. The binds don't end with the death of the older generation. Maybe you can talk to Ciyrs."

"He isn't here," Lynx said.

"What?" Elianna demanded, suddenly appearing at the front of the reflection, "What do you mean he isn't there? Where did he go?"

"We discovered that there is, at least there was, another kingdom relatively nearby. The species that lives there used to maintain a good relationship with the Light Ones. Some of the men left to go there and see if they could find out anything useful. Pyra, Ciyrs, Gyyx, and Ty are all there."

Loralia felt a sudden wash of fear as the mates of the four men Lynx had mentioned straightened, fixating brave faces on the reflection in the compact as they tried to present a sense of calm and control even while they were panicking inside.

"When are they supposed to get back?" Zuri asked.

"We don't know," Ero's voice said and Loralia saw Zuri's face light up as her mate appeared in the mirror, "They weren't sure how long it would take to get there, and they don't know what they would find when they actually got there. I feel like we need more help to figure this out. We need scientific minds and, Elianna, we could really use another healer."

"Are you asking if we will come to the settlement to help you?" Zuri asked.

"Yes. We were only able to defeat the Klimnu because we were all together. Without your help, all of you, there's no way we could have done that. The same goes now. We need you. I need you."

Once they disconnected the communication, the group of women and George stood around Ciyrs' counter looking at each other as if each were waiting for another to start talking so that they would not have to be the one to break the silence and express an opinion.

"Of course, we are going," Elianna finally said.

Everyone looked to her and then Zuri nodded emphatically.

"Of course. The men need us. We have to go," she said, "We need to go talk to Creia about it, but I'm sure that he'll agree to it. We'll spend the rest of the day preparing and we'll leave at sunrise."

"Eden," Loralia said, stilling the sudden flurry of movement that happened as everyone in the shop started getting ready to leave so that they could start their preparations, "you know that you can't go."

Eden's eyes widened slightly and her hands cupped the sides of her belly.

"I want to be with Pyra and to help. I came here to be a scientist and that's what I want to do."

"But now that you are here, you are a mate who is entrusted with the care and protection of your mate's baby, and that is what you are going to have to do."

"I'll stay with her," Leia offered.

"Thank you, Leia," Zuri said, "We'll make sure that your mates know how much you are thinking about them. I'm sure they will be sad not to see you, but, Eden, you know that Pyra wouldn't want you to do anything that would put yourself or the baby in jeopardy in any way, and we don't know what the journey is like to get to the settlement."

"We'll stay here and take care of the compound," Eden finally relented, "but if anything goes wrong, you have to let us know."

"We will," Loralia promised.

With that, the group turned and started toward the main meeting hall where they would tell Creia and Theia that even more of the beloved members of their compound would be venturing outside of it, defying tradition and possibly putting themselves in incredible danger.

8

———

"Do you really think that this is the right thing to do?"

Creia stared down at them from his platform, his hand both cupping over his chin and lifting slightly to cover his mouth as if attempting to conceal how he was feeling.

"Yes, sir," Zuri said, "The goal of the men going on this quest was so that they could learn about the others on this planet and the dangers that we may face. Well, the Covra are one of those dangers."

"By saving the Light Ones, we may also be able to protect ourselves from future attacks," Loralia continued, "and without our help, their entire species will be erased from the planet." She took a steadying breath, trying to control the emotions that rose when she thought of her own kind, destroyed by a virulent disease that left her the only one of her species that still existed. "It is our responsibility to do whatever we can to help them."

"We can't just stand by and allow them all to die and have the new generation of the Covra take over," Samira pointed out. "According to the journal that we found in the prison, once the young have gotten through the first few days of their development, they will be powerful enough to threaten the entire planet."

"We also have no idea about their technology," Elianna continued. "They could have the capacity to travel to other planets and put them at risk as well. If we have even the slightest chance of being able to kill them off now and save the Light Ones, we have to do it. Most of the men are warriors, but we are healers and scientists. This is our duty."

"The way is dangerous and challenging. Are you prepared to handle it?"

"I am sure these women are more than capable of handling the trip," George said, "but I will also be there with them to offer my assistance."

"You will protect them and ensure with the utmost of your ability that they will arrive at their destination and back with their mates safely," Creia said.

"I will," George promised.

"Then you must go."

FOR THE SECOND time in as many days, the group started toward the woods so that they could pass through on the way to the edge of the compound. Each wore bags across their chests or strapped to their backs, filled with as many of the supplies and tools that they could pack. They didn't know what they might need as they travelled or what would be available to them when they arrived at the settlement, so they packed everything that they could in hopes that they wouldn't miss anything.

Zsilvia watched Loralia run her fingertips along the mirror in her compact as she finished her communication with Bannack. He had given them instructions on how to find the settlement and sent good thoughts for a safe and easy trip. Loralia closed the compact and draped it back around her neck, setting her jaw as she continued forward without saying anything to the people around her. Zsilvia looked over Loralia's shoulder to George's back as he led the group. The air around them was slightly cool and he had put on a long-sleeved shirt, but she could still see the shape of his body through the fabric. For a moment she just savored watching him, but then a wave of bitterness flowed over her as she thought of Ivy enjoying his body during their time together on Earth.

She straightened the bag on her shoulder and stepped to the side so that she could focus ahead of her without looking at his back. As they continued to walk she could feel the air around them start to change. The chill became sharper as the air started to spark with intense energy. It was an uncomfortable feeling, like something was building up. The others seemed to notice the change, too, as they slowed and looked around. Suddenly a crack of bright green lightning split the sky above them, crashing with a sound so loud it seemed to shake the ground. Zsilvia heard one of the other women scream just before the sheets of cold, stinging rain came pouring down on them.

Without warning another massive blast of lightning illuminated the sky and a gale of wind rushed past them with enough speed and intensity to nearly push Zsilvia off her feet. Another crack of lightning followed closely after the second and Zsilvia heard the explosive sound of it hitting a nearby tree and shattering the wood.

"We need to find cover," George yelled into the almost screaming sound of the wind, "Now!"

"Come on," Loralia shouted, "Follow me."

They pushed forward into the wind, ducking their heads against the pressure and the pain of the raindrops hitting their skin. Loralia crouched down and ran her hands along the moss at the side of the path. Zsilvia knew what she was doing and recoiled from the rest of the group. She had heard enough about the mirror realm beneath the compound that had been Loralia's home before Bannack had brought her to the surface. She knew that it was a strange and dangerous place where Jem had lost his life and Elianna had nearly followed him. She didn't want to go down into that place.

Finally Loralia pulled aside a piece of the moss, revealing an opening in the ground that led down to the cavern below. She dropped down first, leading the others with the glow of her skin and her movements down into the space.

"Come on, Zsilvia!" Zuri shouted as she started down into the ground.

"Can't we go somewhere else? We could go to the prison. We'll be safe in the dungeon."

"There isn't time. We have to get out of this storm."

Zuri disappeared into the ground and Samira stepped up to the edge behind her, slipping out of sight without hesitation. Zsilvia continued to hesitate despite the soaking of the rain through her clothing and the ache of the wind in her ears. The thought of going beneath the ground into a place she had never been where she couldn't trust anything that she saw was terrifying and she couldn't bring herself to go to the edge of the hole in the ground.

"Get over here, Zsilvia!" George shouted at her.

Instead, she took a step back. Through the driving rain she could see George start to run toward her, his body cutting through the grey to get to her.

"What is wrong with you?" he screamed at her.

"I'm not going down there!"

"Yes, you are."

"No."

Zsilvia took a step back but George had already gotten to her and reached for her.

"You don't have a choice. I won't let you stay out here."

Before Zsilvia knew what he was doing, George tucked his shoulder and pushed it into her belly, sweeping her off of the ground so that she draped over his back. Despite her protests, George took off back toward the hole in the ground. She clung to him, not wanting to touch him, but at the same time afraid to let go. She expected him to put her down when he got to the entrance to the underground mirror realm, but he didn't. Instead, he swung himself down into the gap and she felt them drop for a few seconds before he got his grip on the tree that led them down.

Zsilvia squeezed her eyes closed, trying to fight the tears of fright that threatened them. Finally their downward movement stopped and darkness engulfed them. Zsilvia opened her eyes to see Loralia climbing down toward them after pulling the moss back over the hole in the ground.

"Put me down," Zsilvia demanded.

George complied and she felt the ground beneath her feet again. She looked around and saw the main source of her terror. What should have been the floor of the cavern stretched in front of her a dark, roiling reflection of the storm above them. Grey and purple swirled against a black background, occasionally splitting with lightning that threatened to tear the world to pieces.

The sound of their ragged, uneven breath filled the space. Zsilvia met each of their eyes. She couldn't take it anymore. Taking the light stick from her bag, she illuminated the branches of the trees beneath her and started across them, crossing them as quickly as she could without losing her footing.

"Zsilvia!" George yelled behind her, but she didn't turn back to him.

She heard the sound of his feet pounding on the branches behind her as he followed her.

"George, stop!" Ivy yelled and Zsilvia felt something inside her break.

Closing her eyes, she grabbed onto one of the vines that hung above her, took a breath, and swung herself out over the reflection of the sky that stretched across the ground, allowing the vine to slip from her hand.

9

Zsilvia heard her name tear through the air around her, but she didn't care who had screamed it. Time seemed to have slowed to the point that she could feel each of her heartbeats, sense the blood flowing through her veins, and listen to the breath streaming from her lungs. Though it felt like several minutes, it could have only been seconds before she felt her body start to descend. She didn't know what would happen as she fell. She had thrown herself across the narrowest section of the sky with the goal of reaching the rocky ground on the other side, but she knew that it was possible she wouldn't make it. Though it had been the very fear of that sky that had made her resist going down into the ground, now she almost welcomed the openness of the sky beneath her.

She didn't know what would happen to her when the pull brought her down into the sky, but in that moment she didn't really care. The sky could take her, deliver her from her torment. It wasn't all about George anymore, but the memories and uncertainties that his presence had brought back into her mind. She didn't feel that she could bear them any longer, and if the sky was going to swallow her, it may offer her relief.

Zsilvia drew in a breath and the descent suddenly ended as her body slammed into something hard. She felt herself slipping backwards and clawed for something to hold on to as she opened her eyes to see that she had made it to the other side but was now falling backwards off of the edge of the ground. She could hear George screaming and cursing behind her, but there was nothing he could do. Human legs couldn't jump as far as she just had.

"Help her, Loralia!" Zuri shouted.

"I can't," Loralia yelled back, "If I reflect the wall to create a floor over the sky, it will crush her."

"Get up, Zsilvia," George shouted at her, "Get up!"

Zsilvia's fingers dug deeper into the ground, the instinct to survive taking over the emptiness that had come over her. She grabbed onto a rock jutting out of the dirt and strained her muscles to pull herself up

"The tree, Zsilvia," Samira shouted.

Zsilvia wasn't sure what she meant, but her arms were starting to give out. Her body was weakening beneath her and the tears she had been withholding now slipped down her cheeks. As she felt her hands starting to fall away from the rock, she cried for everything that she had gone through, from what she remembered to the things that she had completely blocked out, and for the life that she had never had the opportunity to live. It was pain that she couldn't explain, and yet feeling it suddenly made her feel free.

A crash beside her brought Zsilvia's attention back to the present moment. Just inches away from her, the roots of one of the large trees on the other side of the reflected sky had dropped onto the dirt.

"Hold on, Zsilvia," George said.

She glanced over her shoulder and saw George scrambling down the length of the tree toward her. Fear rose within her chest. He was moving quickly down the prone tree without holding onto anything. At any second his feet could slip and he would fall into the reflected sky. Her hands slipped again and Zsilvia let out a gasp. She fought to keep her grasp, but her muscles were weak and tired, and the sweat on her palms made them slick. Her eyes closed and she let out the breath that made her lungs burn.

Zsilvia's hands released from the rock and her body began to slide back through the dirt. Her hips had just dropped off of the edge when she felt the movement stop and a strong grasp take hold of her wrist. She looked up and saw George standing on the bank, one hand gripping a piece protruding from the edge of a massive boulder as the other held tightly to her arm. It was the same grip that had frightened her so deeply when she went to his house with him on the first night he was on the compound, the grip that had made her question everything that she had been feeling and everything that she believed about her life and her future. This time, however, it felt protective and safe.

George took a step back, pulling her up slightly. Zsilvia looked into his eyes and felt everything around her disappear.

"Trust me," George whispered.

Zsilvia felt her heart jump, but the words sank into her and she felt herself lift her other hand and grab onto his wrist. The moment of reciprocation exchanged the energy and need between them, encompassing everything that had built within each of them and multiplying it. Zsilvia felt her body pulling up until she was able to dig her knee into the ground and crawl away from the edge. She sagged into the ground, gasping against a breath she didn't realize she was holding, and watching as tears splashed into the dirt beneath her.

The voices of all of the women crashed around her and Zsilvia could hear them coming toward her over the tree. Questions, demands, and shouts seemed to pound around her, pressing down on her until they constricted her lungs and cut off her breath. Finally she held up her hand behind her.

"Stop," she said, her head still hanging.

The voices silenced, but she could still feel that they were standing close behind her.

"Leave her alone," Loralia said, "Let her be." Loralia crouched down beside Zsilvia and placed a hand on her back, "Come with me."

Zsilvia allowed Loralia to help her to her feet and guide her away from the others toward the back of the cavern. The glow from her skin illuminated the darkness around them and Zsilvia followed Loralia into a tunnel that led away from the front chamber and down into another. They walked along in silence, but Zsilvia felt oddly comforted by the quiet, peaceful woman's presence.

Loralia led Zsilvia through a larger chamber and down another tunnel and then a third into a small but high-ceilinged space that felt airy and fresh. The air was cool around her, but she could see steam rising behind a partial wall created by stone formations meeting from the floor and ceiling of the chamber.

"You are safe here, Zsilvia. Relax. Take a bath if you'd like. That storm isn't going to end anytime soon. When you're ready, come back to the main chamber and take the other tunnel down into the second cavern. That's where I'm going to bring the rest of the group."

"Thank you, Loralia," Zsilvia said.

"Of course."

As soon as Loralia left the chamber, Zsilvia started toward the steam at the back of the space. She bathed in the warm, deep water, allowing it to ease the pain and tension in her muscles and wash away the dirt from her hands. By the time she finished her bath, her tears had stopped but she didn't want to go back to the rest of the group. Instead, she stepped out of bath, wrapped herself in one of the wide, thick towels that had been stacked beside the pool, and roamed around the space. It was a strange feeling being there, almost as though she were walking through a memory. She knew this had been the private home of someone once, a space that had been cherished and calming to one of Loralia's kind. She wondered how long it had been since the person who had lived in that particular space had succumbed to the illness, and how long after that it had been before Loralia had stepped into the chamber and claimed it as her own.

"Why won't you speak to me?"

10

────────

The sound of George's voice startled Zsilvia and she turned to him, pulling the towel closer around her to conceal her body completely.

"George," she breathed, not sure what emotion was in the name.

"Why won't you speak to me?" he repeated, stepping closer to her from the entrance to the chamber.

"What are you doing in here? Loralia said that she was bringing everyone to another cavern."

"She did, but she told me where she had brought you so that I could come talk to you."

In that moment Zsilvia realized that Loralia hadn't meant that she alone would be safe in that chamber, but that she would be safe with her thoughts and her words.

"I'm not dressed."

"I don't care."

George took another step closer.

"I do."

"Why are you avoiding me?"

"I'm not avoiding you."

Zsilvia pulled the towel closer, but couldn't bring herself to step away from him even as he drew closer.

"Yes you are. You have barely spoken a word to me since the other night. What happened?"

"Nothing happened. I haven't been avoiding you. I have been with you every day."

"You have been near me, yes, but it's like you put up a wall between us. That first night that I was here, before Zuri came to the house, and then the day before the shuttle came, I thought..."

"You thought what, George? That I could entertain you until Ivy came?"

George looked stung.

"What are you talking about?"

"I've seen the way she looks at you, and of course I can't blame her, but I also can't compete with her. She is so small and delicate and beautiful. She's everything that I'm not, so why would you want anything to do with me now that she's here?"

George took a step to close the space between them.

"Because I love you."

"What?"

Zsilvia couldn't allow herself to believe what she had just heard.

"Ivy means nothing more to me than an assistant. You are everything. You are beautiful and strong and sexy, and I have loved you from the first moment that I saw you. You should never feel anything less than stunning."

"It isn't just that," Zsilvia said.

His declaration of love was entrancing and she wanted to hear it again, but it wasn't enough to erase the fears that still hovered in the back of her mind.

"What is it?"

Zsilvia looked into George's eyes and felt her body respond to him. Knowing that there was nothing left for her to lose, nothing to sacrifice but the pain that had followed her throughout her life, she told him what she had told Eden, detailing the horror she had faced and the betrayal she had felt when there was no one there to believe her, to protect her, or to even care.

By the time she was finished, George's jaw was squared with anger and she could see emotion sparkling in his eyes.

"I am so sorry that you went through that, and if I made it worse for you. I would never have come on to you that strong if I had known."

"You couldn't have known," Zsilvia said.

"I would never hurt you."

George stepped closer to her again.

"George," Zsilvia whispered.

"You never deserved to be treated that way. I wish that I had been here."

Zsilvia could feel her breath slowing and deepening.

"You didn't even know that I existed then."

"I should have. I should have been with you. I should have been the only person to ever touch you."

"I'm sorry," Zsilvia said.

"No," George said, stepping up to her so that his face brushed hers, "Never say you're sorry. You did nothing wrong."

Zsilvia tilted her face toward his to get more of the touch of his skin and the feeling of his breath along her jawline and neck.

"I have known since the moment I saw you that you were meant to be my mate. I've wanted you more than I could ever have imagined wanting anyone or anything. I wish that

I had waited for you, that you could be the only man that has ever touched me."

George nuzzled her nose with his.

"We have lost so much time," he whispered, "let's not lose any more wishing for something that we can't change. I may not be able to take away what was done to you, but I can promise you that from this moment forward I will be the only man who will ever touch you, and that I will never do anything to make you fear me. I want to show you how you should be touched."

"Please."

"But I won't do anything without your permission. I want to bond with you the way you deserve. May I kiss you?"

"Yes."

"Thank you."

George leaned forward and gently caught Zsilvia's lips with his. His mouth moved tenderly over hers, the kiss as rich and luxurious as the one he had given her outside of his cabin the night before Ivy's shuttle arrived. After a moment he lifted his mouth away from hers, giving them both a chance to catch their breath.

"May I kiss you again?"

Zsilvia nodded and George dipped his head to capture her mouth again, bringing his hands to her hips. The tip of his tongue touched the inside of her lips, coaxing her to open them so that he could explore her more thoroughly. Zsilvia complied, opening her mouth and inviting his tongue in across hers. George moaned softly and pulled closer to Zsilvia so that their bodies touched. She could feel the pressure of his erection and her need for him began to spiral, but he moved without urgency.

"May I take your towel off?"

"Yes."

George's hands moved from her hips to the fold of the towel at her breasts and slowly released it, revealing her body reverently.

"You are the most magnificent thing I have ever seen," he said softly and Zsilvia felt her knees weaken slightly.

"I want to see you."

George stepped back to allow Zsilvia to take the hem of his shirt in her hands and peel it off over his head, kicking off his boots and socks and she went to work on his belt. They moved slowly, savoring each moment as they relinquished themselves to the feelings that they had been experiencing since the first second their eyes met.

"May I touch you?"

"I am yours," Zsilvia said, meaning the words with every ounce of her essence, "I have always been yours. You may do with me whatever you'd like."

"You are giving yourself to me?"

"Yes."

"All of you?"

George lifted one hand to stroke along the outer swell of one of her breasts and then brushed the pad of his thumb across her nipple. Zsilvia gasped at the touch and arched her back into it, touching her hands to his shoulders to give herself strength.

"Yes."

George took her hand and led her to the low bed against the far wall. He guided her onto it so that they knelt together in the middle of the mattress, their bodies just touching.

"Forever?"

"Always."

Tucking his hand behind her head, George led her down onto the bed. He lay on his stomach in front of her, slipping his arms beneath her legs so that she bent her knees slightly. Resting one hand to her stomach, George sought hers with the other, intertwining their fingers on the mattress beside her. He looked into her eyes as he leaned forward and drew his tongue through her core. Zsilvia's breath caught in her throat and her body arched off of the bed with the force of the unexpected, unknown touch. George pulled back slightly and blew a gentle stream of air onto her until her body relaxed. He repeated the movement, sweeping his tongue along her folds, tenderly bringing her forward so that her body opened to him.

After a few moments of the delirious feeling of his tongue, Zsilvia felt George sit back on his feet and reach for her hands. He pulled her toward him and their foreheads met. Her body trembled and she closed her eyes to focus on that singular moment.

"Make love to me, George."

Zsilvia handed her control over to him, completely letting go of what lay behind her and offering herself entirely to this man who had proven to her that she no longer had to be afraid.

George cupped his hands around the backs of her thighs and guided her forward, lifting her so that her legs went to either side of his hips where he knelt. His hand touched her lower back and his eyes burned into hers, holding them unwaveringly as he brought her forward so that the warmth of her opening nestled against the tip of his erection. Zsilvia wrapped her arms around his neck, grasping at his back as George eased her hips down so that she enveloped his shaft within her.

Zsilvia gasped at the feeling of him stretching her, filling her after so many years of having no one near her. He held her firmly against him and maneuvered so that he could rest her back against the pillows and come down on top of her without withdrawing from her. She felt shielded by his body, protected by the beautiful muscles and powerful strength rather than intimidated by them. George moved within her slowly and Zsilvia drew her knees up to open further to him. The movement drove him deeper within her and George cried out. He stilled, holding himself deeply inside her but not moving as if fighting to maintain control.

When he seemed to have regained his composure, George began to move again, the long, slow strokes massaging her and building pressure deep in her belly like she had never experienced. She knew that she was climbing toward a climax, but it was the first that she would experience from another person and she felt slightly overwhelmed.

"Are you alright?" George asked, pushing back to look into her face.

"No one has ever..."

He thrust into her and Zsilvia gave a sharp cry.

"Ever?" George asked leadingly.

"No one has ever made me..."

He gave another slightly harder thrust and Zsilvia bit her bottom lip against a moan, allowing her eyes to close as she lifted her hips toward him. George came down over her so that his body touched hers from the chest down and his mouth came to the soft place just beneath her ear.

"I guess that does make me your first."

He touched his mouth to hers, kissing her deeply as he picked up his rhythm. She gave herself over to the sensation of him and let his body nurture hers as she continued to spiral higher. Suddenly the intensity grew to almost unbearable before it shattered around her, releasing into a series of spasms that drew George deeper into her body and brought groans of satisfaction from his chest.

"I love how that feels," he whispered to her, rocking his hips to meet her contractions.

Zsilvia gasped for breath and reached up to take his head in her hands.

"George," she said and then waited until he opened his eyes to look at her, "Fill me."

That simple statement seemed to push George beyond the brink of his control and he gave a deep grunt before starting a faster, harder pace with his hips. Zsilvia writhed beneath him, savoring each fulfilling thrust as his sounds grew louder and more frantic. He gave a final hard thrust and Zsilvia felt his cock throb, pulsing wildly as the heat streamed from his body and filled her just as she had asked.

George dropped down beside her, scooping Zsilvia into his arms so that their legs tangled and her head came to rest on his chest.

"I love you," she finally let herself whisper.

Now that their bond was complete, she felt stronger, better prepared to face whatever challenges lay in their way, and that was put to the test almost immediately.

George reached down to draw the covers up over them, but before Zsilvia could let herself drift to sleep in his arms she heard a frantic shout from the mouth of the cavern.

"Zsilvia! George!"

Loralia's voice sounded terrified and Zsilvia sat upright. She scrambled to grab George's pants and toss them to him so that he was covered by the time Loralia appeared in front of them.

"We need to go," Loralia said.

"Has the storm stopped?" Zsilvia asked.

"It doesn't matter. We need to leave and go to the settlement as fast as we can."

"What's happening?" George asked.

"I just heard from Bannack," Loralia said, sounding as though she was choking back emotion so that she could communicate with them clearly. "The first of the Covra are hatching."

UNTITLED

(To be continued in Part VIII...)

THE ALIEN'S BOND

1

———

The scream from across the settlement was still ringing in Lynx's ears even as he stared down at the lifeless body of the man in the middle of the road. He felt paralyzed even as the other warriors around him tried to get his attention. Finally he felt a hand grab him by the back of the neck and shake him until he turned around and faced Ero.

"What do we do, Lynx?" Ero asked.

Lynx shook his head, trying to regain his focus so that he could think clearly.

"I don't..." he started.

Ero shook him again and a sharp pain shot down Lynx's neck and along his back, helping to cut through the fogginess in his mind.

"You don't get to not know," Ero said. "Pyra left you in charge for a reason and now you have to figure out what we are going to do about this."

Lynx nodded. Ero was right. Pyra had entrusted him with the honor of being in charge of the settlement while he and half of the others had gone off to find a nearby kingdom that had maintained good relations with the Light Ones for the years leading up to the Covra locking the settlement in place. Their powerful leader had overlooked other, older, and potentially more capable warriors to give Lynx control over those who had stayed behind to look after the Light Ones and the settlement. It was his responsibility and his duty to Pyra and the rest of the Denynso to stay calm and help them decide how they were going to move forward.

The cutting, gut-wrenching scream that had shaken Lynx from his vigil over Rain and brought him running down the main street of the settlement as quickly as his legs would carry him was the sound of one of the other warriors. A man bred and trained for battle, screaming in horror as he watched a man die in the few seconds that it took for the Covra eggs implanted within him to hatch and the younglings within to eat their way out of his body.

By the time that Lynx had gotten to the street and found the dead man, Fabian had gotten ahold of himself and was valiantly fighting off the strong, vicious new Covra. Fortunately the voracious appetite that the newborn Covra had in their first moments of life distracted them enough that they were not prepared immediately for the battle that Fabian waged upon them, and with the help of Ero and Bannack he was able to destroy them all by stabbing them directly through the eye, the only way that they knew of to defeat the fearsome creatures.

"Is he the only one?" Lynx asked.

He turned back to the man lying in the dirt at his feet. The slightly swollen, softened area around the puncture wound where the Covra had inserted the eggs was now a gaping hole. The flesh around the hole was tattered, lying open across his torn clothing like ribbons. Lynx noticed immediately, however, that there was no blood. It struck him strangely, making him feel even more uncomfortable than he might have felt if the wounds had bled like he was accustomed to the injured bleeding in battle. Instead, Lynx could look directly into the man's body and see the white of his ribcage and an abdominal cavity left empty by the Covra young eating their way out after hatching.

Who had he been before the Covra froze him? What was his name? Did he have a wife, a family? What was his role within this community? Where was he going as he walked down the street away from the direction of all of the houses in the quickly darkening hours of that evening?

Lynx dug back through is memories to try to remember this man from the night that he had spent making his way throughout the entire settlement reliving the last few moments of the conscious lives of everyone within it. He had used a power that he didn't even know that he had to gain insight into the Covra and how they had managed to completely take over the settlement and lock all of the people in place. Though it had been uncomfortable, almost as though he were prying into these people's existence and digging out information that he had not been given permission to even access much less share with anyone else, it had given them incredibly valuable insight into the Covra that they could then use to defeat them.

No matter how hard he searched, though, Lynx couldn't find this man in the memories of all of those moments. They had been some of the most mundane and unremarkable moments, moments that everyone passes innumerable times each day, but through the Covra toxins they had become the most private and treasured of moments that these people had ever lived. Those few minutes were like shrines, encapsulating all that was each of these individuals in the only way that the world would know them for more than a century. For this man, that shrine had become a tomb for everything that he had been and would never have the opportunity to follow through.

"I don't know," Fabian said from where he stood several feet away from the man and the other warriors, "I found him, but I haven't found anyone else."

"Everyone spread out," Lynx said, pulling his attention away from the man and to the warriors, "Get as many of us that you encounter along the way, but don't go looking for anyone. If these young were just hatched, that means that the other eggs are likely ready to hatch soon. We have to find out if there are any others that have hatched and kill any of the Covra young. Do whatever you can to save the people if you find ones with hatching Covra."

"Which is more important," Ero asked carefully, "killing the Covra or saving the Light Ones?"

Lynx felt his spine straighten and he lowered his shoulders as he resolved to be the strength that the rest of the men needed in that moment.

"Kill the Covra."

2

———————

Zsilvia savored the feeling of George's hand flattened against the small of her back as she climbed back up out of the mirrored realm where they had all been seeking refuge from the storm. The touch was simple, but there was so much in the supportive, protective pressure that it briefly brought tears to her eyes. She had been frustrated and even angry the last few days. It had only been moments when Loralia had stormed into the small cavern where she and George had finally completed their bond and were beginning to drift asleep cradled in each other's arms. It had been Loralia who had led her to that cavern to take a bath and relax after she had run away from the rest of the group, particularly George and Ivy, but at that moment it had been Loralia who was forcing them out of their comfort and telling them that they needed to leave the mirrored realm and keep going toward the settlement where the men were waiting for their help.

Above her Zsilvia could hear that the storm was still raging and she braced herself for the cold of the rain that would soon assault her as it had before they moved down into the safety of the caverns. They had hoped that they would be able to pass the entire storm in the warm, dry chambers where Loralia had lived and then continue on their way in the morning when the weather was more hospitable. They had only been there a short time; however they had to rush out when Loralia got word from Bannack that they needed to get to the settlement as quickly as possible to help them as the new generation of the vicious Covra hatched throughout the settlement.

Even with George's hand on her back and though she didn't want to mention it to anyone, Zsilvia was frightened by the thought of leaving the Denynso compound where she had been her entire life and go to an unknown settlement to help save one strange species from another. She, like the rest of the Denynso women, had only ever encountered her kind until the humans started arriving from Earth to study the planet or bring information about them back to their planet. They had usually only stayed for a short time, however, which meant that she didn't have to interact with them very much. It wasn't until Eden showed up and the king gave her special permission to remain on the planet for as long as she wanted that things began to change.

Once Eden and Pyra had bonded it seemed like everything that Zsilvia had known had started to disappear around her. It was subtle, and she felt that in a way she was being over dramatic about the situation, but the reality was that the influx of humans into the compound as the women appeared for their own reasons and then found their life mates among the men of the Denynso represented a fundamental shift in the lives of the Denynso. What was once a clan that encountered other species only when in battle and never left their compound was suddenly in a situation where they were forced to learn about the ways of another species and assimilate them into their number.

Many found this change exciting and progressive; pointing out that it was the opportunity to learn from one another and eventually cooperate and interact on a regular basis. That was the original point of allowing humans into the compound and then the university exchange program. Zsilvia, though, had been intimidated by the changes and not sure how the others fit in with them. It wasn't that she didn't like them or had a problem with the fact that they were other species. It was more that she felt uncomfortable around those who she didn't understand and who she thought might judge her. Over the weeks, though, she had become more at ease with them and had nearly gotten to the point where she didn't even acknowledge the difference between the other Denynso women and the human women.

Of course, it was the arrival of the humans that had also brought her George, and, for that, she would always be grateful. If it hadn't been for the courage of Creia and Theia and their determination to expand the knowledge and understanding of the Denynso about the people away from their home planet, George never would have come to Uoria and she would have lived the rest of her life completely alone. Deep within her she knew that she needed to do whatever she could to give that same type of chance to the people of the settlement. No matter who or what they were, they should have the opportunity to live the lives that they wanted, not suffer by the whims of others.

Zsilvia took the final step up out of the hole beneath the moss that led out of the underground mirrored realm and cringed as the sharp raindrops hit her face and arms again. She moved out of the way to allow George to climb up behind her and pulled her shirt up as high on her neck as she could, thankful that she had her thick hair down so that it guarded some of her exposed skin.

Everyone else stood closely together, their backs curved and turned against the wind as they tried to protect themselves from the cold. Each of them carried a nervous, uncomfortable expression that bordered on frightened, and as George came up behind her and tucked his hand around her waist again, Zsilvia realized that she was the only one of them who had her mate with her. The others hadn't been able to touch their mates since the men had left on their quest and for the first time Zsilvia was truly feeling the type of impact that that separation had on them. George standing so close to her made her feel safe and secure, and their bodies cut the wind and rain from either side for the other, making them feel warmer and less assaulted by the ever-worsening storm.

Loralia kicked the piece of moss that covered the hole back into place and gestured for them all to continue forward. It was as though none of them wanted to speak. They were all lost in their own worlds, their thoughts controlling them as they ducked their heads and pushed on through the rain and the wind toward the edge of the compound.

Soon they arrived back at the crumbling remnants of the prison where the warriors had found out about the settlement, and where the women and George had gone to find out more about the Light Ones, the Covra, and what might free the people of the settlement from their bonds. Zsilvia had hoped that the rain would have tampered down the burned corpse of the prison enough to keep the acrid, biting smell at bay, but it only seemed to heighten her awareness of the odor, as if the cleanness of the raindrops only accented the ash and charred stone.

"Do we go back inside?" Samira asked, lifting her voice above the sound of the storm.

"No," Zuri answered, shaking her head, "It would be too dangerous to go down there in this weather. The structure isn't sound anymore. You have no idea when the top layer could just crumble in. Besides, we have all of the information that we could find. That's all we need. We need to keep going. Every minute that we delay there is more of a chance of the Light Ones all dying. We have to get there as fast as we can, at least so Lynx knows that we tried."

"What if we don't get there in time?" Elianna asked, giving voice to the worries that all of them held.

"We have to at least do our best."

Silence fell as they started again and Zsilvia tried to block the sound of the creaking branches and tree trunks out of her head. They were out of the densest portion of the forest now, but the trees towered high enough that if one of them broke it could still fall onto them. Though she feared going past the barrier that blocked all of the compound within it, she knew that she was going to feel better when they were finally beyond it and away from the forest.

Suddenly the sky split above them with a flash and a crack of thunder so loud that Zsilvia's ears rang and she turned to look over her shoulder at the row of trees beyond the remnants of the prison. Only seconds later another bolt of lightning shot out of the angry-looking clouds, hitting the center of the pile of rubble that had been the prison. The impact sounded like an explosion and Zsilvia's scream joined the others as she dove away from the exploding stone and wood.

After a few seconds she sat up and looked over at the prison. Flames shot up from the middle and danced across the surface, catching any bits of wood that were dry enough to burn and creating a low glow that was almost mesmerizing. That single, blinding bolt of lightning must have found an area of the decimated floor of the prison that was even weaker than the rest and broken through, igniting everything in the underground labyrinth of corridors and offices that they had not long before been exploring in an effort to find out everything that they could for the men. The flames continued to jump and spit out of the floor, hissing as the rain touched them. New smoke joined the smell of the burned lumber to create an even more choking sensation in the back of Zsilvia's throat.

The thought that they had only moments before contemplated climbing back down into that dungeon made her heart clench painfully and she reached for George's hand. He gripped her firmly, not saying anything as they all rose to their feet from the wet ground. They all stared at the flaming prison with a combination of fascination and horror, locked in place for several long seconds as everything that the ancient Covra had stored inside that building in the generations before the Klimnu had taken over it was engulfed, consumed so that it would never again be seen. Zsilvia found herself hoping that the sight was prophetic, that together they would be able to eliminate the threat of the Covra and let them disappear into the ether of history so that they were never again able to hurt the others that roamed the planet outside of the compound. Whoever those others were.

For the first time since they started toward the settlement Zsilvia thought about Eden. It seemed strange that she wasn't with them. Though she had spent only a short time with them, Zsilvia had become accustomed to the entire group of women being together, from Eden, the first human woman to arrive in the compound, to Loralia, the strange but beautiful creature who the warriors had discovered after their final battle with the Klimnu. She wondered if Eden was worried about them or if her only thoughts were of her mate Pyra and their baby, who she held within her in anticipation of his arrival very soon, too soon for her to brave the walk that would carry them to the settlement or the danger that might face them once they got there. Zsilvia couldn't imagine the type of torment that Eden was feeling then. She had to be not only worried about her mate and wishing that he was home to support and comfort her at the end of her pregnancy, but also afraid that the creatures that were threatening the Light Ones and then warriors trying to defend them would make their way to the compound and put her child's life at risk.

3

Zsilvia was barely paying attention to where they were walking, but suddenly she felt George's hand tighten around hers and she looked up from where she had kept her eyes focused on the ground in front of her so that she could keep the rain out of them. Several feet ahead of them was a massive stone wall. They had finally reached the barrier of the compound.

Everyone stopped walking and stared at the wall. The storm continued to rage around them, but for that moment Zsilvia wasn't even thinking about the crashing of the thunder or the blue and white blasts of light that came from the lightning bolts. Instead all she could think about was what that barrier represented. That was not just a wall or a delineation between abstracts areas of the planet. To her it represented so much more. All her life she had known that her existence was limited just to the compound. It was never something that they spoke about or that had been scared into her like too many lessons parents attempt to teach their children. Rather it was simply a part of life, like an element of her culture that was just as much permeated through all of the tasks of her daily routine as it was passed through the generations and born into her.

Denynso children simply knew that their world was the world of their compound, just as it had been for their parents, and their parents' parents, and on through their ancestors since the beginning of their kind on Uoria. No one ever spoke of what might exist beyond the compound or why they didn't go beyond it. It had never occurred to Zsilvia or anyone that she knew to ask the questions that seemed so obvious to her now that she was an adult and was finally staring at the boundary that had held her back her entire life, whether she realized it or not.

"Are you afraid, love?"

His accent seemed even more pronounced when he whispered to her, and Zsilvia felt herself leaning toward him as if sinking into the soft sound of his voice. She squeezed his hand reassuringly.

"No," she answered, "I'm not afraid. Just," she took a breath, "anxious to see what is on the other side."

George smiled at her and she saw a glint in his eye that told her that despite the storm and the unknown dangers that awaited them right past the stones, he was happy that they were having this experience together, that he was finally by her side to see her through such a momentous moment in her life.

"Who should go first?" Zuri asked, looking back at the rest of the group.

The five other women exchanged glances. Out of the corner of her eye Zsilvia could see George start to open his mouth as if to offer himself as the first to cross the wall.

"I will," Zsilvia said, stepping forward toward the other women.

"Zsilvia?" Zuri said.

"Are you sure?" George asked.

Zsilvia looked into each of the pairs of eyes that stared at her in shock. She could see the surprise and hints of confusion in them, but she was steadfast in her decision.

"I am the only Denynso here," she said in a voice that was calm, steady, and loud enough to rise above the continuing roar of the storm, "This is my compound, my home since the day I was born, and it is my duty to lead. I will go over the wall first."

George looked at her like he wanted to protest, but he knew better than to argue with her. Just as the warriors had the responsibility of taking care of the rest of the clan through their dedication in battle, she felt compelled to step forward and lead in their journey to help the men that awaited them.

She took a breath and released George's hand beside her. Without looking at any of them, Zsilvia strode forward toward the wall. It seemed to grow taller as she approached it, as if trying to intimidate her and convince her to stay back and follow the restrictions that she always had. Tired of being told what to think, how to act, and what to do, she looked at the wall with more determination than she had ever felt, reached forward to grab onto one of the stones protruding just above her head, and planted her foot against it. She blocked everything out of her mind and concentrated for a few seconds on the sound of the raindrops on the rocks. When she had isolated the drops so that she felt she could hear each as they hit the stones rather than just a continuous cascade of water, she brought the focus and clarity within her and pushed herself up.

Suddenly she was perched on the top of the wall and the sound of the raindrops no longer sounded like an assault but a soothing, calming assurance. Zsilvia lifted her eyes from her own legs draped over the top to the land that waited beyond it. Even in the darkness of the storm the open space was beautiful and she felt the tension within her coil up in her belly, shifting from a feeling of nervousness and anxiety to one of potential and excitement.

Zsilvia drew in a breath, swung her legs forward, and released the wall. She felt herself falling and a second later she hit the ground. She was beyond the boundary. There was a moment of still quiet as she stood slowly and looked around. Unlike the compound where there always seemed like something was creating walls around her, whether it was the trees, the cliffs, or the actual buildings of the village, this space was wide and open. It seemed to ripple slightly in front of her and stretched so far it melted into the smoky black line of the horizon.

"I'm over," she finally called to the others on the other side of the wall.

In moments she saw George scramble over the wall and land on the ground beside her. He stood and swept her into his arms. She returned the embrace, tucking her head into the curve of his shoulder and neck so she could draw in the rich scent of him and find stillness in the steady rise and fall of his breath. Around them the other women helped each other over the wall and finally Zuri helped Elianna make her way down and they were all outside of the compound.

It seemed that the intensity of the storm had been, much like her, contained within the compound, and now only clouds and the soft mist of rain lingered. Their pace increased as they continued forward, all of them moving faster despite their exhaustion, compelled and refreshed by the excitement of finally achieving the goal of getting out of the compound.

The sun was halfway behind the horizon when they

finally stopped. Zsilvia didn't realize until then how hungry she was. They hadn't stopped to eat at any other point in the day, though the others might have eaten something when they were in the mirrored realm.

"Where are we going to sleep for the night?" Elianna asked as they all dropped down to the ground to rest.

"I don't see any caves or anything," Samira responded. "I think that we're just going to have to set up our tents and settle in wherever we can."

Despite the wetness of the ground it felt amazing to finally be sitting again after so many hours of trudging along. Zsilvia rested back against her bag and let her eyes drift close for a moment. She didn't really care where they slept as long as they didn't go much further than they were right then. She wanted to sleep like she never had in her life, but as she felt herself drifting away, someone came up beside her.

"Can I talk to you?"

Zsilvia opened her eyes at the sound of Ivy's voice. The blonde woman had settled down beside her and was watching the others digging through their bags to pull out their tents and get started on a fire to heat up their evening meal. Zsilvia pulled herself up so that she was sitting straighter and nodded.

"Sure."

"I just wanted to tell you that I'm sorry about the misunderstanding with George. I didn't mean to upset you. He and I have worked together for a long time at home and are really close, but it has never been anything more than a friendship. I promise you that."

"I know. He explained it all to me."

"If I had known about you before I got here, I never would have acted the way I did with him. I'm really sorry."

Zsilvia shook her head. Now that she understood the entire situation she was starting to realize that Ivy was not at all the type of person she thought she was.

"It's alright, Ivy. There's no way that you would have known. There wasn't really an "us" until today."

"That's not true," Ivy said, the hint of a smile flickering in her eyes. "You might not have acknowledged it, but for George, there was an "us" from the moment that he saw you. I know that man and I have never seen him like he is with you. Just hearing your voice made him light up. It was like his heart wasn't really beating until he was here with you. You brought him to life."

Zsilvia smiled, and then something about the words hit her. She sat up straighter and stared at Ivy.

"What did you just say?"

4

Lynx pulled his dagger up over his head and brought it down with as much force as he could draw into his arms. The sharpened tip burrowed down into the gleaming eye of the young Covra scuttling toward him at a speed that made his skin crawl. The eye split, vibrant green blood splashing out of it and across the ground. A screech poured out of the creature, sending a shudder down Lynx's spine as the creature thrashed for several seconds, fell still, and disintegrated into the floor. Around him Lynx could hear the other warriors grunting and shouting as they fought off the young Covra emerging from the destroyed bodies of the Light Ones that had acted first as the incubators for their eggs, and then as their first meal.

The birth of the new generation of the creatures had thankfully begun slowly. Rather than all of the eggs within all of the Light Ones in the settlement hatching at the same time and releasing all of voracious young Covra, the warriors had only caught three of the sets of eggs hatching. Though the three people who had contained the eggs had died in the wake of the hatching, Lynx knew that they had to concentrate first on killing the Covra as they emerged rather than attempting to save the people. They didn't know what they could do to save them and the risk of allowing any of the creatures to get out of the settlement or have the time to get bigger and even stronger was far too high to allow it to happen.

Lynx tried to block out the image of the woman lying on the steps of her home in front of him, her body contorted in the position where it had fallen when the Covra were born and began eating their way out of her. Though there was no blood, it was a horrific sight and it made his mind wander to Rain lying helplessly in her bed at the other end of the settlement. He knew that there was nothing he could do to help her, and that made him feel helpless, empty, and terrified. Just like the rest of the people in the settlement, her body was harboring a clutch of Covra eggs and those eggs, embedded deeply in her stomach, could hatch at any moment, destroying her before he even had the chance to see her eyes open or hear her voice.

The knowledge that his intended mate could be mere moments from dying a horrific death and that there was nothing he could do to stop it made Lynx feel like he was tied down with invisible ropes, kept from making any move and forced to simply stand by and watch the young Covra destroy her. He knew that he couldn't continue to think about her. He needed to force those thoughts out of his mind and focus on eliminating the Covra as they were born. It would motivate him to keep going and keep him following through with the responsibilities that Pyra had given him.

Lynx ran back down the steps, leaving the woman where she was for the time, and out onto the street. He looked around, waiting to see another of the locked people collapse and release the new wave of young creatures out. For the moment everything seemed still but he couldn't let himself go off guard. He had to remain vigilant or risk one of the creatures surprising him and overtaking him before he was able to fight back. Loralia had warned them that the newborn Covra would be far stronger and more powerful than even the older creatures that they had already encountered, and he had quickly learned that she was absolutely correct. Even though they had just hatched these young were fast, aggressive, and fought with even more intensity than the generation before them even though they had absolutely no knowledge of the conflict of those that came before them. Rather than fighting out of the anger that came from their original conflict with the Light Ones or knowledge of their struggle with the Denynso, the young fought and attempted to kill purely out of inborn compulsion and lust for blood.

"Lynx!"

Lynx turned toward the sound of the frantic voice and saw Bannack running toward him clutching the heavy silver compact that Loralia had given him in his hand. The compact was open, which meant that either he had reached out to the women or they had contacted him. Lynx knew that the women and the new professor who had arrived at the compound after the warriors had left were on their way to the settlement to help them, and something about the possibility of them contacting the men made Lynx feel like there was a rock in his stomach.

"Is there something wrong?" Lynx asked as Bannack got close to him.

"I don't know," Bannack said, "Loralia wouldn't tell me what was going on and immediately handed the compact over to Zsilvia. She said that she needed to talk to you. I have no idea what she needs to tell you."

Lynx nodded and took the compact from Bannack's hand. He was still trying to get used to the idea of communicating through the glass of the mirrors contained in the compact, but it had proven extremely useful in the time that they had been in the settlement and he was thankful for the incredible abilities of his friend's mate.

"Zsilvia?" Lynx said, looking into the compact.

"Lynx, are you anywhere near Rain?"

"No. I haven't been back to the house since the eggs started hatching."

"Get back there."

Before he could ask why Lynx heard the scream of another of the warriors from somewhere in the settlement and he knew that another of the locked people had succumbed to the creatures within them.

"Another set of the eggs has started hatching," he told her.

"Then you need to get back to that house as fast as you can."

"I have to help. Pyra left me in charge."

"Pyra left you to lead and to do what is right for the Light Ones, and in order to do that, you need to get back to Rain. Tell the other warriors to help with the Covra hatchlings. For now, you need to get to the house as fast as you can."

Lynx looked up at Bannack, who nodded at him as if to confirm that he needed to do as the Denynso woman had instructed. Together they started toward the house and Lynx ran up the stairs to Rain's bedroom, terrified that he would find her dead and her room overrun by Covra young.

When he opened the door he felt relief wash over him as she saw her lying in the bed just as he had left her, quiet, peaceful, and oblivious to the chaos going on right outside her window.

"I'm here," he said into the glass.

Zsilvia nodded.

"Show her to me."

Lynx turned the glass so that Rain's reflection appeared in it.

"Can you see her?" he asked.

"Yes. Now say something to her."

The request struck Lynx as odd and he turned the mirror back to himself.

"What do you mean?"

"Turn the mirror back to her and say something to her."

Lynx turned the compact back around, but couldn't think of anything that he wanted to say to her that he would like an audience for.

"What should I say to her?" he asked.

"Anything. Ask her to wake up."

Wishing he could touch her without going into the intense vision of her last several moments before getting locked, Lynx leaned toward Rain and gazed down into her pale, beautiful face.

"Come on, Rain," he said softly, "Wake up."

There was silence for a few seconds and then he heard Zsilvia again.

"Did anything happen?"

"No."

She sighed and then Lynx heard a voice he didn't recognize.

"Lynx, can you show me her injury?"

Lynx pulled the compact up to look at the source of the male voice and saw a middle-aged man looking at him.

"Who are you?" he asked.

"My name is George. I'm the new professor that came to be a part of the university exchange program."

"Lynx," Bannack said softly from beside him, but Lynx gestured for him to be quiet.

"Hi, George. Why do you want to see Rain's injury?"

"I'm a scientist. My research assistant and I have been working with Zuri and the other women to find a solution to the locking of the people in the settlement. Loralia has been the only one to see the Covra injury itself, and it is possible that if I see it, I might gain more insight into it."

"Lynx," Bannack said again, more insistently.

"What?" Lynx demanded, turning to Bannack.

The other warrior's eyes were trained on Rain and when Lynx joined the gaze he didn't need to ask what was causing the shocked reaction.

Rain was moving.

5

———

Lynx could hear George repeating his name, but he couldn't pull his attention away from the subtle flickering of movement behind Rain's eyelids and the occasional tremor of one of her fingers beneath the blanket.

"Lynx!"

Zsilvia's voice startled the Denynso warrior and he looked back into the compact.

"She moved," he said.

Zsilvia smiled broadly.

"When you spoke to her?" she asked.

Lynx shook his head.

"When George was talking."

The smile on Zsilvia's face faded.

"What?"

Her voice sounded lighter and slightly strained.

"When George started talking, I noticed that she was moving," Bannack said.

Lynx nodded.

"I saw it, too. It wasn't much, but she was moving!"

"Is she still moving now?" Zsilvia asked.

Lynx looked down at Rain, but her face had gone just as still as it had always been, and the subtle tremor of movement under the blankets had stopped.

"No. She stopped."

Disappointment washed over him and he felt tears stinging in the corners of his eyes. It suddenly felt even more hopeless. Somehow seeing that little glimmer of possibility, of potential, and then losing it without understanding how it had happened in the first place or what he could do to reclaim it was even worse than not having anything. At least if she had never changed he would always remember her just as she had been and it would be a matter of losing something that he had so desperately wanted and was meant to have, but never really did. Seeing those small movements and then watching them disappear made him feel like he had her in his hand and then watched her slip through his fingers like sand.

"What was he saying when she moved?" Zsilvia asked.

"She started moving as soon as he spoke," Bannack said. "It wasn't any word in particular or anything."

"Oh," Zsilvia said, sounding disappointed.

"What is it, Zsilvia?" Loralia asked.

"I thought," Zsilvia started and then hesitated, "Do you remember what George said about the Light Ones' hearts not beating? That their blood was locked just as much as they were, and that it would take getting their blood flowing again to make them alive?"

"He said that if their hearts had just stopped beating and the blood had stopped flowing because of it, it would have pooled in the lower half of their body and creating dark discoloration," Loralia said.

"That's right," Elianna started and Lynx saw Rain's eyelids flicker again.

"She moved again!" he said, cutting off Elianna before she could say anything else.

"Lynx, turn the compact toward her face and bring it close enough that we can see her eyes," Zsilvia told him.

Once he had followed her instructions, Lynx heard Zsilvia speaking directly to Rain.

"Hello?" she said, "Rain? Can you hear me?"

Rain had no reaction, but Lynx forced the dark brooding thoughts to stay at bay. They had brought the movements back once. They could do it again.

"Rain? This is George."

Rain's eyes fluttered again and Lynx heard the women on the other side of the compact gasp as they noticed the movement for the first time.

"Rain? My name is Loralia. Can you hear me?"

There was no movement and Lynx bit into his bottom lip, trying to hold back the emotions that had started to build up inside of him.

"Hi, Rain," another unfamiliar voice said, "My name is Ivy. Can you hear me?"

Rain's eyelids fluttered again. Lynx heard a few moments of excited chatter but couldn't decipher any words. Suddenly he heard Zsilvia again.

"Lynx, look at us." Lynx turned the compact toward himself. "I'm going to ask you a question and I need you to answer it completely honestly. Do you understand me?"

"Yes."

"Alright. Do you know what species Rain is?"

Lynx felt his heart constrict again just as it had before he admitted to Ero that Rain and the other Light Ones were human. He felt the inexplicable defensiveness again; the resistance to reveal that information to them. Zsilvia must have seen the tension in his face because she tilted her face slightly so that she stared directly into his eyes.

"Tell me, Lynx."

When he didn't respond again, Zsilvia demanded that he give the compact to Bannack.

"What are they, Bannack? Loralia says that you know."

Lynx looked over at Bannack and saw the hint of an apology in his friend's eyes before he nodded.

"They're human."

Lynx could hear the loud jumble of reactions from the women and suddenly George's voice coming through the compact, sounding angry.

"Why didn't you tell us that?" he demanded.

"I didn't know how anyone was going to react," Lynx said.

"Well, because of that you might have killed her and every other person in that compound. If we had known that she was human we might have had a better chance of coming up with an antidote or understanding this situation better."

"What the hell do you want me to do about it now?" Lynx said defensively.

"Go get Ty," Samira suddenly said and everyone fell quiet.

"Ty?" Lynx asked, "Do you seriously think that now is the moment for you to have some sort of reunion with your mate?"

"That's not what this is about," Samira said, sounding slightly disgusted, "Look at Rain."

Lynx looked down at Rain again and saw that her lips had parted and her head seemed to have turned slightly.

"She moved more."

"The more we talk, the more she moves," Samira said. "Get Ty and tell him to bring the box that I gave him."

Bannack rushed out of the room and a few minutes later came back in with Ty, who looked breathless and was carrying a small metal box in his hands. Lynx held the compact out to the young warrior, who took it and smiled down at Samira.

"Hey, Babe. What do you need the box for? What's going on?"

"Ty, did Ciyrs leave any of his healing ointments?" Elianna's voice asked.

"Yeah," Ty answered, "Some. Why?"

"We have an idea," Zuri's voice said, "but it is going to take a lot of courage on the part of one of you. You need to get those ointments and a sharp dagger. Go fast. You don't have much time."

The mention of a dagger made Lynx feel sick. He could only imagine what she had in mind, and the thought was horrific even though he knew it was likely the only option for saving Rain, and possibly the others as well.

Lynx halfway listened to the instructions that George, Zuri, and Elianna gave to the other warriors as he gazed down at Rain. He might have imagined it, but it seemed that her color was slightly pinker and her lips had plumped. He hoped that she could feel him near her and that if she could, he was giving her comfort.

It was nearly an hour later when the warriors had finally gathered everything that they needed and Bannack was standing beside the bed, his hand tightly gripping the handle of a dagger.

"Are you sure that you want me to do this?" he asked,

glancing over his shoulder at Lynx.

"Of course I don't want you to do it," Lynx said, "but it's the only way. Just do it as quickly and carefully as you can."

"Lynx," Elianna's voice came through, "you need to be ready with the bandages and the healing ointments."

"And Ty," Samira said, "be ready with the box."

Lynx wanted to close his eyes and not witness what was about to happen, but just as in the visions, he felt tethered in place, unable to look away and compelled, forced to watch as Bannack carefully pulled back the blankets that covered Rain and respectfully pushed aside the tattered edges of the nightgown near the puncture wound where the Covra had injected her with the clutch of eggs and the locking toxin.

In one swift movement Bannack plunged the tip of the dagger into the puncture wound and drew it back toward him, opening her skin. Lynx felt his stomach turn and the angry, aggressive need to protect her surge up within him, but he held himself back. He knew that this was the only chance. This is what had to be done.

Through the new opening in Rain's stomach Lynx could see the yellow orb that had been attached to the front leg of the massive Covra before the smaller one took it to force it into her so that she could incubate it and then act as the first source of nourishment for the new hatchlings. Bannack tilted his dagger so the blade tucked under the clutch and then pushed, forcing the orb up out of her body and onto the floor. There was a hint of greenish slime and then along with it, a trickle of blood.

"She's bleeding!" he shouted.

"That's good, Lynx!" George's voice yelled from the compact Ty held up so that the professor and Elianna could supervise the procedure. "Now help him finish."

Lynx rushed forward and started applying the healing ointments to the wound, following Elianna's instructions carefully as he packed the wound with a thick herbal paste, covered it with a thinner salve, and then wrapped it carefully. When she was fully bandaged and Bannack had destroyed the eggs, Lynx dropped down on the edge of the bed and looked up at Ty.

"Go ahead and open the box," Samira instructed.

Ty nestled his ring into the top of the box and Lynx watched in awe as the metal gears turned and the sides of the box opened.

"Which disc should I use?" he asked.

"The third one should be fine."

Ty reached into a narrow drawer in the box and Lynx watched him withdraw a small flat object, which he settled into another section of the box. Suddenly Samira's voice filled the room from the box.

"It's working perfectly," Ty said.

"Good," Samira said, "Just put it on the table beside the bed and keep it playing. We have to get some rest and then we will be right back on our way to you in the morning."

"What is that?" Lynx asked.

"It's a voice box," Samira told him. "As long as you restart it when the disc ends, it will continuously play my voice."

"Lynx," Georg said, "watch over Rain. Stay with her as much as you can. With as much of those healing ointments as you have, the other warriors should go see how many others they can save."

Lynx nodded.

"Thank you," he said, turning to watch Rain's movements in response to the sound of Samira's voice. "Thank you so much."

6

Zsilvia watched George close the compact, hand it back to Loralia, and then turn to sweep her into his arms. She clutched at his shoulders, drawing in the scent of his skin and clothes still wet from the rain.

"How did you think of that?" he asked when he stopped hugging her and pushed her back slightly so that he could look at her.

Zsilvia smiled at him and then looked over at Ivy.

"It was something that Ivy said to me."

Ivy looked up, the expression on her face startled.

"It was?" she asked.

"Yes," Zsilvia said. "You told me that when I spoke, George lit up like I was making his heart beat for the first time; that I brought him to life."

Ivy nodded.

"It's true."

George pulled Zsilvia in for another embrace, seeming to pull her even closer now so that her entire body crushed against his.

"It is true," he agreed. "I was nothing before you. I went

about my life and I thought that everything was fine and that I was happy, and then I met you and realized that I hadn't lived a single moment of my existence until the day that I saw you."

Zsilvia rested her lips against his and relaxed into the feeling and taste of his mouth. She knew exactly what he meant because she felt the same way.

"I don't understand, though," Ivy said, breaking the kiss. "George felt that way because Zsilvia is his mate. When Lynx spoke to her, though, she didn't move."

Zsilvia looked over at the lovely blonde woman and realized that in all of the chaos of their conversation with the warriors, they hadn't noticed that Ivy was sinking back away from them. She had spoken up early in the conversation, but had then seemed to disappear. Zsilvia felt guilty that they had pushed her away, whether they realized they had done it or not, simply because she was having difficulty following what was happening.

The rest of them had been living with this problem for longer than Ivy had, and she had not been there for the first talks that they had about the Covra. She didn't know about the creatures or the stories that Loralia's grandfather had always told her and the rest of the young of the species about the fearsome monsters that fought with a skill so terrible he wouldn't even tell them what it was. Of course, they knew now that that weapon was the ability to lock a species in place, take from them their very ability to live without actually killing them, so that they could manipulate them as they wished, or fill them with a virulent toxin that immediately turned the infected person into a vicious, violent killer that would destroy anything he encountered.

"It was not the voice of her mate that Rain needed," Loralia explained. "What she needed was to hear the voice of her kind. My grandfather always told us that the Covra had a single weakness, something that weakened them to the point of barely being able to survive. What if it was that weakness that made them hate the Light Ones so much? And what if they used it when they infected them not just to ensure that their kind would be protected from it, but that the Light Ones would never be able to wake up before the hatchlings arrived?"

"A human voice," Zsilvia said.

Loralia nodded.

"If the Covra are weak to the sound of a human voice, when the Light Ones arrived they would want to eliminate them as quickly as possible. As they got older and weaker, though, they realized that just being near the voices of those people could destroy them before they would be able to actually fight them in battle or have them kill each other. Instead, they could use the technique that they often used to kill their own prey. They locked them in place, knowing that only the voice of their kind could ever awaken them by making their hearts beat again, and that no other humans were on Uoria."

"They had no way of knowing that more would come decades later," Zuri said.

"Just in time for their new generation to be born," Elianna said.

"Exactly," Loralia continued. "But what scared them first was the warriors. A Denynso voice is so similar to a human voice, maybe it has some of the same effect on the Covra. They hated to hear it. So as much as they were trying to protect their young from the men, they were also trying to get rid of the Denynso that weakened them even more than their age already had just by speaking."

Zsilvia shuddered.

"How many of them do you think they will be able to save by getting the egg clutches out of their bodies before they hatch?" she asked.

"A few," Elianna said. "I know that Ciyrs brought enough of his healing ointments for all of the warriors to need them a couple of times during the journey, but Bannack told us that when the others split off to go to that other kingdom that he went with them. He would have brought along half of the supplies. And four of the men have already had to undergo major surgeries. The supplies are likely dwindling now and they won't have enough to treat everyone in the settlement."

"Do we have enough?" Zsilvia asked.

"I think so. We brought three times what Ciyrs did plus enough of the supplies to make more. That should be enough."

She indicated her bag plus the ones that Zuri, Samira, and George had with them.

"We need to get a few hours of rest now before we keep going," George said. "We need to be as strong and ready as we can be when we get there so that we can do everything we can for the Light Ones. I have a feeling that the slow pace of the hatching is just the beginning."

Loralia nodded.

"It will get faster. Remember what those papers we found said. As soon as one set of hatchlings emerges, they begin communicating with the others that are still inside the incubators. It works much the same way as a creature that they lock only responding to the voice of its kind. The sounds of the first hatchlings tell the others that it is time to hatch. The more that get out and have a chance to communicate, the faster the rest will hatch."

7

———

Lynx paced around the room, his hands clenching and stretching as he tried to rid himself of the pent up energy that had built in his chest and wasn't seeming to move no matter what he did. The longer that the box with Samira's voice in it played, the more the aggression and intensity grew within Lynx. It was like he could feel Rain pulling closer and closer to the surface of her consciousness. She was coming out of the locked state and as she did, his mind and body were responding to her even more.

In the days that he had been watching over her, Lynx had been able to suppress much of the feelings that the Denynso men experienced when they were near their intended mate. He could focus on trying to understand why she was locked and what he could do to protect her so his mind didn't wander as much to the thoughts of bonding with her and finally making her fully his mate. Now that they thought that they had discovered what would release the Light Ones from the bonds of the Covra, however, the defensive instinct born into each of the Denynso warriors was giving way to the forceful emotional and physical response of being so close to his intended mate but unable to touch her.

Outside of the window he could hear the gut-wrenching sounds of the rest of the warriors fighting off the newly born Covra. They were hatching at more frequent intervals now, and the young that emerged from the people seemed more aggressive than they had at first, as if simply having others around was giving them even more strength and energy.

He wondered how many of the people in the settlement they had lost now; how many of the people who Rain knew and possibly loved, people who Lynx had felt responsible for since they first encountered the settlement, were now not locked in place, but dead where they had taken their final step.

He wanted to be out with the men fighting, but he knew that he couldn't leave Rain. There was no way of knowing when she might wake up or how she would react when she did. They were still unsure of whether the people would be able to survive even after waking up or how they would respond to the presence of the Denynso. It was possible that as soon as her eyes opened, the age would catch up to her and she would simply die where she lay. The thought was too horrible to contemplate and Lynx forced it out of his mind, replacing it with images of her when she was awake; what he would say to her, how he would explain what was happening to her.

It wasn't until he saw the light against the tightly closed curtains over the window change that he realized he had been holding vigil over Rain throughout the night. He turned off the small lamp on the table and stepped up to the window to push the curtain back. The glint of the sunrise crept into the room, illuminating the wooden floor like liquid. It was a new day.

Just as the sunlight touched Rain's face, he heard a sound come from her that was like a gentle blend of a sigh and a whimper. Lynx knelt by the bed and looked into her face, watching as her head turned gradually from side to side and her body stretched. Rain's face contorted in a cringe and he knew that she was feeling the pain from the incision in her stomach. He inched closer and touched his hand to the pillow beside her head.

"It's alright," he whispered, "I'm here. I'm right here."

Rain made the cooing sound again and her lips parted. She drew in a gasping breath and held it within her for a few seconds. As the breath slid out of her lungs, her eyelids fluttered and then slowly slid up until Lynx finally looked into her eyes.

Lynx felt his heart jump and he straightened slightly so that he could bring his face slightly closer to hers, but not so close that it would frighten her. He didn't know what she was thinking as her eyes explored his face. He resisted the urge to touch her cheek or to lean forward and kiss her. He didn't want to push too far too fast even though now that she was awake and looking at him, he was even more confident than ever before that she was made to be his mate.

Rain's hands slid up from under the blanket and she stretched her fingers, and then her arms. He could see the color coming into her skin as the blood in her body began to flow again and warm her. The gentle pink flush was even more beautiful and he felt himself falling deeper in love with her. She hadn't taken her eyes away from him, and an instant later Lynx felt her hand join her gaze as it came up to rest on his cheek. He closed his eyes and leaned his cheek into her palm, sighing at the touch of her skin. He felt her thumb stroke along his cheekbone and he reached up to cover her hand with his, applying slight pressure to press her skin closer to his.

"Lynx," she whispered and his eyes snapped open. "Lynx," she said again, "is that your name?"

Lynx was so shocked that he could barely bring himself to speak. He nodded, leaning closer to her.

"Yes. How did you know that?"

She smiled at him, the expression further softening her face and making her eyes glitter.

"I could hear you," she said. "Whenever you were talking, I could hear you. It was like I was dreaming. It wasn't quite real and I couldn't wake up or respond to you, but I could listen to you and it comforted me."

The admission made Lynx's heart swell and he smiled at her.

"I'm so glad." Suddenly he felt his mood darken. "Do you know what's happening?"

Rain turned away from him, looking up at the ceiling as if thinking about his question. She started to shift and struggle, and he tucked his hand behind her shoulders as they lifted up off of the mattress so that he could help her sit up. She winced when the pain of her incision hit her, and Lynx reached behind her to fold her pillow so that she could recline back on it. Her body relaxed as the position helped to ease the pain, but her hand dropped away from his face to press to her stomach.

"I only know what I could pick up from listening to you while you were in here with me."

"Do you remember the Covra?" he asked carefully.

Rain nodded, the expression on her face telling Lynx that there were horrific memories of the creatures coursing through her mind as she thought back on them.

"Yes. They did this to me, didn't they?"

"Yes. Everyone in the settlement."

Rain's head dropped back and her eyes closed.

"How long have we been here?" She asked. Lynx hesitated and she lifted her head to look at him. "Lynx? How long?"

"More than a century."

Panic crossed Rain's face and she sat up sharply, gasping in pain as she straightened.

"What happened to me?"

Lynx reached forward and brushed a piece of hair away from her face. Suddenly he realized that he was touching her, but he wasn't having the vision of her last moments as he had every other time he had made contact with her.

"What is it?" she asked, obviously seeing the look of surprise on his face as he continued to touch her hair and stroke her cheek.

"While you were locked, every time I touched you I could see the last few minutes before the Covra injected you. It was how I was able to figure out what had happened. I did it with every person in the settlement and found the weakness of the creatures."

"Their eyes."

"Yes. But now I'm not having the vision. I can touch you without seeing it."

Rain smiled faintly and touched his hand again.

"I guess you don't need to see it anymore."

The need for her surged within him, but he knew that now was not the time. He needed to tell her everything. She deserved to know what had happened to her kind and what they were doing to try to save them. If she remembered the Covra and their weakness, maybe she knew something that would help them as they continued to fight.

8

———

Zsilvia adjusted the bag on her hip and pressed on, walking as fast as she could across the open field. The group had spread out slightly, walking along in pairs or individuals several feet away from each other rather than as a tight group as they had when they were first approaching the boundary of the compound. It seemed like they were at once immersed in their own thoughts and experience of the new space, and trying to take up as much area as they could so that they would be better able to detect any threats that might come their way.

Suddenly she felt George give her hand a shake.

"What?" she asked, looking up at him.

"Look."

Zsilvia followed his point and saw the arch looming ahead of them. A figure appeared in the arch and Zsilvia heard Samira gasp behind them.

"Ty!"

The figure looked up and in an instant was running toward them. Samira ran ahead, dropping her bag so that she could move faster. When they reached each other, Ty swept Samira up into his arms and kissed her deeply, holding her a few inches off of the ground until their mouths parted and he lowered her to her feet.

"You're here!" Ty said happily, "I missed you so much."

"I missed you, too."

The rest of the group sped up to meet them and Zsilvia watched George approach Ty, holding out his hand.

"Hello," he said, "I'm George."

"He's the new professor for the university exchange program," Samira explained.

Ty nodded and took George's hand, shaking it firmly.

"I'm Ty. It's nice to meet you. Thanks for taking care of the girls for us."

George laughed.

"They've been taking care of me just as much. How are things in there?"

Ty glanced over his shoulder.

"They aren't good. It seems to be getting worse. Three more died this morning."

"How is Rain? Did the voice box work?" Samira asked.

"I don't know," Ty said, taking her hand and starting to guide them toward the arch. "Lynx hasn't let anyone in since last night."

"Have you been able to do surgery on any of the others and get the eggs out of them?" Zuri asked.

Ty nodded.

"We did all of the children first. None of them have died and we just couldn't bear the thought of that happening to any of them. We had enough of the ointments to take care of all of them and about ten of the adults. There are so many more, though."

There was a shout from the arch just ahead and they all took off running toward the settlement. As soon as they got through the arch they saw a man lying on the ground ahead of them, his leg splitting open as horrific-looking black creatures emerged. Zsilvia recoiled, but George ran forward, his hand unhooking the blade at his hip as he went. Ero shouted again as he slashed at one of the creatures, missing its eye but severing one of its legs. The Covra hissed and reared back, presenting the sharp points on the ends of its legs. George skidded to a stop beside it and brought the tip of his blade down into the creature's eye, holding it in place as the Covra thrashed and hissed.

Zuri ran forward and joined the fight, pulling a short spear from her bag and tossing it toward one of the other creatures as it scurried in their direction. The spear embedded itself in the Covra's eye, but the spider-like creature continued. Ero lunged forward, pressing the Covra to the ground and pressing the spear deeper into its eye until the gleaming black body stilled and disintegrated into the ground.

With the final young Covra dead, Zsilvia watched Elianna drop her bag to the ground and start digging through it. She pulled out containers of ointments and a roll of long bandages.

"What are you doing?" Zuri asked.

The man's hand twitched slightly and Elianna nodded toward it.

"The eggs were in this man's leg, not in his abdominal cavity. The Covra didn't have far to go to get out, which means that they didn't eat through vital organs or arteries. This injury isn't life threatening and he's responding to our voices. I think we can save him."

George took his blade and cut away the leg of the man's pants so that they could better access the wounded area. His skin looked tattered and the muscles lay open, but Zsilvia had seen far worse injuries on some of the warriors when they returned home from battle. She knew that if they were able to get the right healing ointments onto him and bind it up quickly, he could be spared.

Ero and Zuri stepped away from the rest of the group to embrace and Zsilvia watched as he wiped a tear away from her cheek. Even in the horror of what was going on around them, the pair had found a moment of peace to enjoy together.

"Rain's awake!"

The sound of another voice coming toward them brought Zsilvia's attention away from Zuri and Ero and toward the settlement that lay below. Vax ran up to them and touched Ero's back.

"Rain is awake," he repeated. "Lynx sent me to tell you."

"Start talking!" Ivy said, reaching out to rest her hand on George's arm briefly where he crouched, packing ointment into the wound as Elianna cleaned the skin around it, "Now! Start talking!"

"She's right," Zuri said. "If Rain is awake, that means that the voice worked. Maybe it works like the Covra hatching. The more voices, the stronger the effect. Everyone talk. It doesn't matter what you say, just talk to him."

"Zsilvia, can you go with Vax and find somewhere that we can bring this man when we are finished with him? If we can get him awake, he's going to need rest to recover."

"Absolutely."

Zsilvia kissed George on the top of his head not wanting to stop him from his reassurances to the man that they continued to work on. She followed Vax swiftly down the hill and into the settlement, looking around her in shock at the unmoving people that dotted the street. It was just as the men had described it, and yet seeing it made it even more horrifying. She could see a few children in positions that indicated they had been playing when the Covra had gotten them, and the sight of the bandages wrapped tightly around their little bodies from where Ty and the others had cut out the eggs was at once comforting and disturbing.

"Where is Lynx?" she asked.

Vax pointed out one of the buildings and Zsilvia ran toward it. She knew that she was supposed to be finding a place for the man at the entrance to the settlement to rest, but something compelled her to see Lynx and Rain. She entered the house and climbed up the stairs toward the sound of voices. The door to a bedroom on the upper hallway stood halfway open and she knocked on it carefully before pushing it open.

"Hello?"

"Zsilvia!" Lynx said in surprise, "When did you get here?"

He had been kneeling on the floor beside the bed and now climbed to his feet to greet her.

"Just now. The others are still up the hill."

"This is Zsilvia," Lynx said, looking at the pretty woman sitting in the bed. "She is the one who had the idea about you needing a human voice to unlock you. Zsilvia, this is Rain."

"Thank you," Rain said, reaching for her hand.

Zsilvia took her hand and squeezed it.

"Of course. Now I must ask a favor of you."

Rain looked at her quizzically.

"What?"

"The rest of my group is at the entrance to the settlement trying to save a man that is up there. The Covra put their eggs in his leg rather than in his stomach so when they hatched they didn't kill him. They are talking to him now trying to unlock him and when they do they want to bring him somewhere to rest so that he can recover. They sent me here to find him a place, but I think that he should be back in his own home. If he can't tell us, can you tell us who he is and where he lives?"

Rain nodded.

"I can." She paused and looked at Lynx, and then back at Zsilvia. "How many have died?"

"I don't know," Zsilvia said quietly, wanting to keep her as calm as she could, "but we are going to do everything we can to keep anyone else from dying. You can trust us."

9

―――――

Loralia stepped back from the woman stretched across the wooden floor and tied her hair up so that it was out of the way. Bannack knelt on the floor beside the prone woman and carefully cut into the area around the puncture wound that the Covra had created. He moved cautiously but swiftly, removing the clutch of eggs with the fast, confident motion that came from having performed the same procedure several times before.

Outside Loralia could hear Zuri, Elianna, Samira, Ivy, and George shouting as they moved up and down the street. After the man who they had encountered when they first entered the settlement woke and was strong enough for them to settle him back into his own bed in his home, they realized that Elianna had been right. Their plan became to focus their surgical efforts on those who contained the Covra eggs in the most vulnerable areas of their body including their backs and their stomachs while also using their voices as much as possible to wake the people as quickly as they could. This allowed them to save those who would have died almost instantly when the Covra young hatched and then react if the eggs within any of the others hatched, leaving injuries that wouldn't threaten their lives.

The hiss of Covra young falling under the blades of the warriors echoed around her, but Loralia tried to concentrate on the songs the humans sang instead. They had been shouting for some time now and had suddenly started singing songs that they remembered from Earth, which struck Loralia as strangely funny. The Light Ones would never have heard those songs, except for the few ancient lullabies that the women and George cobbled together with the few words or partial lines that each of them remembered, but somehow the loud, jubilant singing seemed to be working even more powerfully than just them shouting out words and greetings. The woman that lay on the floor as she tended to her incision while Bannack destroyed the eggs was shifting and murmuring slightly, and Loralia knew that she would wake soon. She poured a small amount of serum between her lips to keep down the pain of the procedure and finished wrapping her in the bandages.

Just as she did with the others that they had helped over the course of the day and a half since they had arrived in the settlement, Loralia would sit with the woman until she was fully awake, find out her name, and give her a brief explanation of what was happening. She would help her into her bedroom, bring her water and food, and encourage her to get some rest so that her body could heal. Then she would move on to the next. Loralia was hoping that they were making fast enough progress through the Light Ones and would soon finish. The count of the dead was already so high, and she didn't know if she could bear to see the tears of another wife who realized her husband had died, or the look of terror on the face of a man who didn't know where his wife and children were.

"Pyra?"

Loralia was climbing down the stairs of the house after helping tuck the woman who had told them her name was Andrea into her bed. Bannack had left the room to give the two women privacy to talk and now was standing at the front door of the house looking out over the street.

"They're back!" he exclaimed and ran out of the house.

Loralia followed after him, picking up her skirt so that it wouldn't tangle around her feet. Pyra was standing in the middle of the street with the other warriors who had gone with him to the other kingdom around him. Behind them was a group of people who she didn't recognize. One of them turned to look at her and Loralia immediately stopped. She was struck by the ethereal beauty of the man looking at her, but there was something else. Something radiated off of him, something inherent and inexplicable that made Loralia not want to get any closer to them.

"Bannack," she called out to her mate, stopping him before he got all the way to his leader and the others.

Bannack turned and came back to her, a questioning look on his face.

"What is it, Loralia?"

"There is something strange about them, Bannack," she said, taking hold of his arm, but not looking away from the beautiful creatures who crowded behind the warriors.

"What do you mean?" he asked.

"I don't know, but there is something really odd about them."

Bannack took her hand and moved it off of his arm.

"Do they seem dangerous?" he asked.

"Not really."

"Then there are more important things that we need to be doing than thinking about them."

Bannack walked away and Loralia felt her stomach turn slightly. She knew that he was right. There were still people throughout the settlement who needed their help and Covra young were hatching at a far faster pace than they had, making it essential that they all work together to ensure that they destroyed all of them and saved the Light Ones. She took a hesitant step forward and then followed Bannack, trying to trust him as much as she had always asked him to trust her.

"They've agreed to come help us," Pyra was saying as Loralia approached. "They say that their elders told them stories about the Light Ones and the war. They sent explorers to try to help them when they stopped hearing from the Light Ones, but none of them were ever able to find the settlement. None of them who were alive at that time were ever able to see the settlement or any of the Light Ones again."

Bannack looked out over the group of the beautiful strangers and Loralia saw him nod.

"We really appreciate you coming," he told them, "We need all the help we can get."

As he explained what needed to be done to save the people and kill off the Covra, Loralia backed away from Bannack and made her way away from the main street. She needed to get away for just a moment. The sounds of death and pain around her had become too much, and now the uncomfortable sense radiating off of the strangers pushed her past what she felt like she could handle. She needed to

get away from the fear and the chaos, to take a second to
breathe.

"You're up!" Lynx said as Rain made her way carefully down the stairs.

He got up from the chair where he had been sitting in the living room and rushed up to her, wrapping an arm around her to offer support and help her the rest of the way down.

"I'm alright," Rain laughed, "I feel fine."

Despite the reassuring words, Lynx wouldn't let go of her until he got her all the way to the sofa and lowered her down.

"Are you hungry?"

"Starving."

Lynx rushed into the kitchen and brought her a plate of the lunch he had prepared for himself while she was still sleeping. She had spent much of the time since she had first woken up resting, but her occasional soft sighs and movements took away his fear that she was sinking back into the lock that had kept her away from him. They ate quietly together and then Lynx put the dishes back into the sink before sitting beside her and taking her hands.

"The warriors killed the last of the Covra this morning," he said.

Rain's eyes widened and a smile broke across her face.

"That's amazing."

Lynx opened her arms and Rain dove forward into them. He swept her against him, wrapping her arms around him like he had wanted to since the first time he saw her. He buried his face in her hair and rested a kiss to the side of her neck.

At the feeling of his lips on her skin, Rain stilled. She pulled back slowly, lifting her eyes to his. Lynx hesitated for a moment, then leaned forward and touched a kiss to her lips. Rain drew in a breath and then looked at him again.

"I heard you talking to the other men," she said softly. "You called me your mate."

"Yes," he said.

"I don't understand what you mean by that."

"You realize that I am not human. None of us who were here first are."

"I know. Even a century isn't long enough for us to evolve that much."

Lynx smiled and shook his head.

"No."

"What are you?"

"Denynso. Our kind mate for life. There is one other person who was made for each of us, and once we find that person and bond, we are together for the rest of our existence."

"And you believe that I am that for you?"

"I don't believe it," Lynx said, "I know it. I have been waiting for you my entire life. I knew it the moment that I saw you."

"How did you know?" Rain asked breathlessly.

Their faces had started to move toward each other and Lynx indulged his desire for her by sweeping the tip of his tongue along the center of her lips.

"I could feel it," he responded. "When my kind find our intended mates, we immediately know. We become aggressive," he kissed her softly, "and protective," he kissed her again, "and we can't think of anything but our need to bond with that mate."

"Is that all?" Rain asked, her face now so close that his forehead rested against hers.

"No," he said, sliding closer to her, "I knew when I saw you that you were meant to be my mate," he took her hand and placed it on the inside of his thigh, flattening his hand over hers so that he could slide her palm up, "because my body has never needed someone like it needs you."

Lynx brought her hand up to rest on the hard swell that had formed at the front of his pants. She gasped and he pressed her hand down more insistently, cupping it so that she held his surging erection against her palm. He moaned as she gave a slight squeeze and turned her hand to better hold him.

Rain looked into his eyes and buried her other fingers into his hair. She held his head firmly and their mouths met again. Lynx touched the tip of his tongue to her lips and she complied with the gentle pressure, opening her mouth to allow his tongue in to massage hers. As their kiss deepened, Lynx tucked an arm around her waist and stood, sweeping her up so that he cradled her against the front his body as he made his way across the living room and up the stairs to the bedroom.

The light from outside was rich and golden, filling the room with the same glow as the day that the Covra had locked her. Lynx kicked the door closed behind them and crossed the room to lie her down on the bed. He lifted his mouth away from hers and looked down at her. There was a nervous look on her face and he stroked her cheek tenderly.

"What's wrong?"

"I was just lying down to take a nap that day," she said softly, obviously reminded the same way he was of the day that the Covra locked her, "I had been working most of the night the night before and I was tired. I had no idea that I wasn't going to wake up the next day."

"I promise that you will wake up tomorrow," Lynx whispered, "and I will be lying right beside you."

Rain lifted her mouth to his, tucking her hand behind his head to bring him back down onto the pillow with her. They kissed languidly, their mouths moving across each other without hurry as if they were trying to make up for all of the time that they missed with one another. Filled with the intense need for one another, and a sense of awe that they were finally able to touch one another, their hands moved along each other's bodies, removing clothing slowly and trailing kisses along the skin that they exposed.

Lynx nurtured her with his tongue, tracing the curves and folds of her core to patiently bring her forward and prepare her for him. She writhed against the bed, her hands grasping at the blankets beside her as sounds of intense pleasure filled the space around them. The sounds lifted Lynx further, making him almost ache with the need for her. He wanted to bring her all the way, to carry her to the heights that he had been dreaming about since the moment that his eyes touched her.

Just before she reached the peak of her pleasure, Lynx took his mouth from her and slid up on the bed. He turned her carefully onto her side so that he could tuck his body around hers protectively. She nestled back into him, the softness of her body massaging against his. Lynx stroked his hand from her thigh over her hip and into her waist, then onto her stomach and up onto her breast so that his hand cupped it, allowing his to knead into her flesh. Rain whimpered and tilted her head back so that she could kiss him, coaxing him with her tongue and the roll of her hips.

Lynx moved her hand down her body again and tucked it between her thighs so that he could part them slightly. Pulling the top leg back so that it draped over his thighs, Lynx brought his hips forward so that the tip of his erection touched her opening. They both groaned at the feeling and he struggled to maintain his control. Finally Rain arched her back, pressing her hips further against him so that he sank deeply into her.

Moving her leg back down into place, Lynx cuddled closer to Rain's back, cradling her against his body as he began to roll his hips so that he moved within her in long, deep strokes. His mouth played along the curve of her shoulder and neck, and he could feel the pounding of her heart against his hand as he pressed it to the center of her chest to keep her against him. Lynx could feel the wet heat of her body increase as he moved, and he reached down to stroke his fingers along the sensitive pearl of flesh at her peak. She rolled her hips against his touch, gasping as Lynx increased his pace and pushed deeper into her with each thrust.

Suddenly she let out a strangled cry and Lynx felt Rain's body contract around him, gripping him tightly and pulling her more deeply into her. The sensation was too much for Lynx to handle, and he crashed into his own climax, meeting each of her rapid tremors with pulses that filled her and bonded their bodies and their souls.

11

Ivy stepped up to the stone wall at the back of the settlement and rested her hands against it. She took a breath, letting the cool air wash over her. The weather on Uoria was proving incredibly challenging to her. She was accustomed to the weather on Earth where she could predict the temperature and any impending storms by the time of year. On this planet, however, the weather seemed to change and shift on whim, though the Denynso didn't seem confused or taken aback by it.

"It is a wonderful night."

Ivy turned to the sound of the voice behind her and saw one of the stunningly beautiful strangers Pyra and the other warriors had brought back approaching her. This man had caught her eye the first time she had seen them standing in the street when they arrived back to the settlement, and she hadn't been able to stop thinking of him since. His eyes were like honey and when they met hers, Ivy felt like the breath couldn't find its way out of her lungs.

"It is," she said when she could finally manage to speak.

"May I join you?"

"Yes."

"Your name is Ivy."

"Yes."

It seemed ridiculous that she couldn't find any better words, but his intense beauty seemed to steal them from her.

"I'm Maxim," the man said.

He reached his hand forward and Ivy reached forward to shake it, but Maxim caught hers and lifted their hands between them. She felt him press his palm to hers and align their fingers. The touch of his skin was warm and smooth, almost sultry against hers. She remembered the gesture from when the rest of his kind was meeting the warriors who had stayed behind. It had seemed a strange, foreign ritual when she first saw it, but now that she was doing it with Maxim it was intoxicating.

"I was going to take a walk," she said softly. "Would you like to come along with me?"

"I'd be honored."

Their hands parted and Ivy felt a flicker of disappointment, but she could still feel the tingle on her skin where it had touched his and as they turned to walk he drew close enough that their shoulders brushed against each other.

"Where should we go?" she asked, looking around the unfamiliar surroundings.

"Away from the graves," Maxim said solemnly, "I have seen enough of those."

Ivy nodded, the words sinking deeply into her like a chill. She turned to look at Maxim, allowing herself to drift away into his eyes so that she could pretend that just below them the Light Ones hadn't gathered in the glow of a Denynso-built fire to bury their dead, placing them alongside the first victims of the Covra in a cemetery that had waited more than a century to see the end of the war.

There was still space in the field, though, still room among the graves.

It wasn't over yet, but Ivy wouldn't let herself think anything of it. She would think only of Maxim until she closed her eyes and allow whatever awaited them tomorrow to exist only after she opened them.

UNTITLED

(To be continued in Part IX...)

THE ALIEN'S TRUTH

1

———

"Has it changed much?"

Lynx felt Rain intertwine her fingers with his and heard her give a sigh that sounded somewhere between contemplation and resignation. She looked out over the settlement from their vantage point at the top of the hill, her bright blue eyes scanning the streets and buildings newly alive again after more than a century of forced slumber. Those eyes were one of the greatest delights that Lynx had discovered since Rain had awoken. Though he had seen them briefly reflected in the mirror during his visits in the moments that led to the Covra locking her along with the rest of the Light Ones in the settlement, those fleeting glimpses didn't even begin to compare to how they looked when she was gazing directly at him.

"It has and it hasn't," Rain said, turning to look at him. "It's strange because it doesn't seem at all like it has been so long, but at the same time everywhere I look I can see the years. Does that make sense? I feel like I just went to sleep that day and then woke up the next morning. Like maybe my nap went on too long and I ended up sleeping through the night and then woke up in the morning just like I would have, but instead of waking up the next morning I woke up a hundred years later. The buildings look older. The plants look bigger.

Strangely, though, things don't look as different as I would think that they would look after a century passed. I don't know. You have this concept of a hundred years being so long and that everything will just disintegrate in that long if you weren't around. But I opened my eyes and found out that the world had just gone right on without me. It survived. Everything went on without us as if we were never here. I noticed vines climbing up the back of one of the buildings yesterday. They had started to creep into one of the windows. It's like the planet is just moving on, trying to take back over and go forward."

Lynx gave Rain's hand a gentle pull to draw her up against him so that he could wrap his arms around her. She curled into his chest, tucking herself as closely against him as she could and wrapping her arms around his waist as he rested his chin on the top of her head and gazed out around the settlement just as she had. He tried to imagine what it would have looked like when they first arrived, whenever that was. What did the roads look like? The buildings? The arch leading into the settlement? In all of the time that the warriors had spent in the settlement among the Light Ones trying to figure out how to save them from the Covra and unlock them, Lynx hadn't really thought much about the settlement itself. He had been so focused on freeing his mate that he had pushed aside the lingering questions about why they were there and what the settlement meant for the rest of Uoria and the relationship between the Denynso and the people of Earth.

Though when he first discovered that Rain and all of the

other Light Ones within the settlement were actually humans who had come from Earth Lynx had wondered why they were there and how they got there, especially considering Creia, who the Denynso respected and honored as their knowledgeable and powerful king, didn't know that they had been there for more than a century, he had quickly turned his attention back to her and to all of his efforts to kill off the gruesome creatures that locked her and bring her back to life.

Now that she was free and they were gradually rebuilding their lives, all of these thoughts began to creep back into his mind, making him feel uneasy. The Denynso warriors had embarked on their journey around the planet with the intention of finding out about what other species might inhabit Uoria and determining if those species posed any threat to the Denynso, their compound, or the mates who had joined them in the last year. They had anticipated encountering creatures they had never seen and potentially engaging in battle in order to exhibit their dominance and show why they were considered the most fearsome and skilled warriors of the entire galaxy in order to dissuade those creatures from getting near their compound. They had not, however, anticipated encountering a species with whom they were already familiar with but also who they were told had not come onto the planet at all before Creia began allowing specific representatives to come for short periods of time to research.

The fact that the Light Ones were human and had been on the planet for more than a century was in a way unnerving to Lynx. It meant that either they had arrived on the planet without the Denynso knowing it and carried on with their existence without ever making their presence known to the Denynso or anyone other than the beautiful creatures who they had connected with at the other kingdom. Or Creia already knew that they were there all along and knew about their conflict with the Covra and had simply chosen not to tell the warriors. And if he did know, that meant that he either figured that they would not exist any longer once the warriors left the Denynso compound for what was supposedly the first time in the history of their kind, or that he intended for them to go and encounter the Covra and the humans for reasons that Lynx couldn't fathom.

"What's wrong?" Rain asked.

Lynx didn't realize that Rain had stepped slightly back and was now looking up at him, her expression telling him that she was concerned about his sudden quiet. He stroked the backs of his fingers along her cheek and gazed into her eyes.

"I was just thinking," he said softly.

"What about?"

Lynx let the air stream out of his lungs. He had just found his mate, just completed his bond with her, and he didn't want to do anything that he thought might alienate or offend her. Now that he finally had her in his arms he couldn't bear the thought of losing her just because of something that he said.

"I don't know much about you," he admitted. He stepped back away from her so that he could reach into his bag and pull out the picture of her that he had taken from her nightstand. "I know that you're human, but how did you get here? Why are you here?"

Rain took the picture from his hand and looked down at it, a faintly homesick expression on her face. She paused for a moment and then looked up at him.

"You want to know about me and my group?"

"Yes. I mean, you are my mate. I was intended to be with you from the moment I was born even though you were laying here locked in place then. I love you no matter what, but I do want to know more about you."

Rain smiled softly.

"You love me?"

Lynx hadn't realized that he had used those words. He hadn't really meant to even though he meant them with every ounce of his being. He wanted to give her more time and allow her to better assimilate to opening her eyes in a time that was unfamiliar and a situation that might be truly terrifying for her before he had that moment with her, but he hadn't been able to stop himself.

"Yes. With everything that is within me. I have since the moment I was born and will for the rest of my life."

"I love you, too."

Lynx ducked his head and touched a kiss to her lips. She nuzzled her nose against his and sighed contentedly.

"I guess it's time that we all sit down for a talk," she said as she pulled her face away from his. "I think there are some things that we all need to know a little bit more about.

Lynx nodded, tucking the picture back into his bag and then taking her hand so that they could walk down into the heart of the settlement where the rest of the warriors, the teachers, healers, and scientists, the surviving Light Ones, and the beautiful creatures from the nearby kingdom roamed and tried to make connections.

2

Ivy leaned against the wall surrounding the settlement and felt the pressure of Maxim's body rest into her. His hands came to her hips as his face nuzzled gently into the curve of her neck and shoulder. The touch was tender and soft, but it sent a shiver through her body as she felt his skin touch hers and the warmth of his breath ripple down between her breasts. The pads of his thumbs massaged into the fronts of her hipbones and she could feel each steady rise and fall of his belly on hers as he breathed. As his lips touched her collarbone Ivy lifted her hands to bury them in the thick, silky strands of his hair and stroke them down along the back of his neck.

"Tell me more about you," Maxim whispered against her neck.

Ivy smiled, subtly lifting her body up so that it touched his more fully. The beautiful man in front of her responded with the press of his body and a tender touch of the tip of his tongue along her skin.

"What do you want to know?" she asked.

His hands slid around to the small of her back.

"Everything. Where is your home? Why did you come to Uoria? Why did you come here with the Denynso?"

Ivy laughed at the stream of questions, each punctuated by a kiss along her chest until he reached the soft dip at the base of her throat and stroked it with his tongue. She gently pushed Maxim away so that she could stand up straight.

"Let's take a walk," she said, taking his hand and starting to guide him around the edge of the wall, "I need to get outside of this wall for just a little while. Have you ever been out there?"

Max looked out over the wall.

"Only for the time that we were walking from the kingdom here. It used to be that my kind moved in and out of the kingdom freely, but that has changed in recent years. Now the younger generations are expected to stay inside the kingdom until they are fully grown and then they are allowed to leave."

Ivy laughed.

"Fully grown? Aren't you fully grown?"

The concept of being contained within one small area until she was an adult seemed so strange to Ivy, but when she stopped to think about it she realized it really was no different than being expected to stay close to home when she was young. The thought of never leaving the equivalent of her small hometown, though, seemed unfathomable.

"What do you think?" Maxim asked, "Do you think I'm fully grown?"

The suggestion in those words brought the smile off of Ivy's lips as her breath deepened and her eyelashes lowered. Her steps paused and she felt Maxim pull slightly on her hand so that she turned into him. Ivy's breasts crushed against his chest and she kept her eyes trained on the sliver of skin revealed at the top of his shirt to keep herself under control. She felt Maxim tuck one finger under her chin and tilt her face up to look at him. The color of his eyes seemed to deepen as though it were melting as he gazed at her. He brought his mouth forward and Ivy lifted her face more to meet it.

Their lips met and she relaxed into his kiss, allowing him to coax her lips apart with the tip of his tongue so that he could delve deeply into her mouth and explore her. Ivy heard Maxim moan into the kiss and the sound sent fire through her. She gripped his shoulders, rising up onto the balls of her feet to lessen the space between them and press her mouth harder against his. She needed him like she had never needed anything, and the pounding of his heart against her ribcage told her that he was feeling the same thing for her.

When the kiss ended, Maxim took his lips from Ivy's slowly as if he were trying to savor the last taste of her lingering in his mouth. He kept his face close enough to hers as he whispered to her that she could still feel his lips softly brush hers with each word.

"Come on," he said "let's go explore."

Ivy happily linked her hand with his and allowed the gorgeous man to guide her along the edge of the wall and toward the small gate that they had discovered the night before. Though it had only been a few days since they had first met during her late night walk to the back of the settlement to escape the choking emotions and smoke of the funeral below, she felt like she had known Maxim for much longer. They had spent nearly all of their time together since that first moment when he approached her, startling her out of her musings and bringing her into very sudden, very intense reality with the beauty of his face and the stare in his eyes. It wasn't until tonight, though, that he had finally kissed her.

Maxim's contact with her had been slow and careful. Though she had craved more of his touch from the moment that he lifted their hands and pressed their palms and fingers together in the intimate gesture of greeting traditional among his kind, Ivy felt adored and honored with the slow and tender way that he approached her. Each touch was an indulgence, only pushing her further into her desire for him rather than satiating it. Unlike the human men she had dealt with at home on Earth and the Denynso warriors she had watched in the brief time she had been in contact with them, who seemed to show their strength and dominance loudly, aggressively, and forcefully, it was Maxim's patience and quiet steadiness that had her under his control. He never felt intimidating or hurried, yet he was the strongest, most entrancingly powerful man she had ever encountered.

His hand rested for a moment on the latch to the small gate before he tried to push it open. The ancient hinges groaned in protest of trying to move after so many years of abandonment, but he pushed against the door again and Ivy saw them give, allowing the door to creak open enough for them to pass through. Maxim closed the gate behind them and they started away from the wall, neither of them knowing where they were going but only caring that they were by each other's side.

"Why are you here, Ivy?" Maxim asked after they had walked along in silence for several minutes.

"I am a scientific research assistant. I came here to be a

part of an exchange program with the Denynso. The scientist that I work under is doing some extensive research into their kind and why they are such powerful warriors, and I came to help."

"The scientist... the rather intense man with the streaks of silver through his hair."

Ivy gave a short laugh.

"Yes. George can be a bit much to handle when you first get around him, especially when he is focused on a research project or has something to figure out. He has gotten much more bearable now that he has Zsilvia, though."

"Is that the tall woman who looks like the warriors?"

Ivy was amused by the way that Maxim saw the world and the straightforward, unapologetic way he spoke about it.

"Yes. She is his mate. Or maybe he is hers. I'm not entirely positive how that works when both of them aren't Denynso."

"What do you mean?"

"Where we're from, finding someone to spend your life with is a bit of a gamble. You kind of just wing it and choose someone to be with. That isn't the way it is with the Denynso. They have one person in all of existence who they are meant to be with, and there is no one else. They know as soon as they meet that person that they have found their mate, and they will be with that person for the rest of their lives, or they will be alone. It just isn't like that back home, so I'm not sure if she is his mate, or if he is just hers."

"I think they are each other's," Maxim said and Ivy felt her heartbeat quicken slightly.

"I like that."

"What is it like at home? How is it different from the Denynso finding their mates?"

"All throughout your life you meet people, but with the exception for the butterflies in your stomach when you are really attracted to someone, or the tremble in your heart when you realize that you have feelings for another person, there is no single moment that you for sure know you have found anyone special. So, you date. Sometimes that is just a few people, and sometimes you have more dates than you have friends. If you are very, very lucky you find a person who you fall in love with and make a commitment to. You may get married, you may not. Either way, you spend every day after that hoping that you are going to be able to keep it together and that this person you chose is the right one, the one who will give you the best possible life, and who you can give the best possible life. Sometimes that works and people are together for their entire lives and are completely fulfilled by each other and can't imagine a single second of existence without the other. Sometimes it doesn't and people realize that they didn't choose the right person. They live questioning what could have been better if they had found someone else. They might divorce and try again. It can be very complicated."

"We are more like the Denynso," Maxim told her. "We create lifelong partnerships with a single other person that was meant for us from birth. Finding that person, though, isn't always as easy as just looking at them. It isn't instant. We have to fall in love."

They had wandered into a broad patch of lush, velvety purple flowers and Maxim lowered himself to the ground, gently pulling her down along with him so that she sat on her knees facing him.

"Where did you come from, Ivy?"

"Earth. This is the first time I've ever left."

"Did you come here the same way the other humans did?"

Ivy's eyes snapped from the plush petal she rubbed between her fingers to Maxim's face.

"What do you mean?" she asked. "How did the others get here?"

"Pyra," Lynx said, walking up to the leader of the Denynso warriors where he stood in the kitchen of Rain's house.

Pyra put the piece of fruit he was eating down on the counter and took a step toward Lynx, a look of concern on his face. It was an immediate reaction, one that came from the fear and confusion surrounding them from the moment that they entered the settlement. Though everything had been going fairly well since they followed Zsilvia's recommendation and used Samira's voice recording to unlock the Light Ones, Pyra had still not put down his guard. Any time someone approached him, the look of worry tightened his face and he looked ready to spring into action to handle whatever emergency might have befallen them.

"What's wrong? Did something happen?"

Lynx held up a hand to calm the massive warrior and stepped up closer to him.

"Everything's fine, Pyra. Nothing happened. Rain just thinks that we should all get together and talk."

"Talk about what?" Pyra asked, picking the fruit back up and biting into it.

"I pointed out that we still don't know why they are here or how they got here, or even how we didn't know that they have been here for this whole time. She said that she thinks it would be best if we all sat down together, cleared the air a bit. I think that there are questions that the Light Ones have of us, too."

Pyra seemed to be thinking about this for a moment and then he nodded, swallowing the bite of fruit, taking another, and tossing the remaining core into the chute that led directly into a compost pile outside of the house.

"She's right. Now that everyone is awake again and there doesn't seem to be any adverse reactions to the locking or unlocking, I think that we all have questions that need to be answered. Help me get everyone together. We'll meet in the hall on Main Street in half an hour. Do you think that Rain is willing to talk to everyone?"

Lynx nodded, turning toward the door to the kitchen so that they could leave the house and start gathering all of the different creatures now roaming throughout the settlement for the meeting.

"I'm sure she will."

He was very aware as his own leader stepped out of the house and started down the street toward the next house that the Light Ones were without any form of authority to guide them. They had learned quickly after destroying the final Covra hatchlings and unlocking the last of the Light Ones that the leader of the settlement had been one of those who had died as a result of the eggs hatching within him before they were able to rescue him. The loss had been a deep and painful blow to everyone in the settlement, and Lynx felt more than ever that the Denynso would have to help these people find their stability and organization again before they could even consider leaving the settlement and continuing on with their journey. He couldn't imagine the Denynso warriors without Pyra, and the entirety of the clan without Creia and Theia. The thought that the Light Ones were without that strength and control made him worry about the safety and security of their future.

"What did he say?"

Rain stepped up beside Lynx and took his hand, reaching up to brush a strand of his hair back off of his shoulder. The gesture was intimate in a comfortable, content way that seemed to underscore the deep connection that they had created through their bond. It was these little things, tiny gestures and details that he had noticed her doing over the last several days, that made him feel more nurtured and cared for than he could have ever imagined and he felt his body relax as her presence released all of the stress and tension that had begun to build within him as he thought of the chaos that could ensue within the settlement at any time.

"He wants to gather everyone in the meeting hall. Do you mind being the one that does the talking about the Light Ones and why you are here? There needs to be one person who can act as the voice for everyone."

Rain took a long breath, her eyes clouding slightly as if the comment had made her think of the leader who they had lost.

"Absolutely," she said. "I'll do whatever you need me to do."

Lynx squeezed her hand and they started off together in the opposite direction that Pyra had gone so that they could spread the word to everyone about the meeting. As they walked along the road, encountering small clusters of people as they went, Lynx began to realize how strange it seemed to him that each of the species had broken out of their main groups and were now mingling together without any sense of structure. So accustomed to living in the compound where he had encountered only his own kind except in the context of battle before the humans started to arrive, Lynx found it strange and even unnerving that they had all seemed to assimilate so easily into blending together. He naturally sought out structure, order, and hierarchy, yet here there seemed to be none of that. Rather than clear divisions and easily recognizable forms of authority and control, there was fluidity and a type of tenuous cooperation as four different species from two different times tried to learn one another and find the connections that had once existed and that were still building.

HALF AN HOUR later Lynx stepped into the large open room at the center of the meeting hall. It was arranged like an amphitheater with a deep well in the center of the room and a series of thickly carpeted steps leading down toward a small platform at the bottom. A few people wandered around the room, some talking casually with each other while others seemed lost in their own thoughts as they explored the space that had been untouched for more than a century. He noticed that a few of the Light Ones were moving around the room with purpose, cleaning the walls and the carpet as they tried to remove all signs of the abandonment as if they were reminders of the time that they spent locked out of existence and the painful losses that followed.

Lynx followed Rain down into the well and perched at the edge of the bottom step. Everyone was filtering into the room and he watched as they took their seats on the steps. It was fascinating to watch as they parted and came together, divided and melded, sitting individually or coming into groups around the room. He glanced at Rain. In all of the confusion around him, she was a moment of peace and stability. As he looked at her, though, he realized that she was just as out of the realm of his sense of normalcy as everything else that was going on around him. She was not only a different species than he was, but she was also from a completely different time. Had the Covra not locked her when they did, she would have been long interred in that cemetery before he was even born. In that moment Rain turned to him and offered a calm and reassuring smile and for a moment Lynx felt like he was looking at a picture of her, gazing through the years to her last smile before the Covra attacked.

"I love you," she mouthed, and in that instant, the years disappeared, the discomfort and confusion faded, and Lynx was finally present in changes that no longer seemed as terrifying.

4

Zsilvia settled onto the low carpeted step beside George and settled into the crook of his side as he wrapped his arm around her and drew her close. She rested her head on his chest and took a breath. The warmth of his body against hers and his smell filling her lungs was calming and comforting in a way that she had never experienced. George kissed the top of her head and she smiled, tilting her head back so that she could kiss him.

"Is everyone here?"

The sound of Pyra's booming voice brought her attention away from George and down to the platform at the bottom of the well. The tremendous Denynso warrior leader stood in the middle of the platform with Rain, looking around at the steps that had filled over the last few minutes with the all of the people that had filled the settlement since the warriors had found it. She looked at each of the different species, noting the subtle differences in their appearances that separated them. It seemed strange to her as she realized that it was the Denynso that stood out the most from the others.

Having spent her entire life on the compound, far enough separated from even the battles that the warriors waged against the species that tried to invade and take over the land that she never even saw a different species until the first of the human researchers arrived well into her adulthood, she somehow thought that every other species that existed on Uoria or any of the other planets throughout the galaxy would look extremely different. When the first humans arrived, they did look different. Perhaps not as much as she would have anticipated, but enough that they were distinctly separate. Even the largest of the men that visited the planet were smaller than the Denynso warriors, and they didn't have the distinctive white hair and shifting eyes of the men of her kind.

When they encountered Loralia for the first time she realized that this creature looked very much like the humans, with only her flowing silver hair, lavender eyes, and luminescent skin to set her apart. Now that she was sitting in the settlement looking out over a group comprised of four species, she noticed even fewer differences. Except for their clothing, the Light Ones and the contemporary humans were indistinguishable. Even the beautiful creatures from the other kingdom simply looked like exquisite, almost painfully lovely versions of the humans.

Though the realization that it was the Denynso that were so far different than the others and not the other way around should have been unnerving to Zsilvia, something about it was strangely reassuring. She couldn't quite explain it, but as she sat in the well cradled against her mate, the consistency of the others and the smooth, easy way that they all seemed to assimilate into their newly shared existence put her at ease.

"Ivy isn't here," George muttered.

Zsilvia looked around and realized that he was right. Since the time that they had all spent in the settlement had been focused not on research, but on making sure that the Light Ones recovered and gradually rebuilding the connections that had once existed while discovering new ones among the groups. This meant that the women and George weren't spending as much time together as they had been as the human women reunited with their mates and parted ways to spend time with them while exploring the settlement. Zsilvia realized that she hadn't seen Ivy at all that day.

"When was the last time that you saw her?" Zsilvia asked, glancing around again just to make sure that she hadn't simply overlooked the slight blond sitting somewhere amongst the group that had filled the well.

"Yesterday," George told her. "We were doing some research after breakfast in that little clinic that I found, but one of the men from the other kingdom showed up and she ran off with him."

"One of the men from the other kingdom?" Zsilvia asked.

It was somewhat surprising to her that Ivy would wander off with one of the almost ethereal men who had come to the settlement from the kingdom that had once maintained good relations with the Light Ones and their settlement. Even though Ivy had assured her that there was nothing romantic in the relationship between her and George, that his role in her life was nothing more than a mentor who was guiding her through the beginning of her scientific career, Zsilvia had seen the look in the young woman's eyes when she looked at George.

She no longer felt any form of jealousy or concern toward Ivy, but Zsilvia could recognize the admiration and attraction Ivy had for the dignified, sexy older man. It was the type of attraction that often smoldered within young women for impressive older men in their lives, but now Zsilvia understood that this was not the type of attraction that Ivy would ever act on, or even want to. It was that attraction, however, that made it unexpected that Ivy would fall for a man who was so different from George. These men were young and quiet, and though from what she could tell their bodies were as beautifully crafted as their faces, they lacked the primal, rough-edged intensity of George.

Just thinking about the comparison between the two men made Zsilvia think about George's body when she had him naked in her arms and could draw her fingernails through the coarse dark hair that covered his chiseled chest, flat belly, and lead down from his navel... These thoughts got her feeling intoxicated and made her feel weak in the knees and she wanted the meeting to be over as soon as possible so that she could drag him back to the house that they had been sharing and indulge her need for him.

Her hand had drifted onto his inner thigh and the backs of her fingers brushed the front of his pants. George cleared his throat softly and Zsilivia felt his thighs part slightly as he pressed against her hand. Her hand massaged into the gradually hardening bulge with the pad of her thumb and sighed as George's mouth came close enough to her ear that she could feel his breath on her neck and his lips touch her skin.

"You better stop that right now," he whispered, "if we are going to have any hope of making it through this meeting."

"Maybe I don't want to get through the meeting," she whispered back.

The sound of Pyra getting their attention again stopped Zsilvia's giggles and she looked back at the warrior who was giving her a look like he had been watching their interaction the entire time. A heated blush burned across her cheeks and Zsilvia tucked her head into George's shoulder to wait until the feeling of Pyra's eyes on her disappeared.

"It seems that we are missing a couple of people," Pyra finally said, "but we're just going to go on without them. I called everyone here because we think it is time that we talked all of this through and made sense of what has been happening on Uoria. It's obvious that none of us know as much about the planet or what is on it as we thought we did, so we need to get everything out in the open. Since the leader of the Light Ones was lost to the Covra, Rain has agreed to be their voice and tell us about what led up to the conflict."

Rain stepped forward with a tense look on her face and scanned the crowd slowly. Her eyes seemed to settle on each person individually as her gaze moved gradually across them. Finally they landed on Lynx and stayed there for a few beats longer, the look on her face softening slightly as she looked at him.

"First," she said, her voice lifting higher and stronger than Zsilvia would have expected it to, "I want to set the record straight about who we are and ask that no one refer to us as the Light Ones again. This is a name that was given to us by the Covra and it spread so quickly that it became our identity. Continuing to use that name is only perpetuating their memory and continuing to give them power that we should have taken back long ago."

Pyra stepped closer to Rain and placed a hand on her shoulder.

"I'm sorry," he said, lowering his voice slightly, "I didn't know."

"I know you didn't," she said, her voice holding both determination and forgiveness, "and that's why it's so important that we come together and talk. We really know nothing about each other. If we are honest we'll admit that each group either didn't know that the others either existed, or thought that they were myths and legends before encountering each other. I think it's time that we all knew more, and that should start with us." She turned to look at Pyra. "Tell me what you want to know."

Pyra glanced out at the crowd and then back at Rain.

"How long were you here before the Covra locked you?"

"Fifteen years," Rain said, "but we had been in conflict with them for several years before that."

"Where did you come from?"

"Earth originally."

"What do you mean 'originally'?"

"Our group left Earth on a research mission to what everyone thought was a previously unexplored planet, but that we believed was being used as an illegal prisoner of war compound."

Behind her Zsilvia heard a low gasp. She turned to see Zuri and Samira sitting at the edge of their steps, grasping each other between them with one hand while the others clasped tightly over their mouths. Zuri's eyes were wide with shock as she stared at Rain.

"Project Nyx 23," Zuri whispered.

Rain's eyes lifted to Zuri, some of the same shock registering in her eyes.

"Yes," she said, taking a step forward, "Yes! That's us!"

Whispers and gasps rippled through the crowd. Elianna crossed the room to sit beside Samira, muttering something in her ear as she grasped onto her hand. Zsilvia watched

Zuri stand up and step around her so that she could move closer to Rain. There was something significant happening, but Zsilvia didn't quite understand what.

"You are in our textbooks. Everyone learns about you in school, especially the ones in the sciences. We thought that something horrific happened to you. Most people think that you went off course and your ship was destroyed in a meteor shower or that you were captured on the planet and killed." Zuri looked out over the rest of the people staring at them, trying to understand the exchange. "The people on Earth didn't even know that Uoria existed when Project Nyx 23 left on the recognizance mission to Penthos."

"Penthos?" Rain asked quizzically.

Zuri nodded and Zsilvia saw a soft smile cross her lips.

"When your group didn't return and mission command couldn't make contact with you, they sent a rescue team to the planet that you were supposed to be exploring. They obviously didn't find you, but they did find the prisoner compounds that you thought were there. They sent back war units and freed the prisoners. Once it was over, they named the planet in honor of you."

"Penthos was the Greek god of mourning and lamentation," Rain said.

Zuri nodded.

"The world mourned for you. The whole world. It was considered one of the greatest losses of the time and for a long time after. What happened? How did you completely lose contact with mission control?"

Rain sighed and looked out over the crowd again. Pyra looked at Zuri and she settled onto the step beside Zsilvia where she put her hand back over her mouth and continued to stare at Rain, her head shaking back and forth slowly as if she still couldn't believe what she was seeing or hearing.

"While we were on our way to the planet now known as Penthos someone tipped off the Valdicians, the ones that had turned it into a prisoner of war colony. We still don't know who it was or why they did it, but by the time we got there, there was an army waiting for us. We saw everything that we needed to in order to know that we were absolutely right about what they had done to all of the prisoners of war that they had captured themselves and that they had bought or stolen from other planets. There was very little that we could do, though. We pushed hard enough into the planet that we were able to get some weapons and supplies to a few of the prisoners and freed a few more, but the army was too strong for us. We had to leave before they killed all of us, or worse, captured us and put us in the colony.

As we left the planet the Valdicians damaged our ship. They embedded it with timed weapons that would take over the operation of the ship and destroy all communication equipment once we were a certain distance from the planet. These weapons redirected the ship so that it followed a path that the Validicians had programmed into them, forcing us to come here. Once the ship was within the atmosphere of the planet, the weapons released control and the ship crashed. Not everyone survived."

"You were the first humans to step foot on Uoria," Elianna said. "You were here long before we even knew that this planet was here."

"Yes."

"But why?" Samira asked. "Why did the Validicians send you here? If they wanted to kill you, why didn't they do it while you were on Penthos, or destroy the ship all together after you left?"

"They sent us here as an offering to one of their allies," Rain said.

Zsilvia saw Pyra tense, his shoulders straightening and his jaw setting.

"The Covra."

Rain glanced over her shoulder at him.

"Yes."

5

Ivy's heart pounded as she looked into Maxim's eyes. The comment about how the Light Ones had arrived on the planet was so cryptic, and it made her nervous. A second later, though, he smiled and reached out to stroke the curve of her face with one hand. He shook his head slightly.

"It doesn't matter how they got here," he said. "That was a long time ago. It doesn't even matter how you got here. All I care about is that you are here with me now."

Any concern that Ivy felt about his question melted into Maxim's eyes and she reached forward to mimic his touch on her face. His skin felt soft and smooth beneath her hand and when he turned his face to press a kiss to the center of her palm Ivy felt a surge of desire go through her. Maxim's eyes closed and he took his hand from her cheek to press it over the one she held to his face. Ivy eased closer to him so that they sat with their thighs touching, bringing their chests close together and making it so that she could hear the breath sliding in and out of his lungs in slow, deep rhythm. They sat still like this for several long seconds until their breath synchronized, filling the space around them with one blended sound of breath and heartbeats.

Maxim's eyes opened gradually and he lifted them to Ivy's. She could feel them meeting hers, connecting them with some invisible force that bonded them into that moment. He leaned toward her, tenderly touching her lips with his, and nothing else mattered. It was as if everything around them had been cast in watercolors and his kiss had dissolved it, leaving only them alone in an indistinct wash of color.

The kiss deepened slowly, their bodies moving toward each other carefully as they tasted one another and shared their breath, filling their lungs with each other. As the kiss ended, Maxim moved slowly around her until he was at her back. Ivy felt his hands touch the zipper at the top of her dress and begin to draw it down. There was no urgency or impatience in his touch, only calm and reverence that carried over into his kiss as he lowered his mouth to graze along her skin as the zipper exposed it.

Ivy let her head fall forward as Maxim's lips traveled down her spine, carefully kissing each bone and gently glazing the skin with the tip of his tongue. Finally her dress was completely open and she allowed him to push it forward over her shoulders and off. She had worn only panties beneath the dress so the soft breeze that blew over them brushed against her bare nipples, making them even more taut and sensitive than they already were in response to his touch. Ivy lifted her hips slightly and Maxim eased her dress the rest of the way off of her, pausing to also remove her shoes and toss them aside.

Now in nothing but pale pink panties, Ivy shifted her weight so that she could turn around to face Maxim. His eyes traveled over her body reverently and she lifted her hands to the front of his shirt so that she could release buttons. He sat still as she worked her way down the shirt, allowing her to take as much time as she wanted to reveal his body. The buttons finished, she slipped her hands through the open sides and ran them up his chest and back over his shoulders so that the shirt came off and she could drop it onto her own dress beside them.

Ivy touched a kiss to the spot just above his heart and then lifted her head to look at him. Narrowing her eyes slightly, she reached forward and ran her fingertips along the smooth, undisturbed plane of his stomach.

"Is something wrong?" he asked softly.

"It's just," she paused, laughing at herself quietly, "you don't have a belly button."

Maxim smiled at her.

"My kind aren't born the same way yours are," he told her. He took her hand from his belly and eased it down to the button at the front of his pants, leaving it there and tucking his hand behind her so that he could knead her gently through her panties. "Does that bother you?"

"Should it?" she asked, raising her eyes to look into his.

"No."

"Then it doesn't."

Maxim kissed her again and Ivy followed the suggestion he had made with her hand, releasing the fastenings at the front of his pants so she could push them over his hips and off as he kicked off his shoes. The flowers were plush and warm beneath her as Maxim deepened their kiss and eased her back so that she stretched onto her back. His body came down onto hers and he took his mouth from hers so that he could kiss along the outside of her neck, still moving so gradually Ivy could savor each tiny feeling that his lips created as they moved down.

One hand cupped Ivy's breast as Maxim's mouth came down to cover the other. Ivy let out a long breath as his tongue swept over her nipple. He moved over to repeat the attention on her other breast, mimicking with the pad of his thumb on the first nipple as his tongue encircled and traced each side of the hardened point. Maxim pushed back to sit on his thighs and grasped the sides of her panties. She lifted her hips so that he could remove them and then he came back to his position over her, returning his mouth to her breast as his fingers tenderly ran along the side of her ribcage, into the dip of her waist, and over the swell of her hip, then back.

Ivy parted her thighs slightly and felt Maxim still over her. Up until now he had been lying on her legs, his erection cradled against her thighs, but that small shift had caused his hips to settle down between them so that his tip brushed down over her core. Maxim lifted his head and without taking his eyes off of her, moved his body up further so that his chest hovered over hers. He lowered himself to his elbows, bringing his body closer. Ivy brushed her lips across his and rested her hands on his back, running them along his sides so that she could feel the tense muscles beneath his skin.

In one smooth, slow movement, Maxim sank into her. Ivy arched slightly as he filled her and she felt her body wrapping around him as if it had been made to welcome him inside. Maxim tucked his head into the curve of her shoulder and reached down to grip her hips as he began to roll his hips against her. With each deep stroke she felt his hard, thick length massaging her, nurturing her. Ivy's hands dropped away from his back and Maxim met them, pressing his palms to hers and intertwining their fingers so that he could bring her arms up beside her head. The position gave him more leverage and he pushed back slightly, the angle sending him even deeper. Ivy cried out as he pressed completely inside her so that her body stretched to hold him.

Maxim rocked into her a few more times and then lowered his body fully onto hers and rolled to his side, sweeping her leg up over his hips and wrapping his arm around her waist so that he held her tightly against him. Their bodies meshed together, Maxim's legs tangling with Ivy's and their arms grasping each other close. Ivy could feel his heart pounding against hers and hear his low, rhythmic sounds as he continued to stroke inside her in thrusts that kept their bodies tightly connected. She tucked her head onto his shoulder, kissing along the firm muscle as she subtly rolled her hips to meet his.

The pressure within her was building to an almost over-whelming intensity and Ivy whimpered as Maxim took hold of the thigh rested over his hip and used it to hold her still so that he could push into her even more intensely. Ivy's head fell back, a gasping cry pouring from her lips, and he thrust into her again, his own groan joining hers. As he buried himself almost impossibly deep within her, Ivy felt the incredible sensations he was creating within her spiral upwards and reach a mind-erasing peak, then crash around her in a series of spasms that pulled him closer and drew him to the edge of his own climax. Maxim groaned, suddenly throbbing within her as he released, spilling into her body and clutching her as tightly to his chest as she could get.

Ivy clung to him, kissing his neck and licking the sweat from his shoulder as she luxuriated in the continuing waves of her orgasm. Finally her breath settled and her body relaxed, and she felt Maxim calm beside her. They remained entwined with one another, staring into each other's eyes and occasionally kissing as their hands explored the curves and planes of each other's bodies. Ivy let her eyes drift closed, drawing in breaths of the fragrance of the velvety purple flowers mixed with the scent of Maxim.

"What will happen when it's time for me to leave and go back to the Denynso settlement?"

"I'll go with you."

Ivy opened her eyes again and found Maxim still gazing at her.

"And when it's time to go back to Earth? I'm only on Uoria for a short time."

"I'll go with you then, too."

"You will?"

"Yes. Or you can stay here with me. Look at everything that had to happen so perfectly so that we would be here, now, together. I won't let anything happen that will change that."

Ivy leaned forward and rested her lips to Maxim's. He was still cradled within her and she felt him twitch as he hardened again in response to her kiss. His hands moved to her hips and Ivy let him lift her as he rolled to his back so that she came down on top of him, straddling his hips. This was ecstasy, perfection, and she knew at that moment that she wouldn't allow anything to take her from his arms.

6

"What do you mean you were sent as an offering to the Covra?" Lynx asked.

He could feel the anger building up within him, but he fought it. The Covra were dead. There was nothing more that he could do to them now, and losing control of his own aggression would only make it more difficult for him to understand what Rain was telling them.

"The Valdicians and the Covra had formed an alliance years before. The Covra were ancient, vicious creatures, but a species that most others new little to nothing about. I know that we hadn't even heard of them even though we had been researching the Valdicians after we received intelligence that they were using that planet essentially for slave labor from the prisoners of war they brought there. The two species formed an alliance for the purpose of taking over as many planets and species as they could throughout the galaxy. They wanted to rule over it and control its entirety. They sent us here so that the Covra could use us as slaves and mercenaries to take over Uoria and put it into the power of the Covra. The Valdicians considered it the jewel of this area of the galaxy. They believed that once they had it and everyone on it under their control, the other planets would fall."

"You said that you didn't come into conflict with the Covra until several years after you crashed here, though. If you were sent for the Covra, why didn't they attack as soon as you got here?" Lynx asked.

"The Valdicians didn't know that the Covra had already started a war of their own on Uoria and the numbers of their adults had dwindled down to nearly nonexistent. What was left was weak and unable to fight, but there was a new generation coming. They had never really intended to cooperate with the Valdicians. They were going to go along with what the Valdicians planned just until they had them in the ideal position, and then take them over just as they already had begun to do with the other species that inhabited nearby on Uoria at the time. All they had to do was wait."

"What species?" Pyra asked.

Lynx knew that it couldn't have been the Denynso, but remembering what Loralia had said about her grandfather's stories, he thought it must be her kind. He turned to look at her across the room where she was sitting beside Bannack, but before she could acknowledge him, he heard a voice from his other side.

"Us."

Lynx turned sharply, startled to see one of the men from the other kingdom standing as he looked out over the rest of the group. Whispers swelled around them as members of the crowd shifted uncomfortably.

"You?" Pyra asked incredulously.

The man nodded and recognition finally set in for Lynx. This was Rey, the leader of the kingdom who had offered himself and his own men to come back with Pyra and the Denynso warriors so that they could help the people of the settlement.

"Yes," Rey said, turning his eyes back to Pyra.

"You told me that you knew nothing of the Covra," Pyra said, his voice low and the familiar growl of his anger bringing edge to each word. "You said that you had heard the name and that you knew of the war that they had with the Li—" he stopped himself short of using the phrase for which Rain had shown so much disdain, "the people of this settlement, but that you didn't know anything about them and that you never even got to find out anything about them before your communication with them cut off."

Rey's face looked sad and strained. He nodded again, his hands coming in front of him as if imploring Pyra to listen to his explanation.

"I know. I'm sorry that I lied to you, but the history with the Covra is something that is extremely painful for my kind. When the last of the elders who were alive during our conflict with them died, our kind hoped that the memory and history of that time would die, too. Very few of us now even know the whole story. I do only because I am the leader and come from the same line that led then. That was nearly two hundred years before the crash that brought the first humans here. I didn't want to dishonor the memory of our ancestors by recounting those dark times."

"I asked for your help and you lied to me," Pyra said. "You might have been able to help us save more of these people."

"No," Rey insisted, shaking his head, "it wouldn't have mattered even if I had told you. We knew that the Covra locked people, yes, but we didn't know how to save them. None of our kind that were taken by the Covra survived."

"Taken?" Pyra asked.

Rey nodded.

"When the Covra attacked, they didn't kill immediately. Instead, they took the strongest, both men and women, and forced them to work. They spoke of visions that they had for the future of the planet, compounds and buildings that they would use to conquer anything and anyone that stood in their way. They forced the captives to build the first of the buildings that they planned."

"What was it?"

"A fortress."

"A prison," Gyyx said.

"What?" said Pyra, looking up at the massive warrior who had stood and was moving down the steps toward the platform.

"The building that they forced the captives to build. It was the prison. Remember how we thought that the Covra had forced the humans to build the prison for them because they didn't have the hands to do it themselves?"

"They couldn't have," Lynx said, his thoughts starting to align with Gyyx's. "That prison is far older than the length of time that that the humans have been here. Rain and the others couldn't have been the ones to build it. It had to be someone else, someone who had been here longer but had the same abilities. Like them."

He pointed at Rey, who nodded.

"When the building was finished, our kind never saw the captives again. The war between the species had been hard on both sides, but the Covra had become weaker as the years progressed and soon after the captives disappeared, the rest of the Covra were either killed or died off. By then there had been turmoil amongst our kind. After the final battle with the Covra, our kingdom split and a group left."

"You told me that," Pyra said, "but what happened to them? Where did they go?"

"I told you that we didn't know what happened to them after they left, and that was the truth. After the division, our kind didn't hear from the traitors or the Covra again. Everything was quiet."

"For how long?" Lynx asked.

"Nearly two centuries. When the humans crashed, our kind reached out to them. They didn't seem to pose any threat, and when one mentioned the name of the Covra, something that they had heard from the species that sent them here, our kind knew it was essential to protect them as best we could."

"We had no form of communication," Rain said. "The Valdicians had made it so that all of our equipment on the ship was completely destroyed when their weapons took over control. When we crashed here it was a planet that none of us had ever heard of and even our personal communicators couldn't make contact with Earth. There was no way for us to let anyone know that we were here, or to travel off of the planet."

"Our kind didn't leave the planet," Rey continued. "We originated here, had always been here. We had the technology to travel to other planets, but all of our ships had been destroyed during the war with the Covra and we never built another."

"And even if there had been, we wouldn't have known how to get back to Earth. On a planet that we hadn't even known existed, we had no way of orienting ourselves or figuring out where to go. It was pretty soon after we got here that we decided it would be a waste of our time, energy, and resources to try to find a way to get back to Earth. So we just stopped and focused on surviving. We settled in, assimilated to the planet, and built up a relationship with the people who were already here. We were here for ten years before we saw the first Covra."

"Ten years?" Lynx asked. "Why didn't they come sooner?"

"Rey, you said that the Covra were weak by the time you had your last battle with them, but that they said a new generation was coming."

"Yes."

"And that was just after the captives finished building the prison."

"The cells didn't have chains."

Elianna was gripping Ciyrs's hand and Lynx could see the look of fear in her eyes as painful memories swept through her mind.

"They didn't?" Pyra asked.

Elianna's eyes lifted to meet Pyra's and she shook her head.

"Some of them did, but they didn't look anywhere near as old as the rest of the building. When I was escaping I looked into a lot of the cells, and I didn't see chains. No hooks, no bars except for the ones on the main doors. There wasn't anything to hold a person there."

"What if they didn't need to be held?" Lynx asked. "What if the people who they were holding in those cells couldn't have escaped even if the Covra left the doors standing wide open all day and all night?"

"They were locked, just like us," Rain said, her voice powdery.

"Not just that," Lynx said, looking over to Rey where the man stood with his hands now gripping each other as if trying to let out the pain and frustration he was feeling through the tension. "They were locked for the same reason."

"Rey said that the Covra were weak when they were fighting them and that there was another generation coming. That means that they had to have somewhere to protect their eggs and something to feed their hatchlings," Lynx continued. "They took the strongest men and women from the kingdom because they would be able to build the prison that the Covra planned to use when they were fighting other species, but first it was going to be a hatchery. The reason that those slaves never came back is that they fell victim to the hatchlings."

Rey's hand lifted to cover his mouth and several people around Lynx gasped. It was horrific enough to think of the people in the settlement getting locked by the Covra and used as incubators for their young. Now they were realizing that this was not the only time that it had been done and that even more lives had been lost in the gruesome way.

"Was it those hatchlings that eventually came and attacked the humans?" Elianna asked.

Loralia stepped forward into Lynx's periphery and he noticed that the shimmering glow from her skin seemed fainter than usual as if it were reacting to the tense emotion swelling through the room.

"No," she said. "It couldn't have been. The Covra have long lives, but not two hundred years. If they did, they would have more than one set of hatchlings. The young who were born from that group had at least ten years before they would need to lay their eggs and then another century before they would become weak and die off. These people," she gestured toward Rey and the others of his kind that had gradually moved toward him as they spoke, "are not the only species that was on the planet at the time that the Covra were at their most powerful. There's a reason that they chose that particular spot to build their prison fortress. It wasn't an accident. They had begun their plans to take over Uoria long before they became allies with the Valdicians so that they could conquer them as well, and they made sure that they set up their strongest building close to the species that they intended their hatchlings to conquer first...my kind."

"Your kind?" Bannack asked, obviously shocked by what he was hearing his mate say.

She turned to him, nodding.

"We didn't always live under the ground," she told him. "The caverns where I grew up were a refuge, an escape from a war that had waged for far too long and was claiming far too many of us. My grandmother told me when I was young that going below ground to live was one of the most painful decisions that our kind had had to make. They loved the land where they had lived. So deeply, in fact, that they created a mirror within the cavern that would make their new home a reflection of the home that they had lost."

"The Denynso compound," Zuri said softly.

Loralia nodded, turning back to Rain and Pyra on the platform.

"The war with the Covra was only part of what they were fighting. A plague had broken out among them, killing off members of the community seemingly indiscriminately. People were dying faster than the healers could find ways to help them, and more often than not, as soon as a person died, the Covra would take the body and drag it away so they didn't even have the opportunity to honor those who were lost. My kind fled beneath the group, hoping that the Covra would simply forget about them. It seemed to work. Going below ground even seemed to rid the clan of the plague that had tormented them."

Loralia fell silent and Lynx shifted uncomfortably. He knew that she was thinking of that plague now. The illness may have disappeared when they first went below ground, but two centuries later it would return, rising up in the caverns and killing every one of her kind except for her.

"You knew all of this and didn't tell us when we first started talking to you about the Covra?" Pyra demanded.

"I didn't make the connection until now," Loralia insisted. "I only remembered the stories that my grandmother had told me about how our kind ended up in the mirrored world beneath the ground, but she never called the enemies by name. When my grandfather spoke of the Covra, he only said that they were vicious and hated, never that they had been the cause of our kind going beneath the ground or that they had been the source of such devastation. He did tell me, though, that they had come into contact with an enemy that weakened them. That after years of fighting enemies with the cruelest of their weapons and taking some domination over the planet, they had encountered a species that forced them back and took some of their power." She took a step forward, looking directly at Rain. "It was you. You were the first humans that the Covra ever encountered and it was your voices that weakened them to the point that they knew they couldn't defeat you. There was no way for the Valdicians to know that when they sent you thinking that they would be able to take control of you so easily. You are the reason that the rest of us survived. If you hadn't fought them off..."

Loralia's voice trailed off and Lynx saw Bannack step up beside her, wrapping his arm around her waist tightly as if in an effort to hold her up. Lynx's mind was spinning. He was having difficulty putting all of the pieces together as they realized little by little just how intricately connected they truly were.

"We didn't fight them off," Rain said. "They came slowly at first. Coming into the settlement a few times and then leaving. Then they descended on us. Rather than fighting against us themselves, they wounded the men. Something in their talons made them lose all control. They fought against each other with viciousness that I can't even describe."

"We've seen it," Lynx said. "They did it to me right after I found you when we first got here. Then to two other men during our last battle with the last generation before the hatchlings. Ciyrs saved us."

"We couldn't save any of them," Rain said, the emotion catching in her throat. "What started as a team of more than 200 on one of the most advanced clandestine mission Star-City ships of the time became a group of fewer than 100 in a settlement built from the wreckage."

Lynx looked around him at the room where they sat and thought of the houses where they had been living. It sent a chill through him to think of the survivors of the crash dismantling their ship, knowing that they were taking apart the only hope that they had to get off of the strange and completely unknown planet. He couldn't imagine having to move aside the bodies of those who hadn't made it through the crash and wipe away the blood before using the pieces to cobble together the buildings they knew would be their homes for the rest of their lives.

"You survived," he said, climbing to his feet so he could step onto the platform and take her hands, "You fought off enough of them and weakened them to the point that they were forced to lock you in place and use you for their hatchlings rather than keeping you as the slaves that they intended." Lynx leaned forward and kissed her, resting his forehead against hers. "You survived."

Rain pulled away from Lynx and looked over his shoulder at Zuri.

"What happened after the war units released the prisoners? Where did they go?"

"They dispersed back to their original planets, mostly. There weren't many left by the time the war units got there."

"And none of them mentioned that we survived getting there?"

"The official story is that they said a group came to free them but the Valdicians forced them off of the planet."

Rain pushed around Lynx and stepped to the edge of the platform.

"When did the people of Earth find out about Uoria?"

"They first recognized that the planet was here sixty years ago. The only species that they could make contact with was the Denynso and it wasn't until ten years later that any humans received permission to visit."

Lynx felt his chest constrict as he thought of the only stories he had ever heard of those first visitors. It was a small group, a collective of journalists and scientists who received permission to be on the planet for one month to bring back whatever information they could about Uoria and the Denynso to the researchers on Earth. It was one of these women, a journalist in her early twenties who fell in love with a warrior and was cast aside, who became the grandmother of the woman who nearly led to the destruction of the entire clan. The flight attendant who had served Eden, Leia, Elianna, Zuri, and Samira on their way from Earth manipulated a traitor from the Denynso and cooperated with him to aid the Klimnu and help them to wage battle against the warriors. It was a sensitive topic, but one that was even more painful to them now.

"Humans have been coming to this planet for 50 years," Rain said, her voice so low now that they could barely hear her, "Fifty years that we have been lying here. Fifty years of people telling stories about us and turning us into these legends when we were right here. All they had to do was leave the compound and they could have found us."

"They weren't allowed to leave the compound," Pyra said, sounding slightly defensive at Rain's accusatory tone. "That was the part of the restrictions that applied to people who wanted to come here. They were very well controlled and could only move in certain areas of the compound. Every visitor had a warrior assigned as guard and protector so that they stayed in the constraints of their visitation permissions. If they tried to move beyond those constraints, they were kept in custody until a shuttle could bring them back to Earth. At that time it was a more than 10 day journey. Certain rule violations warranted more than rescinding of permissions. Very few people ever tried anything."

"Even if they had found you," Ciyrs said from where he stood next to Elianna, still gripping her hand tightly, "they wouldn't have been able to do anything for you. Humans even now know nothing about the Covra. They wouldn't have known what had happened to you or what to do to help you. If they hadn't assumed you dead and buried you alive right here in the settlement, they would have brought you back to Earth to memorialize you and the Covra young would have hatched there. The entire planet would have been at risk."

Silence fell over the room and Lynx could feel Rain tense further beside him.

"What do we do now?"

"It's up to you," Pyra said. "The warriors left the compound to explore the planet and this is as far as we've gotten. I have decided that we should move on as soon as possible so that we can continue our original mission and get back to the compound with our findings. You are free from the Covra now. You can do whatever you want to. You can stay here and continue life the way you had been living before the war and rebuild your connections with your allies, or you can come along with us. We will see to it that a shuttle will come and return you to Earth when we get back to the compound."

Though it seemed like this would be exactly what Rain wanted, her face suddenly darkened at Pyra's suggestion.

"Stay here? Go back to Earth? And do what? We don't know anything about this planet or that one anymore. How much has changed? Would we even have a life to go back to? And if we stayed here, what would we do?"

For the first time since the meeting started Lynx became very aware of the children in the room with them. Obviously born in the years after the crash, some of them were young enough to be playing in the corners and running along the top edge of the well, oblivious to what was going on around them with the adults."

"I can't answer that for you," Pyra said. "We did what we could. It is up to you now what you do. Everyone is dismissed now. Please take some time to make your decision as quickly as possible. We leave in two days."

Pyra stepped off of the platform and stalked out of the room. Lynx recognized the intensity in his stride and the broadness of his shoulders. He was feeling angry and likely longing for Eden. As much as Lynx was sure that their leader wanted to continue on with the mission that they had originally set out for themselves and bring back as much information about the planet as possible, he knew that Pyra was also eager to get home to Eden before their baby was born. Now that Pyra had seen some of the brutality and coldness that had existed on the planet in years that were far too recent for his comfort, he would want to be near his mate and their vulnerable newborn in order to protect them from a world in which he thought he was the fiercest of warriors, but was beginning to question that truth.

Slowly the group dissipated around them. Rain curled into Lynx's chest and he held her against him as the crowd gradually filtered out of the room and out into the settlement to discuss and decide their fate. He didn't know what would be the right decision. He knew that he needed to be with Rain, that no matter what decision was made, he wouldn't leave his mate's side. For the rest of them, though, the decision didn't seem as clear.

"Rain?"

Rain eased off Lynx's chest but he kept his hands on her as she turned to Ciyrs's voice.

"I can't even begin to imagine what you're going through," the healer said in the calm, soothing voice that he always used when talking to someone who was suffering and who he was trying to help. "I wouldn't know what decision to make either. While you are making it, though, you deserve to know as much as you can."

Ciyrs reached into the bag at his hip and withdrew the book that Elianna had given to him before the men left the compound. He held it out to Rain.

"My mate wrote this. She is from Earth and she came here to learn about the Denynso. The beginning of her time in the compound was very difficult, but she has overcome it and integrated into our kind. This book is about her and what she went through herself, as well as what the other human women went through when they came to live on the compound. There is some information in there about Earth now. It might help you."

Rain took the book and gave Ciyrs a slightly teary smile.

"Thank you."

8

———

Ivy felt the first rays of sunlight touch her eyes and she stretched, reaching beside her to touch Maxim. Her hand fell to the sheet and she opened her eyes sharply, finding the bed beside her empty and cold. Outside of the window she could hear the street coming alive with people preparing to leave the settlement. They group had come to a largely split decision over what to do now that the Covra were gone. Many of the humans from the settlement wanted to join the Denynso on their continued quest around Uoria, eager to explore more of the planet that they themselves had hardly ventured into, while others, particularly the families of the children born to the settlement after the crash, decided that they had established their lives on Uoria and wanted to focus on rebuilding the settlement and continuing life there.

Rey had assigned several of the men to stay behind in the settlement to help the humans find their footing again and to work on reconnecting the two species so that they could hopefully reform the relationship that had once existed between. Those who had families back in the kingdom would return there, while Rey and the others would journey with the Denynso at least as far as the other side of Uoria. Though none had mentioned taking Pyra up on his offer of traveling to Earth, Ivy felt like some of them, even some of those who had chosen to stay behind in the settlement, still harbored the desire, or at least the curiosity, to go.

At that moment, Ivy was thinking of Maxim, worried that he had changed his mind about returning to the compound and then to Earth with her. Even though Maxim had mentioned that she could stay behind and live in the kingdom with him and the rest of his kind, there was never a question that she would be returning to Earth just as she had planned. He had agreed to go with her without hesitation, but now that she had woken up to him being missing from the bed they had shared for the last few nights she was concerned that he had changed his mind and was at that moment preparing to join the ranks returning to the kingdom.

Dressing as quickly as she could, Ivy ran out of the house and onto the street. Her eyes scanned the faces around her until finally they settled on Maxim's. Her heart pounded harder in her chest as she saw him hand the man beside her a bag. As if he could feel her staring at him, Maxim's eyes lifted and met hers. He smiled and started toward her, opening his arms as he crossed the street. Ivy felt the fear in her body ease away as she stepped into his arms and let him gather her against his chest.

"I was afraid you were leaving," she whispered into his shoulder.

"Didn't I tell you that I was coming with you?" he asked.

"Well, yes," she said, "but..."

"But nothing," Maxim said, taking her by the shoulders and carefully pushing her back so that he could look into her eyes. "I have not questioned my decision for even a second. I love you and I want to be with you, whether that is here in the settlement, back in the kingdom, on the Denynso compound, or on your planet. I just came out here to say goodbye to my brother."

Maxim stroked her cheek with his thumb and Ivy smiled.

"I love you, too."

Out of the corner of her eye Ivy saw Loralia standing several feet away, her eyes locked on Maxim. Ivy turned her face to look at her and saw an expression of distrust furrowing Loralia's brow. She had released her flowing hair from the tight knot she had taken to wearing and strands of silver now trailed in the slight breeze around her, furthering the ephemeral quality of the gorgeous, if strange, woman.

"Loralia?" Ivy said, "Are you alright?"

Loralia's face relaxed and she looked to Ivy as if the question had startled her out of some kind of deep concentration. She took a step closer, but Ivy noticed that she hadn't taken her eyes off of Maxim. She wasn't gazing at him as though admiring him, but staring at him with a look almost as though she were looking past his face into what was inside him.

"This is Maxim," Ivy introduced, reaching to take Maxim's hand. "Maxim, this is Loralia, Bannack's mate."

"Hello," Maxim said, extending his hand.

"What are you hiding from her?" Loralia demanded before he could even get the full word out.

Maxim stepped back slightly as if stunned and Ivy shot a glare at Loralia.

"Loralia!"

"He's hiding something from you," Loralia insisted. "I can feel him worrying. He doesn't want to tell you."

"Loralia, stop..."

"No," Maxim said, cutting her off and holding a hand in between the two women. "She's right."

"What?"

Ivy felt her heart sink as Maxim's hand slid out of hers and he took a step back from her side. He extended his arm and began to roll the sleeve up from his wrist. As it got closer to his elbow Ivy saw a thick white bandage wrapped around his forearm. Panic rose in her and she reached for his arm.

"What happened?" she asked.

Maxim pulled his arm away from her, pushing the sleeve back down to cover the bandage.

"I don't know."

"Let me see it."

"What's going on?"

Pyra stepped up beside Ivy and looked between her and Maxim. His face was stern and cold, the look of a warrior preparing to lead his men forward.

"Maxim is hurt," she told him.

"I'm not hurt," Maxim said with a tone in his voice that sounded like he was trying to hush her.

"Then why is your arm bandaged? And why were you trying to hide it from me?"

"I'm not hurt," Maxim said again, calmer this time, "There's something wrong with my arm. It's having a reaction to something."

"Show it to me," Ivy insisted again.

Maxim looked between Ivy and Pyra, and his shoulders dropped. Ivy could feel her body shaking with worry as she watched Maxim roll his sleeve up again to reveal the bandage on his arm. He grasped at the end of the bandage with his fingers, freeing it so that he could begin to uncoil the layers. Finally the bandage fell away and Ivy stepped back, her hand coming up to cover her mouth.

9

"When did this start happening?" Pyra asked.

He was looking down at the man's arm and could feel the tendrils of panic beginning to coil their way up from his belly into his throat. Maxim looked into his eyes.

"I first noticed it yesterday. It was just a small spot, but then by this morning it was like this."

"Come with me," Pyra demanded and then glanced over his shoulder to where the other Denynso were gathering their supplies and preparing for the journey ahead. "Ciyrs!"

The healer looked up from his bag and Pyra gestured at him to follow. Just as he always did, Cirys draped his bag across his chest before following. Pyra felt a sense of relief at the gesture. They may be in serious need of his healing abilities very soon.

He led them toward Rain's house. They were still using her living room as their main meeting space rather than the meeting hall when it was just the Denynso, and the smaller space felt more comforting than the large empty well would have. As soon as they were all in the living room and the door to the house was closed behind them, Pyra gestured to Maxim.

"Show Ciyrs your arm."

Maxim extended his arm and Pyra's eyes fell again on the area of skin that he had covered with the bandage. The patch was slightly depressed as though some of his flesh had dissolved away, revealing only slimy white skin.

"Is this the only place on your body that this is happening?" Ciyrs asked, dropping his bag to his feet and stepping forward to look more closely at Maxim's arm.

"There is a small place on my back and one on my leg."

"And it started yesterday?"

"Yes. It wasn't this bad until this morning, though. When I woke up to help my brother get ready to go back to the kingdom I noticed that it had gotten much worse overnight."

"What did you do over the last few days?" Ciyrs asked. "Did you come into contact with anything strange? Any animals or plants? Did you eat anything that you haven't before?"

"I've stayed in the settlement for the most part."

"The most part?"

Realization seemed to dawn on Maxim and he glanced at Ivy before looking back at the Denynso healer who had crouched down and was pulling items out of his bag.

"Ivy and I went for a walk outside of the settlement walls the day before yesterday."

"While everyone else was in the meeting hall?" Pyra asked.

"Yes. We didn't realize that there was going to be a meeting. We were taking a walk and when we got to the fence at the back of the settlement we decided to go out and explore a little."

"Did you touch anything strange?"

"The only thing that I didn't recognize was the flowers."

"What flowers?"

"There were purple flowers. We sat down in them."

Pyra saw Ivy glance away and noticed a blaze of color stretch across her cheeks. From her response and the fact that the reaction of his skin had spread onto his back and leg told Pyra that they had done more in those flowers than just sit, but these were not his warriors. He would have to remain discreet.

"What do you think Ciyrs?" Pyra asked.

His voice had the slightest hint of a tremble in it, not as though he might cry, but like he was trying to hold in a flood of emotion that he didn't know how to properly express.

"It doesn't make sense to me, Pyra."

"But you see what I am seeing."

"Of course, I do. But how? How is that even possible? Rey said himself that his kind originated here, that they have always been here and that even though they had the technology to travel to other planets, they didn't. It just doesn't square up."

"But what about what Leia told us about how she came to Uoria? They talked about how they were beautiful once, but that had all been destroyed because of a toxin that interacted with their skin."

"That doesn't explain the origin, Pyra. They're from Ynn, a completely different planet."

Their voices grew faster with each exchange and Pyra could see out of the corner of his eye that Ivy was shaking, her face strained with fear as she tried to listen to what the two Denynso men were saying and glean any type of meaning from it, though Pyra knew that she wouldn't be able to. She hadn't been in the compound long enough. She could never understand.

"How long ago did they get to Uoria?" Pyra asked. "When did Creia say that they got here?"

Ciyrs seemed to stop and think for a minute.

"I don't know."

"Exactly. His conflict with them wasn't very long ago, but he never told us when they actually came here from Ynn."

"I don't understand."

"Rey said that their group split after the war with the Covra and that the part that left completely disappeared. They never heard from them again."

"Right."

"So what if they didn't just disappear onto Uoria? What if they used their knowledge of technology to create a ship that would bring them to another planet, only to destroy that planet and have to return here."

"She said they were beautiful once," Ciyrs repeated, his eyes scanning Maxim's face. "So what if they didn't come here from Ynn, but came back?"

"And began to change so rapidly that they were unrecognizable."

Ciyrs tucked everything he had taken out of his bag back into it and stood. He rubbed his hands together as he continued to stare at the strange patch of slimy white skin on Maxim's arm.

"I'm sorry," he said, glancing up at Maxim's eyes before grasping onto his wrist and pressing the pads of two fingers directly onto the skin.

As soon as Ciyrs's fingers touched his arm Maxim's back arched and he screamed. Smoke rose from his arm and a sickening hiss filled the air.

"Maxim!" Ivy screamed. "Stop!"

After a few seconds, Ciyrs took his hand away from Maxim's arm. Pyra watched the younger man collapse into

Ivy's arms, clutching at the place on his arm that was still smoking. Ivy lowered to the floor, taking Maxim with her so that she held him in her lap.

"How could you do that?" she screamed up at Ciyrs, tears streaming down her face as she held Maxim.

Pyra ignored her and took a step closer to Ciyrs.

"Find Rey and tell him to gather every single one of his men and bring them to the meeting hall, then find Gyyx, Ero, Ty, Bannack, and Lynx and bring them to me. Tell them that the Klimnu have returned."

UNTITLED

(To be continued in Part X...)

THE ALIEN'S LIBERATOR

The *Klimnu.* Ivy shuddered at the sound of the word. She had heard it before during her short time on the compound though she hadn't ever gotten the full story about them. She only knew that it was these creatures who the Denynso had fought against in their biggest and most intense war, the creatures who they had been fighting against when they climbed beneath the ground for the first time and discovered the mirrored realm that was home to Loralia and who were the cause of the death of Jem, one of their most treasured warriors. The rest of the details about them were shaky at best, but from the fire in Pyra's eyes and the growl in his voice, she knew that these were not creatures that should be taken lightly.

She looked down at Maxim who she still cradled in her arms, his head rested back on her shoulder as he gripped the arm that Ciyrs had just so brutally injured. The respect that she had initially held for Ciyrs had faded as soon as she watched his hand touch Maxim's arm and his scream of agony filled the air around them. Elianna had spoken of her mate as such a great and powerful healer, compassionate and nurturing in a way that was truly astonishing. He was the man who all of the warriors depended on to help them when they were injured or ill, the reason Elianna herself as well as Eden and Leia were still alive. Without him they would have succumbed to the injuries inflicted by the vicious Klimnu, and the men would have torn each other apart after being poisoned by the Covra and forced to fight against each other. He had seemed to be such an incredible person, yet now she had seen him coldly and without cause inflict horrific pain on the man who she loved.

"What is wrong with you?" she asked through gritted teeth, the tears still pouring down her cheeks as she looked up at Ciyrs.

He stared down at her, his orange eyes chilling in their lack of emotion. He didn't have the aggressive, searing anger in them that Pyra had in his own round, almost neon eyes. The color in them was unique to the Denynso, something that she had learned soon after her arrival among them. Not all of them had the rich orange color, a shade that was reminiscent of the last light of the sunset at night or the first rays of the sunrise in the morning. That glow was reserved only for the Denynso who had found their lifelong mates and completed their bond with them. It was an important distinction that showed that these men and women were set apart from the others and given the tremendous responsibility that came along with the bond.

When Ivy had first learned the significance of the orange colorations she thought that it was endearing, a sweet testament to the union of the two mates, but now that she was seeing it through the veil of cold emptiness in Ciyrs' expression, the color was a frightening, chilling reminder that the Denynso were not human, and were not like her. They were creatures that the humans were just beginning to really understand even after decades of contact. The thought hadn't mattered to her when she first began to plan for her visit to Uoria, or when she arrived and met the king and queen. Even though they had not been welcoming when she first encountered them, she knew that it was her fault. She hadn't followed the proper protocol in giving them notice about her arrival, and that is something that had been clearly and explicitly explained to her before she ever made arrangements to be a part of the exchange program. The Denynso were an extraordinarily regimented and structured society that lived their entire lives by the sense of responsibility and duty that was born into them. Their fate would be decided for them at birth and it was that role that they would spend their entire lives working to fulfill. By not telling them that she was coming she was putting this order and control at risk, something that could have resulted in her immediate expulsion from the planet. They only allowed her to stay because George had stood up for her and she agreed to their stringent regulations.

"Answer me," she said, the tension in her jaw causing pain to radiate down the sides of her neck.

Without acknowledging her any further, Ciyrs turned sharply and walked out of the house, letting the door slam behind him.

"Get up," Pyra said down to Maxim.

As soon as Maxim was out of her lap Ivy jumped to her feet and stepped up to Pyra.

"What is going on?" she demanded.

Pyra turned away from her and Ivy reached out to grab his arm. Pyra thrashed his arm out of her grip, turning and pulling his hand back as if he was going to strike her, but then lowered it to his side. Ivy stared up at him unwaveringly. Even his tremendous size and aggression weren't frightening her. She didn't care about the reputation he had built as the most forceful and violent of all of the Denynso warriors, or the fact that he was leader of the group of men. He wasn't going to force her back.

"He is expected at the meeting hall with the others."

"He has a name."

"I don't care what his name is," Pyra said, glaring over her shoulder at Maxim. "That creature will go to the meeting hall with the others of his kind."

"And who are you to demand I, or any of my kind, do anything?" Maxim demanded, stepping up behind Ivy close enough that she could feel his chest touch her back.

His hand rested protectively on her hip and Ivy found comfort in the touch.

"I am the lead warrior of the Denynso. I am who brought them here and I am who came to your kingdom and brought you here. Where there is no control, I am that control. You will do as I say or I will eliminate you now."

Ivy felt her spine straighten and her chest swell angrily toward Pyra. She knew that she was tiny compared to him, but at that moment she felt like anything that he had was little compared to the anger that was swelling inside her. She no longer felt compelled to follow him, to assimilate to the ways of the compound or to even follow through with her part in the university program. This was not what she had intended when she agreed to come along to help George with his research. She thought that she would be coming to the beautiful and mysterious planet of Uoria to learn more about the Denynso and the planet itself. She thought that perhaps they would do experiments that would teach them more about the environment, the plant life, and how the Denynso and another creatures they encountered lived and be able to record enough information that they could write up reports that would finally get her name in the scientific publications at home. She had not anticipated the turmoil that she would walk into or the tumultuous journey that she would have to go on to go to the settlement to help the lost humans locked there. She had not anticipated meeting another species, one that was so like her own and yet still different, and falling so deeply in love with one of those people. She had especially not anticipated listening to the rage in Pyra's voice or standing in the middle of what was becoming an impending war.

Ivy felt Maxim's hand tighten on her hip and apply pressure so that he guided her back toward him rather than allowing her to advance toward Pyra like she wanted to. She could hear him making soothing, quieting sounds into her ear as if attempting to quell the words that hadn't even started out of her mouth yet. She wanted to lash out at Pyra, to tell him that this was not the way that the world worked, but she realized that when she was on Uoria, this was the way the world worked. She was at the mercy of other species who lived a life so incredibly different from hers it was nearly impossible to reconcile them from many angles. As much as she had dreamed of coming to Uoria and had been so looking forward to the time that she would get to spend on the planet, now all she wanted was to bring Maxim back to Earth with her and pretend that, other than him, the time on the strange planet hadn't happened.

"You aren't going to threaten him," Ivy hissed.

"It's alright, Ivy," Maxim said, tightening his grip even more. "I have nothing to hide and neither does any other member of my kind. We are a peaceful kind. We will go to the meeting hall like he asks and hear what he has to say. We can decide then what we will do from there."

2

"Pyra, how can you know what you are saying is true?"

Pyra looked up from where he stood on the platform in the well of the meeting hall and met eyes with Gyyx. They were gathered in the meeting hall as they had been just a few days before, but the feeling was completely different than it had been then. In that first meeting there was a feeling of tenuous connection and the beginning of hope for a cooperative future. The steps of the well had been a mix of the different species as they mingled amongst each other, created new groups and pairs, and sat independently without the need to be aligned with their own kind that had defined everything Pyra was accustomed to. There had been a sense of excitement then, even as they remained cautious and somewhat unsure about how they would proceed forward, but now there was a feeling of tension and suspicion hanging heavily in the air around them.

Rey and his men were clustered in the first few rows of the well while the Denynso warriors created a wall around them, a few of the humans filling in the spaces between the larger, more aggressive warriors to create a physical barrier that surrounded the beautiful creatures that had become such as source of suspicion and terror for Pyra. His eyes fell on each of them in turn, evaluating them, scrutinizing them. Finally they rested on the young man who sat beside Ivy, the angry open wound on his arm evident and visible. He searched for the man's name in his mind, but the level of anger and sheer aggression within him kept it from his lips. Finally his attention returned to Gyyx.

"There has only been one other time in my life, in any of our lives that we have heard of a creature that changed from being beautiful and kind to being a disgusting, vile species set on only destruction and bloodshed. One species that has been the scourge of our kind since before any of us were born." He turned back to the injured man and saw his eyes meet his without hesitation. The lack of fear, intimidation, or even a sense of shame that should come from him knowing what they were spurned Pyra's anger on even further and he pointed at him forcefully. "What is your name?"

"Maxim," he responded evenly.

"Come here."

Maxim didn't move, but continued to stare at him defiantly. Pyra felt the frustration building in his belly and the tension of the anger tightening his chest. For a moment he was angry with himself for leaving his weapons at the house, but then he thought of Eden and forced the feeling away. He gripped the necklace that she had Jem make for her, stroking the pendant that represented the two of them and the child that they would be welcoming soon, telling himself that he had to calm down. Starting a war now would only put him and the other men in danger, and create danger for the rest of the compound, including Eden and the baby, and that was something that he had to try to avoid as best as he could.

"Maxim," Rey said calmly. Pyra watched Maxim turn to look at his own leader. "Do as Pyra asks. We agreed to come here to help him with what he needed. Let him assuage his fears so that we can all move on from this."

Maxim rose to his feet and walked down the steps of the well until he was standing at the base of the platform. Pyra stepped aside to provide more space and Maxim stepped up to stand beside him. The younger man's jaw was set firmly, but he was still showing no fear. It was defiance that seemed to be a silent threat.

"You wanted something with me?" Maxim finally asked, his voice low and controlled.

"Show them your arm."

Maxim remained still, continuing to stare up into Pyra's face as if he were evaluating the Denynso warrior just as he was being evaluated.

"Maxim," Rey said leadingly, "go on."

Pyra watched as Maxim turned to the rest of the group in the room and extended his arm, revealing the wound. The area that Ciyrs had touched was burned so deeply it revealed the bone of his arm while the area around it maintained the slimy white texture that seemed to be expanding. Several people in the crowd gasped and Pyra heard a few of the warriors mutter obscenities under their breath when they saw the wound. He knew that his men recognized the color of the skin immediately.

"Now you see," Pyra said. "You see the way his skin is changing. What else have you ever seen that looks like that?"

"What happened to you, Maxim?" Rey asked, the concern in his voice evident.

"I went for a walk outside of the boundary of the settlement. I took a rest in a field of flowers that I've never seen before."

"When was this?"

"The day of the first meeting."

"And when did you start noticing the reaction on your skin?"

"The first small spot appeared two days later. It has gotten worse since then."

"And it burned down to the bone?"

At this point Rey was walking toward Maxim, the worry in his voice now reflected in his eyes.

"No," Maxim said, lowering his arm and turning to glare at Ciyrs. "The great healer of the Denynso did this to me."

He spat the words with such viciousness and disdain that Pyra felt his hands clenching again and the desire for vengeance taking over his need to control himself.

"He was testing what we know now to be true," he said angrily, stepping in the way of Rey so that he couldn't get closer to Maxim.

"And what is it that you think is true about our kind?" Rey asked.

The soft gentleness in the man's eyes had faded and been replaced by sharpness that seemed to exaggerate the clear blue color that had so fascinated Pyra when he first saw them. Pyra straightened, squaring his chest to the smaller man in a show of dominance.

"What I know is true about your kind is that you are the Klimnu, the vilest, disgusting, and hated of all of the species that the Denynso have encountered."

There was a rush of voices through the well and several of Rey's men stood to their feet. The Denynso warriors and the human men stepped toward them, some touching the weapons that they wore at their hips. Pyra could see that there was a violent and potentially bloody conflict stirring and he raised his hand to stop the warriors and bring them under control. He knew what he wanted to do with these creatures, but before that happened, he needed answers, and the only way that that was going to happen was if he kept these men alive long enough to confront them.

"How dare you bring such accusations against us? What could you possibly have that would support that?"

"The reaction on that man's arm is exactly what the skin of the Klimnu looked like."

"You have decided that we are some sort of fearsome, bloodthirsty race based on a reaction to some flowers that has damaged Maxim's skin?" Rey asked incredulously.

"We know what the skin of the Klimnu looks like," Ty said from the back of the crowd.

There were a few shouts of agreement among the warriors.

"We have been up close to them in battle," Ero added, "killed them with our own hands so that they couldn't kills us."

"Rescued our women from their grasp, including my own who suffered nearly to death in that prison that your kind built," Gyyx added.

"Our kind has lived in the same kingdom for the entirety of our existence. We told you that during our last meeting when we were discussing the Covra and our history with them. We live in the same place, in the same homes, and with the same traditions of our ancestors. We have never once transformed into any type of gruesome creature and waged war with you," Rey said. "Don't you remember when we first met? I told you that my kind has revered the Denynso as legends, almost myths. If we had been at war with you, don't you think that we would have remembered?"

"You told me yourself that half of your group split off from the others after the war with the Covra ended."

"Yes, they did, but no one knows what happened to them after they left the kingdom. We never heard from them again. We assumed that they fell victim to their own vices and simply died off."

"What do you mean their vices?"

"After the war with the Covra, some of our kind felt that it was our peaceful, accepting ways that had made us so vulnerable to the Covra. They were angry and aggressive, and wanted to take back the power that the Covra had taken from us. My elders once told me that it seemed like the ones of that group had been infected by the Covra in that cruel and horrible way that they forced our kind to fight with one another so that that Covra didn't have to do it themselves. Rather than fighting with each other, however, this group seemed to be filled with the greed and cruelty of the Covra. They said they wanted more than just our kingdom. The other group refused. They told them that we had won our freedom from the Covra and that we should go back to living the way that we always had, just putting that dark time behind us. There was no agreement and the other group left the kingdom, vowing that they would be back to reclaim the land and the rest of the species. They never returned."

Pyra drew in a deep breath, his eyes narrowing as he looked at Rey.

"You have just confirmed everything that I thought."

3

The coldness in Pyra's voice was more frightening than any of the words that he said and Ivy felt her breath catching in her throat. She wanted to go to Maxim, to be close enough to touch him. What could Pyra have meant by what he had said?

"I don't understand," Rey said, seeming to take a small step back away from the Denynso leader. "What do you mean I have confirmed everything that you thought?"

"The half of your group that split off from you didn't just disappear, and they didn't die out there on Uoria. With your resources and technology you couldn't have honestly believed that they would just go out there and die. They would be far too prepared, and far too smart, for that. The reason that they didn't ever return to your kingdom was that they didn't stay on Uoria."

"I still don't understand."

"My mate was held captive by the Klimnu for nearly two months in the prison that you built," Gyyx said. "During that time the one who captured her told her about the origins of the Klimnu. He didn't say anything about a kingdom or a war with the Covra. What he did say, however, was that their kind knew our king before, when they were still beautiful and happy. He said that they had come in contact with toxins that had begun to eat away at their skin and turn them into gruesome, slimy creatures."

Ivy felt like she couldn't breathe. The tension in the room was building so intensely that she was afraid at any moment one of the men was going to break out of the hold that the conversation seemed to be having over all of them and attack the others. She didn't want to be witness to a battle, but she also couldn't even think about leaving Maxim behind. He was obviously in serious danger even if she was still unsure of what was happening. Her hands gripped the front of the step in front of her so tightly her knuckles were white and she could feel the joints ache. She watched Pyra nod at Gyyx as if acknowledging what he said.

"You said that the half of your group that had split off learned from the Covra. The Covra wanted to rule every-thing. The wanted to take over the entirety of the planet."

"If the rogue group wanted to take over the planet, don't you think that we would have heard from them again? We would have known that they were taking over areas of land and that they were fighting. They would have come back here and tried to dominate us," Rey said as if he were pointing out something that completely explained away everything that Pyra and Gyyx had said.

"That's true," Pyra said.

Rey smiled, but Ivy was too suspicious of Pyra to think that it was that simple. He was far too determined to just allow the situation to drop that easily.

"If this was the planet that they were trying to take over," Ciyrs said.

The smugness in his voice made the hatred and anger

toward him surge even more within Ivy and she fought with herself to stay where she was sitting.

"I don't understand. We already told you that we can't travel off of the planet."

"No," Pyra said, "you didn't tell us that you can't travel off of the planet. You told us that you choose not to. You have the technology and are more than capable of leaving Uoria and that is exactly what happened. You're right that if the rogue group decided to take over Uoria, you would have heard from them again. They would have come back to take over the kingdom. They wouldn't have just let you stay here undisturbed while they fought with the other species of the planet and took over just those areas. If they were going to take over a planet, it wasn't Uoria."

"Then where did they go?" Rey asked.

Ivy would have expected him to sound angry, even defiant of the warriors who were making such horrible accusations of his kind, but instead, Rey sounded sad and somewhat wistful. She realized as she looked at him, his eyes wide as he waited for Pyra to tell him what happened to the group that left the kingdom, that he was feeling the same way that the humans had about the Nyx 23 crew. They had built a sense of attachment toward those that they had lost and the thought of knowing what had happened to them was an emotional moment for Rey even if the revelation wasn't something that any of them wanted to hear.

"Ynn," Gyyx said.

"Exactly," Pyra responded, nodding. "We always thought that the Klimnu originated on Ynn, but that isn't the case. They didn't start there, they went there. Unless I miss my guess, your kind is able to live on very little and can deal with temperatures and conditions that would wipe out other species."

"Yes," Rey said. "When necessary, we can go for long stretches of time without eating, can make food out of things that others aren't able to digest, and can tolerate extreme climates."

"That's exactly why it doesn't make sense that you would think that they had died when they went off on their own. This planet is far too lush and mild for them to be anything but comfortable even if they went to the harshest corners. No. They used the technology that they already knew. Knowing that it was a largely uninhabitable planet, but one that they could endure, they chose Ynn. Without many other species being able to endure the conditions of the planet, they knew that they would be able to completely take it over and create a paradise where they would be safe from any other invaders. They were prepared to fight any other species that might already be there or who attempted to come, but they knew the chances of that happening were slim."

"But you said that they had some sort of conflict with your king. How did that happen if they left Uoria for another planet?" Rey asked.

"They intended on staying on Ynn permanently. That is where they gave themselves the name of the Klimnu and trained their warriors. After several generations passed, however, they realized that they had destroyed the planet. Their greed and lack of regard for anything but themselves turned the entire planet of Ynn into a wasteland. It started to become uncomfortable even for them, so they decided that it was time that they returned to Uoria."

"Why Uoria? If you think that they fled to Ynn because they were so afraid of the Covra and didn't want to put themselves in a position of ever having another species take them over again, why would they come right back to the planet where it had happened to them, and where they knew that they would encounter other species who were just as strong?"

"They knew that they were already familiar with the planet. It would be easier for them to establish themselves, regroup, and possibly collect a few slaves of their own. Maybe they intended to only be here for a short time before finding another planet to take over. The point is that they came back here to take over and take advantage of the comfort and resources of the planet, but Uoria itself fought back almost as soon as they arrived."

"The flowers," Maxim said softly.

Ivy's stomach turned. The accusations had seemed so wild, so completely unfounded when she first heard them, but now Pyra's words were sinking into her brain, coming together and forcing her to acknowledge that what he was saying was true. These beautiful, peaceful people, including Maxim, were what had turned into the vicious and disgusting Klimnu.

"The flowers," Pyra repeated. "They were scouring the planet for a new place to settle, and naturally they moved toward the area of the planet where they would be most comfortable, near where their ancestors had lived. Where they chose to settle, though, put them in contact with the one thing that they didn't know would be a danger to them; lovely purple flowers."

Pyra ended with a tone of mocking in his voice and Ivy saw Maxim's jaw twitch.

"Once they came into contact with those flowers, the reaction began. They knew that Creia, the king from the nearby compound of Denynso, had healing powers. They went to him to ask that he stop and reverse the reaction so that it would restore their beauty," Ciyrs continued. "Creia had no tolerance for their behavior since they arrived on the planet, however. He told them that he would heal them if they agreed to stop their plans to take over the planet and leave Uoria. Instead, they chose to embrace the brutality that was coming over them. It was not just taking over the planet any longer. They would also eliminate the powerful Denynso warriors. They had discovered something about them that made it even more appealing to stay and wage war with them rather than establishing their own planet."

"What do you think they discovered?"

"Leia said her captor told her that the Klimnu thrived off of the anger, torment, and blood of the Denynso."

Rey shook his head, stepping back as if the words forced him backwards.

"No."

4

Ivy's hand covered her mouth as she fought the sick feeling that welled up within her at the words.

"No," Rey said again.

"Yes," Gyyx said. "The Klimnu knew that if they could take over the Denynso they would have the strongest and most feared warriors in the galaxy to do their bidding, and the harder they fought us, the stronger they got. They thrived off of the anger, fear, and anxiety that they were able to instill in us, and when we fought, they had access to the greatest source of power and strength that they could ever find: our blood."

"No," Rey said again, sounding more desperate with each word that tumbled from his slightly quavering lips, "our kind hasn't resorted to consuming the emotions and the blood of others to survive since the earliest of our days when survival was all that mattered. It isn't done anymore. It isn't what we are."

"It is exactly what you are!" Pyra roared, all of the aggression and anger that had been fairly well controlled up until this point suddenly exploding out of him and silencing everyone in the room. "Your kind took over another planet and then destroyed it because of your greed so you came back here to try to start over. When the toxins from those flowers started to dissolve away the beauty that you hold so precious and Creia refused to help you because of the darkness and cruelty in your hearts, you vowed to take revenge of him and the rest of the planet in the best way that you could, by feeding off of the emotional torture and the blood of the Denynso that came after him."

"We did nothing of the kind!" Rey argued.

"Yes, you did! We always wondered why the Klimnu didn't wage war on us like the other species did. They came in droves, fighting us in tremendous battles over short periods of time until they fell. The fighting didn't end until we had defeated them. The Klimnu, though, were different. They came slowly and periodically, one or two creeping into the compound and assuming the appearance of one of our own in order to gain trust and then attacking, or engaging in brief battles that could be months or even years apart. It never made sense why a species that had proclaimed themselves as our most hated enemy wouldn't just engage themselves fully in combat with us. It was because we were too strong. We fought back harder than anyone else the Klimnu had ever encountered and you needed the time to restore your strength. Keeping us constantly guessing and wondering when the next attack would be, where it would happen, and how severe it would be kept all of us anxious and made the fighting even angrier and more aggressive. As we fought you, we were feeding you."

"That wasn't us!"

"If it isn't you now, it will be. Those flowers only changed their skin, not who they were inside. It was their own twisted minds and the way that they let the Covra get into them that changed them into the vicious, cruel monsters that we have fought for as long as we can remember, and that we thought we had eliminated in battle. Coming into contact with those toxins only made them look the way they should. All of you may still be as beautiful and perfect as they once were, but inside you are all the same. You are all Klimnu."

The roar that came up from the Denynso warriors shook through Ivy and contracted around her heart, making it difficult to breathe. She could feel the tension of the room building even more intensely around her, as if the fury, fear, and aggression from all of the men in the room were pouring out of them so that it could crash and struggle together without the benefit of their physical bodies. The wall of warriors and human men was starting to crumble as the massive warriors stepped down into the crowd of beautiful, confused men being declared Klimnu and the human men took a step back, unsure of what was happening.

"We are not Klimnu!" one of the men yelled, trying to scramble away from Gyyx's tremendous hand as it reached down to grab him by the front of the shirt and yank him up to face him.

Ivy anticipated fear and horror from these men, but what she was seeing was a chaos of emotions. Some seemed paralyzed in place, staring ahead of them as if watching images that no one else could see as they grappled with their own emotions and tried to make sense out of everything that was happening around them. Others stood, the fear in their eyes mixed with a level of anger that rivaled even that in the eyes of the Denynso. Others pulled together, standing in clusters and looking around them as if planning an escape. The warriors closed in, their chests heaving with ragged breaths of anger. As she looked at them, Ivy noticed something that she hadn't before. Some wore black bands around their upper arms, a sign of mourning. She wondered if those were worn for the warrior she had heard them mention, the man who had lost his life in the final conflict with the Klimnu.

Was this why Maxim had been so reluctant to tell her how the humans arrived on the planet in the first place? Did he know that if he told her about the Valdicians and their alliance with the Covra that she would eventually realize what he really was? Her eyes lifted to him standing on the platform in front of her and his eyes met hers. She could see the torment in his gaze as his hand moved to cover the place on his arm that proved their origins. Guilt filled her painfully. If she hadn't brought him out of the settlement and into that field of flowers, this wouldn't be happening.

"We came on this quest because of the Klimnu," Pyra told them. "We left our compound and came out onto Uoria because of the war and what was lost in it. The blood, the betrayal, and the death was too much for us to bear and continue to remain right where we had always been. It was our mission to come out onto the planet and find what other threats might be here so that we could eliminate them before they could invade our land and threaten our families. We were prepared to encounter creatures that we had never seen and threats that we didn't understand. Who would have known that this journey would bring us face to face again with the very enemy that brought us here? Our warriors failed to purge Uoria of the scourge of the Klimnu once. We will not make that mistake again."

Ivy's eyes snapped to the huge Denynso warrior leader and saw his eyes flash. His hand moved to the dagger at his side, but just before he was able to raise it, Zuri flung herself onto the platform, stepping between him and Rey.

"What are you doing?" she screamed.

Her sudden appearance on the platform and the power in her voice made everyone in the room fall silent. All movement stopped and the divisions in the species seemed even starker than they had before.

"Zuri, come back here," Ero demanded.

"No," Zuri said, not even turning to look at her mate. "What the hell do you think that you are doing, Pyra?"

Ivy stood and ran down the steps toward the platform, suddenly mobilized by the silence in the room. She pushed through the people in the well indiscriminately, not caring who she was shoving past to make her way to Maxim. He reached his arms out to her and Ivy fell into them, clutching him to her chest as she finally allowed the tears that were building in her eyes to fall.

"Get her away from him!" Pyra growled.

Ivy felt Maxim pull her back several steps and when she looked over her shoulder she saw two of the warriors advancing toward her.

"Leave her alone!" George said, standing from his position on the steps and advancing toward them. "You have no authority over her. She is a citizen of Earth, not of the Denynso compound."

"She is a visitor of the Denynso compound," Pyra said, "which means that she is under the command of our rules and our authority."

"No," Zsilvia said, stepping up beside her mate. "She is under the command of her guard and protector. She must only abide by that protector and the king and queen themselves. Those are the terms of the treaty with Earth, you should know that. You have no command over her."

"Who is her guard and protector?" Pyra asked slowly, his teeth gritted so hard that Ivy felt certain they would break.

She could see the bands of muscle and tendons in Pyra's arms straining against the skin and his hand flexing and relaxing around the handle of the knife that he held. Through her studies Ivy had learned that it was not the tradition of the Denynso to carry their weapons with them, and they rarely even used them in battle. They far preferred hand to hand combat, yet somehow since their time leaving the compound these warriors had turned to their weapons as their constant companions.

"I am." Zsilvia said evenly.

She showed no fear of Pyra and Ivy felt her heart lift. George looked at her softly and turned to his mate, touching an appreciative kiss to her cheek before whispering something in her ear.

"Then control her," Pyra demanded.

"She is doing nothing that requires control, Pyra. We are not in a sanctioned state. No crimes have been committed. There is no war."

"And there won't be, because I won't allow it," Pyra responded.

5

———

"What are you talking about, Pyra?" Zuri asked, still keeping herself firmly positioned between the two men.

"Our entire lives we have been fighting the Klimnu. We have lost people who we love and nearly lost many others. These creatures are the bane of the existence of all who live on this planet and I will not allow them to continue on and put all of our kind, and anyone else, at risk."

"Kill them all!" a voice shouted from one side of the platform.

Several more voices joined the first, shouting for them to kill off all of the men who the warriors had declared where the predecessors of the Klimnu. Zuri felt her stomach clench and a bitter taste flooded her mouth as she realized that she was hearing nearly all of the voices of the warriors. These were men who she had grown to know and trust in even her short time on the compound. She had seen them as powerful and protective, but now she was watching as they crowded on a people who they had known only a matter of days, dissolving into a frenzy of wanting to simply cut them down.

"No!"

Ivy's scream cut through the uproar of voices and Zuri looked around Pyra to see her clutching the man beside her, a look of sheer terror on her face.

"Stop!" George yelled, holding up his hands to stop the warriors who were moving toward the men.

"These are the creatures that we have hated more than anything in our entire existence," Pyra said, his voice now a snarl that seemed to perfectly embody the coldness and anger that he was expressing in his words. "Each and every one of you saw how the skin on this one's arm is changing. He said himself that it is happening because of his reaction to the flowers that he touched when he was outside of the settlement. You know what they are."

"We can't let them live," one of the other warriors agreed. "We fought too long and too hard to just let them live."

"You went to them for help," Ivy said, her voice choked with emotion.

"Ivy's right," Zuri said. "When you needed help to rescue the humans from this settlement, you went to their kingdom and you asked them to help you. They came here to give you that help. They have been nothing but kind and supportive since they arrived."

"It doesn't matter," Pyra said. "I will admit that they came to help us, but we can't let that influence us. We have to protect what is ours. We have to be loyal to the Denynso and do what is right for our kind."

"Is it truly loyalty?" Ivy asked. "Or are you mistaking fear for what you think is loyalty?"

"Denynso fear nothing."

"Yes, they do." Zsilvia said.

Zuri felt her heart skip at that statement. She knew exactly the fear that Zsilvia was talking about and the thought of it still made Zuri feel slightly sick.

"Denynso warriors fear nothing," Pyra said, slowing his voice as if in concession to the statement.

"Yet you are so willing to kill off an entire species because of what part of their group did. Something that started hundreds of years ago and didn't involve any of these people," Zuri said.

"You saw his skin," Pyra repeated. "You weren't around during the attacks, Zuri. You don't have any idea what they were like. You don't know what we went through."

"I most certainly was there," Zuri said, her fists clenching with anger as she realized that Pyra could so easily forget her contribution to the war against the Klimnu. "I was attacked by one in the forest and I was there when the women explored that tunnel that led down into the mirrored realm where you fought the final battle. The only reason that I wasn't there for the battle was that I was recovering from the wound in my chest one of the Klimnu created. I wasn't there to watch Jem die, but I was certainly there to watch him sink into that whirlpool. I cried the same tears as everyone else. Don't tell me that I don't know what the Denynso went through. I might not be one of you and I might not have lived on the compound for as long, but I have lived it every second that I have been there."

The silence in the room was so deep that Zuri could hear her own ragged breathing.

"None of our kind knew what happened to the rest of our group when it split off," Rey said. He seemed to be fighting to control the emotion that he had to be experiencing at that moment and was speaking in a voice that was slow and controlled. "I am being honest with you when I tell you that those of our kind who were living at the time and every generation that has followed thought that they had died out in the wilds of the planet. There are areas of Uoria that are not nearly as beautiful and welcoming as this area, and we feared that with the avarice and cruelty that had taken over them since the conflict with the Covra they would have gone straight for those areas, hoping to conquer them and enslave whoever may live there. You have to know that we are not the same as those creatures."

"We know nothing about you," Pyra hissed, his voice filled with offense that Rey would even suggest some sort of camaraderie between the groups even though this was exactly what had been building just days before.

"You knew nothing about the humans of this settlement, and yet you were willing to risk your lives to help them."

"That's different."

"How?"

"We stayed here to help the people we found here because one of our own discovered his mate in their number. If we had not helped and had left Rain here to suffer and die, Lynx would have lived out the rest of his life alone. Several of us have humans as mates, including me. Our connections with that species are strong."

"It seems that Ivy has found her mate among these people," Zsilvia pointed out.

Pyra turned and Zuri watched as he locked eyes on the pair, their arms entangled around each other. Though it didn't seem to soften him at all, it did make him pause.

"You can't simply kill an entire species based on what they could be," Ivy said. "You can only judge them based on what they are. They have done nothing to prove that they are anything but peaceful. How can you justify killing them based off of what a small portion of them became?"

"Even Ulli betrayed us," Zsilvia said.

"Don't speak his name," spat Pyra.

"Why? Because you don't want to hear it, or because you don't want to admit to yourself that one of your kind, one of your warriors, the closest people to you, could turn his back and become something that you would ever have expected him to be?"

"Everyone has the potential for darkness," Zuri said. "That exists in each one of us. It doesn't justify preemptive killing."

6

———

"You can't listen to them, Pyra," Vax said.

Pyra turned to the warrior and stared at him. He had never been the same after the attack from the Covra that left him trying to tear the other warriors limb from limb. Something in him had gone, like it had been torn away the moment that the sharpened black point of the creature's leg dug into his back.

"Pyra," Vax said again, his hand tightening around the throat of the man he was holding in place beneath him," these things will destroy us. If you show them even a moment's leniency, you are offering yourself and your family to death. They will become Klimnu and they will infiltrate our compound. They know more about us now and will be able to torture and kill us without a second thought. If we don't kill them all now, we won't survive."

"Stop it. All of you."

The voice was powdery, but powerful enough that everyone turned. Loralia stood at the back of the room behind everyone, the faint pearlescent glow of her skin seeming to grow stronger as she looked out over them.

"Loralia, please," Bannack said, trying to take a step toward her, but Loralia held up a hand to stop him.

"I have never felt such fear and hatred in a single place. Never have I been so overcome by such a feeling of pure, blind instinct for survival. I was at the last battle between the Denynso and the Klimnu. No one knew I was there, but I watched as the men fought. I witnessed a level of absolute disdain for another living being that I didn't know existed and have not seen rivaled until I heard of the Covra. It is impossible to think clearly and really know what choices you are making when you are so absolutely overtaken by this type of turmoil. The decisions that are made here must be the ones of men, not of emotion."

Pyra felt Loralia's words burn into him. He looked around at the people in the room, registering all of their emotions, their body language, where they were looking. Though he would have hoped to see a united front among his warriors and submission and control through Rey and his men, he realized that he didn't see either. The warriors had scattered through the room, those with mates hovering close to them, others looming over some of the men, and others pulling away from the others, seeming to withdraw from the situation. Though the disgust was evident on the faces of those who were already gripping the necks or arms of the men near them, there were questions in the eyes of some of the others. He noticed that most of the warriors with human mates hadn't said anything and were standing somewhat apart from the rest, not like they were aligning themselves with Rey and his group, but also not like they were fully invested in what Pyra was saying either.

He knew that Loralia was right. It was his responsibility as the leader of the Denynso warriors to lead with strength and honor. He couldn't act rashly. The experience with Ulli and the Klimnu, and then the Covra had proven that what he first thought he knew and believed was not always what was. Though he was steadfast in his belief that these precursors of the vile Klimnu should be eliminated before they had the chance to cause more problems, he also knew that making that decision when he was this angry and when his men were so divided was not in keeping with his role as their leader, or with the responsibility and trust that Creia had placed in him when he stepped up into the role that he was born to assume.

"Loralia is right," Pyra said.

He could hear the tangle of discordant voices rise in the room, expressing the conflicting emotions and opinions of everyone in the well.

"You can't be serious, Pyra!" Vax shouted. "You are just going to let them be so that they can slaughter us all?" Pyra stared at him silently, not feeling the need to justify his decision. "Well, I'm not going to."

In one fast movement Vax lifted the man who he was holding by his throat and tightened his grip until the man thrashed and fought for breath, his hands clawing at Vax's arm in an attempt to release himself from the much larger man's hold. Before Pyra could take a step toward him, Vax flew backwards, the sudden movement causing him to drop the man he was holding. Vax slammed into the wall with a deep grunt and slid to the carpet where he huddled.

Pyra turned sharply and saw Ty staring at Vax, his eyes focused so intensely it was as though he were looking through the man. He knew that it was the young warrior who had caused Vax to slam into the wall, releasing the captive that almost certainly would have died in moments by Vax's hand crushing his throat.

"You will do as Pyra says," Ty said.

"All of you will," Pyra said. "From this moment I am taking over official command. Rey and all of his men will be quarantined here in the meeting hall until a final decision is made regarding their future. I will lead this settlement and everyone who is in it. If anyone has a problem with that or does not intend to comply with my leadership, you are to leave now, but be warned that I now consider us to be in a war state. Anyone who leaves this settlement will no longer be under the protection or assistance of anyone who remains. You will be on your own."

Pyra fell silent for several seconds, letting his eyes scan over the room so that he could watch the reactions of everyone. No one moved. He couldn't tell if it was because no one wanted to or if it was simply that those who did want to leave were too wary of what may happen to them as soon as they took a step toward the door.

"How will we keep them quarantined?" Gyyx asked.

Pyra glanced around the walls of the room, noticing that there were several doors along them, each of which led to hallways he assumed contained more rooms and possibly exits out of the building. It would take every one of his warriors to guard these exits and even then there would likely not be enough men to keep them under supervision.

"Let me," Loralia said.

Pyra watched the ethereal woman walk slowly down the steps of the well, keeping her eyes focused ahead of her rather than watching where she was stepping as if she just knew that everyone she passed would move out of her way as she walked. She climbed onto the platform beside him and looked out over the well.

"What are you going to do?" Pyra asked.

"I will block off half of this room so that the men have access to part of the building during their quarantine, but that they will be limited and only a few of the warriors will be necessary to guard them. This way not all of the men must be on duty at all times but Rey and his men will be kept completely under control."

"Why should we do anything that you tell us to do? What makes you think that we will just let you tell us where to stay?" one of the men asked.

"Because you have no choice," Loralia said. The sternness in her voice was startling to Pyra and he found himself speechless. "Bannack," she said, turning to look at her mate, "I'm going to need your help."

7

Ivy could feel herself trembling and even though Maxim tightened his arm around her to support her, her body shook with fear and anger. This was not what she wanted out of her experience on Uoria. These were not the images that she had had in her mind when she was in the shuttle, filled with anticipation and excitement. Part of her wished that Creia had not listened to what George had to say about her and simply put her back on the shuttle so that she would be back on Earth away from all of this turmoil. The other part of her, however, could not imagine drawing in another breath without Maxim and was willing to go through anything to keep him close to her.

"Ivy."

She looked up at the sound of her name and saw Loralia staring at her. Bannack was standing beside her and both held their silver compacts in their hands.

"You have to go," Maxim whispered in her ear.

"No," she said, shaking her head and holding him closer.

"Go," he said again, gently pushing her toward Loralia

and Bannack. "You have to. You don't want to make this any worse. Everything will be fine. I promise. Go."

Finally Ivy complied, stepping away from Maxim and allowing Loralia to take her gently by the wrist and pull her behind her. As she stepped past her, Ivy noticed Loralia's striking lavender eyes meet hers briefly. There was something in that gaze that she didn't quite understand, but that gave her a moment of calm.

"Everyone go to that side of the room," Loralia said.

Ivy watched as the other men climbed onto the platform and then past it so that they were scattered on the other side of the steps. Maxim remained in place, standing strong in the center of the platform where he didn't take his eyes off of her. Ivy felt another hand on her wrist and she looked over her shoulder to see Zuri standing close behind her. She followed the guidance of her hand as Zuri led her off of the platform and up several of the steps along the side of the well.

"What is she doing?" Ivy asked, watching Loralia look around the room carefully as if looking for something very specific.

Before Zuri had a chance to answer, Loralia leaned over to whisper something in Bannack's ear and they both opened their compacts, tilting them carefully. Ivy watched in fascination as they moved the mirrors in minute amounts, shifting them slightly, staring into them, and then shifting them again. Suddenly they stopped moving the compacts and Ivy saw the glow of Loralia's skin pulsate slightly. Between blinks a wall appeared in the center of the room, crashing down to the middle of the platform so that it cut the wood and molded to the shape of the steps, creating a tight seal.

Ivy screamed, pulling herself out of Zuri's hand as the

larger woman tried to grab onto her and hold her back. She ran up onto the remaining half of the platform and slammed her hands on the cold, solid white wall. Tears burned into her skin, stinging as they dropped onto her chest and blurring her vision. She ran along the length of the wall, running her hands across the surface, desperately trying to find a door, a window, any opening, but there was nothing but the solid white expanse.

"Ivy," George's voice said from behind her, "Ivy."

She felt his strong hands wrap around the tops of her arms and she thrashed, trying to shake them loose, but finally relenting and allowing him to guide her back until she sat on one of the steps. Ivy dropped her head forward onto her thighs, gasping for breath and trying to force down the sickness rolling through her.

"It's going to be alright, Ivy," Zsilvia said as the Denynso woman settled down beside her. "He's not gone. He's right on the other side of the ceiling."

The sentence startled her and she looked up at Zsilvia.

"The ceiling?" she asked.

Zsilvia nodded and glanced up and then back at the solid white wall. Ivy followed her gaze and realized that every detail of the two surfaces was exactly the same.

"It's a reflection," Zsilvia told her. "Loralia made it to divide the building. The other side of the room is still there, and Maxim is fine."

"But they have no food, no water, nothing that they are going to need to survive. How long does Pyra plan on keeping them in there?"

"No one knows anything that Pyra will do, but there are doors on the outside of the building that the Denynso warriors will guard. We will use those doors to bring them the supplies that they need when they need them."

Ivy stood and rushed back up the stairs to the wall, pounding her fists on it.

"I need Maxim," she said, the tears beginning to trickle from her eyes again.

"Ivy?"

The muffled sound of Maxim's voice came through the wall and Ivy gasped, pressing her hands harder against the surface in an effort to be closer to him even through the solid expanse.

"Maxim?"

"I'm right here," he said, "I'm fine."

"Everyone is to leave the meeting hall now," Pyra commanded. "Rain, tell the people who were not here what happened and ensure that they understand I am in charge now. This situation will remain under control. I will no longer have any tolerance."

"I don't want to leave," Ivy said through the wall to Maxim.

"Ivy, you need to come on," George called to her.

Ivy shook her head and rested it against the wall, closing her eyes so that she could focus on the presence of Max so close to her.

"I said everyone," Pyra shouted from the back. "I will have compliance or the Denynso will leave and continue on our path around the planet. We will seal the doors and let the life leave them slowly."

"Go," Max said to her again. "I promise you, everything will be fine. Please just go."

Ivy turned away from the wall and climbed to steps, her eyes searing into Pyra as she went. All fear of the man was gone. Now she felt only disdain. He followed her eyes as she walked past him, but she refused to give him the satisfaction of seeing a single tear fall. She would comply with his commands, but he would not control her. She would find a way to overcome him and leave with Maxim.

She stepped out of the building and into the bright day. The tension inside the meeting hall had been so intense she had forgotten that it was only morning when they went inside and now the blazing light of an afternoon sun was beating down on her face. She closed her eyes and let it warm her, drying the tears on her cheeks and soothing the chill that had seemed to settle into her bones.

"If only you didn't believe that wall was there. Just for a moment, if part of it would simply fade away."

Ivy heard the words but it was as if the wind had spoken them into her ear. She looked over her shoulder and didn't see anyone, but as she turned in the other direction she saw Loralia walking slowly down the street, her fingers lightly intertwined with Bannack's. The words sank into her, digging into her heart until she felt a stab of pain go through her. On their surface they seemed like a cruel taunt, but the more she thought of the tone behind them, the more they seemed like a veiled message, something that Loralia wanted to tell her but couldn't risk saying.

THE DAY CREPT by in painful near-silence. A heavy, almost palpable cloud of tension had fallen over the settlement and everyone moved through it as if fighting the air, pushing aside the suspicion, accusations, and worry that hung in simply so that they could breathe. Everyone had worked throughout the day, tending the gardens that they had started, gathering food from the trees at the edge of the settlement that still bore fruit, and sorting through the homes of those who had died in the Covra hatching to find anything useful. Ivy felt like she was picking their bones, giving them a final indignity in a death that was already almost too gruesome to bear, but Rain had broken through the suffocating silence for a few moments to reassure her that those who had died would have wanted to help the survivors in any way that they could. Even then, however, it felt like another exertion of control.

There was a sense of relief when darkness finally fell over the settlement and Ivy stepped into the bedroom where she had been sleeping, closing the door behind her so that she could be alone. She peeled off the clothing that she had been wearing all day and stepped into the small bathroom alcove on the side of the room. Touching her hand to a panel on the wall she released a stream of water over herself, allowing it to rinse away the dirt, sweat, and tears coating her skin.

She closed her eyes as the water glazed across her skin and pooled onto the floor beneath her feet before washing way into the purification drain beneath her feet. For a moment she didn't want to see the purple color of the Uoria water. She didn't want the reminder of where she was and everything that she was going through. For just a moment she wanted to pretend that she was back home, grabbing a fast shower in one of the tiny university laboratory showers on one of the long nights that George insisted that they continue working hours after everyone else had left. As she stood there, the water beginning to cool as she used up all of the reserves in the solar tank, her mind wandered back to what Loralia had said to her when they left the meeting hall.

If only you didn't believe that wall was there. Just for a moment, if part of it would simply fade away.

She let the words run through her head and across her skin like the water, moving them around in her mind, separating them into letters, into sounds, into different phrases.

Finally she brought them back together and whispered them. The cool water touched her lips as she formed the words and suddenly, as if the droplets of water had brought the memories forward, she remembered something that the women had told her during their walk toward the settlement. It had been an offhand detail, something that was part of a much larger story Elianna told her as they hid in the caverns away from the raging storm.

She forced herself to remember everything that Elianna had said. The memories were hazy, colored and fogged by the tense emotions of that journey. As she was listening to that story she was also worrying about Zsilvia and her reaction to her, and George and how angry he seemed. All of the heat ran out of the water, but she continued to stand in it, allowing the biting cold to clarify her mind and sharpen the memories. She could see Elianna crouched in the cavern, her small body tucked close to a fire that Loralia had built in the center of the floor, trying to get dry after the sudden deluge above ground. She could hear her talking about going down into that place when they first found it and how the sky had seemed so terrifying to her as it stretched across the ground.

She remembered Elianna talking about the first time that she had seen Loralia reflect something, creating the stone floor out of the wall behind them. This had been what had seemed familiar about the white wall appearing in the meeting hall, but the fear and disgust that tormented her when it appeared had washed that thought from her mind. Now the memories flowed in more rapid succession. She heard Elianna tell her about watching others walk across the stone floor and about taking her first steps onto it. Then she heard Elianna's voice, clear and almost tangible as if she were standing right there in the room with her.

"I will never forget taking a step and wondering if the floor was going to be underneath my foot when I lowered it. Even though I could feel the floor beneath my feet, in that one moment I questioned whether that piece of the floor was going to be as solid. I didn't believe it would be. And then I stepped and it wasn't there."

Ivy turned off the water and jumped out of the shower. Drying off as quickly as she could, she threw on her clothes, dragged her bag out from where she had tucked it beneath the bed when she first chose that room and started shoving the rest of her belongings inside. She took her second bag from the hook where it hung on the back of the door and checked the items that were still tucked inside. Tossing both bags over her shoulder, she rolled the blanket on the bed into a tight ball, held it beneath her arm, and stepped quietly out into the hallway.

The rest of the house was silent, but she still held her breath as she crept down the hallway toward the next bedroom. The door was slightly open and she eased it just enough that she was able to step inside. Though the room was darkened, she could tell by the slow, even breathing coming from the area of the bed that Elianna and Ciyrs were sleeping, exhausted from the day that was now grinding to a close. Watching carefully in the faint light from the moon allowed in through the window to make sure that neither of them moved, Ivy lifted Ciyrs' bag off of the floor, added a few items from another on the door, and slipped back out.

Downstairs Ivy unrolled her blanket on the floor and filled it with as much food and as many metal cylinders of water as she could before rolling it back up and heading outside. The street was deserted. Not even the sound of one of the children laughing or a couple whispering as they settled down for the night drifted on the soft wind that was blowing around her. Feeling more confident know that she was out of the house, Ivy began to run. She moved as quickly as she could despite being weighed down by the bags and the now-heavy blanket. Finally she found herself at the front of the meeting hall.

Ivy slowed as she approached the building, looking around for the warriors that were guarding the building. It seemed that because the wall Loralia created intersected the main room, making it impossible for the people to get to the front door that Pyra hadn't insisted on any guard being there. Whispering her thanks into the night air, she rushed up the stairs of the meeting hall and pulled the door open, slipping through as soon as there was enough space for her body to fit. She stopped the door with her back, easing it closed so that it wouldn't make a sound loud enough to alert the guards at the back of the building.

Knowing that this was the only chance she had, Ivy didn't let her nerves slow her. She hurried into the main room, running down the steps so fast that he worried she would lose her balance along the way. As soon as she made it onto the platform she lowered her blanket and two of the bags to the floor, then approached the wall.

"Maxim?" she said, raising her voice as loud as she dared.

There was a long moment of quiet from the other side of the wall and Ivy felt her heart pounding in her chest. She repeated his name, turning her mouth closer to the wall to help her voice get through it, all the while trying to convince herself to believe that that wall wasn't there. Another few seconds passed without a response and the panic began to creep up her spine again as she wondered if something had happened and Pyra had changed his mind about taking some time to think the decision through.

"Ivy?"

She heard the hiss of Maxim's voice come through the wall and nearly sobbed with relief. She pressed her palm against the surface, spreading her fingers as she had with Maxim when he introduced himself, and rested her cheek beside it.

"I'm here," she said. "Are you alright?"

"I'm fine. We've spread out through the other rooms that we can access and some of the men are trying to get some sleep. I couldn't rest. I can't stop thinking about you."

"I'm so sorry. If we hadn't gone outside of the settlement, if I hadn't insisted on going for a walk, this never would have happened."

"Shhhh," Maxim comforted her. "This isn't your fault. You didn't do anything wrong. I wanted to be there with you. I wanted to hold you. I wanted to kiss you."

As Maxim spoke Ivy let her eyes close and her mind wandered to the afternoon that they had spent together. She sought each sensory detail of him, from the warmth of his skin to the touch of his lips and the smell of his hair.

"I wanted that, too," she said.

"I wanted to spend every moment that I had cherishing you. I wanted to run my hands across you and feel your skin against mine. I wanted to make love to you."

Ivy felt her breath catch in her throat. She could feel Maxim near her, hear his voice, but the wall was still solid beneath her hand. No matter how hard she tried to convince herself not to believe that it was there, even to question that it was there, she couldn't. It felt too imposing, too forceful in how it blocked her from him.

"I have wanted you since the first moment that I saw you," she told him.

"You have?"

"Yes."

"I love you, Ivy."

"I love you."

Suddenly Ivy was no longer touching the cold of the wall. Her hand moved through open space and her body tipped forward, coming into contact with the warmth of Maxim's chest. He pushed her backward, stepping out onto the other side of the platform just as the wall behind him solidified again. Ivy threw her arms around him, clutching at his shirt and burying her face into the curve of his neck. She hadn't been able to bring herself to believe that the wall wasn't there, but with those few words, Maxim had made her believe, fully and completely, that she was with him again.

8

"Ivy!" Maxim exclaimed, gathering her close to his body.

Ivy pressed herself to him until she could barely breathe, but she didn't care about breathing. She didn't care about anything except that she had gotten Maxim out of the room.

"I love you," she said again as she pushed back to look at him, wanting to be able to look into his eyes as she said it.

"I love you, too," he said. "How did you do that?"

"It doesn't matter right now," she told him, releasing him so that she could pick up the bags she had dropped and hand them to him. "Right now we have to get out of here. If Pyra catches us, both of us are dead."

"What about the rest of my men?"

"I can't help them," Ivy said. She took a moment, letting a painful, difficult breath seep out of her lungs. "I got you out. Now what you do is your choice. You can stay here and try to fight the guards and get the rest of your men out, or you can come with me. It's up to you."

Maxim didn't hesitate. He reached up and she felt his hand cup her cheek.

"I will always choose you."

He slung one of her bags over his bag and took the blanket from her so that he could tuck it under his arm. Feeling a surge of energy as if she had already slept through the night rather than worked the entire day, Ivy ran back through the main room and to the front door of the building, knowing that Maxim was right behind her. She paused at the door, waiting for any sound that might tell her one of the guards had come around front to check on the surrounding area. When several seconds of silence passed without her hearing anything, she opened the door and both of them eased out, closing the door carefully behind them.

The ground seemed to unravel beneath her feet as she ran down the street toward the back of the settlement. Though they knew that this would put Maxim at further risk of coming into contact with more of the flowers, it was safer to disappear into the darkness away from the houses and buildings and slip out of the gate at the back of the settlement than it would be to try to go through the front. This way they had a better chance of getting out without being detected. As they moved she repeated milestones to herself.

Beyond the houses.

The base of the hill.

The stone wall.

The back gate.

They burst through the gate with such speed Ivy didn't even remember unlatching it. She didn't slow down as the ground began to be illuminated more by the moonlight than by the torches lining the main street of the settlement and the faint glow of the solar lights from some of the windows. The bottoms of her feet ached from the weight of the bag and the pressure of her pace, but she pushed herself harder, putting more and more space between her back and the buildings at the bottom of the hill.

"This way," Maxim said behind her and Ivy looked over her shoulder to see which direction he had gone.

She fell back slightly so that she could follow him, trusting his knowledge of the planet as they moved into the darkness.

She didn't know how long they had been running, but when she finally dared a moment to look back, she could no longer see the line of the settlement against the moonlight on the horizon. Ivy turned back to look ahead of her and saw that they were running toward what looked like a rock ledge and the open mouth of a small cave. The thought of stopping somewhere safe forced her to push even harder and soon she felt the softness of the grass beneath her feet change to the grit of dirt leading into the cavern.

They didn't stop as soon as they entered the cave, but continued in, weaving their way down a narrow passage that seemed to lead slightly upward until they stepped out into an open chamber. It wasn't filled with rock formations like the cavern where Loralia once lived. Instead, it seemed to be nearly empty, the floor smooth and the ceiling low enough that a crack allowed the moonlight to wash in. Ivy dropped the bag to the floor and let out a long breath. In front of her Maxim lowered the blanket and the bags he was carrying.

He turned to face her and an instant later he rushed toward her, closing the space between them in two long strides. His arms wrapped around her waist and he lifted her off of her feet, turning her so that he could press her back against the wall closest to them. Ivy welcomed his mouth as it crushed down on hers, drinking him in as she felt his hands leave her waist and go to the hem of his shirt so that he could pull it off over his head. Their mouths parted only long enough for both to shed their shirts, and then tangled again as Ivy kicked out of her shoes and socks and reached forward for the front of Maxim's pants.

Her fingers worked across the buttons, tearing them open so that she could push the pants off of his hips and let them fall to the floor. Maxim returned the gesture, peeling her pants off of her until she was able to kick them off. He kissed her feverishly until her lips felt bruised beneath his. She felt his hands at the fastening on the back of her bra. When the garment fell away, revealing her breasts to him, Maxim groaned low in his throat and bent down to capture one taut peak in his mouth. His tongue roved over the tip of her sensitized nipple, causing Ivy to arch against him. Though the feeling of his mouth was dizzying in its pleasure, his gorgeous body was naked in front of her and she couldn't wait another moment to have him inside her.

As if he could sense her desperation, Maxim swept her off of her feet again, using one arm around her waist to support her, and the other to open her thighs so that they settled onto either side of his hips. He sank into her without hesitation and Ivy cried out as her body stretched to accommodate him. Already hot and wet, she hugged him close, gripping his length as he thrust into her relentlessly. She clutched the hard curves of his shoulders, biting into one of them as the sensation of him inside her spiraled into an incredible peak and she felt herself crash around him in an all-consuming orgasm. Seconds later she felt his cock pulse within her and Maxim pressed as deeply as he could, tucking his head against her chest as he let a primal yell pour out of him.

Ivy crossed her ankles and wrapped her arms around his neck, holding Maxim close and allowing him to pull her carefully away from the wall and turn so that he could lower both of them to the ground and stretch over her without separating their bodies. They kissed languidly and Ivy savored the feeling of his tongue tenderly massaging hers as he gently rocked his hips against her in long, slow strokes. When their bodies had cooled and relaxed, Maxim lowered himself onto her so that she cradled his head against her heartbeat. Ivy ran her fingers through his sweat-damp strands of hair and let the feeling of his belly rising and falling against her with each breath soothe her.

"I didn't know," Maxim said after a few long moments of quiet.

"What didn't you know?" Ivy asked.

"Any of it," Maxim said. "I didn't know that the group that had split off had become those creatures that went to war with the Denynso."

"I know you didn't."

"I'm sorry I didn't tell you more about the humans from the settlement. I know that you wanted to know and I should have told you."

"Why didn't you?"

Maxim touched a kiss to the side of her breast and sat up on one elbow. She looked at his honey colored eyes and felt a surge of love wash through her.

"It wasn't that I was trying to hide anything from you. It is just a horrible thing that happened to my kind and something that we don't like to talk about very much. Especially those of us who are not supposed to know about it all in the first place."

"What do you mean?" Ivy asked.

"Not everyone in the kingdom learns about the conflict

with the Covra, the prison that my kind built so many centuries ago, or how the humans got here. It is information that is kept closely guarded only for specific families. I have never understood why I couldn't know, so I have spent a lot of time eavesdropping on my elders. I was only ever able to pick up small bits of information so I don't know all of the details. I felt guilty that I betrayed my elders and I didn't want you to think badly of me."

Ivy gave a soft smile and followed the curve of Maxim's face with her fingertips.

"I could never think badly of you, my love. There's nothing wrong with wanting to know what is happening around you."

Maxim leaned down and nuzzled the tip of her nose with his.

"What are we going to do?" he asked.

Ivy sighed. What she wanted was to stay curled up with Maxim just like this and not have to face everything that was happening around them, but that wasn't an option. They had made the decision to run, and now they had to make the decision of what they were going to do next.

9

———

"Where is she?" Pyra roared.

He crashed through the bedroom, knocking over the small table to one side and flipping the bed up so that he could look under it. It had been less than twenty-four hours since he had put Rey and his men into quarantine and somehow one of them, the young one who had been the cause of this disaster in the first place, had managed to escape despite the seemingly impenetrable wall Loralia had created and the guards positioned at every possible exit that they could access.

"I don't know, Pyra," Loralia responded.

Usually her calm, quiet demeanor was comforting to everyone who she encountered, but now it was only infuriating to Pyra. It was as if she were mocking him with her complete lack of concern that not only had Maxim somehow escaped from the quarantine in the meeting hall, but Ivy, the woman who had fought so hard for him, was also gone.

"You did this," Pyra accused, turning to her. "You did

something to that wall to make it so that he could escape with her."

"How could that possibly be true?" Loralia asked. "You watched me make that wall yourself, and Bannack was right there with me helping to create the proper reflective angle so that we could specifically reflect the portion of the ceiling that did not have any vents or skylights that could be used as escape hatches. Bannack does not have the control over the reflections that my kind does. He could not have managed to do that himself."

"Then you must have helped her. You went down to the meeting hall last night and you helped her free him."

"Pyra, that is impossible," Bannack said, stepping forward. "She was with me for the entire night. You are accomplishing nothing by accusing my mate of something that she obviously had no part in. We made that wall together and it was just as real as the one that we made to fight the Covra on the street. Besides, don't you think that if Loralia and Ivy were going to go down to the meeting hall to somehow change the wall to get Maxim free that she would have just released all of them? There's no secret that she disagrees with your thoughts on them."

"She wouldn't have freed all of them because she knows that she would be starting a war that would put all of us at risk. With you as her mate she is loyal to us and she wouldn't compromise that."

"I am loyal to Bannack, Pyra. Not to this. Not to everything that has been happening in this settlement. I didn't free all of the men, but I didn't free Maxim, either."

"Then where are they?" Pyra demanded.

"I don't know. I've told you many times. I can't read minds. I can read only emotions and feelings. I have no way of knowing where she is."

"Wherever she is," Ciyrs said, walking into the room with an empty bag, "she has enough supplies to survive for quite some time without having to settle anywhere. She took my entire bag plus extra ointments and supplies, and almost all of the food and the water reserves from the kitchen."

"Where are the other human women?" Pyra asked.

"In their houses."

"Bring them to me."

As Ciyrs rushed down the stairs and out of the house, Pyra swiped his hand across the small table beside the bed, knocking everything to the floor with a cry of rage.

"What are you so afraid of, Pyra?"

He turned to Loralia and glared at her, the fury radiating off of him with such intensity that he could feel himself shaking.

"The Denynso fear nothing," he growled, repeating the words that he had said just the day before in the meeting hall.

"That's not true," Loralia said.

She took a step toward him and Pyra felt unnerved. Bannack had stepped out of the room so he was alone with the strange woman and the evaluating way that she was looking at him made Pyra uncomfortable.

"I have run into battle with more species than any other warrior leader. I have led my men into the depths of hell and back. I have killed and I have bled and kept going. I have looked creatures in the eye and watched as the life drained out of them, leaving them empty shells. I am not afraid of anything."

"You cannot convince me, Pyra. I know that you are a great and powerful leader. You have achieved amazing things and protected your kind courageously. Courage, however, is not the lack of fear. It is the willingness to be afraid and still do what needs to be done. I can feel that you are tremendously brave and do not fear things that most people would. But I also feel that you are tremendously courageous. There is something inside of you that is very afraid and you have not faced it."

Fear was something that the Denynso were taught from a very young age to push aside. If asked most could not even remember a time in their lives when they were genuinely fearful of something. Fear would keep them from their tasks as warriors, which was what these men were born to do. The more Loralia spoke to him, however, the more Pyra wondered what she was feeling and how much of him she really understood.

A sense of relief washed over him as the human women arrived, breaking the uncomfortable tension that had built in the room. He wanted to get away from Loralia. He pushed out of the room and down the stairs so that he could talk to Zuri, Samira, and Elianna.

"Where's George?" he asked.

"You asked for the human women," Ciyrs told him.

"He knows her better than any of them do. Go find him."

Pyra sat down on the edge of one of the large chairs so that he could face the women lined up along the sofa staring back at him.

"I suppose you all know now that Ivy is missing."

The women nodded.

"Elianna told us that she woke up this morning and Ivy was gone," Samira said.

"It is not just her," Pyra said. "That man who she has been with is also gone."

"His name is Maxim," Zuri said.

Pyra turned to her slowly.

"Maxim," he said. "They somehow got him past the wall

that Loralia made and the warrior guards that I positioned at the windows and doors. Did she mention to any of you that she was planning an escape?"

"An escape?" Zuri asked in a shocked voice. "You said that anyone who wanted to was free to go. That is not escaping."

"I said that they could go at that moment, and that didn't include the men who were under quarantine."

"You called for me?"

Pyra turned toward the masculine voice and saw George standing at the entrance of the living room. He stood and faced the man.

"Do you know where Ivy is?"

Genuine shock crossed George's face.

"What do you mean do I know where Ivy is?"

"No one told you?" Zuri asked.

"Told me what?"

"Ivy and Maxim are missing."

"How did Maxim get out?"

"We don't know."

"You didn't know that she was missing?" Pyra asked.

"No. She was so devastated after your outburst yesterday that I thought it might be better to give her some time to herself. I haven't spoken to her since we were in the meeting hall. "

Pyra felt anger twist in his stomach at George's choice of words, but he pushed the feelings down.

"We need to find her," he said, keeping his voice as calm and even as he could. "If he keeps changing, she will be in serious danger before too long, and if she somehow finds a way to make it back to Earth with him along, all hell is going to break loose."

"Do you really think that it is a good idea for us to go back to your kingdom? If we are trying to get away from everyone, why would we go to the first place that they would probably look for us?"

Ivy watched Maxim rearrange the supplies tucked inside the blanket and roll it back up so that it was more compact.

"I don't think that they are going to look for us there," he said, giving the ends of the blanket a final tug to ensure that it wouldn't unravel.

"Why not?"

"Because I think that they are going to think in the exact same way that you do," he said, walking up to her and tucking a finger under her chin so that she lifted her face to his. "They are going to think that since we are trying to get away it would be far too obvious to go right back to my home. They would assume that even if a despicable creature like me would want to go back there, that a level-minded and in control of all of her faculties human such as yourself would discourage me because that is the first place that they would look."

"So they won't go looking in the first place that they would look?" Ivy asked, feeling slightly dazed.

"Exactly."

Maxim touched a kiss to her lips and Ivy smiled. It made her happy to hear Maxim being playful about the situation, but she still had a heavy feeling in her stomach thinking about going to the kingdom where he grew up. Not only would traveling there require them to go very close to the settlement again, but it would also put them somewhere that Pyra knew how to get to and where they could not easily escape. Considering she knew nothing about Uoria and had no other options, however, Ivy knew that all she could do is place her trust in the man she had fallen in love with and hope that he was right, or that if he wasn't, they would be able to protect each other again.

Stepping out into the brightness of the new morning made Ivy feel far more exposed than when they were running toward the cave under the protective cover of the night. She felt like there were eyes looking at her from every angle, watching her as they walked away from their shelter. It was as though the blades of grass themselves could see her and were whispering to each other as they bent with the breeze, passing along the information so that they could betray them to Pyra.

"How far is the kingdom from here?" she asked.

She hoped that she could distract herself enough to shake the uncomfortable feeling off of her and keep moving ahead more confidently.

"A few days' walk," Maxim told her. "We should go for a few hours, rest for the afternoon, and then go as late into the night as we can. It will be better if we sleep during the day and travel at night until we get there."

She felt like Maxim had heard her thoughts and though

she knew that he hadn't actually been able to hear her, unlike the Denynso warriors and their mates who actually could communicate with one another simply through their thoughts, it was comforting that he was responding to her needs. She was ashamed to admit it, even to herself, but part of her had taken what Pyra said about his kind deeply to heart. She hadn't wanted to believe a word of it, and still didn't, but when she saw the damaged area of his skin continue to spread and the upheaval in the meeting hall, part of her began to wonder if he really did have the capacity to devolve into something gruesome and terrifying. With each kind word and tender gesture, however, he was separating himself further from this fear and she had the ability to concentrate just on her love for him.

They walked largely in silence, each concentrating on the area around them and using all of their senses to try to detect if the warriors had found them and were coming after them. The sun was already well into its descent from its noon peak when they found a thicket of trees with a small creek nestled in the moss-covered ground and took refuge in the shade. Ivy rested back against the moss, closing her eyes for a moment and becoming highly aware of a bead of sweat that trickled from her hairline and made its way across her forehead, down her cheek, and onto her lips. She licked it, noting the saltiness that was so close to tears.

"Is there ever any pattern to the weather here?" she asked.

Just a few days before she had shivered with the cold wind that whipped around her as she walked through the settlement, and now she felt like the sun was singeing her skin with every moment. It was disorienting in a way that seemed to blend time so that she had difficulty knowing just how long it had been since she arrived on the planet or even since she and Maxim had met. She disliked the feeling and again found herself missing Earth, if this time only for the predictability and structure of the seasons.

Maxim laughed as he carefully unrolled the blanket and removed a few containers including the water canisters that they had already emptied.

"You'll get used to it," he said.

"If there's no pattern, there's nothing to get used to," she argued.

He glanced up at her as he removed the cap from one of the canisters and leaned down toward the creek to fill it with water that was rushing past over the rocks so quickly it faded from its usual jewel tone to a softer lavender that reminded her of Loralia's eyes.

"That is what you will get used to."

Ivy smiled at him and took the water that he offered her. She tilted her head back and let a large sip fill her dry mouth and wash down her throat. The taste was pure and slightly sweet, unlike any water that she had ever had at home. It cooled and revived her, and Ivy felt better instantly. She sat up and helped Maxim spread out the food he had chosen for their midday meal.

"You'll have to let me cook for you sometime," she told him. "I think that you would really like the food on Earth."

Their eyes met and she saw the hint of sadness in his. Her mood lowered and she reached for his hand.

"You know that you may never make it back to Earth, right?" Maxim asked softly. "Without the benefit of the university shuttle that brought you here, you really have no transport. And it's not like we can go to the Denynso compound and ask them to call the shuttle for us."

"I know," Ivy said.

Though she had been fighting hard with herself trying

not to admit it, deep inside she knew that the chances of her getting off of Uoria were very slim. Her decision to run from the settlement was not just running from Pyra and the rest of the Denynso for that moment. It was a decision to run from life as she knew it and everything that she had imagined for her future. She had taken a leap that had her tumbling through the complete unknown.

Maxim reached for another container out of the blanket and she heard him hiss in pain as the injured area of his arm touched the fabric. He pulled his arm back protectively, clutching it close to him and covering the area with his hand. His eyes slid up to Ivy, his gaze filled with concern as if worried that she had forgotten about the injury and was now going to leave. Ivy put the canister in her hand onto the ground and slid closer to him, resting her head comfortingly on his shoulder.

"Let's see if we can make that better," she said.

She reached for his arm, but he pulled it back like he had when he first showed the reaction to her back at the settlement.

"You can't fix it," he said.

"Ivy reached again and took his arm, gently pulling it towards her so that she could look at the skin.

"I can try."

The place that Ciyrs had touched was still deep, but it no longer looked like an angry open wound. Instead, it had turned to ash, creating a powdery grey gash in the white expanse of skin. She ran the pad of her thumb along the skin. It felt cold and slick, and for a moment she had to withhold a shudder that threatened to roll down her spine. Forcing herself to stay calm, she continued to touch the skin and looked up into Maxim's eyes. As she gazed at him, the uncomfortable reaction to the texture of the skin eased. She took Ciyrs' bag and searched through it, pulling out containers of the healing ointment, additional herbs, and strips of fabric.

She dipped one of the pieces of cloth into the creek and used it to gently clean the wound, then patted it dry. Remembering how Ciyrs and Elianna had treated the surgical sites of the people after removing the Covra eggs, Ivy coated the wound with the healing ointment, packed it with the herbs, and wrapped it with the other strips of fabric. When she was finished, Maxim drew it against his stomach again and rested his hand against the new bandage.

"Thank you," he said softly.

As they walked over the next few days Ivy changed the bandage each time they stopped to rest. The white area of the skin seemed to be getting smaller with each application, and the wound less deep. On the third morning, just after the sun came up, they stepped down into a deep burrow where Maxim said that they could sleep.

"Are you sure that whatever made this burrow isn't here anymore?" Ivy asked nervously as she followed Maxim down into the dirt cave.

Maxim laughed and dropped the bags and blanket to the ground.

"What made this burrow hasn't been here in a very long time. I promise that you are safe."

"Let me change your bandage before we go to sleep."

Even though she was exhausted after traversing a particularly rough and hilly area of the planet, she didn't want to neglect the care of his wound, especially when it was responding so well to the ointments that Ciyrs and the women had made. Maxim sighed and sat down, extending his arm to her dramatically.

"Don't be like that," she said playfully, taking the end of the bandage and starting to unravel it. "How much farther do we have to go?"

"Not too far now," Maxim said.

"You told me that you had never left your kingdom before you started toward the settlement. How do you know how to get around the planet so well?"

"That is one of the strange things about our elders. They teach us that we should never leave the kingdom, that we should remain close to home except in urgent situations, but they also insist that we know the surrounding areas to the detail. As children we learn the different lands and how to access them as quickly as possible from the kingdom."

"Maybe that's so if there ever is an emergency, that you will all be safe."

"I suppose so. With as much as our elders choose to keep from us, I'm glad that they at least gave us that."

Ivy nodded as the released the final layer of the bandage and pulled it away from Maxim's arm. She gasped, her hand immediately going to touch his skin. The area that had been white and slimy was completely healed. All that was left of the injury was a depression where Ciyrs had burned away Maxim's skin with his touch, and even that was covered over with smooth, even skin. She ran her hand along it, tears forming in her eyes. She kissed his arm tenderly and looked up at him smiling. There was no sign of the horrible reaction to the flowers. Ivy felt her heart soar. This confirmed to her even further that Maxim was not one of the vicious creatures that Pyra said that he was. The transformation from such peaceful beauty to one of the Klimnu was not inevitable, it was not something that they just had to accept and wait for, but something that they could change.

"Were you really worried that what Pyra said was true?" Maxim asked.

He didn't sound upset with her, but Ivy felt a tinge of guilt anyway.

"I don't know anything about this planet, Maxim. I don't know about anything about your kind or the Klimnu or anything. I might for a moment have worried that the reaction was going to spread even more, but I still came for you and I am with you now. Your heart didn't change. Even as the reaction on your skin got worse, you didn't change. You never showed the cruelty or disregard that the Denynso have described in the Klimnu." Her head dropped and she continued to stroke his skin with her fingertips. "I'm sorry."

"It's alright," he said soothingly. "It's expected for you to worry about something that you don't understand. You didn't lose faith in me, and that's all that matters. No matter what any of them were saying, you knew who I really was and you never let go of that." He tucked a finger beneath her chin and lifted her face to look at him. "I will never be able to thank you enough for that."

11

———

Maxim and Ivy were awake and packing their supplies late that afternoon. Just as the final flashes of the sunset sank beneath the edge of ground in front of them, they stepped out of the burrow and continued on toward the kingdom. Ivy walked with a renewed sense of purpose, the complete healing of his skin removing the last lingering hints of trepidation that had been tormenting her during their journey. She knew that they were still in danger if Pyra and the other Denynso found them, but at least now she had the confidence of knowing that Maxim was whole and unchanging, that they only needed to find a way to get beyond the seeking eyes of the warriors and they could start their own lives together. She was no longer afraid that she would soon be alone.

It was nearly midday when Ivy felt Maxim's hand touch her wrist. She looked up from where she had been watching her feet tamping down the blades of grass to mark their progress across the wide, smooth pasture that they were crossing. Ahead of them she saw a faint outline against the sky. It was in the distance, far enough away that she couldn't make out the distinct shapes of anything, but close enough that it was definitely a break in the even monotony of the meadow.

"That's it," he said, his voice lowered to an almost conspiratorial whisper. "That's home."

Ivy turned her hand so that she could intertwine her fingers with Maxim's and they started toward the kingdom, their pace quickened by the anticipation of arriving after such a long journey. They closed the distance in what seemed like a matter of moments and finally Ivy could see the kingdom that she had been thinking of since they huddled in the cave wondering what they were going to do next. It was smaller than she had imagined, but beautiful in its meticulous care, and even more so by simply being there. They seemed to be approaching it from one side rather than the front because all Ivy could see was the tops of buildings over a stone wall that was much taller and more pristine than the one at the settlement.

"Now that I have been to the settlement with the humans I can see just how similar the two places are," Maxim said. "My kind did all that they could to help them make their home here and survive their first years. It had to be terrifying to suddenly be in such an unfamiliar place and know that you are most likely never going to be able to leave it, that it has to be your home whether you want it to be or not."

"It is," Ivy said quietly.

Maxim released her hand to wrap an arm around her shoulders and pull her close to him. He kissed the top of her head and she heard him take in a deep breath.

"I can't wait for you to meet my mother," he said.

She was suddenly self-conscious. They had only had the opportunity to bathe once since leaving the settlement, and even that was just a brief dip in the creek with a cake of hard soap that she had tucked into her bag. It made her uncomfortable that she was going to meet the people of Maxim's home looking far less than her best.

"Is there somewhere that I can take a bath or a shower before I meet her? I'm sure that becoming fugitives that very well might have a price on our heads is not the best impression that I can make in the first place, but I would rather not look like one."

She tried to smooth some of the strands of hair that wriggled their way out of her braid and Maxim laughed.

"You are the most beautiful fugitive that I have ever seen," he said.

"Have you known many fugitives in your time?"

She asked the question only half in jest. With everything that she had learned about his kind in the last few days, she was very aware of the possibility that he had in fact come into contact with fugitives of more than one species. His noncommittal shrug was not as comforting as she would like it to be, but before she could take too much time to contemplate it, they approached the stone wall. He guided her along it for several feet until they came to a gate embedded in the stone. An aging man stood beside it. Even with his silver hair and weathered face, this man had the same type of beauty as the other men.

"Maxim!" the man said when he caught sight of them. "What are you doing? Where are the others?"

"Athan, I need you to get us to my house without anyone seeing us, and if anyone comes here asking, you didn't see us."

"What's happening, Maxim? What's wrong?"

Maxim gripped the black bars of the gate and stared into the older man's face. Ivy could see the desperation in his eyes. Even though he believed they would be safe in the kingdom, at least for a time, she knew there was a part of him that worried they had been gone long enough that the Denynso may come here looking for them.

"Please, Athan. I can't explain right now."

Athan paused for another moment, glancing between Maxim and Ivy, then nodded, reaching down to release the lock on the gate and pushing it open to allow them inside. He glanced around as if checking to see if there was anyone that might be watching them, and then placed his hands on their backs, guiding them to one side of the gate.

"I can't be gone from my post for long. I can take you as far as the tunnels. Will you be able to make it from there?"

"Yes. Thank you, Athan."

Athan nodded at Maxim and started along the edge of the wall, his stride so long that Ivy almost needed to jog to keep up with them. Suddenly the older man stopped and Ivy crashed into Maxim's back. He reached back, grabbing onto the back of her thigh and giving her an affectionate squeeze. She watched over his shoulder as Athan pressed his fingertips to a stone in the wall. The stone shifted, revealing what looked like a small keypad made with different colors of gems. Athan touched them in sequence and stepped back. A section of the grass sank and then tilted, creating a ramp down into the ground.

"There shouldn't be anyone else in the tunnels at this time of day. Once the access hatch is locked in place, there is a five minute lock-out when the doors cannot be opened from the outside again, so you have that amount of time to get to the exit before anyone else would be able to get inside."

"Thank you so much."

Maxim started down the ramp, but Athan reached out and touched his back to stop him.

"Maxim, I don't have to tell you how dangerous it would be if someone found out that I allowed you into the tunnels."

"I know, Athan. You can trust me."

"I know that I can." Athan touched Maxim's cheek and Ivy noticed how much older his hand looked when it was against the smooth, young skin of Maxim's face. "You look so much like your father." As if startled, Athan let his hand drop away from Maxim's cheek and stepped back. "Go on. Hurry."

Ivy let Maxim take her hand and lead her down the steep ramp into the tunnel below. She glanced up a final time to watch Athan's face disappear as the section of grass moved back into place and the access hatch again become undetectable in the rest of the grass. She had expected that the tunnels would have been dug directly into the ground and be dirt, but was relieved to find that it had been reinforced with smooth sheets of stone and seemed to glow with recessed lights at the tops of the walls, but only in the first several feet.

"Come on," Maxm urged, tugging on her hand and starting down the tunnel.

As they moved along the passageway the lights overhead illuminated and the sections of the tunnel behind them extinguished. She noticed that each section glowed with a different color of light, apparently indicating where along the path of the tunnels they were.

"What did Athan mean that it would be dangerous if anyone found out that he had let you into the tunnels?" Ivy asked.

"These tunnels were designed for use by the elders and a

secret segment of the military that the rest of us are not even supposed to know about. Allowing someone who is not authorized into them is considered a high form of treason."

"How did you know about them?"

"My father was a member of the Order. He told me about them when I was a child."

"Your father was in it, but you aren't?"

"My father. My grandfather. His father before him. I wasn't selected."

"By who?"

"I don't know."

"Rey?"

"Rey doesn't control the Order."

"But if all of those generations have been in it, why weren't you selected?"

Maxim stopped and turned toward her sharply. Ivy saw a moment of frustrated anger flicker over his face, and she knew that she had pressed too far.

"The circumstances of my father's death changed the Order. Athan is the only person who was in it with him who still is, and I do not know who else is a part of it. He won't tell me, and I wouldn't ask him."

Ivy nodded and Maxim turned away from her again, stepping into a section of the tunnel that glowed red as he passed through. He had only taken a few steps when Ivy heard the sound of muffled voices ahead of them. A look of panic crossed Maxim's face and Ivy realized that there were people coming toward them from the other end of the tunnel. Maxim looked around and then she saw his eyes lock on something above him. He jumped up and grabbed a metal bar that was barely perceptible in the vibrancy of the red light and yanked it down. A narrow ladder followed him down and he started up it without another word. Ivy followed, keeping as close to Maxim as the bags on his back and the rolled blanket beneath his arm would allow.

At the top of the ladder Maxim pushed against the ceiling. The lights went out around them and the sudden darkness made it so that Ivy could see the hint of purple light from a section of the tunnel several yards away. She could hear Maxim muttering to himself, commanding the ceiling to move. The purple light gave way to yellow and the voices of whoever was in the tunnel grew louder. An instant later the light shifted to green. They were moving quickly now and Ivy felt her heart pounding against her ribs with such intensity that the bones seemed to tremble in her chest. The light shifted to blue and she could hear their voices distinctly now.

"There is someone here. I'm telling you. I heard footsteps."

"There's no one that would come down here. Athan and Vitri are on guard. The rest are with Rey."

The light shifted to white and Maxim's muttering became more frantic. Above her she heard a scraping sound like stone grinding against stone.

"That's why it is so troublesome."

The light shifted to orange and the sound above her reached a peak, then she heard Maxim let out a breath and felt him moving up the ladder again. She followed as quickly as she could, letting him grab her by the arm and pull her up. The ladder came up with her feet and just as the door they had climbed through closed, she saw a flash of red light.

"We have to get out of here," Maxim hissed.

Ivy scrambled after him through the dark room where they had come up out of the tunnel. By the piles of cartons and cloth-covered forms scattered throughout the space Ivy assumed that they were in some sort of storage room, but she didn't ask Maxim. He weaved his way through the room until he reached a small window on the far wall and she saw him release the three latches holding it closed before tossing everything he was carrying through and then following. Ivy followed his lead, handing her bag through and then pulling herself up and through the window.

The window led out onto what looked like a screened-in porch. As soon as Ivy dropped down onto the wood-planked floor, Maxim grabbed up the bags and blanket and started for a door at the far end. A crash behind her made Ivy jump.

"They followed us," Maxim said.

Ivy picked up her bag and they ran down the length of the porch. Instead of going through the door, however, Maxim turned and ducked through a small archway in the wall that reminded Ivy of the dog door she had had in her kitchen door when she was a child. It led to a small, dark stone chamber that didn't seem to have any other exits and Ivy felt panic rise in her throat. She watched Maxim brush dust away from one of the walls and a metal ring came into view. He yanked on it and the wall gave way, opening so that they could slip through. The door closed behind them and brilliant pink light disoriented Ivy for a moment.

"Are we back in the tunnel?"

"Yes. Come on."

"If they are coming after us for being in the tunnel, why did we go back into it?"

"No one knows about that door. My grandfather created it long before anyone but Athan was a part of the Order and he didn't tell anyone except my father about it. I wasn't even sure if it would still work."

"What would have happened if it hadn't?"

Maxim shook his head and she didn't press any further.

They were only in the tunnel for a few moments before Maxim pulled down another ladder and they hurried up into a cool, faintly lit room. The hatch to the tunnel had just closed when Ivy heard a door above them open, she braced herself, but Maxim didn't seem concerned. He walked toward the bottom of a set of stairs across the room and smiled up into the light that came down into the room.

"Maxim?" a woman's voice said incredulously.

"Hello, Mother."

A stunningly beautiful woman who vaguely resembled Maxim rushed down the stairs and gathered him into an embrace.

"What are you doing here?" she asked as she pushed back to look at him.

"Mother, this is Ivy," he said, carefully stepping out of his mother's arms and turning to gesture at Ivy.

Ivy brushed at her clothing, hoping to get as much of the dirt off as she could and smoothed her hair back again before stepping toward her.

"Hello, Ivy," Maxim's mother said, "I'm Ellora." She looked at Ivy carefully and then glanced back at Maxim. "Maxim, she's lovely."

Maxim smiled and ran the backs of his fingers tenderly along Ivy's cheek. Despite the grime of her travels, she had never felt more beautiful than she did at that moment.

"It's nice to meet you, Ellora," Ivy said.

"You, too. But, Maxim, what are you doing here without the others, and why did you come through that door? I told you when you were just a boy that you were not to go into those tunnels."

"Father showed them to me."

"Your father..." her voice trailed off and Ivy could see Ellora trying to control a sudden wave of emotion.

"Mother, it is absolutely essential that you do not tell anyone that we are here. There were members of the Order down in the tunnels. We only got past them by using the door that Grandfather built."

"The Order!" Ellora gasped. "You know the difficulties that this family has dealt with because of them. I had hoped that you would remember that and stay away from them."

"The only reason that we made it even this far without someone seeing us is because of Athan."

Ellora seemed to contemplate this for a moment, weighing what she should say to her son, and then she shook her head and gestured at the steps.

"Come on. Come upstairs. You two need to get cleaned up and then I want to hear what's going on."

Ivy followed Maxim and Ellora upstairs into a home that felt so warm and inviting it was almost as if she had stepped off of Uoria and into her grandmother's house on Earth. She relaxed as soon as she walked into the kitchen and the smell of something very close to coffee touched her nose. She drew in a deep breath and saw Ellora smile.

"Would you like a cup?" the beautiful woman asked.

Ivy was startled.

"You have coffee?" she asked.

"Yes," Ellora said with a laugh. "We've been growing it here for generations."

Ivy glanced at Maxim who was giving her a look that said she shouldn't ask any more questions about it. She assumed that meant that it had something to do with the unspoken history of their kind. The plant had to have come from Earth, and as Ellora filled a delicate cup that seemed to be crafted out of thin blue shell and handed it to her, Ivy could imagine that she was drinking coffee from plants originally grown from beans carried to Uoria by Project Nyx 23.

The thought was oddly comforting, as if the drink was a thread connecting herself back to Earth at a time well before she existed. She took a sip of the coffee. It was stronger and silkier in her mouth than the coffee at home, but she credited that, and the slightly different fragrance, to the lush growing environment on the planet.

"When you're finished with that, why don't you take a shower?" Maxim offered. "I know you would feel better and it'll give me a chance to explain everything to Mother."

"Is that alright?" Ivy asked, lowering the cup carefully to the table where they had sat.

"Of course it is," Ellora said. "Whenever you're ready, you just go on up. The bathroom is at the end of the hallway."

Ivy finished her coffee in one long sip, thanked Ellora, and headed up to the bathroom. She stood under the water for several minutes until she finally felt clean again, and then stepped out. She pulled fresh clothing out of her bag and stepped into it, luxuriating in the feeling of the clean fabric against her now-clean skin. Not knowing how long it would be until she had a chance to bathe or wash her clothing, she had avoided changing out of what she had been wearing when they left the settlement, and the feeling of the clean clothing was nearly as refreshing as the shower.

Gathering her clothing under her arm, she took the strap of her bag in her palm. She couldn't stand to have it over her shoulder for another moment, not until she absolutely had to. She started down the steps back toward the kitchen and was startled by Maxim's heated whisper.

"You mean they knew?"

"Of course they knew!" Ellora responded. "The Order knows everything. Why do you think that your father died the way that he did?"

Ivy wasn't sure if she should continue into the room or

just pretend that she was still in the shower. The way they were speaking seemed to mean that they didn't want to be overheard, but she was as involved in this as Maxim was, which meant she needed to know as much as she could in order to protect herself.

"If the Order knew about what happened to the group that split off, why didn't they do anything about it?"

"They tried, Maxim. They made alliances in the badlands and it drove them off of Uoria. When they came back and their bodies began to change, there was little anyone could do. By then they didn't even know about the Order anymore. They destroyed the Order's original allies because it was only war and hatred that the generations taught each other."

"Who were their allies?"

Ivy couldn't stay out of the room any longer. What Ellora was saying completely changed what Pyra had believed about the Klimnu and their evolution.

"I don't know," Ellora told her. "I am not privy to the details of the Order. I never have been. I only know what little I was able to pick up from Maxim's father."

"Rey said that he didn't know anything about the Klimnu," Ivy said, turning to Maxim.

"He doesn't," Ellora confirmed. "Rey is not a part of the Order. He leads the kingdom, but in many ways the Order is above him."

"Why did the Klimnu not come after the rest of the kingdom when they came back?"

"They didn't remember us. The generations that came before them had only told them of the conflict, not of their origins. They didn't know where to find us, and once their transformation began, they were too distracted by the new war they waged to care about continuing to look."

"The Denynso," Ivy said. "That is who the new war was with. Because Creia wouldn't rescue them from their change."

"So the Order just pretended that they didn't exist?" Maxim demanded. "They knew that these creatures were out there and they did nothing to protect anyone from them?"

"Some of them did, Maxim. There was tremendous conflict. It was violent..." her voice weakened and she stopped. She looked back and forth between the two of them. "If they found you here, Maxim. If they knew what you had done, that you came through those tunnels..."

"We won't put you in any danger, Mother," Maxim promised. "We'll just stay here for the rest of the night and tomorrow to get some sleep, but then we will leave and continue on our way."

"Where are you going?" Ellora asked.

"We don't know. We just have to go. The Denynso will be looking for us and we can't let them find us."

"You can't run forever, Maxim."

"We can't let them catch us."

"No. They shouldn't catch you. You should go back to them."

"Mother—"

"You can't spend your entire life running. You have to go back and stand up for what you know is right. Do what your father didn't have the chance to. This isn't time for another war. It's time that this planet finally comes together."

12

———

"It's been four days."

Pyra slammed his hands on the counter and stared at the men sitting in the living room.

"We've looked, Pyra," Gyyx said. "We don't know this planet and without a guide there is no way that we can go too far from the settlement. Maxim knows this planet better than we do and he would be able to get them somewhere that we didn't know much faster than we are going to be able to find them."

"By now their supplies will be running out."

Pyra looked at George who stood away from the rest of the group, his arms crossed over his chest. He looked stony and defensive, refusing to make eye contact with any of the men. Zsilvia stood beside him, rubbing his back. After a moment she lifted her eyes to stare at Pyra.

"We're trying to find them," Pyra said.

"You aren't trying to find them," George said. "You're hunting them. They would rather die out in the badlands than have you get to them and kill them. They won't let you control what people will know about this. They will do this on their own terms and then at least history will remember them."

As soon as he said those words, George straightened. Pyra noticed the change in his posture and watched as he turned to Zsilvia. He wondered if they were communicating in the same unspoken way that he was able to with Eden. He had never really paid attention to the other couples communicating in this way, but now that he knew that Zsilvia and George were likely talking to one another about Ivy and Maxim, he wanted to know exactly what was passing between their minds.

"Are we finished here?" Ty asked.

Pyra looked at him, taking a moment to register what he had asked him.

"What?"

"Are we finished? We have to go switch out the guards at the meeting hall in less than an hour and Samira has lunch waiting for me."

It seemed such a mundane sentiment in the military state that Pyra had created and for a moment the Denynso warrior leader wondered if Ty was joking. The young warrior stood and faced him, though, his face showing that he was anticipating a response.

"Yes. We're done. Be sure that you aren't late to your posts. Any of you."

The group dispersed and headed out of the house, George and Zsilvia rushing out first ahead of the warriors. As Gyyx walked past him Pyra grabbed onto his arm, pulling him into the kitchen so that he could speak to him without the others hearing.

"George and Zsilvia know something about Ivy and Maxim. Follow them. Report to me what you hear."

· · ·

PYRA PACED through the living room, his hands clenched. It had been almost two hours since the men had left, but Gyyx hadn't come back. He was starting toward the door when it opened and Gyyx came back inside.

"What the hell took you so long?" Pyra demanded.

"I'm sorry, Pyra. When they left here they went to the clinic and started working on more of the healing ointments just like they were supposed to. It wasn't until they left to go to the garden that I heard anything."

"What did you hear?"

"They ran into Zuri on the way and I was too far away to hear everything. All I could catch was George mentioning the wreckage."

"The wreckage?" Pyra asked.

Gyyx nodded.

"I don't know what he meant by it, but I think that they are planning on going there tonight."

"Rain said that they used the wreckage to build the settlement."

"I don't know."

"Find Lynx. Have him bring Rain to me."

Gyyx rushed out of the house again and Pyra went back to pacing through the room. He felt like his was mind was spinning. He was losing control of his hatred for the Klimnu and the only thing that was keeping him from decimating the entire group still quarantined in the meeting hall was the feeling of the pendant around his neck and the thought that he owed it to Eden and to their baby to make sure that every last one of the creatures was gone. And that meant finding Maxim before he and Ivy had a chance to escape.

Twenty minutes later Rain came into the house with Lynx close behind her.

"What's going on, Pyra?" Lynx asked.

Pyra gestured toward the furniture arranged in the middle of the living room.

"I just need to talk to Rain for a minute."

"What is it?" Rain asked, sitting down on the edge of one of the sofas.

"You told me that you and the rest of the humans here used the wreckage to build the settlement."

"We did."

"All of it?"

"What do you mean?"

"Did you use all of the wreckage?"

"Most of it. There were pieces that were too large to move so we left them where they were. I think that some people still had hope that one day we might be able to salvage it and return to Earth."

"Can you lead me to what was left?"

Rain nodded.

"I think that I could. I haven't been back there since the last time that I took pieces for the building projects. It was too painful for me to even think about going back. I'm sure that I would remember once I started. Why do you want to go to the wreckage?"

"I think that that's where Ivy and Maxim are."

"I don't understand."

"You don't need to."

"Pyra, if you are going to ask my mate for help, you will show her the respect that she deserves." Lynx said, stepping up beside the sofa so that he could look into Pyra's face.

Pyra tensed, feeling his jaw set as he looked into Lynx's glowing orange eyes. He didn't appreciate one of his warriors standing up to him that way, but he knew that when it came to the mate of a Denynso, calm and tenderness did not extend beyond that mate. A warrior's primary duty was to fight. His primary responsibility was to his mate.

"I'm sorry," Pyra said, choking out the words through the angry tension in his throat.

As much as he didn't want to give Lynx even the smallest amount of leeway, he knew that Rain was his only chance to get to the wreckage and possibly find Ivy and the creature she had chosen. At this point, it was all he had to go on and he couldn't risk it.

"I will bring you to the wreckage," Rain agreed. "If you promise that you won't hurt either of them if you find them there."

Pyra's jaw twitched. He was not accustomed to being told what to do, especially by a woman, and it had happened with disturbing frequency since they had encountered the other species in the settlement, though he had primarily received obedience since declaring himself leader.

"I will bring them back here unharmed."

13

———

Ivy rested her hand on the metal shell of what used to be the main cabin of the ship. The moss that covered it felt soft and warm beneath her palm as if the planet itself were trying to shield it. She moved aside the vines that had grown up over the shattered entrance to the cabin and gazed itself. Even crushed it was massive, like a tremendous metal and glass cave. The plants had completely covered the outside and were creeping along the interior, tangling around the single seat that was left and weaved through the structures inside the wall.

"I can't believe I'm looking at this," she said softly. "We learned about this ship through school. There's even a monument of it at the university."

"Why?" Maxim asked.

"They were pioneers, a team of researchers and para-military forces who left Earth to explore a planet that had recently been identified. The government and most of the scientific community believed that the planet was empty and barren, but this group, Project Nyx 23, was made up of people who believed that it was not only not barren, but that it was being used as an illegal prisoner of war camp against the most recent incarnation of the galaxy peace treaty. They left with the mission of exploring the planet and confirming their suspicions. They never came back."

"What is 'Nyx'?"

"She was the Greek goddess of the night."

"I like it. That is what we should name our daughter."

Ivy looked at him sharply and saw Maxim gazing back at her softly. He extended his hand toward her and she placed her fingers against his palm, allowing him to draw her against his chest and tilting her mouth up to accept his. She relaxed into his kiss, parting her lips to draw his tongue in against her own.

"Ivy!"

Ivy's mouth tore away from Maxim's and she turned to see George rushing toward him through the scattered pieces of the wreckage. She ran toward him, jumping into his arms.

"George!"

George released her and Ivy reached up to embrace Zsilvia.

"Are you alright? Both of you?"

"Yes," Ivy said, stepping back so that she could take Maxim's hand and pull him closer to George and Zsilvia. "We're fine. Look."

She held Maxim's arm out so that they could see the healed skin.

"That's amazing. You only used the healing ointments?"

"And some extra herbs."

"How long did it take?"

"Three days." She lowered Maxim's arm. "How did you find us?"

"I remembered how much this story fascinated you. It

suddenly occurred to me that no matter what, if you had the opportunity to see this wreck, you would."

"And that is exactly what you did."

George whipped around and over his shoulder Ivy could see Pyra standing at the edge of the wreckage, his hands on his hips and a cruel, satisfied smile curving his lips.

"I didn't tell them, Ivy," George said. "I promise you, I didn't tell them."

"That's right," Pyra said, taking a step toward them. Now Ivy could see Gyyx and Lynx behind him. "He didn't tell me. But he did make it really easy to figure out."

He started toward them and Ivy felt Maxim step up beside her, carefully pushing her back behind him.

"Stay back, Pyra," he said.

"You're going to come along with us now," Pyra said. "We're going back to the settlement and you are going back into quarantine where you belong. As for you," he said, looking sharply at Ivy, "I don't know how you got him out, but you are never going to have that opportunity again. You went against the command of the king by leaving the super-vision of your guard and protector. You will be put into isolation with a warrior guard until we can return you to the compound for Creia to deal with you."

"You can't force them to go anywhere," Zsilvia said.

"I wouldn't test me if I were you, Zsilvia. As a guard and protector who has failed in your duties, you are subject to even more severe punishments than Ivy. All of you come now or we will bring you with us by force."

Maxim launched toward Pyra and the two crashed into each other. Despite being much larger, Pyra was taken aback by Maxim's sudden attack and stumbled. They fell to the ground and Maxim slammed his hand into Pyra's face, sending blood splattering across his chest. Pyra reached up and clutched the front of Maxim's throat, gripping him hard enough that Ivy could hear the choking sounds coming across the space toward her. She screamed and ran toward them, but Zsilvia grabbed her by her waist and pulled her back.

"Pyra!" Rain shouted. Ivy hadn't even realized the other woman was there until she heard her voice and saw her rushing toward the men. "You promised me that you wouldn't hurt them. Let him go!"

Pyra hesitated for a moment, then dropped Maxim. He clambered to his feet and pointed down at Maxim where he still crouched on the ground, gasping for breath as he held his bruised neck.

"All of you saw that," he said, hissing through his ragged breaths. "All of you saw this creature attack me. It is absolute proof of everything I have said about him and all of his kind."

"You provoked him!" George argued. "Any man would respond as he did."

Pyra took a step toward George, lifting his hand to point into the older man's face.

"You would do very well to remember whose planet you are on. I am stronger and more powerful than you will ever be and you are under my control."

"You may be bigger, Pyra, but I will never be under the control of someone with a mind that would find it justifiable to kill an entire species because of simple prejudice and fear."

"The Denynso fear nothing."

"You fear everything!" George spat back. "You want to kill off all of those men because you are so afraid of what they might turn into. You haven't even stopped to notice that Maxim is fully healed. His skin is fully repaired."

"I don't care about his skin," Pyra fumed. "It wasn't the Klimnu skin that waged war against us, that tortured our women, or that shed our blood. Nothing will change what he was born to be. We know what he is, and that means that he and all of the others deserve to die before they are able to destroy any more lives."

"Stop it!" Ivy screamed. "All of you. Stop this now. You say that you have the right to kill all of these men because you think that they are inherently cruel and destructive, but you have never stopped to think of how everyone sees you and your kind. You are considered the most fearsome warriors in the galaxy, not because of your training or your precision, but because of your cruelty and unstoppable viciousness in battle. I know that the other human women have chosen men among you as their mates and that they wouldn't have devoted themselves to you so deeply if you were nothing but that level of violence and aggression. But since that is the way that the rest of the galaxy sees you, are those species who you have decimated in battle entitled to come here and kill you all one by one?" Pyra shifted uncomfortably, his eyes flashing at Ivy, and she took another step toward him. "This is not your planet, Pyra. You are the leader of one group of one species who lives on one compound."

"If anything," Zsilvia said, her strong voice showing that she would no longer give Pyra or any of the warriors the satisfaction of her fear, "this decision belongs to Creia, not yours. He gave you permission to come out onto the planet to explore and find other species. What is done with any of them is still up to him."

14

———

"You're right," Pyra said after a long pause. "This decision belongs to Creia. We will go back to the compound and he will settle it from there."

Pyra turned on his heel and stomped away from the rest of the group, seething with fury so intense that it felt like it was burning through his muscles and consuming everything that was within him. His grasp on everything was slipping. He longed for Eden, to hold her and rest his head on the belly that cradled his child, the first baby to be born to the Denynso since the last of his generation. He had been away from her for so long and it made him feel like he was losing his grip on his mind. His need to protect her had become even more desperate as the days past, and soon had turned to obsession. He wanted to rid the world of anything that could put the most treasured beings in his life, his mate and his baby, at risk.

The walk from the site of the wreckage back to the settlement took a few hours and he remained in absolute silence throughout it. The conflict at the site tumbled through his mind as he tried to piece together everything that was said. Now that Maxim was healed, he couldn't stop thinking about Creia. The king of the Denynso compound, he had been at the center of the war with the Klimnu. He had the capability, or at least the Klimnu perceived that he had the capability, to heal them and reverse the gruesome reaction to the flowers. When he refused, telling them that if they wanted his help they would have to leave Uoria and vow to stop all attempts to take over the planet, they had turned all of their hatred and violence toward him. This conflict had been long and destructive, and when they finally thought that they had eliminated the Klimnu in that last battle in Loralia's mirrored realm, Creia had been so proud of them. He had honored them highly and granted them permission to leave the boundaries of the compound, something that they had never been allowed to do. By all rights, it truly was Creia's situation to handle. It was as though he had the same decision to make as he had during that fateful meeting, only this time he was making it in advance. He was owed that moment to look at the men who held within them the potential to become Klimnu and decide what he thought should be done.

THEY GATHERED everyone who was to make the journey back to the compound as quickly as they could. The remnants of their abandoned plans to travel throughout the planet cast aside at the entrance to the settlement, the warriors, the human women from the compound, Loralia, George, Ivy, Maxim, Rain, and Rey started back toward the Denynso compound. Pyra had left eight of the warriors in the settlement to continue to guard the men in the meeting hall, instructing the human men from the settlement to take shifts as necessary. He knew that the authority that they saw in him was enough that they would comply with this command. Even if there was dissention in the settlement, those who protested would not be able to stand up against those who followed the orders and the warriors who had been left in Pyra's place.

A heavy, thick silence defined their travel back to the compound. It seemed to pull on all of them until their bodies barely moved and their pace was so slow it felt as though they would never make it back. Pyra scarcely slept along the way. Maxim and Ivy had gotten away from him once before, he wouldn't give them, or any of the others, the opportunity to do it again. At night he wandered through the rows of tents and pallets, listening for whispers, or sat in the center near the fire, losing himself in the flicker of the flames. Sometimes he could see Eden's face in the colors and it fueled him forward.

He kept them traveling throughout the day and late into the night, and they began again in the morning before the sun was fully up. It was grueling, but it was necessary. Until he got all of them back into the compound, Pyra would not feel at ease.

The moon was high above them when he finally saw the stone wall of the compound in front of them. It was so similar to the one that surrounded the settlement, and yet so distinctly different that he knew he would be able to recognize it no matter what. Their pace quickened as a group when they saw it and soon they stood at its base. The warriors stepped up to it and rested their foreheads against it, each immersed in his own thoughts and feelings about finally being home.

Pyra stood watching each person climb and cross the wall into the compound until he was the only one left that was not inside. When he was confident that they had all made it into the boundaries of the compound, he launched himself over the top and dropped to his feet on Denynso ground for the first time in what seemed like a lifetime. The feeling was not as joyous as he thought that it would be. Instead it felt like a film of dust from the other part of the planet had coated him, following him into the compound and showing him that life was not as it was, and would never again be what it was before they had climbed that wall for the first time. Things were completely different now and it felt almost as though he were stepping into the past, a past that didn't fully remember him.

They walked until they neared the remnants of the prison and Pyra heard choking sound from behind him. He turned to see Maxim and Rey kneeling at the edge of the charred remains of the building, their faces registering shock and devastation. Maxim's hand covered his mouth and nose as he stared out over the blackness and Rey seemed to be trembling. It was in that moment that Pyra realized the cruel irony that it was their kind who had built the prison for the Covra and lost their lives to them, but then the twisted evolution of the contemporaries of those same creatures reclaimed that prison later to imprison, torment, and destroy another species.

Pyra started to say something to them, to force them onward, but Ivy knelt down beside Maxim and Zsilvia lowered to Rey's side, both woman stroking the backs of the men, and Pyra stopped. For those moments, he would allow them to grieve.

WHEN MAXIM and Rey stood again, they continued on their way, walking into the depths of the forest that seemed so much thicker now after spending so much time in open, endless spaces. The moon came through the leaves, dappling their skin and illuminating the path in front of them. Suddenly Pyra noticed movement ahead. He heard a small gasp and watched the tiny creature several yards away drop a basket to the ground. It started running toward them and he realized in moments that it was Leia. She ran to Gyyx, who scooped his mate into his arms and held her several feet off of the ground, kissing her tenderly as she gripped his massive neck with both arms.

"Leia," Pyra said, trying to get the tiny woman's attention. "Leia." Finally she turned to look at him. "Where is Eden?"

Leia had stayed behind while the rest of them left the compound so that she could take care of Eden who could be in the last stages of her pregnancy. It was one of the reasons that Pyra had been so on edge the entire time that they were gone. Eden's pregnancy was unique in that she was born human but somehow transformed to Denynso when Ciyrs healed her after a Klimnu attack. Her DNA said that she was now Denynso, but the transformation had not changed her body much. There was no way to know if she would carry this baby like she would have if she was still completely human, or if she would carry it more like the Denynso women. This meant that the time that she could deliver varied widely, making it unnerving to leave her alone for even a few moments.

"She's at home. She's sleeping."

"Is she alright? Why did you leave her?"

"She's fine, Pyra. She's just sleeping. It's the middle of the night. I came out here to get some fruit for her. It is all she has wanted to eat for a few days, but it is very hard to find. The best time is by moonlight, so when she falls asleep, I come out here to try to find it for her.

"Thank you for doing so much to take care of her," Pyra said.

"What are you doing back so soon?" Leia asked. "We didn't expect you for several more weeks."

"There's been a situation," Gyyx told her, gently lowering her to the ground.

"We need to see Creia," Pyra said. "Immediately."

"Is everything alright?" Leia asked, the concern evident on her face.

"Go home, Baby," Gyyx told her. "Get some sleep. I will explain everything to you tomorrow."

"I don't want to go home," Leia protested.

"Home," Gyyx repeated, tucking his hand around her chin and gazing into her face. "Build up some energy for when I get home."

Leia gave him a mischievous smile and walked back to the basket that she had dropped, scooping the fruit that had rolled across the ground back into it before walking away in the direction of the houses. Pyra continued toward their meeting hall, somewhat feeling like he was walking through a drawing. Everything was still around him, unmoving, unchanged. It was so calm, but he knew that in moments it wouldn't be any longer.

15

———

Ivy at once felt stifled and had chills running through her as she stood in the grand hall again, waiting for Creia and Theia to appear. Her first time standing in that hall had not been pleasant, but even that was nothing compared to why she was standing there now. She looked across the room at Maxim where he and Rey stood, flanked by Pyra and Gyyx. He stared at the elevated platform at the far end of the room, his eyes trained on the massive thrones that sat there as if he were waiting for the monarchs to simply materialize in front of him. In that moment, after everything that she had gone through and seen in her time on Uoria, it likely wouldn't have even fazed her if they did.

Just then the heavy curtains at the back of the platform opened and Creia and Theia swept through. Neither looked terribly rested, but the worry etched deeply onto Creia's face told her that he was responding more intensely to the sudden reappearance of his warriors and those who had ventured out of the compound with them.

"Pyra?" Creia said.

"Yes, sir," Pyra said, stepping forward.

"What are you doing back here so soon?" he asked.

"There's been a situation, sir. Something gravely serious and we have come to you to ask your help in resolving it."

"What has happened? The last I heard of what you were doing, the women and George were leaving to help you with the Light Ones and the Covra."

"Yes, sir," Pyra said and Ivy saw him glance back over his shoulder toward Rain, who stepped forward to stand beside him. "This is Rain. She is one of them. They are human."

Creia took a slight step back and Ivy saw Theia straighten in her throne as if trying to get a better look at Rain.

"Human?" Creia asked.

"Yes, sir."

Ivy listened as Pyra recounted the story of how the humans had found their way onto the planet and what had happened leading up to the locking by the Covra. By the time he finished Creia had walked backwards until he sank into his throne and was looking at them with a strange look on his face.

"They are not why we've come to you, though."

"Then why?"

Pyra looked by at Gyyx who stepped behind Rey and Maxim to lead them forward. As soon as Creia saw them Ivy saw the expression on his face darken even further and he seemed to shrink slightly back into his throne. Pyra began to explain how they had come into contact with the beautiful creatures in their kingdom and brought them to help with the people in the settlement because of their history of alliances, but Maxim suddenly spoke over him.

"You know exactly who we are, don't you, Creia?"

Ivy gasped and she took a step forward, but stepped back again when she felt Ero's hand touch her elbow. The guard that Pyra had assigned to her, Ero had been kind to her, but Ivy knew that he would also be steadfast in his responsibilities, especially now that they were back on the compound and in the presence of the king and queen.

"Be quiet," Pyra demanded.

"Why don't you tell them, Creia?" Maxim continued, ignoring Pyra. "Why don't you tell them about what really happened so long ago? I wasn't sure at first, but I'm putting all of the pieces together now and I'm finally seeing the full picture, so why don't you enlighten all of them as well? Go ahead and tell them about the real origin of the Denynso."

"Be quiet," Pyra demanded again.

"How long have the Denynso been on this compound, Creia?" Max continued. "Your kind didn't always live here. It was once home to another species. So when did your kind take over, and why?"

"I am not going to tell you again," Pyra said, reaching for his dagger.

"Don't you dare touch that weapon, Pyra," Creia said. "This man is absolutely right. There are many things about the Denynso that I have never told you, but you have the right to know."

"What is it?"

"Come with me."

The king came down off of the platform and crossed the hall with purpose, not looking any of them in the eye as he passed through the huge arched doors and out of the hall. Ivy felt so exhausted that she didn't feel like she could take another step, but she forced herself to follow the rest of the people gathered in the hall as they streamed out after Creia.

16

———

Pyra followed closely after Creia, trusting Gyyx to properly watch over Maxim and Rey. His mind was reeling after what had just happened. He had spent his entire life respecting Creia as their wisest and most powerful. He was not just his king, but his father, and the thought that he had been hiding something from him and from the rest of the clan made him feel like there was a weight in his belly.

He was moving down the steps when he saw Eden coming toward him. Flooded with love, relief, and a mix of emotions that he couldn't quite identify, Pyra ran off of the steps and across the dirt to her, sweeping her into his arms and catching her lips in a kiss before she could even say a word to him. He turned her in his arms so that he cradled her under her back and knees and pulled her higher so that he could rest his ear against her swollen belly. It was even larger than when he had left the compound and it took only a second for him to hear the shifting of the baby inside and feel the pressure of a kick against him. He kissed it, whispering the words he had as he was saying goodbye before he left.

"What is going on?" Eden asked, her hand stroking through his white Mohawk and tangling in the hairs at the nape of his neck that had grown out slightly since he had been off the compound.

Pyra looked over and noticed that everyone had paused, waiting for him. He rushed back to his position behind Creia, comfortably carrying Eden along with him so that she didn't have to rush to keep up with his much longer strides. When they had first met and even after they completed their bond and became lifetime mates, Eden was extremely stubborn and resistant to allowing him to carry her. Now she was going along with it without even a moment's protest. That told him more than words ever could how much she was struggling in this end phase of her pregnancy.

He tried to catch her up as quickly as he could with a brief version of what happened.

"You promised me that if anything went wrong, you would let me know," Eden said accusingly to Loralia who had walked up behind them to greet her.

"Everything was moving far too quickly. There was no way to get in touch with you. Besides, Pyra was not in danger."

"It was like I could feel you whenever you were thinking about me," Eden said to Pyra.

"I thought about you all the time," he told her and she shook her head at him.

"No. There were moments when it was like you were right here with me. Like I could open my eyes and you would be lying in bed with me."

"Take my necklace out of my shirt," he told her.

Eden reached into his shirt with one of her slim hands and withdrew the chain and pendant. He adjusted her weight so that he supported her with one arm and took the pendant from her hand. He touched the pendant with the pad of his thumb just like he had when they were on the settlement and he heard Eden gasps slightly.

"That's it," she told him. "Whenever you touched the pendant, I could feel it."

Pyra felt his heart fill. It made him feel better to know that she could sense him so strongly, especially in the moments when he needed her the most. Suddenly he realized that they were walking away from the main center of the compound and toward the cliffs at the back corner where anyone rarely went. These cliffs were not like the ones closer to the center of the compound. Though steep and tall, those cliffs were relatively smooth and hospitable. The cliffs at the back, however, were sharp and jagged, the terrain threatening for even the warriors. They had to walk along the edge of the funeral lake to get to the cliffs and as they did Pyra avoided looking into the water, not wanting to think about Jem.

Pyra gave a small leap to one side to avoid stepping into a massive tangle of underwater plants and Eden gasped in his arms.

"Are you alright?" he asked.

She nodded and gave him a slightly strained smile.

"I'm fine."

They finally reached the base of the tallest cliff and Creia turned to look at them.

"Pyra, Gyyx, Ty, I will need your help."

Pyra lowered Eden to the ground and walked through the group to where Creia was standing. The king walked up to what looked like a broken-off piece of the cliff and turned back to the warriors.

"Move this."

The warriors looked at each other incredulously, but none of them protested. They walked up to the rock and positioned themselves so that Pyra and Ty were on either side and Gyyx was on the front, pressing his palms flat to the surface so that he could apply pressure up to lift from the center. They groaned and strained with the incredible weight of the rock, but finally it began to move. Pyra dug in and pulled harder, easing the rock toward himself as the other men pushed it toward him.

"That's enough," Creia said.

Pyra allowed his arms to fall away from the rock with relief and stepped around it to look back at Creia. What he found was the king standing beside the mouth of a narrow pathway winding its way up the cliffs.

"I didn't even know this was here," Pyra said as he stepped onto the path behind Creia.

"No one does anymore," Creia replied. "The rock was put there to block it, but it has been so long since then, no one is around any longer that even remembers it is here. No one but me and Theia."

Pyra followed the king up the path, trusting that the others would help Eden along behind him. It seemed that the path wound on endlessly through the fiercely sharp points that rose out of the rocks and jagged edges of the small ravines between the cliffs. Finally they turned a corner beside a towering rock spike and the path straightened and opened onto a plateau. Pyra's stomach sank as he looked out over the edge through the mist of a low-hanging cloud.

The ground beneath them was blackened, areas of

bright, glowing orange showing through cracks in the surface. Smoke billowed up in pillars that mixed with the clouds to create a sooty streak that blotted out the stars. In the distance Pyra could see what looked like the darkened metal and stone skeletons of buildings. Others lay crumbled against the ground, spread out in pieces like the wreckage of the human ship.

"These," Creia said, "are the real badlands."

17
___

"What is this, father?" Pyra asked.

"There was a time," the aging king said, gazing out over the destroyed land, his voice suddenly sounding for the first time like it was carrying all of the years that he had lived within it, "when there was more than one clan of the Denynso. There were three, positioned throughout the planet in the places that offered what each of those clans considered the most beautiful and productive of surroundings. The largest of the clans lived here."

"Why would they live somewhere like that? It doesn't even look inhabitable," Ero said.

"It wasn't always like this. It was once lush and beautiful, even more so than our own compound. The clan that lived here was powerful, honored above the other two. They knew that there was another species living on the land just on the other side of these cliffs, but rarely interacted with them. Then the strangers came."

"The Covra," Pyra said.

Creia nodded.

"Yes," he said, "the Covra came for the species that lived on that side of the cliffs, the side that is now our compound, but they were not the only ones to invade this part of Uoria. As they fought the Covra, the Denynso on the other side of the cliffs encountered strangers that came from another planet, something they had never encountered. They called themselves the Valdicians."

Pyra felt like someone had punched him directly in the gut. Behind him he heard Rain gasp and a moment later she was standing beside him, searching Creia's face.

"They are the reason that we're here," Rain told him. "They are the ones that had built the prison camp on that planet and then took over our ship so that it crashed here as part of their alliance with the Covra."

"But that was 200 years after my kind went beneath the ground," Loralia said, seeming to materialize out of the group who stood listening intently to what was happening. "They couldn't have been the same ones."

"You're right," Creia said. "They weren't. The Valdicians came with the hopes of aligning themselves with the Denynso. Almost as soon as they arrived, the people who were living on this side of the cliff, your people, Loralia, started to become very sick. The plague lasted for as long as the Valdicians were here and drove the entire species underground. Soon after, the Denynso convinced the Valdicians that there would be no alliance and forced them to leave."

"That was the first time that the Valdicians and the Covra encountered each other," Rain said.

Creia nodded again.

"Everything seemed peaceful once both the Valdicians and the Covra left this area of the planet. The quiet didn't last for long, however. Soon more strangers came onto the compound with the Denynso. These people were incredibly beautiful, but also incredibly cold."

Pyra's eyes drifted to Maxim, who kept his eyes trained on Creia, his hand holding Ivy's tightly.

"The Klimnu," Pyra said.

"What would become the Klimnu, yes. They used their own understanding of technology and the Denynso resources to build a ship, intending on using it to scout other planets for slaves that they could force into their service as they took over Uoria. Soon another group arrived. They seemed to be the same species as the first, but they were brave and honorable. Their number was very small, but they reached out to the Denynso to create an alliance that would force the cold, greedy ones out of the compound. Half of the Denynso agreed to the alliance, but the other half didn't want anything to do with what was quickly escalating to a civil war. The clan split and the half that didn't want to be involved in the conflict crossed the cliffs to the land that had been left behind by the victims of the Covra."

"The Denynso split just like the Klimnu," Gyyx said.

"They did," Creia said. "Those in the original compound worked with their small group of allies to force the creatures that would become the Klimnu off of the planet and everything seemed quiet again. On the new compound, however, two new babies were born just a few months apart. They weren't like all of the other children, but no one spoke of it. Nearly two and a half centuries passed. The two smaller Denynso clans disappeared and the others continued to build their reputation for war. Species from other planets would hear of the beauty of Uoria and come to invade. By then this compound had been walled in and the prison that had been built on the far end was largely forgotten. What we didn't know was that during that time, the Covra had reemerged and a misdirected ship of humans had crashed on the planet."

"What do you mean the other two Denynso clans disappeared? What happened to them?"

"No one knows. The clans were highly separated. There was rarely any communication and by the time the clan from the other side attempted to reach out to them, their compounds had been empty for years."

"What happened to this compound?" Pyra asked. "If it was once so beautiful, what turned it into the badlands?"

"You know that the first human visitors were allowed to Uoria around 50 years ago."

"Yes."

"Those visits lasted fewer than 10 years before we had to suspend them. That is when the Klimnu returned. While they were still beautiful, the years had only intensified the avarice and lust for violence and dominance within them. The first thing that they did was come to the people who had rejected the offer of alliance from their ancestors and destroy it. They buried weapons in the ground and detonated them, triggering the volcanos beneath the surface to erupt and burn the compound to skeletons and ash. That is when they learned that they could feed off of the high emotions of the Denynso and that the blood of the warriors would give them unimaginable power. The fire has not stopped burning since. It was only two years later; they came to me after coming into contact with the flowers and wanted my help to heal them.

By then those two strange babies who were the first born on this compound had grown up and several generations of their families had been born after them without any indications of the oddness of those children. There were two young men in the compound then, however, the youngest of those two family lines, who would grow up to have babies of their own and each of those children would show the same extraordinary characteristics that their ancestors had two centuries before. Not fully Denynso, these children would grow to be men, both losing their fathers far too young. From them, however, we got one warrior with the smaller size, beautiful face, and incredible speed of the Mikana tribe, this tribe," Creia said, gesturing toward Maxim and Rey, "and one with the gentle, kind heart of his mother but the astonishing ability to control objects of a father with Valdician blood, blood that was shed when the Valdicians returned for his son and he gave his life to protect him."

Pyra felt like he couldn't breathe. He turned slowly and faced his warriors. Ero and Ty stood in the center of the group, visibly shaking. Their mates clutched them, trying to offer them strength. Two of his dearest friends, men raised like his brothers, men who had fought alongside him in battle, had the blood of the worst enemies that the Denynso had ever encountered flowing through their veins. He opened his mouth to speak, but the words disappeared in the sound of a scream from the back of the crowd.

Loralia felt Eden's fingernails dig into her arm, breaking through the painful, foggy thoughts that were filling her mind. She knew now what had restarted the plague that had killed her family, and though it still didn't explain why she had been the only one to survive, the very fact that she now knew what was behind it seemed to give those deaths more meaning, as truly pointless as that meaning was. At that moment, however, she pushed those thoughts aside so that she could turn to Eden. The smaller woman was clutching Loralia's arm with one hand and holding her own belly with the other, terror in her eyes as she looked up at Loralia.

"Eden, what's wrong?"

Pyra crashed through the crowd and made it to Eden's side just as Loralia was lowering her to the ground. She placed her hands over Eden's belly, pressing her compact to it with one palm, and focused in on the baby inside, blocking out all of the emotions and thoughts of the adults around her so that she could only feel the growing child.

"She's in labor," Loralia said, running her hands down to

the side of Eden's belly so that she could continue to follow the baby as it rocked with the contractions clutching his mother's body.

"What?" Pyra nearly shrieked.

"This baby is coming," Loralia said pointedly. "He's not going to wait any longer."

"This means that you are carrying like a Denynso," Zsilvia said, rushing to Eden's side, "but if so you would have been feeling labor pains for several days now."

Eden looked up and nodded, then took a breath and arched as her belly visibly tightened.

"I have been," she admitted. "I didn't want to say anything."

"Why?" Zsilvia asked.

"I wanted Pyra," Eden said. "It's ridiculous, I know, but I felt like if I didn't say anything, it couldn't be real and then maybe he would make it home so I didn't have to go through this without him."

"I did make it home," Pyra said, reaching down to take Eden's hand.

Loralia could feel Eden calming as soon as Pyra touched her and she nodded at him.

"That's helping, Pyra. Keep touching her. Elianna, go get the midwives."

Elianna took off running down the path, but Loralia could feel the doubt and fear rising off of Eden. She knew that she wasn't going to make it long enough for the midwives to arrive.

"Can you stand up and try to make it back to the house?" Loralia asked, wanting to keep Eden calm by giving her as many options as much control as she could.

"I can't," Eden gasped.

"What if I carry you?" Pyra asked.

"No, please. I can't go that far."

"Is there somewhere we can bring her?" Pyra asked.

Creia stepped forward and pointed across the plateau.

"There's a cave over there. It's not very large, but it will get her out of the open."

Loralia and Zsilvia stepped back so that Pyra could scoop Eden up and rush her across the plateau to the cave. She settled onto her knees beside Eden and a moment later saw Ivy rush up to the mouth of the cave. She took the bag off of her shoulder and held it out to Loralia.

"There are clothes, a sheet, and some medical supplies in there," Ivy said. "Use whatever you need."

Loralia thanked her and opened the bag, taking out the clothes and balling them up so that she could tuck them under Eden's head. Next she withdrew the sheet, the ointments, the herbs, and the strips of bandage and laid them to the side. Eden cried out as another contraction coursed through her body and Loralia rested a hand on her shoulder to calm her. Almost as soon as her back rested onto the ground again, Eden bucked again, screaming more loudly and reaching out for Pyra.

"The midwives aren't going to make it here in time," Eden sobbed.

"I can help you."

Loralia looked up toward the voice and saw Rey standing at the mouth of the cave.

"No," Pyra said harshly.

"My great-grandmother was midwife to the human women in the settlement after the crash. She taught my grandmother, who taught my mother, who taught me. They said that if I was to lead in the footsteps of my father, it was a skill that would make me stronger. I have attended several births."

"Human?" Loralia asked.

"No," Rey said, "but my mother taught me the differences very carefully."

"No," Pyra growled again, starting to stand.

Eden yanked him back down to the ground beside her and nodded.

"Yes. Thank you."

"He's a man!" Pyra protested.

"He is the closest thing that I have to a midwife who can help me deliver this baby. The Denynso midwives have never delivered a human either, so how is this so different?"

"Those midwives aren't men," Pyra said, "and you aren't human anymore."

"My body is, Pyra, and I don't care if he's a man as long as he gets the baby here safely."

Loralia rested her compact over Eden's belly again and then nodded to Rey.

"He's ready."

"Are you still sure that it's a boy?" Pyra asked.

Loralia smiled up at him as Rey helped Eden get into position to push.

"You'll find out in just a few minutes."

19

———

Ivy stood in Maxim's arms, her forehead rested against his as he gently rocked her back and forth. She had only been able to hold his hand behind Gyyx's back, but in the chaos of everything that had happened on the plateau, Gyyx had stepped away from Maxim and she had immediately curled into his arms. She took a deep breath of him, filling her lungs with the smell that she never wanted to spend another moment without. He ducked his head and touched a kiss to her lips. Her mind was spinning with everything that was happening around them, but that simple kiss soothed her.

The high sound of a baby crying suddenly cut through the air and everyone turned expectantly toward the direction of the cave. The crying quieted and there was still silence for several long seconds before Pyra walked around the corner, a tiny, sheet-wrapped form tucked in his elbow. He carried it carefully over to Creia and Ivy watched as he lowered himself to his knees in front of his father and king. The first light of the morning was just coming over the cliff as Pyra lifted the baby into his hands and held it up to Creia.